# SLANT

SLANT
First published in 2023 by
New Island Books
Glenshesk House
10 Richview Office Park
Clonskeagh
Dublin D14 V8C4
Republic of Ireland
www.newisland.ie

Copyright © Katherine O'Donnell, 2023

The right of Katherine O'Donnell to be identified as the author of this work has been asserted in accordance with the provisions of the Copyright and Related Rights Act, 2000.

Print ISBN: 978-1-84840-838-8
eBook ISBN: 978-1-84840-839-5

All rights reserved. The material in this publication is protected by copyright law. Except as may be permitted by law, no part of the material may be reproduced (including by storage in a retrieval system) or transmitted in any form or by any means; adapted; rented or lent without the written permission of the copyright owners.

This book is a work of fiction. Names, characters, businesses, organisations, places and events are either the product of the author's imagination or are used fictitiously. Any resemblance to actual persons, living or dead, events or locales is entirely coincidental.

British Library Cataloguing in Publication Data. A CIP catalogue record for this book is available from the British Library.

Lines from 'Tell all the truth but tell it slant —' (1263) and 'Wild nights – wild nights!' (269) by Emily Dickinson which appear in *The Poems of Emily Dickinson: Reading Edition*, edited by Ralph W. Franklin, Cambridge, Mass.: The Belknap Press of Harvard University Press, Copyright © 1998, 1999 by the President and Fellows of Harvard College. Copyright © 1951, 1955 by the President and Fellows of Harvard College. Copyright © renewed 1979, 1983 by the President and Fellows of Harvard College. Copyright © 1914, 1918, 1919, 1924, 1929, 1930, 1932, 1935, 1937, 1942 by Martha Dickinson Bianchi. Copyright © 1952, 1957, 1958, 1963, 1965 by Mary L. Hampson are used by permission. All rights reserved.

Set in 12 on 15pt Sabon and ITC Franklin Gothic
Typeset by JVR Creative India
Edited by Rachel Pierce, verba.ie
Cover design by Fiachra McCarthy, fiachramccarthy.com
Cover image by Chloe Sherman, 'On the way to Folsom St. Fair. San Francisco 1994', courtesy of the artist.
Printed by Scandbook, Sweden, scandbook.com

New Island received financial assistance from The Arts Council (An Chomhairle Ealaíon), Dublin, Ireland.

New Island Books is a member of Publishing Ireland.

10 9 8 7 6 5 4 3 2 1

# SLANT

**KATHERINE O'DONNELL**

*K. O'Donnell*

NEW ISLAND

*For the first readers:*
*Liz Evers, Hilary Kneale, Soren Mayes, Joan McCarthy,*
*Elixxchel Levy, Anto Gibbs, Ruth Vanita, Evelyn Quinlan,*
*Rachel Morton, Valerie Coogan & Martha Breen*

*Tell all the truth but tell it slant—*

**Emily Dickinson**

# CORK NORTH CENTRAL
# ELECTORAL CONSTITUENCY

## 2015

It became addictive: the canvassing.
I seemed to need to have my nostrils fill with their discomfort, their distaste, their disgust. I didn't go on those rounds of door-knocking for the moments when they said 'Yes', 'Of course', 'Yes.'

Most of the moments at the beginning of my long, solo months of campaigning were quiet moments. Quiet knock on the door, slow and deep inhalations while waiting for it to be opened. The soft, deferential introduction, 'I'm looking for a Yes vote in the Referendum on Marriage Equality.' A shy proffering of a flyer. A gentle offer to answer questions. Waiting. Watching their caught-off-guard embarrassment. Waiting to answer their questions. They nodded. They had heard you ask for their vote. They took the flyer. They had no questions. They closed the door. They went back into their home.

I started canvassing months out from the referendum date. I was becoming demented with anxiety. I kept telling friends – dykes my own age – that we were all going to lose, big time, that the only hope was to go knocking on doors.

My friends didn't want to listen.

'We don't have enough people,' they said.

'Straight people will have to do it too. I said It's their issue, homophobia. Wherever there's straight people there's homophobia. They've to work to get rid of it.'

'That's not a great argument to win them to our team,' my friends said. 'And you know right well they sue if we use the word homophobia. They are not homophobic, they just work against us.' My old comrades told me the polls looked good. It looked like it would pass.

'Do you believe the polls?' I asked.

Nobody believed the polls.

My best friend, Chris, said, 'Look, Ro, I just can't face it. I've got in a couple of TV box sets to watch for the next few months, all the Agatha Christies, *Miss Marple* and *Murder, She Wrote*. Otherwise, I'm just not turning on the TV. I'm not turning on the radio. I'm not looking at Facebook. We've done enough, Ro. We really have. We stayed standing. We're still here, we kept on going as well as we could and that's really enough now. We've got to look after ourselves. And sure, you don't believe in marriage anyway.'

I had an anti-marriage rant to hand, and once I started it I just could not stop:

'I don't believe the State should give all of the goodies and incentives to married couples. I don't think our culture should incessantly promote, romanticise, idealise, privilege and sell marriage from the day we are born. And I just see a lot of straight people lying through their teeth, miserable, lonely, fed-up, bored and feeling shite while pretending they live a happily married life. Nobody is even allowed to say they're in a "good enough" marriage, that, on balance, all things considered, it's probably OK, or that they are so institutionalised now they couldn't face changing it. And the people they feel most relaxed and happiest with are their trusted same-gender buddies. And lesbians are better than all that, we've loved each other better than that. We have family models and real partnerships that the straights could learn from ...'

I lost them, always, my pals, during that lesbian chauvinist rant – they had heard it too often from me and my raw emotion made them uncomfortable. And the young lesbians and gay boys mostly seemed to really want it – to get married. They wanted weddings like their siblings had. They wanted to be like their straight parents. They didn't want the extended families of the older dykes, all those complex arrangements to raise children and share houses, loans, savings and pensions: no one should blame them, the younger lesbians and gays, for wanting clear and straight lines. 'They want to belong,' Chris said, 'they want to belong to the whole world.'

The early weeks on the canvass were fascinating. People said things like, 'Well, the gays will get such a land if they get married. It's not all about showy weddings and a big party and loads of presents and a honeymoon in the Maldives. They'll get a great, big land when they realise what marriage is all about.'

This was one of my favourite openings. I had a few counters.

'Vote Yes then to teach us!'

A few of them were surprised to find they were talking to a real-life lesbian. 'You're the first one I've ever actually met, except for seeing them on the telly.'

'That you know of,' I would reply. More smiles and laughter.

'Oh! You won't be long not being called gays – you'll be as miserable as the rest of us!'

As they were chuckling along I would say something like, 'Lots of lesbians and gay men are in committed relationships for years, decades. They would like the same chance to organise their lives and to have their commitment respected.'

Some people would say they could easily see themselves living with their best friend happily for years, it would be wonderful, so much easier, but it wasn't the same thing as marriage.

'Vote Yes, get a divorce and marry your best friend, then.' That often got a laugh.

'Who knows what passes between couples?' I would say. 'Many gay men and women say they love each other and want to have the benefits and security of marriage. Why don't you let us?'

'Well, ye can't have children.'

'But many of us already have children. Some of them are fine big adults now.'

'The poor children.'

That always hurt.

I loved when they arrived at the crux – the real nub, when they said, 'But can't the gays already get a kind of marriage? I thought they could, that they had something already, civil partnership?'

They generally were agreed that civil partnership was a good enough thing for the gays.

And so I would say, in a casual, desultory fashion, 'You think marriage should just be for a man and woman couple and that gays should have a lower-order civil partnership?'

They would invariably say: 'Yeah, yes, I suppose so, well, it kind of makes sense.'

And, in a laidback manner, I would ask, 'Why do you think that?'

And they would reply, 'Well, because a man and woman is a natural thing/a better thing/it's always been that way/we were told that was the better thing/we were told that is what is good/society needs men and women to have children.'

Or best of all, 'I just think that we should be the ones who have marriage.'

I would stay quiet then and just gently look at them. Many of them seemed relieved to have sorted it out for themselves. It was the right order – the straights were better, everyone knew that, and the homos just had to accept it. They just hadn't thought about it much or at all before I had come knocking. Some would look immediately stricken – they were not happy with the assumption of superiority, their guts were turning over. Others got more expansive, more puffed up – everything was right with the world, there was an order and a ranking, and they were on the top of this particular heap. I would wave a cheery goodbye, thank them for their time and leave them with a small leaflet I had written and got printed.

I would say, 'Look, it's a while to the referendum, but there's a phone number and a website listed on the leaflet, I'm sure you'll be in loads of conversations about this, so if you want to find out more or settle any arguments – that's a good place to go for genuine information.'

I had been out so long that straight people around me talked freely about what they really thought about 'the gays'. I was part of the furniture. My older brother and sister and their spouses casually told me that they would be voting against equal marriage. Of course my parents were voting No, and all of their friends and their neighbours were voting No.

In the early weeks of my canvassing I had started to talk with them, my mam, my dad, my aunts and uncles, the neighbours around my folks' place who had watched me grow up. There wasn't a Yes vote among them, which wasn't a surprise. I knew I would need to have a long lead-in to the day of the vote in order to change their minds, and so I started the conversations early in the year. But after three or four weeks of chatting with them and planting seeds as to why they might consider voting Yes, I just wasn't able to do any more follow-up. I became incapable of engaging with them. I nodded mutely over the next number of months while they took me aside, individually, or in couples, threesomes, or gangs of four, to explain to me, in a concert of great detail, why they were voting No. They all started in the same way:

'I mean, remember when you were a young one and we found out – you know – that you're a gay, like?'

'You didn't find out. I told you.'

'God, I know – you were fierce adamant.'

'Yeah.'

'Like, other people had problems then with you, but I never did.'

They did not notice my silence. They continued, 'I always stuck up for you. I mean, people were terrible back then. But sure it's all grand now. I mean, I never gave a toss, like, one way or another, it's all the one to me. But, like, there has to be some kind of limit. Like, if this goes through – what next?! Like, ye all hate the Church and the clergy. God help us. And now ye want to be married there! Sure, it's against Church teaching! They can't be forced into that!'

'It's not about getting married in churches. It's only about getting married in a registry office,' I said.

'But it won't stop there, will it?'

'What do you mean?'

'I mean people will want to marry their dogs and cats and all kinds of things.'

On those occasions the only way for me to get them to stop talking at me was to say:

'But do you really think you're going to lose? I mean, I think you're going to win.'

'Really? The polls all say we'll lose. And all the young ones, regardless of their species, are mad for the equal marriage.'

'Do you think the young ones will actually get registered and actually vote?'

No one was too sure of that happening.

'There seems to be a lot of people keeping silent,' I said.

They agreed. 'They are probably afraid of being called homophobic just because they are doing the right thing. Because nobody hates the gays. It isn't that at all.'

'Yeah. Do you believe the polls?' I asked.

Nobody, actually, believed the polls.

In early March I confessed to Chris that I was getting out canvassing at every opportunity, anxious with the clock ticking down the referendum date at the end of May.

'I'm down to three night shifts every ten days and I can keep it like that until referendum day. I've piled in holidays all around the Easter break so I have extra time to go canvassing. You know I never take all my holidays and time off in lieu, so management at the home are being decent in leaving me have this time.'

'Gosh, Ro, you'll be missed by all the residents,' Chris said.

We were sitting out in her small back garden, waiting for our china mugs of tea to cool, happy with the springing primroses.

'I miss them, to be honest. And I miss the calm the work brings. I miss my time writing. I miss the regularity of a week of night shifts on and then a whole week off to myself. I miss all the time I have at work in the dead of night to spend over my jotter. But it's easier to manage the anxiety by actually being out on the canvass.'

Chris indulged me by pretending to listen to the stories I gathered while knocking on doors.

'I'm telling you,' I told her, 'they think we're not the same, that we're hardwired differently. They don't think very deeply but just go with "the gays have different feelings". They think we can't understand what marriage is all about. They think we don't know about the hard graft of commitment, they think we are only about sexual desire. They are freaked out to hear we're raising children, they don't think we fall in love, that we're there for the everyday, the domestic, the mundane, for the detail and duty.'

'Yeah,' Chris said.

I called into Chris most evenings before, after, or even during bouts of canvassing. She became an unwilling witness to how I was becoming preoccupied, even possessed, by times past. I had begun to relive events, episodes, days and some weeks from my twenties. I relived those times, but now I had the perspective of someone who was over fifty, and what I had experienced in my twenties with wonder and joy I was now reliving as horror.

I told Chris that when I was out on the canvass, I could feel again what it felt like to be twenty-odd: the rush of that intoxicating cocktail of optimism, gratitude, joy for the love I had found, the dancing superpowers of being a lesbian. I remembered what it had been like to feel the tenderness, craving, passion, lust, risk, vulnerability, hormone highs and deep satiety, the swagger, the fusion of sex and love-making. Liquid heat.

Walking around looking for votes, I felt again that clear grief for the boys my age lost to AIDS and the holy cleanliness of the rage that had fuelled the resistance. I experienced again the shocking awakening from a gormless naivety to the realisation of how much hate there was for us fags and dykes, how awful it was to have had to witness and endure the banal viciousness my kind were subjected to by those who had so much power over us. In remembering what had happened to me and my friends at the hands of employers, landlords, publicans, doctors, social workers, Gardaí, judges, B&B owners, shop-keepers, taxi drivers, teachers, classmates, bankers, funeral directors, priests, neighbours, relations, siblings, parents – I had this awful experience of receiving the insults, the dismissals, the mocking and degradation as if for the first time.

I tried to tell Chris about the flashbacks: I was hit by that sharp green sensation of meeting the world with an expanded, curious heart like when I was a young one. I had felt then that I was part of a tribe moving as wind: sometimes salty, sometimes rain-drenched, sometimes howling, then playful, tickling, a gentle breeze, but always bringing more oxygen and possibility to the world, changing the atmosphere and dappling the light. And as I felt once again all of those times that were already an overlooked history, not remembered enough to be called forgotten, I felt the dissonance of that time with my life as I now lived it. I felt now, once again and as if for the first time, the shadows looming, the forces threatening my youth. Those forces still lived and still threatened and now I was getting older. My quiet life, marshalled by contented daily and seasonal rituals, was again up for grabs by those who wanted to press me down and away from sight.

I began to get taken over with memories, disassociated from the present, reliving my past with the hindsight of how very tough those times had been. In my twenties and thirties, a kind of magic shroud, a patina of grace, had sheltered and buffered me from feeling the full force of the blows but now as a woman in her fifties I had no such force-field. I realised that I had endured cuts and breaks and deep injuries after all.

Jenny, Jenny.

The ghost of Jenny walked beside me, although she had been gone for the war. There had been a war but Jenny had remained safe, and I was so relieved that Jenny had been safe.

I had become a soldier, I really had no choice, and I had stayed standing. Yet on those awful canvasses I realised that I had been wounded, repeatedly, over decades. I just hadn't taken the time to feel the hurts. I had thought a lot of the war might be over now or maybe it was just a ceasefire or maybe the battle boom had left me deaf? But I knew now I was one of the walking wounded.

Jenny, Jenny.

She would often come to mind and I was glad she had missed the war, that she didn't know what this pain was like. That she was protected in her safe life. Jenny had no need of superpowers. I was haunted by Jenny. I had forgotten how I had spun carefully threaded stories to hold the sadness leaking from the pit of my stomach. The fine weave of those threads was now unravelled and wrapped around me. The sticky web of grief confused me.

Chris tried to get me to stop canvassing. I wouldn't. Well, I couldn't. Like I said, I was addicted.

'Why don't you write your way through it like you always do?' she implored. 'Go write a story that will contain all the experiences, the feelings?'

'I'm trying,' I kept saying. 'I can't, though. I can't write at all.'

'Maybe that's why you're having this nervous breakdown.'

'Is that what you'd call it?'

'I would, yes.'

She looked at me softly but steadily, her blue eyes forcing me to hold her gaze.

'You've got to stop, Ro,' she said gently.

In the end I had to go back there. To the past. To Boston. I can say now that I did have a kind of a breakdown of sorts, though

I would call it a burnout. It was nothing dramatic, that's not my style. Just, I was too exhausted to operate most of the ways that I had of being in the world. I was both stuck and spinning. Stuck, and compulsively and exhaustedly spinning.

I recovered again, and completely, after I had cycled out to Herring Cove, which forms the curving arc that is the tip of Cape Cod. I sat listening to the thump and sizzle of the waves and I watched that immense optical illusion of the sun setting below the ocean. I knew stars were already in the night skies on the further reaches of that same ocean as it flooded into Cork harbour.

We seem to forget we are on a turning globe, and we bury our lives seeking stable forevers.

I sat on the beach and read and re-read an old postcard from Jenny and the note I had written to her in return but, as so often, had never sent. I had to start there, with Jenny's words and my reply. I had to pick up and follow those lines to remember again, to literally re-member me, to put my limbs and body, my mind and memory, back together again. To begin again.

# FOSTER STREET

1984

# 1
# (There's) Always Something There To Remind Me

'*Ro McCarthy?!* What the hell are you doing here? It's gone the hour – your team is already on the corridor!'

Helen Keogh, cleaning supervisor at the Copley Plaza Hotel, generally felt the need to put a rocket under my arse. And I suppose, in fairness, I regularly enough gave her sufficient cause for having that feeling.

'Oh hi, Hel!' I said, as I shut my jotter, stashed my biro in my coat pocket and slipped off the large laundry sack overstuffed with used sheets.

'I'm actually finished my shift,' I said. 'I've punched out, like. I just had to write something down in case I forgot it.'

'Is that for your college course?' said Helen.

'Yeah, it is. Well, kind of.' I said. 'Well … it's related to it.'

Back then I never told anyone I wrote fiction. Most people thought my only creative streak was that I liked to cut my own hair (invariably ending up very short as I sought to correct the mistakes I made). I secretly wrote stories to contain emotions I had nearly or really experienced or to record things I had seen. I wrote stories to get a kind of a handle on things that puzzled me, to wrap a cordon around the things I didn't yet understand.

'Go on off home now and get some kip,' said Helen. 'Everyone else from the early shift is long gone and you'll only be after confusing me, I'll be giving you more work if you stay around here.'

'Grand so.' I grinned at her. 'Have a nice day!' I said in a mock-American accent.

'Oh have a nice day, honey!' she sang back at me.

When I got down to the hotel lobby I found a chaos of people my own age happily anticipating having a party on someone else's expense account. I had heard this crowd was going to be here for the weekend. These international students were already on full scholarships at universities across America. They were to have three days and two nights in Boston, all on the tab of the Fulbright Commission. I was fascinated by the fizzing variety of nationalities. Everyone was 'psyched' as the Americans liked to say, and the happiness was contagious.

I mingled among the crowd and surveyed the groups milling around the reception desk, and that's when I saw her. She stood alone between her suitcase and an aggressively large rubber plant, a little apart from the throng. She stood stiffly and at odd angles to herself, looking past the clutches of students introducing themselves to each other while waiting to check in. She was smoking a cigarette and the light coming in through the lobby's high glass atrium caught the trail of smoke and made copper and gold glints in her astonishing halo of curls.

My gaze kept snagging on this girl, who seemed to be waiting for the melee to soften before attempting to register. She wore a long black jacket with shoulder pads and the sleeves, with striped lining, were folded up to her mid-arm. Her flowing white shirt reached below a stretchy black mini-skirt, she wore black leggings and dark-green pixie boots.

I said a swift prayer that this girl was able to speak good English and I half-skated and nearly tripped across the lobby tiles to talk with her.

She made a polite reply to my 'hello'. She had an English accent, which was disconcerting. Her afro head of curls was also much more blonde close-up.

'I actually thought you might be Danish,' I said, and I have absolutely no idea why I said that.

'No, I'm English,' she replied, in a very English voice.

'Do you have Danish ancestry?' Apparently I couldn't just shut up.

'None.'

There was a tinge of silence for some moments.

'So where did you get your amazing hair?'

'My parents. Sorry, that's obvious,' the girl said, blushing. 'As far as we know all the ancestors are English. Though in Boston, I am surprised some people think I am Irish.' She smiled.

'Really?'

'Yes. They hear an accent.'

'You're definitely not Irish, though.'

'No.'

'I'm Irish,' I said.

'Yes, I thought so. I mean, sorry, I presumed.'

'D'you think I have an Irish accent?'

'Yes. I mean it's a very nice accent. I like it.'

'I'm Ro, by the way.' I put out my hand to shake and immediately felt an even worse eejit, but thankfully the English girl shook my hand in a firm and formal manner.

'Please call me Jenny. My friends call me Jenny.'

'My friends, and everyone else, call me Ro.'

'R-O-W? R-O-E?'

'Even simpler – R-O.'

'Would you like me to call you Ro?'

I shrugged. 'Well, Jenny, we'd be friends if you did, but I answer to many names. In work situations I'm often called Rosie or Rose, but I'm also called Roz or Róisín. I was christened Rosemary. Take your pick.'

Jenny answered, 'There's Rosemary, that's for remembrance.'

We finished the quote together, both careful with the careful comma.

'Pray you, love, remember.'

We relaxed in a comfortable silence, letting the frisson of poetry percolate. We stood next to each other and contentedly watched the students piling around the registration desk. I was glad I had found someone who liked to quote poetry. It is always good to find your own kind.

After a brief pause I asked, 'Did you have far to travel today?'

'Just across the river. Harvard.'

'That's a big suitcase you have.'

'I know. It was hellish to take on the T. I suppose I should have taken a taxi, but it seemed it would be a simple commute. I should have just brought my satchel as you have.'

I deflected from admitting I was not, in fact, checking in.

'What are you studying in Harvard?'

'I'm not studying anything there really. I mean, I'm not registered for any degree, nor taking any courses. I'm just using my time there to finish up my Doctorate in English Lit.'

I could tell Jenny was assiduous in being pleasant, she was doing her best to be that English thing of being 'cheery' in the way people on British TV quiz shows make the best of a bad lot and show they are good sports.

'A doctorate, like a PhD? Fantastic! So you're doing that for college back home? Where do you go to college?'

'Newnham, Cambridge.'

'Wow, Cambridge! That's wonderful. I love those opening scenes in *Brideshead Revisited*, where Sebastian atones for vomiting in the window by covering Charles's room in flowers.

I have a friend who watches those scenes from the TV series over and over again – he has it on video. Anytime he's feeling a bit under the weather he sticks it on and it's on rewind until he feels better. He had to get a second copy of the video because it started jumping, he rewound it so much. He's a gay, of course.'

Jenny nodded. 'Yes indeed, the architecture of Oxford and Cambridge can be very similar.'

Jenny smiled and nodded. Nodded and smiled.

I was about to explain that I was not one of the students checking in, that in fact I had just punched out from my cleaning shift.

'You're checked in?' Jenny asked.

And with an electric prickle of all-over shame I copied Jenny's nod. I nodded. Yes. I pushed out of my head, the fib, the untruth, the obfuscation, the misunderstanding, the joke (which would it be?) that I had just passed by Jenny.

I tried to say that I was studying part-time at the University of Massachusetts, that I was registered on the master's programme in English literature and I should have it done within two years, but that felt like a lie even though it was, in fact, factual. The actual truth was that I was one of the 40,000 'New Irish' in Boston. (I might say 'undocumented' or 'don't actually have my own Green Card'. I wouldn't say 'illegal'.) Jenny must surely have noticed the Irish people her age who were working all over Boston: if she had bought a coffee or a beer in Harvard Square, she would most likely have been served by an Irish person in their twenties. I tried to tell her I was one of the New Irish, but I felt a weird disjunction, a kind of shame, and it wasn't only that I had just pulled a fast one in trying to pass myself off as a Fulbright scholar, it was simply that it was embarrassing to be from a country that was so patently failing at sorting itself out.

'Where are you studying, Ro?'

'Eh, same as yourself.'

'You're in Harvard too!'

'Eh, no, like, I'm in Boston too. UMASS. And I'm also studying English. I'm nearly fluent.'

Jenny didn't seem to get the joke, she nodded sagely.

'What's your dissertation topic?'

'Well, eh, it's a master's I'm doing, so it's all courses, like, no thesis as such.'

I tried to tell Jenny that I was a part-time student, but instead I ended up in a very long explanation about how I had tried my hand at waitressing.

'I was crap at it. You know, I worked with brilliant girls – they could shimmy around and have banter with the customers and let them know the specials and sort out all the different options and combos and remember what to hold, what to put on the side, what to substitute, and they could get all the plates out and back without a bead of sweat breaking or a hair falling out of place. But me? I was a mess. I could only do a quarter of the tables everyone else could do. It just took me ages to get the orders down properly while remaining any way civil. If I speeded up it was just a disaster – I couldn't say, "Hello, I'm Ro, your server for today," without making it sound like a threat. And I would come back to them stressed as high as a harp string with entirely wrong orders all round. No tips then. I think I only ever got tips out of pity. So I wasn't able to make any money. My only regret is that The Purple Shamrock fired me before I got organised enough to quit.'

I didn't know why I had gone into such detail or why I had ever begun to talk about my waitressing failings. Jenny listened with an expression of polite concern. When she was certain I had finished she replied, 'I've been rather boring in not taking up the opportunity to take a part-time job. I've just spent my time in the libraries.' Her polite reply seemed to seal my lie that I was a Fulbright scholar studying at UMASS.

I tried again, I tried to tell Jenny that I had a job caring for an elderly woman called Clara Goldfarb, but I just moved my hands around without getting any words out. Jenny was kind – she smiled and nodded again as I seemed about to say something but didn't. I was acutely aware that I liked Jenny. I liked and admired her politeness. After an awkward period of silent nodding and smiling, I lowered my head and stepped away, and I could feel relief, both my own and Jenny's. It really was a bit of bad luck that the person I spoke to was English, out of all of the two or three hundred-plus nationalities crowding around I had to land up talking to the polite and uptight English one.

However, before I finally left Jenny, I had a pressing question to ask her.

'What are you writing on, Jenny, for your thesis?'

She announced in a voice used to performing in competitive tutorials that she was working on the poetry of Emily Dickinson. Apparently everyone was wrong about Emily D. Jenny said that 'the editorial presentation and reception of her work has mispresented and misunderstood her radical innovations in poetic metre and subject matter'.

I was impressed. 'Jenny, I love her! I just love Emily Dickinson!' And I began to recite:

'Wild nights – Wild nights!
Were I with thee
Wild nights should be
Our luxury!

Futile – the winds –
To a Heart in port –
Done with the Compass –
Done with the Chart!'

I stopped short, feeling a complete and utter eejit, but Jenny stared at me intently and answered:

'Rowing in Eden –
Ah – the Sea!
Might I but moor – tonight –
In thee!'

We smiled. The poetry absolutely sealed it. We were friends now.

I hung back while Jenny checked in. The entire front of house staff of the Copley Plaza Hotel was Irish. The hotel was owned by an Irish-American and he had some deal going with US Immigration which allowed him to employ Irish people who had trained in hospitality and catering. I didn't work for the hotel, I worked for an agency that supplied cleaners, but I knew the two girls at the reception desk. When Jenny went off to her room I slipped in behind the desk.

'How's it goin'?' I murmured to Sinead, one of the receptionists, as I picked up a Fulbright conference pack from a leftover pile.

'Ro, love, I think they all have names on them,' said Sinead.

I dug through the pile until I found a few that didn't have a registered *Student name* and *Home country* at the front of the pack.

'This is spare,' I said to Sinead. 'And if there is any hassle, sure I can hand it back in.'

Sinead looked doubtful. 'Why do you want it, Ro?'

'I'm just interested,' I replied.

I read through the schedule of events for the Fulbright students while I was walking across icy Copley Square to the Boston Public Library. I was thinking of what Fulbright student cultural events and talks I would be free to attend between my cleaning jobs and taking care of Clara Goldfarb. My idle daydreaming was beginning to shape itself into a plan as I climbed up the steps of the library and swung in through the heavy doors.

I had got used to referring to the library as the BPL. Entering the BPL had become a ritual for me. I loved that moment of putting my body weight behind the cold wrought-iron trellis of the doors and pushing my way through to the marble hall. As I climbed the wide and worn stone steps of the staircase, I liked to put my hand on the shiny brass rail that ran down the centre of it, to touch the dreams of all the other readers who had gone before me. I always paused at the entrance to the Central Reading Room, I liked to take a moment to delight in the sight of the room which was a dreamy fusion of an Italian Renaissance palace with a French Baroque ballroom.

I had come to the library in the last week in August, the very first week I had arrived in Boston, nearly seven months ago. The library and reading room had been a culture shock. I thought there was no way I would ever be able to read in that room bigger than a football pitch, with its wide oak tables. The weather on that August day had also been shocking: the heat was so wet it was like breathing through an old facecloth. I could smell the tang of Boston harbour creeping through the artery of the Charles River, the pungency of rapidly rotting seaweed, the crawl of flies on dead molluscs, the diesel of giant cargo ships. I hadn't realised the spinning Earth could generate such a mix of acid daylight, beating heat and waves of sweating moisture. The air conditioning of the library had hummed a welcome chill, but I needed to get out. I had stumbled out of the building but instead of finding the street I was in the open centre of the BPL, a prairie of a formal garden, all neat rows of calf-high box hedging, triangles of lawn and a playing fountain with the requisite hunted nymph. I had sat on the marble floor under the colonnade of arches, squinting up at the glinting edifice of the library towering around the cloistered garden. I missed home. I missed dampness that was cold. I missed soft, bending, dipping light, the slow colours. I missed nooks and crannies and clogged ditches, the dripping of rain from hedges and the steady thickness of quiet dying, the heavy air of the long gone.

I hadn't returned to the library until February, until I was four weeks into my classes: ENG 527 The American Gothic and ENG

553 The Harlem Renaissance. I had made my peace with the BPL reading room. The acres of space above my head still felt wrong, but I had settled on my spot. My ritual now was to walk down the long length of the room to the last tables and camp on either one of the furthest corners facing back into the room.

Today, both of my spots were already occupied. I took that as an encouraging sign to put my sketchy plan into action and I swivelled back towards the Copley Plaza Hotel. I entered by a side door and made a deft dash into the function room where the Fulbright scholars were having a buffet lunch. I couldn't see any hotel workers in evidence and regarded that as another good sign. I picked up a plate and a bread roll and joined the queue for the buffet of cold meats and cheeses.

'Hello.'

The good-looking blond boy in front of me had turned around. His name tag proclaimed 'AUSTRIA' in large capital letters but it was difficult to read his name, which was in much smaller lettering.

'Hans,' he said, when he saw me trying to decipher the script.

'And I'm Ro.'

We shook hands.

'Where are you from, Ro?'

'Oh Ireland, I took off the tag, I didn't like people staring at my breasts.'

Hans laughed and introduced me to the boy standing next to him.

'Here is my fellow Austrian, Feet.'

I turned to shake his hand. 'Feet? Hans and Feet? Really?'

'Not Feet. FRITZ.' The boys laughed, a bit manically I thought.

They looked a pair: slim with blond floppy hair, smooth skin, blue eyes, wide smiles, crisp chinos and light blue shirts. The Austrian boys were both studying International Human Rights Law at Harvard. They declared it very funny that an Irish girl was studying English literature in America. I told them I was nearly fluent in English and thankfully they understood the joke, although their hilarity was a tad disconcerting. One of them said that even though they were Austrian they were both nearly fluent in German, and the two of them cracked up.

I liked the lads, they were shiny with the ease of affluence and they instantly included me in their pairing, so I was now one of a trio, which was very handy as the boys took on the job of introducing me to other students. Hans and Fritz were wonderful at mingling. They told me they both planned to be diplomats and it seemed they had already started accomplishing the soft skills of that smooth profession. I was enjoying myself, except for those times when Hans and Fritz gave me credit for making a witty pun with their names and it was my sad fate they shared the joke with all the other students we met. 'Hands and Feet! Hands and Feet!' Only the two Japanese students seemed to genuinely think it funny.

I was anxious about bumping into the genuine Fulbright scholars from Ireland, if indeed there were such creatures. I also shimmied away from the Fulbright administrators who brandished clipboards, as they obviously had lists that no doubt had tick marks. I thought I might be able to blag my way out of any possible query by just pulling out my cleaning agency staff ID and saying I was … I didn't know exactly what I would say, but something would come to me, it always did.

After lunch the plan was that the students were going to board buses to take them to the Science Museum for a guided tour and a special screening in the IMAX cinema of the documentary film *Race for the Moon*.

'Hi.' I fell in next to Jenny as the students were filing out of the hall.

'Oh hello!'

'Are you actually going to go to the Science Museum?' I asked.

'I expect so, that's where the buses are going,' replied Jenny.

'Yeah, but I'm sure you've been there before?'

'No, actually. It was never on my list.'

'You see, I was thinking we could go down to Haymarket and visit the Friday market and get some oysters and go on the ferry that goes over to Logan, the ferry is free if you get a transfer at Haymarket T, we wouldn't get off, of course, we would travel back. The view of the city from the harbour is so different, it's beautiful and it's so good to be on the water. It'll be cold, of course. You'll need a warmer jacket.'

'Oh. I see. I don't actually have a warmer coat. Not with me.'

I realised I was scaring Jenny. She did not seem to be the kind of girl who skipped out of a printed schedule and besides, she didn't know me from a hole in the wall. I bit back questioning Jenny on what kind of warm coat she had and if she had actually managed to survive Boston's winter with just an English winter coat. My friends, Eily and Mels, had taken pity on me when I had arrived at their apartment one morning in winter, crunching through the early snow wearing only a parka jacket. Mels had insisted on giving me a duck-down coat that reached below my knees.

'Well, OK so,' I said as I tried to push away the intensifying realisation that, best-case scenario, Jenny was thinking I was just a bit of an eejit and harmless.

'That does sound a lot more fun than a Science Museum trip,' she said. 'I'm afraid I haven't been terribly adventurous in my time here.'

I drifted along with Jenny towards the three buses lined up outside the hotel. The Fulbright administrators seemed to be counting people. Hans and Fritz called me over, they were just about to embark on the second bus. I followed the boys, Jenny followed me, and before I quite knew what was happening I was on the bus in the company of the Fulbright scholars.

I spent the rest of the afternoon trying not to follow Jenny around the Science Museum but only occasionally succeeded.

Jenny often laughed at one of my questions or in the middle of a serious story when I was explaining something. Seeing my perplexity, she would say, 'Oh. You were serious? Were you serious? Oh, you were serious. I am so sorry.'

'I wasn't serious if you're laughing. I love hearing you laugh.'

'Oh, I'm so sorry, Ro, I really thought you were being funny.'

I wasn't often sure what Jenny found funny but I had become addicted to her laughter, it was deep and gentle. Jenny had beautiful brown eyes. Jenny's laughter made up for all of the times when she failed to recognise I was joking.

'Yes. Yes,' Jenny would say, nodding earnestly in a concentrated fashion, and I knew she hadn't a clue what I was on about.

Even as we continually missed the beat of understanding each other, we continued to circle around each other. Or rather, I kept returning to Jenny's side.

I got the Fulbright bus back to the hotel and as it shuddered to a stop I snapped out of my fantasy date with Jenny. I realised with a jolt I would have to scarper fast to go to my next job. I muttered, 'I've to go Jenny,' and I was the first off the coach when its door sighed open. I was slipping across the dark cold of Copley Square, walking towards the T with a familiar chorus of self-recrimination resounding in my head (*Why the fuck did I not think about how much of a tool I was until after the event?*), when I heard my name being called in that strangely lovely English accent.

'Ro? Are you going to Haymarket now?'

'No, sure it's dark, Jenny.'

'The ferry? It might be nice to see the city at night?'

'Eh. Well. I can't go right now.'

'Where *are* you going?'

OK, now it was time to come clean, to confess all.

'You know Jenny, I actually work.'

'What?'

'Like, part-time.' I was backsliding, but I stuck to some factual truths. 'I have a job looking after a Jewish lady out in Brookline, the three weekend nights. I usually stay over, Friday, Saturday, Sunday, 8.00 p.m. to 8.00 a.m. Though this weekend I've Sunday free. I'm off there now.'

'Oh.'

'Yeah.'

'So you won't be around for tonight's trip to Fulbright Alumni homes?'

'Eh ...' (*just feckin' tell her*, said the voice in my head) ... 'no.'

'You couldn't get the weekend off?'

'Well ...' This was it. I was going to come clean. I looked at Jenny's face under the halogen glare and shadow of the lights of Copley Square. It was time to step up and be a grown-up and own up to being a total messer.

'... Well, as it's Easter it was hard, you know, everyone else who looks after Clara is Irish and they all want to go to the pubs today, it being Good Friday.' *(Just tell her, you langer!)* And I really like Clara. She's amazing actually.' I felt shit.

'You're very conscientious,' said Jenny with an admiration so sincere it stabbed me.

'I'm a langer,' I announced, without explanation as to what that might mean. I dumped my bag on the ground and shrugged off my duck-down coat.

'Here, girl, this was given to me out of the kindness of someone who took pity on me. It's time I passed it on and got my own coat. They tell me we could have another month of this beyond baltic weather. Put this on. You can't be wandering around freezing Boston in thin jackets and English wool coats.'

Jenny seemed somewhat stunned. I put the coat around her shoulders and pressed the top fastener closed around her throat.

I laughed. 'Nice cloak, Jenny!'

'I can't take this from you. What are you going to wear?'

'Don't thank me, thank the woman who gave it to me in the first place, her name is Mels Gallagher, that's who you should thank. And I'm alright to get to Clara's house. The T takes me nearly to her door. And I've my hat.' I placed my hand on top of my Army surplus hat with ear-flaps tied under my chin.

'That is quite a hat.'

'My pals call me Amelia Airhead when they see me in it. But I don't care. It does the job.'

'I shall see you tomorrow, Ro. You are coming back in the morning, no?'

I heard myself saying, 'I am, yes. Of course. See you then.' *(Why the fuck did I say that?)*

I thought about Jenny for the entire journey as the swaying carriages of the T carried me out to Brookline.

# 2
## Everyday I Write The Book

I was perished by the time I arrived at Clara Goldfarb's. I was early by over an hour. It was going to be a treat for Jacinta, I would let her off early. Clara's daughter paid the bills but Jacinta Fitzsimons was in charge of organising the roster of Irishwomen who cared for Clara. As I arrived at the apartment building a resident was coming out the front door so I was able to slip inside and get the lift straight to Clara's apartment, where I cheerily rang the front doorbell. Jacinta was smiling a pretty smile as she opened the door but when she saw me she flashed a look of derision.

'What are you doing here?' she said.

'Surprise! I thought I'd let you off early. You can start the weekend early.'

'Daniel is collecting me here so I'm going to have to stay anyway. That's typical of you, Ro, you suit yourself but let on like you're doing a favour for other people.'

'Sorry. I thought it would be a nice surprise.'

'At the very least you should have phoned. Do you think you'll get paid extra? It's all money with you, isn't it?'

'No.' I was getting pissed off but also fearful of Jacinta getting even more cross. 'Look, I'll head. I'll come back at ten to eight.'

'I'll phone Daniel,' said Jacinta. 'He might be able to get here earlier. Wait downstairs at the front door. How did you get up here anyway?'

'Somebody let me in.'

'That's illegal, Ro, as you well know!'

I didn't know but I nodded anyway and turned and made my way towards the lift of the apartment complex.

It was a touchy subject with Jacinta, illegality. She and her boyfriend, Big Dan, both had legitimate visas and they were being sponsored by American relatives. They had been going out together since they'd met at University College Cork, where both of them had studied Economics. Jacinta and I had known each other slightly in UCC, we had friends in common, and Jacinta had seemed keen to help me when I'd first arrived in Boston. We had bumped into each other in the Tristram Shandy and Jacinta had said she could line me up with shifts looking after an old lady ('very easy gig'), but only if I was legal.

'Oh yeah, I'm legal,' I'd said. 'I've a Green Card through my auntie.'

'The illegals are giving the whole lot of us a bad name,' said Jacinta. 'Some of us are here legitimately but now all of us are tarnished with a bad brush because of the yokes who come in and overstay their welcome!'

I nodded. Jacinta was a bit of a dose, but I needed work.

'I remember you were a bit of a leftie, weren't you? I remember you protesting about the US and El Salvador or Nicaragua with the student hippies. But I'm glad to see you got over that and came to work here. Good! Well, it's rational for everyone to maximise their own interest,' said Jacinta with a clipped nod of approval.

I was uneasy being praised for hypocrisy. I had not tried to get a sponsored visa. I didn't know how, and anyway, there was no way in the wide earthly world I would want to live in America: that right-wing, global war-sponsoring, polluting, capitalist-racist state, founded on genocide with no social welfare system to speak of. America! A place full of wilfully deluded people who bought the bullshit that riches would invariably arrive if an individual worked hard enough. America!

Yet here I was. In America.

Even if Jacinta had been half-decent about her fellow Irish who were working without papers, I couldn't tell her that I was using my Auntie Kathleen's Green Card, which Kathleen had got when she had worked in the States in the 1950s. Kathleen would get a better pension if I got a job that paid taxes. So my secret was implicated in my Auntie Kathleen's scam. Green Cards were actually very basic affairs, they had no photograph, no date of birth, no information but a social security number. When I went for the interview with the cleaning agency, there were no questions asked once I could produce a Green Card. Kenny Flanagan, the owner, was Irish-American and he liked to give jobs to the New Irish who were coming in droves which hadn't been seen in Boston since the influx that had brought Auntie Kathleen and her friends thirty years previously.

Kenny Flanagan had shaken my hand and said, 'Welcome to the greatest country on earth, Kathleen. I'm Irish, too. We both survived the Famine.'

It was hard to imagine Kenny Flanagan had ever been within a time zone of a famine. He looked the quintessential Irish-American, that is, he looked absolutely Irish except more spruce, 20 per cent taller and 40 per cent wider than the average Irish man, and he had also benefited from the kind of orthodontic care not normally on display in an Irish mouth.

I swore curses at Jacinta Fitzsimons as I took the lift back down to the lobby. I sat down on the floor under the mail boxes and took out a collection of poetry by Langston Hughes and I was soon contentedly learning lines of his elegy for Billie Holiday. It wasn't a requirement to learn the poetry by heart but it was a habit I had got into as a child, and I loved the ways in which the poetry I had memorised took on more and different resonances within me as I got older. It seemed with every passing year I was able to hear something extra in the lines hardwired into my memory. And so the words of the dead are modified in the guts of the living.

I jumped when I heard Jacinta's voice. She was standing in front of me and declared, 'You can't sit here. Get outside the building.'

'It's too cold. I'm not doing that,' I said quietly, not looking up from my book.

Jacinta was not used to me being anything other than compliant with her wishes and appeasing her aggravation. She may have registered some shock as there was a brief pause before she began to berate me. However, I have excellent skills of zoning out when trouble comes visiting and I knew Jacinta would not leave Clara unattended for very long. I just had to wait this one out. I stared at her feet clad in white court shoes and nylon tights. I noticed that she'd actually ironed a crease into her denim jeans.

Sure enough, it was mere minutes before Jacinta had to leave, though not before she bent down to hiss in my face. 'You deserve everything that's coming to you, Rosemary McCarthy.'

I remained impassive, but Jacinta did freak me out. What did Jacinta Fitzsimons know about what was coming down the tracks for me? Jesus. It was not unheard of that people who had grudges would call US Immigration and those scary fellas would do a raid on a place of work or land in at 4.00 a.m. into the apartments of the illegal Irish. There was the awful story about four lads, brothers from Connemara, stopped as they came back into Logan airport, returning from their father's funeral, and they were put straight back onto the plane they had flown in on. Apparently they had got on the wrong side of some Irish-Americans on a job. Of course, they had all been able to get back in by going through Canada. They got collected by their buddies at Niagara Falls. But still. Was that what Jacinta was planning?

If I hadn't been so happy with Clara Goldfarb I would have walked off the job to leave Jacinta with the run of things, but I was mad about Clara – spending time with Clara was the highlight of my week. If my Granny McCarthy hadn't died she would be the same age as Clara Goldfarb. They were both born in December 1902: one was the daughter of a lobster fisherman in the Beara peninsula off west Cork and the other was the youngest daughter to the furrier in Moscow who supplied the Tsar and all his royal cousins throughout Europe with their fur coats and ermine trim. I believed my granny had sent Clara to me. Clara thought that idea was crazy Irish girl talk, but she did seem to half-like the notion. Whatever else happened with Jacinta Fitzsimons, I would always have to thank her for introducing me to Clara Goldfarb.

It wasn't long before Big Dan pulled up outside the building. He left the car running and ran gingerly across the frozen ground to the front door intercom. He was finding it difficult to tap in the numbers with his gloves on. I opened up the door for him. Big Dan was a nice fella.

'Hiya, Ro.'

'Dan.'

'Sound of you to let us off early.'

'Of course. Big parties tonight. Where are ye going?'

'Well. No plans as such.'

Jacinta and Big Dan were one of those couples who kept a tight ration on going out. They were saving. Big Dan was working in a bank, which was a crap job really, not paid well at all, not like at home, but Jacinta said it would look great on his CV when they went back to Ireland. Big Dan was also studying for a master's in actuarial science, whatever that was, but Jacinta said once he had the degree they would be coining money.

'How's the study going, Dan?'

'God, it's hard, you know, Ro! Not easy at all.'

We took the lift up together, chatting idly as we walked down the corridor to Clara's apartment. Jacinta opened the door. 'What are ye doing lurking at the door? And don't ye know it's illegal not to be buzzed into the building! I could see the car at the door on the intercom camera. Daniel, you've left it running, anyone could hop into it.'

'Sorry,' Big Dan and I replied in unison and I wanted to kick myself for saying sorry.

Jacinta gave a curt twitch of her head and walked rapidly towards the stairs and Big Dan waved absentmindedly at me as he hurried along behind her.

Clara was standing by her Zimmer frame in the kitchen. I gave her a hug and a kiss on the forehead and another on the top of her head. Clara was tiny. I was prone to declaring (out of Clara's earshot) that Clara was as cute as a mantelpiece ornament, like one of those little Russian Babushka dolls you find nesting inside a bigger Babushka (if the Babushkas wore Chanel, both the perfume and the twin-sets).

'Darling, happy birthday weekend!' said Clara as I planted kisses.

'Wow, Clara! I'm impressed you remembered!'

'Of course I remember! I'm not gone in the head. Not yet.'

'I think I forgot myself, to be honest.'

Clara started to direct me on what to take out of the fridge. We had a routine and on Fridays: it was always fillet steak and I made French fries with real potatoes, following Clara's precise instructions. I would pull one of the La-Z-Boy armchairs into the kitchen so Clara could see exactly what I was doing. We had a glass of Burgundy with our steaks from a half bottle and the remainder of the wine would go into a Bolognese sauce on Monday.

When we were settled into our meal I declared, 'I've a confession, Clara.'

'Honey?'

'Have you heard of Fulbright fellowships?'

'Yes, honey. For the smart students.'

'Well. I ended up crashing their conference today. All the international Fulbright students are in Boston for a weekend of networking and entertainment and I came across them when I was clocking out of my shift at the hotel and I just found myself talking to one of them and I just went along with them. I had the buffet lunch and I went to the Science Museum.'

I was ashamed. My voice was low and I couldn't look at Clara, though it was a relief to make the full confession.

'Honey! That is good! You should be with the smart kids! That's where you belong. You need to make friends there. Stop hanging out with the Irish. You know enough Irish.'

'Ah Clara, you don't get it. I crashed their gig. I'm not meant to be there. And Clara, anyway you know I haven't been in the pub in weeks.'

'Keep it like that, honey!'

Clara left me to my own thoughts as I prepared the meal. Clara knew that sometimes I needed to be quiet to drop the churning thoughts and shake my thinking back to being in good form. She just watched the TV in the meantime. Clara was actually in quite good health except that arthritis had gripped her joints, making movement painful and forcing her to be humiliatingly dependent on others to dress and undress her and to help her go to the bathroom. I loved Clara's stock grouchy line which admitted she needed to use the toilet: 'I need to go to the john, or the loo, or the bog, or the jax, whatever you Irish say. Such a lot of names so as not to have to say piss and shit!'

The only routine I didn't like was the argument Clara and her daughter Sophia regularly had on the phone. 'Honey!' Clara would protest. 'I really don't need someone here all the time. All day and all night! It's too much, darling! The expense!'

Clara would hold the phone away from her ear as Sophia worked herself up to a frenzy of anxiety. I didn't know why Clara ever started these arguments with Sophia. They invariably took the turn of Clara being threatened with Velcro clothing and adult diapers. Clara's weak point was her love of cloth, its texture, colour, the cut and line – in her gnarled bones she would always be a rag trade merchant and so the arguments always ended with Clara agreeing to put up with the Irish girls.

When Clara had first laid eyes on me she had been disturbed. After a few awkward minutes when I was trying to introduce myself Clara had limped off with her Zimmer frame to her bedroom to phone Sophia, who was with her family in their holiday home in Florida.

I was punished for my creeping earwigging at her bedroom door by hearing Clara declare, 'Darling, this Irish girl is not like the other ones. She looks like a young boy and I think she has the depression. She tells me it is a headache, but I think it is the depression or a hangover, she looks sick. It's a long time, this holiday season: two weeks of this I cannot stand.'

Clara repeatedly refused to have Sophia come and collect her and bring her to Florida. She agreed to give me a chance. She would give me twenty-four hours and then Sophia would phone around the agencies. Clara made an offer of going to a hotel.

'For a week, honey! Room service! I can stay in my nightdress, what would be the problem!?'

Clara had stayed in her room after the call and I had dithered about what to do. Clara was right, I had a ferocious hangover and only the dregs like myself would be available to work over Christmas. But the fact is that we were both just stuck with me. There was simply no one else to step in. I had asked some of the others what Clara liked and had brought her some chocolate-covered prunes and I had made gingerbread, which didn't work out all that well. I set about brewing up a stew of tea in the way I was told she liked it. I had finally got the prunes, gingerbread and tea all decked out on a tray by the time Clara shuffled back into the room.

'Lookit,' I declared, 'I know it's not much of a holiday time with me here, but maybe we can make the best of it?'

'What you got there, honey?'

'Well, I don't know how to celebrate Hanukkah, but I thought tea and cake might be a start.'

Clara had sighed as she'd struggled to get into her La-Z-Boy armchair. 'I don't do that Hanukkah anymore. I never did Hanukkah before I married my husband, Lenny, and I was already thirty-six! Before then I celebrated sixth of January, that was always the holiday when I was a girl. Now I don't really do anything.' She looked at the prunes and gingerbread and gave a half-smile. 'You're a nice kid.'

I poured her a cup of tea through a strainer. She scooped a spoon of strawberry jam from the glass jar I had put on the tray and stirred it in. She sat back and sipped, then she smiled at me.

'You make good tea! You can stay.'

I had loved those first two weeks I had with Clara. We got on mightily. I had asked Clara if it would be possible for me to use the phone to call home to Ireland on Christmas Eve.

'It is possible, yes it is possible! But you're not asking me if it's possible. You say to me you want to use the phone!'

'Eh. Only if it's no bother and I will pay of course.'

'Whaddya mean *bother*? You Irish don't speak straight up. It makes no trouble for me. No of course you don't pay! You use the phone anytime! You phone your family!'

I thought I had spoken very clearly, but apparently not by Clara's grammar. It took a lot for me to ask to use the phone. Transatlantic calls were so expensive.

'Thanks a million, Clara. I'll phone home so, and I'll keep it brief.'

'That's all right, honey.'

But I hadn't called home on Christmas Eve, and I woke on Christmas Day with the guilty weight of not having phoned the family as I had written to them that I would.

Clara had asked me how the call had gone, and I'd had to admit I hadn't phoned. I didn't tell her that I felt paralysed with being a fuckup. And so it continued, most days I assured Clara that I would phone home, but each day it never happened, and each day I felt more oppressed by having let down my family.

On the sixth of January, Clara had insisted that I had to phone home. It was a holiday in Cork, Nollaig na mBan (Women's Christmas). It was the middle of the day in Ireland and everyone else was out of the house except for my mother, who had started to cry when she heard my voice. Mam stopped crying as quickly as she had started and became anxious as to why I was phoning home: she kept asking what was wrong, but I told her everything was fine.

'Really. Grand, actually.'

Mam told me about the weather in Cork (it was raining) and I told her about the weather in Boston (very cold, but no snow).

Christmas was 'Grand, grand,' she said. 'We got through it fine, everyone came to us for the dinner. Your father kept on expecting you to phone. But I told him it wouldn't cross your mind.'

Neither of us could think what else to say to each other. Clara took the phone, and she held my hand while she told my mother what a good girl she had, very polite and hard-working, and a master's student too! Mam was rightly surprised at that information as I had never admitted that when I wrote home. Mam said she'd heard studying was expensive in America. She asked Clara if it meant I would stay longer in the States.

'Do you know that she had a good job here?' Mam said. 'Well, the job was in Dublin, but it was a very good one.'

Mam had asked Clara if I was eating well, she had asked if I was warm and without waiting for an answer she had asked how I looked, if I had let my hair grow. Mam apologised and said she should have asked me these questions but she never could think what to say to me on the phone. She thanked Clara for looking after me.

'We're all laughing here at the idea that Rosemary is being paid to look after someone. I'm quite sure it's the other way around. I know full well that you'll be the one taking care of her. I just hope she's not too much of a burden to you, Mrs Goldfarb. Though I'm sure she's entertaining enough with all her stories.'

'You have raised a good daughter, Mrs McCarthy. She is caring for me very well. She has a very good heart and she is a smart girl.'

'Oh, she's smart alright,' said Mam.

Clara seemed to understand the jibe. She jerked the phone receiver from her ear, held it in front of her and shook her head at it. She passed the receiver to me.

'Hi Mam.'

'God, you're a dark horse. What are you doing a master's in?'

'English.'

'Jesus, Mary and Joseph. I thought you already did English! What kind of job can you get with that?'

'I just like doing it.'

We were both silent then.

'I thought you said you were only going to be over there for three years,' Mam said softly.

'That's the plan.'

'It doesn't sound like that's the plan if you're spending money on doing more college.'

'I am saving,' I said as I swore to myself that I would begin saving.

There was more silence then.

'It's a pity there's only me here,' said Mam eventually, 'your dad will be sorry not to have talked to you, and Mossy and Ger too.'

I gave a sob then. That shocked me. I think I was going to say something but whatever it was got drowned in a big sob. I tried to catch my breath, but I was full on silently heaving with tears on my face. I missed my brothers. I missed my dad. I missed Mam.

'Rosemary, are you alright?' asked Mam. She had sounded upset.

I sucked in and held it together. 'Grand, Mam, really grand.'

'We don't know what's going on with you over there,' she said. 'Your letters tell us nothing, they're full of descriptions of things. No real news.'

'I'll write better letters.'

'Do.'

'Tell everyone I was asking for them.'

'Oh, are you going so?'

'No. I don't have to.'

There was more silence.

Mam sighed. 'You had better go. This is costing a fortune. I'll think of all the news after I put the phone down.'

'I know.'

'Bye so. Be careful, Ro. Mind yourself. You can come home anytime, you know that right? There's always a place for you here.'

'Thanks, Mam. Bye, Mam.'

'Bye.'

'Bye.'

Mam sighed. 'Bye so, bye, bye.'

'Bye.'

'Bye.'

I put the phone down as gently as I could, it gave the softest click. I was wrecked.

Over the course of those two weeks, while the rest of the world celebrated the holidays, Clara answered the long stream of questions I had about her life. At any moment I was prepared for her to tell me to shut up but, in fairness, she answered every question. She talked about 'the Terror' as if I knew what that meant and said her family had stayed on too long. There had been a particularly bad night. Clara didn't say much directly about it, but I guessed that rape was involved. I didn't know what questions to ask about that. It seemed she needed my questions to tell the story but I didn't know how to ask about that night.

Clara sat in her armchair and spoke up at the ceiling.

'After that night, when my soul went straight up and I could look down and see what they were doing to me, since then I stand next to myself. And I keep standing and I keep going, you know? And it's like a habit now and I don't know how to stop it. I don't wanna step back into myself, but I don't wanna be so bored and so tired anymore. Not to be waiting: that would be good. Just to stop.'

I had held one of Clara's twisted hands between my own hands as she kept talking. Eventually she told me about Pyotr, Petya. She didn't tell me everything, in fact, she didn't tell me much.

'Was he your boyfriend?' I asked.

'Boyfriend? Yes. I think that's how you say it.'

Clara told me how she had waited for him when she lived in Paris for years with her broken father.

'They held Papa that night, you know, and they made him watch what they did. And he kept screaming, "Kill me! Kill me!" Afterwards it was like he never could see anything else. I could see that night still on his eyeballs. He stared, always terrified at the world. When he looked at me he had horror stuck on his eyes. I tried never to look in his eyes.'

Clara waited in Paris, among the other Russians, for news of Petya. But there was never any news, of any kind. She told me how she had exhausted the patience and interest of all the emigré Russians by not marrying. But how could she?

Clara hadn't wanted to go to America. She was employing seamstresses in Paris, but her father didn't realise that Clara's girls were mainly making blue overalls for workmen. It was a good business, but if he knew her business was overalls for workmen, he would be completely defeated. Her girls also made ball gowns – that business her father knew of – and the crazy new dresses for the jazz girls. Her father begged her to take him to America. Clara believed he hoped she would forget Petya when she had to learn English. But Petya wasn't the only reason Clara could not face suitors. She believed her father knew this and it kept him broken. She eventually agreed to go to America because maybe he was right. Maybe moving again would change everything.

Her father died during the crossing. Clara said, 'They say buried at sea, but they fed Papa to the fishes.' Her father's body was wrapped in winding sheets that twisted away as he was swung out over and down into the salt water, somewhere that was nowhere among the sighing waves. The white sky breathed snow which dissolved into the wrinkling black ocean. A chaplain said prayers in English. He was the last of her family. She was alone in the world, so maybe it was just as well she was going to the New World. At least she would no longer have to look at that reflection of herself on his scorched eyeballs. He had long ceased to be a father to her. But he had been her father when she was a girl and needed a father. She would always be grateful for that. She was going to the so-called New World although she felt more ancient than fog. She was twenty-eight.

'When I come to Boston, I learn I'm not a Russian. No! Only a Jew! The Russians already here in Boston had no time for a Jew. Jews were Bolsheviks.' Clara had shrugged.

'So I don't meet with the Russians. Why would I explain when they already knew what they knew? I come here to this country just in time for the Great Depression, that was what they called it. And that was no matter to me. I made my business. I married a good man.'

Lenny was from Lithuania, he was saving to bring his family over. Clara was able to pay to bring them all over, and everyone came except the grandmothers.

'We never ask about the old ladies because our family story is such a lucky one and we want to keep that lucky story. And maybe the old ladies die of old age, in their beds, in the quiet winter. That's what we say. Now Sophia has lots of cousins and not every Jew her age can say that.'

The last big business Clara had made was detachable shoulder pads. She sold them in tubes to busy young women, the shoulder pads had Velcro strips. She let her son-in-law into the business and he persuaded her to take on money-men partners. The money-men took over the business, they had to pay big, big money to take her business, but they took it. The shmucks didn't understand it was actually Clara who made the business, they thought she was just the cranky old mother-in-law. They moved the factories to the Philippines.

'They do nothing now but T-shirts. T-shirts! What kind of business is that?!'

Clara liked to repeat her worries about her grandsons who were going to a college in the hills of Western Massachusetts.

'So they themselves decide the name of their degrees! What do you think of that?!'

I had to admit I'd never heard the like.

'They are nice boys, but with degrees they name themselves they will never be taken on to manage anything. But maybe they will be artists? That is not such a bad thing.'

Clara liked to ask me to tell her stories about my family, but I often didn't know what to say. She would give me prompts.

'Describe the Corrrrk!'

'It's just Cork, there's no 'the' and there's only one 'r', it's just Cork.'

'See! You say rrrrr: Corrrrrk!'

There was never any point in arguing with her. I would describe Cork, safe in the knowledge that she would never get to visit the place for herself.

'It's the capital city of Ireland and there are 365 bridges which criss-cross the city's fifty-two islands. There are four rivers that flow in from the north, the south, the east and the west and they conjoin to form a new and mighty river called the Lee. This huge river flows from the city four miles down to the harbour, which is the second largest in the world but much more beautiful than Sydney. We sing the song 'The Banks' to celebrate the rivers. There are seven hills encircling the city and they are each so steep that houses have to be built into the cliff faces because otherwise the buildings would topple over. We walk up the hills by hanging on to metal handrails.'

Clara never seemed to tire of that description. I would describe the college I went to, UCC, in quite factual terms.

'The revolutionaries took the statue of the Famine Queen from the top of the college tower and buried her in a secret location under rose bushes. They replaced her with a statue of the saint who founded a monastery there centuries before and now, where he once taught, all from the Munster region go to learn.'

'The College of Knowledge! That's good!' Clara would say.

I had only been in Dublin for less than a year, but I had some stories from there as well. I told her that Dublin was not the real capital of Ireland, but it's where the parliament meets, and it constantly smelled of coal fires and occasionally the sharp roasting of green hops. When it rained your clothes got stained with soot. My job as a civil servant in the Department of Education was boring. My boss, a woman, Miss McInerney, kept ducking down behind her desk to secretly massage her face with Johnson's Baby Lotion. She was silent for days on end and then would erupt into whispered hours of warning me against having sex outside marriage and 'winding up pregnant'. She said she would help me if I ended up 'in that sad fate'.

Clara thought it clear that Miss McInerney was mad, and she tried to point this out to me. However, I knew Maura McInerney was merely lonely and I felt obliged to keep in touch with her. I wrote to her fairly regularly from Boston and she always wrote back immediately, typed, detailed pages, although she never actually had any news except what work was passing through the department and who had been interviewed by Gay Byrne on *The Late Late Show* and what they had said to Gay and what he had said back to them. Miss McInerney was from the countryside, somewhere in Westmeath, but she didn't go back to her family for the holidays. I had to explain to Clara that this was a very unusual state of affairs in Ireland.

'Even if you don't get on with your family, you still spend the holidays with them.'

Clara said, 'What happens if you hate them?'

'You don't hate them,' I said. 'Well, maybe if you hate them, you just emigrate.'

I said Miss McInerney probably had a baby outside wedlock and had to give it up for adoption. Clara wasn't sure she had ever heard the phrase 'an illegitimate child'.

Clara thought having four siblings meant I was from a very big family. Eventually she had to leave me insist that five children in a family was not counted as an especially large family in Ireland. I told her my parents thought that their first two children, my brother Mick and sister Mags, were no problem at all but that they must have done something wrong with me and my two younger brothers, Mossy and Ger. The hardest thing was trying to explain to Clara how I had disappointed and upset my parents.

'Well, you see Mick works in accounts in a pharmaceutical firm and Mags is a nurse.'

'So!?'

'Well, you see. They're respectable. Right? Like, they've done the right things.'

No matter how much I explained, she didn't seem to understand that I hadn't done the right things.

'They just think I'm a bit of an eejit. They didn't know why I wanted to go to college if I didn't want to be a teacher. They really were shocked when I gave up my job in the Civil Service. I think they think I might have got fired.'

I had finally admitted to Clara that I was not (strictly speaking) a 'legal' worker and how upset my mam and dad would be if they ever found out that I had lied about having a visa to work in America. I was relieved Clara brushed aside the matter of my lack of papers.

'So, they don't know about the deal with your shady aunt. That's good! You're doing good. You're studying, you can get legal in a few years if you pay your taxes, and you will do that. Why do you think your parents think you are a no good? That I don't know! Maybe your soft heart makes you soft in the head.'

The only other thing that puzzled Clara was when I told her my dad was a police sergeant. Why, wondered Clara, are all the Irish police?

I had to learn to step back and leave Clara get herself onto her La-Z-Boy chair without any assistance. It was hard to stand by and just watch as Clara struggled to lever herself onto the chair. I was always relieved to hear her satisfied sigh as she settled in and tilted back to a recline. The chair was positioned in front of the TV, and as far back as the wire of the fancy channel changer would allow. Clara liked pressing the button on the channel changer and she liked to shout 'So long, sucker!' at those dumb TV people when she switched from their channel.

Clara maintained she could walk without the Zimmer frame, but it was good to have it to rest on. Mostly she just watched TV or read newspapers for a bit. I had got her some books on tape, and Clara liked the Dickens guy, but sometimes he was confusing. She dozed and napped a lot, she was mostly bored but didn't know what to do about that. We both enjoyed despising Ronald Reagan and we shared our gathered intelligence and most recent opinions while eating the suppers I cooked.

Recently, I had started to bring LP records and tape cassettes from the library to play for myself and Clara. I had given a lot of thought as to what I would bring to play over my birthday weekend. It would have to be something we could both love. The music librarian had been very patient with me and had finally and definitively recommended Tchaikovsky. Clara wasn't immediately impressed.

'Me and Lenny went to the Symphony just about every week during the season, but not to the Russian music.'

'Why?'

'Why! I don't know. Why?! We just didn't go to the Russian music. Especially not to the ballet music, not even to *The Nutcracker*, which they do every single holiday time.'

'Well this isn't ballet music. This is for a string orchestra.'

'Every orchestra has strings!'

'Just humour me, Clara, it's my birthday weekend.'

'Tchaikovsky? OK. I will listen. It might be a good thing, you seem so jumpy tonight, honey. You know it is good you are hanging out with the smart kids. That's where you should be!'

I sighed and shrugged.

Clara persisted. 'I'm an old lady, so I know things. I see what you should do with your life!'

I said, 'It's funny how it is so much easier to see what someone else should do with their life and so difficult to see what you should do with your own.'

'That's normal. That's what life is.'

'What do *you* want from your life, Clara?'

'Honey!' Clara snapped. She took a breath and tried to speak more evenly.

'When I wake up I think, "Oh! I'm still here!" I watch myself, I see myself continuing on and on and not knowing how to stop.'

I nodded though I didn't really understand what Clara was saying to me.

I turned off the overhead lights and put on the lamps. I tucked up Clara under a mohair blanket which helped just a little to soothe her ribs which seared when she forgot not to sigh. I put on the music: *Andante Cantabile*.

When Clara heard the cello she smiled at me – and nodded. I watched her as she closed her eyes and settled back further into her armchair.

'I am back a long time ago, Ro, sitting in the red velvet seats, with my sister Anna and all of the people of the city are in the theatre.'

I curled up in my own armchair and thought of Clara and Anna and all of Moscow in the auditorium and I let the cello catch my breath. The cello took the breathing of the entire audience and brought us outside, into the thickness and silence of snow, we saw the orioles of light around the gas street lamps and we drifted beyond the square through the criss-crossing facets of streets under the diamond glint of moon. The world was still. There was a breaking. A staccato breaking open. Dawning. Dawn. Daybreak. A flood of unexpected warmth, a crashing forth of blossom. And still the hearts beat. Strings are plucked. The hearts beat because they have to. The breath comes in, because it must. A resonance lingers in the moisture of the air and in the breathing of those who were there.

I woke with a jolt. I had fallen asleep in the La-Z-Boy chair next to Clara. The needle was hissing on the warmth of the vinyl. I was kinked at an awkward angle and my neck hurt. I couldn't remember what I had been dreaming about, but it had been very important. I tried to recall the last sensations, to trace the dream back into my consciousness, but all the vivid dream-knowing was now lost. Clara had thrown a small blanket over me and gone to bed.

I tilted up my chair and dug myself upright and set about going to bed. First, I checked on Clara. She was in her room, fast asleep on her bed, lying on her back, softly snoring and fully clothed. I felt shit at being such a crap care assistant.

When I was changed into my night-time tracksuit bottoms and sloppy T-shirt, I sat up in the kingsize bed in one of the spare rooms that was my bedroom when I stayed over. So much had happened today. I would never get it all down in my diary but I should write some headlines. I held a pen over the blank pages of my jotter. I was too tired to write anything other than: *Day before my Birthday, Good Friday, April 20th 1984* and *HUGE day. I met Jenny*. I realised I didn't know Jenny's surname. I would ask her tomorrow. I would go back to the Fulbright Experience just so I could get Jenny's surname, and then I would leave her alone and not be a further langer.

# 3
# Nothing But The Same Old Story

Early the next morning I woke with a wisp of a story in my head that I tried to chase down in the pages of my jotter.

I tried to describe a day in Boston in late November. My central character was cycling down the steep hill to the house on Foster Street, which is where I lived, in a house share with six Irish lads. The lads declared that 'officially' they lived in Foster Street though 'actually' they lived at a different address with their girlfriends. I regularly had the large house entirely to myself, unless one of the lads was temporarily on the wrong side of the girlfriend. It was the girlfriends who seemed to want to be able to say to their parents back home that they didn't (*officially*) live with their fellas. The difference between 'official' and 'actual' seemed to sum up an awful lot about being Irish.

In the draft of my story I had my central character, Patsy, speed down Foster Street hill on her bike. She (or maybe it was he?) squeezed too hard on the crap brakes and the cables popped out and they dangled, clanking against the spokes of the front wheel as the bicycle took her on down the hill. Patsy prayed the cables wouldn't wrap around the wheel and cause the bike to stop at high speed: s/he/they would be fucked off in no time, and royally fucked. They could feel the sharp air scissor their cheeks.

The hill was very steep at the top but over a mile long and the slope lessened gradually before it hit the busy intersection down at Brighton Center. Patsy knew they needed to hold their nerve and pray nothing would cross their path.

The story was based, perhaps too precisely, on something that had happened to me. As Foster Street went on and on and took Patsy's bike and them with it, they resolved to get sober. There was no point in avoiding their life. They may as well face it all, it was going to happen anyway, with or without their full participation.

Before the end of the street, Patsy managed to curve the bike off to the right and up a steep incline into a small enclave of houses where they were able to jump off. Patsy's legs were trembling as they wheeled the bike back up Foster Street but they began to feel their spine straighten and shoulders relax as they faced the fact they had to go back to college again, it was the only thing they were really any good at, even if it was kind of a useless thing to be good at. And moreover, they knew they would have to find the lesbians. Yeah. Patsy was going to have to be a lesbian.

Before I got out of bed, I quickly read over the draft of my story. My stories regularly surprised me. Would *I* really have to find the lesbians, or was that what fictional Patsy had to do? I mean, Patsy's story really was *my* story. I had nearly killed myself, or rather an accident had nearly killed me, when my brakes had popped going down Foster Street on Thanksgiving Thursday and with my new resolve after the bike incident I again made enquiries at the University of Massachusetts to see if I could sign on to their master's programme in English literature.

Almost as soon as I had arrived in Boston last August, I had made my way out to the UMASS campus, but the bureaucracy of making an application had been too daunting. American bureaucracy was a whole load more complex and exact than the casual Irish approach to form-filling. At least UMASS didn't ask you if you were legal – there was no requirement to show them a Green Card, which was a relief – but they did want all kinds of documents from Ireland, like birth certs and transcripts of my degree, which also had to be notarised. I wasn't even sure if there was such a thing as a notary in Cork or if UCC actually did 'transcripts'. It was impossible to organise.

However, following the near-bike accident in November and with all the energy of making a fresh start, I had managed to get my brother Mossy on the case. I phoned him at his job, where he worked as a car mechanic. He was astonished to get a call from me.

'Long distance!' was all he could repeat for an expensive few minutes.

I had begged Mossy to help and he heard me. He took down the list of what was needed and set about doing it. Our parents thought that Mossy was a bit thick, that there was an unequal distribution of brain cells between me and him, that I had ended up with too much brain power and Mossy too little. But Mossy was sound. He had managed to get all the pieces of paper, including the required notarisation, and he had put them all in an envelope and posted them to Foster Street. He enclosed a John Hinde postcard of Patrick's Bridge. The camera that took the picture must have had some odd lens on it because the postcard made the bridge look an acre wide.

He wrote: *Remember your the best. And we all love you here.* He enclosed a book of poetry by Pam Ayres with another note written on the back of invoice paper from the garage he worked in: *You might have this one already Ro but I'm taking a punt on it. The lady in Easons says its good.*

I kept that postcard tucked into my jotter and regularly stared at it and at Mossy's precious greased thumbprint. The inside of the padded envelope smelled of Mossy: engine oil and metal, Clinic hair shampoo, Swarfega and goodness. I breathed in the molecules of Mossy's precious scent until all that was left was padded-envelope dust. Thanks to Mossy, I had managed to get enrolled at UMASS.

I closed up the jotter, tucking inside it the precious postcard. I scrambled into my clothes and peeped in at Clara – she was half awake.

'Oh Clara! I am so sorry I fell asleep! When I woke up you were already in bed. And you've had to sleep the night in your clothes!'

'Stop! Stop!' said Clara. 'I need no help to go to bed! I keep telling all you guys that!'

I winced. 'OK. But do let me help you with the buttons and zips, I know that is the only thing that can be a bit tricky for you. Let me help with your clothes so you can have a shower.'

Clara was silent as I helped her undress. I brought her Zimmer frame to her and hovered around while she made her way to her walk-in shower. She sat on the safety stool, I handed a facecloth and soap to her, took down the shower head from its wall mount and turned on the shower. Clara always stayed quiet when I helped her undress and shower. She started talking again once she had dried herself and I was helping her dress.

'I liked that music last night, honey.'

'Oh! I'm glad, Clara!'

'Yes. I'm gonna ask Sophia to get me that record. We can play it here then anytime we want. But I don't want to listen to it a lot. Just sometimes.'

'OK.'

I made Clara her favourite breakfast: warmed rye bread with scrambled eggs and smoked salmon. I gobbled mine quickly, becoming worried that the next carer, Helena Mulcahy, might be late. When Helena came in the door, I bade Clara the swiftest of goodbyes.

'Have fun, honey!' she yelled as I galloped out the door.

I rushed to the T. If I didn't hurry I would be late for my next Fulbright Experience.

I used my time on the T to do my usual thinking – it was about the only time in the day I had for thinking. I thought back to those months before I came to work for Clara. I was pathetic. I had given up a permanent and pensionable job with the Civil Service; I had colluded with Auntie Kathleen and lied to the parents about getting a Green Card visa; I had made this huge effort to get the hell out of the damp hole that was Direland but there I was in Boston, which turned out to be the capital of Galway. All I was doing was hanging out with Irish people in Irish bars, listening to Thin Lizzy, Paul Brady, the Boomtown Rats, and traditional diddly-idley music (the kind I never had time for at home), catching up on the Irish news (all bad), drinking gallons of Guinness and paying a dollar a pop for a bag of Tayto crisps. Whenever someone reminded me of some mad incident from those first four months in Boston (like driving up to Montreal with Ciarán Sully, coked out of our brains for the entire journey, up and back, and singing mad nationalist songs with some dodgy Québécoises in an underground bar with vaulted ceilings), or when someone recalled stories from drunken nights lost to me in blackouts, it was then I believed in guardian angels, holy spirits. The ghost of my dead grandmother was surely looking over me and had miraculously kept me from what should have been inevitable, disastrous harm. It was because of Clara and her eagle eye that I managed to sober up. She always knew if I had even the vaguest of hangovers and that was a bit mortifying. Of course I still took a drink, but not every night. I had even managed to pay visits to the Tristram Shandy and nurse the one pint without anyone actually noticing I wasn't lashing into the porter. I had avoided a slippery slope, a bad mangling crash in more ways than one.

 I ran off the T and up the stairs to Copley Square and arrived just as the last bus was leaving. The Fulbright students were going to get guided tours of Salem and Concord. Jenny and Hans and Fritz were waiting for me, standing on the steps of the coach.

 'Run!' the boys yelled.

 I mounted the bus without any thought other than I must talk with Jenny.

I sat in the seat next to Jenny and we talked for the next hour, in total agreement, about *Little Women*. I had a big passion for Thoreau, I had taken a copy of *Walden Pond* from Clara's house. I suspected I was at least slightly boring the arse off Jenny, but in any case she indulged me by letting me read out my favourite sections.

We walked together around the grand towns, talking constantly. I remembered to ask Jenny what her surname was.

'I go by Archer,' replied Jenny.

'Very Henry James.' I nodded approvingly.

'Most people say very Radio 4,' laughed Jenny.

I didn't know what Jenny was referring to, but I laughed regardless.

'What do you mean you "go by" Archer?'

'The full name is Cottington Archer.'

'Oh.'

'And your surname?' asked Jenny, somewhat shyly.

'McCarthy.'

Jenny nodded in a concentrated manner and seemed to hesitate. There was a pause between us and I guessed correctly.

'You're trying to avoid saying McCarthyism, aren't you?'

Jenny blushed and then couldn't stop laughing.

On the bus trip back to Boston, Jenny and I remained in deep conversation.

'I've a habit of making Irish friends,' she announced.

'Oh?'

'Yes, in college there was a boy from Liverpool called Tommy. I liked him. When my parents came I introduced them. My mother was so shocked.' Jenny laughed.

'Why?'

'Oh, you know, Irish Catholics, leaving the lights on during the war so the Luftwaffe could come and bomb Britain.'

I was stunned. 'I don't think that happened, Jenny.'

'My mother seems to think so,' Jenny nodded airily. 'She's got quite this thing about the Irish.'

I nodded as if I understood and accepted.

'My mother stays out of the sun. My father says she turns dark brown in the sun. And she is constantly oiling her hair – if she didn't, it would have tighter curls than my own frizz.'

'Is she mixed race?' I asked.

'Not on your life! She's from Cheltenham for generations. Her family has land.'

'Oh!' I nodded.

'Never there for the festival, though!' Jenny continued, perhaps mimicking her mother, her voice sounded overly correct. 'Too many Irish in the atmosphere!'

I felt a little deflated. Jenny looked at me and announced quite defensively, 'My father is quite cruel to my mother.'

'Oh!' I nodded again.

'She can never get cross with him, because if she does make a slip he is so pleased to tell her that her "bad blood" is showing. She stays rather quiet with him as a result. He is happy to have her cross about other things, just not with him. They both seem to rather enjoy being cross.'

'Do you have any brothers or sisters?'

'None. The parents were engaged for quite a while but married rather late. I think each was rather hoping someone better would come along.'

I didn't know what to say.

'Do your parents get on?' asked Jenny.

'Eh. I think so.'

Jenny laughed. 'What do you mean?'

'Like, I've never noticed them *not* getting on. Like, they just get on with things,' I floundered.

'It must be nice to be from a happy family,' said Jenny.

'We're just a family,' I replied weakly. 'Like, it's a mix of things.' I shut up. I would have to think about families. It was something I had never really thought about. Families were like weather – just something always there and going on mostly as usual.

The buses deposited us at the Isabella Stewart Gardner Museum. Afterwards there would be a reception at the Boston Museum of Fine Arts. I had decided it would be taking the piss entirely to stay for the reception and the free drink. In making the decision not to crash the reception, I felt virtuous and more at ease in being with the Fulbrighters on their tours. I told Jenny I was going to head away just before the reception but I would see her again the following day. Jenny became very grave. She put both her hands under my left elbow and seemed to want to steer me back outside the front door.

'What's up, Jen?'

'I have something I must say to you.'

My knees bent in the opposite direction to their usual fashion. The Fulbright students milled all around us.

Shite, I thought, it was good while it lasted. Fuck, so she figured it out. She'll never want to see me again. Jenny bowed her head and chewed her lower lip. We were standing in front of the Singer Sargent portrait, *Mrs Gardner in White*, the one where she looks like a drag queen before the wig goes on. The yards of curvy whiteness in the painting did nothing to ruffle Jenny, she gazed over my head into the middle distance to announce she was, in fact, a lesbian. Jenny had delivered this spiel before, or maybe she had just practised saying it a lot.

'Ah sure, Jenny, I know that,' I replied. 'I knew that when I went over to you at the check-in yesterday. That's why I went over to talk to you.'

Jenny seemed very pleased. 'Most people don't realise. It comes as quite a shock. They think not having your hair shorn and wearing a skirt means you can't be a lesbian.'

I digested this new information, it was awful to think Jenny would ever cut into her density of curls. I hadn't quite realised there was a lesbian uniform, but it seemed perhaps to be short hair and jeans which was good, that suited me. I would think about this later.

'I thought maybe you hadn't picked it up, it didn't seem to strike you,' said Jenny.

I repeated myself. 'No, I knew, I knew at check-in. That's why I went over to talk to you.'

'Why did you want to talk to a lesbian?' asked Jenny.

I was at a loss as to what to say. Why, why exactly did I want to talk to a lesbian? I hoped Jenny would know, but I didn't know what it was that I hoped Jenny would know. The only answer that rattled in my throat was 'because you looked so beautiful', and of course there was no way on God's green earth I was going to say that.

'Emmmm,' I replied, and I heard the words 'because you looked so beautiful' and it was me who had said them: out loud, straight from my heart, bypassing the protective conduits of common sense.

I wanted to claw the clammy phrase out of the air but Jenny was already laughing, she thought I was joking. She didn't seem to realise that anyone looking at her would be stunned by her beauty.

I kept a smile rigid on my face and surreptitiously breathed through my skin. We walked back down the stairs to join the rest of the group.

I persuaded Jenny not to get back on the bus, I said that it was just a short walk to the Boston Museum of Fine Arts and if she came with me we would, in all likelihood, be there before the buses arrived. I liked how myself and Jenny fell into step with each other. I liked that Jenny always crossed to be at my left-hand side. I felt protective. I was ready to put my left arm around Jenny and be ready with my right hand to defend and shield her from all comers.

I knew I needed to tell Jenny about Fionnuala, although I didn't know where that story actually started.

I gave it my best shot. 'D'you know, Jen, that there was a woman in Dublin that I was mad about?'

'Did you make your feelings quite clear?' queried Jenny.

I nodded.

'How clear did you make them?'

'Very clear.'

We walked on. I realised Jenny expected more detail.

'I told her.'

I wished Jenny would help me out by asking questions, but there was nothing but a listening silence coming from her. We walked on while my thoughts jumped like bed fleas. The only way I seemed able to talk was to punctuate the coughed-up phrases with strangulated *'eeh'* sounds: I had to keep making those sounds because otherwise the words would dry up. Somehow I told Jenny about how I met Fionnuala. I didn't, of course, use Fionnuala's name. I called her 'this girl'.

'So, my path kept *eeh*-crossing with this girl. We did sort of kiss a bit. Her hair smelled of geraniums. And I did tell her I loved her. She did know. But she couldn't love me like that.'

'What was this girl's name?' Jenny asked.

I was so used to keeping Fionnuala and my feelings for her secret it felt blasphemous to use her name.

'Fionnuala,' I said, reciting her name like a magic charm, a prayer. Fionnuala's name, spoken aloud, still had a powerful charge. I didn't give her surname or any other incriminatory details on her identity.

Jenny laughed.

'What's funny, Jenny?'

'Fionnuala. The name Fionnuala. It is such an Irish name.'

We walked on in a silence, yet in my head there was an incessant nonsensical chatter directed at Jenny.

Eventually I heard Jenny confess she was finding it difficult to call me Ro.

'I know all your friends call you Ro, but I'm finding it difficult, I just keep thinking of *Row, row, row your boat / Gently down the stream,* and it just goes on and on in my head.'

'*Merrily, Merrily, Merrily / Life is but a dream.* Oh God, Jen, I'm going to be so pissed off if it stays in my ear,' I moaned.

'Sorry!' said Jenny. 'But that does bring me to my request. May I call you R.M., the initials for Rose Mary? I think I would be the only person to call you that. Would I?'

When I heard R.M., I thought of Major Sinclair Yeates, the resident magistrate dreamed up by the Anglo-Irish authors, Somerville and Ross. The Irish R.M. was frequently deceived by the devious human fox, Flurry Knox. Flurry Knox was a better name for me than R.M.

'R.M?' I said. 'Perfect.'

For a moment it looked like Jenny would seal the deal with a hug or an embrace of some kind, but the moment passed.

We walked on in silence, drifting towards the front of the museum. The buses were disgorging the Fulbrighters. Our pace had meandered into a dawdle, we were going to say goodbye.

I announced, 'You're broken-hearted.'

I was sorry when I saw Jenny jump.

'Is it really that obvious?'

'It is really,' I replied.

Jenny didn't ask me how her sadness was so evident and I would not have been able to produce a list of defining symptoms, all I would have been able to say was that I could see Jenny was hurt, that there were parts of Jenny where her skin had dissolved in shadow and her ribcage was not bone but petrified coral with the cold winds of the world seeping through. I could see a hesitation in the light of Jenny's eyes, a bruised tenderness in some of her gestures. I could hear a catch in Jenny's breath. Jenny was broken-hearted, and I recognised a fellow traveller.

# 4
# Girls Just Want To Have Fun

I left Jenny to take the T and for the second evening in a row I got to Clara's early. This time the carer, Helena Mulcahy, was very glad to get away over an hour early. Helena Mulcahy was one of those people who everyone called by their full title: first name, surname. She was a big-boned girl from North Cork, the epitome of a dairy farmer's daughter – curvy, with rosy cheeks and dancing eyes.

'You're sound, Ro! I owe you! Thanks a million!'

The ritual for Saturday nights was that myself and Clara would have a glass of vodka (neat, in small metal tumblers, straight from the freezer), but tonight there was an extra treat for the birthday girl: two jars of premium Beluga caviar. I shook my head when I saw it.

'Clara, I told you not to be giving me this.'

'Honey!

'I just keep thinking that you could get a return flight to Ireland for two small jars of this.'

Clara's grandsons had taken her out for brunch and then had hung around with her for most of the day, so she was quite worn out. We usually had long chats on Saturday night, but it seemed that it was going to be an early night for Clara. She tried to rouse herself by repeating some of her favourite observations on the similarities and differences between the Irish and Jews.

'When you Irish girls talk you just keep talking – telling such dramatic stories, on and on, laughing, explaining one story with another story, raising up your voices and making your voices low, and so on and on, so you are like Jews in that way of stories.'

Clara tiredly declared that the Irish girls often seemed lonely, they missed their home, they were young, they missed their parents and their families, but they weren't like the older Irish: full of grief for things they couldn't say, just like Jews. The older Irish, the men, would get so angry, such rages and tempers, but us girls didn't seem to be like that. Clara presumed alcohol made the Irishmen fiery and maybe they were afraid they would drown in cold despair and that's why the Irishmen drank the way they did. When Clara lived in Roxbury, when she was first in Boston and she was pushing the pram from door to door, buying old clothes for pennies to fashion into new pieces, she had seen the marks of the rage often enough on the streets and in the broken doors and windows and on the faces and bodies of their women and children, navy blue and yellow marks, red cuts. It was worst in the darkness of the nights, when outside or underneath or overhead, you could hear the banging of rages.

Clara prided herself on not bothering us Irish girls who were brought in to care for her, she liked to leave us in whatever one of the large bedrooms we chose. We could watch TV there or do whatever else it was that we wanted to do.

I let Clara talk without any interruption and stood back while she got herself onto her La-Z-Boy. She fell asleep within moments, in the middle of a sentence telling me to eat up the caviar.

I gently roused her. 'Come on, Clara, you really need to be in your bed.'

She let me help her move to her bedroom and get into her nightdress. The fact she let me help her without any protest was a dramatic symptom of her exhaustion. Just as I was turning out the light, she roused herself one last time.

'Happy birthday, honey.'

I made a camp for myself on the sofa out on the balcony, where there was a kind of glass conservatory that really only worked as a place to sit in the late spring and autumn, otherwise it was too boiling hot or too baltic to sit there. I took a pile of fur coats from one of the closets. I sat on some of them and buried myself beneath others. I had my pen and jotter.

My brain was melting and I was grateful for the cold of the conservatory. There was so much on my mind I didn't know where I would begin. Mr Darcy was on my mind. Mr Darcy was, in fact, never far from my mind. I wanted to be like Darcy: taciturn but liberal in judgement, of few words yet decisive in action, the hero who saves the day, the one who is allowed to adore the heroine. Mr Darcy is self-contained, leak-free, utterly dependable, and patently, unabashedly devoted, and that was what I wanted to be allowed to be. It was my secret pleasure that I knew that I was in truth, in my heart, in my dreaming, that guy, that hero, that gentleman.

I headed the blank jotter page with Mr Darcy's declaration to Elizabeth: 'My real purpose was to see you and to judge, if I could, whether I might ever hope to make you love me.' I ran a line down the centre of the page, dividing it in two and making lists under the quote. On one side of the page ran the list: *What I could offer Jenny?: the pluses*. On the other side of the page was the list: *Barriers to being with Jenny/ things I need to improve on and change: the minuses*. I wrote constantly, amending, crossing out – it took me a surprising amount of time.

The first two things I wrote in the plus list were:

1. I am mostly very good at taking care of people. I would cherish/mind you, Jenny.
2. I know if I was to be with you/Jen I would have to be both honest and brave. These are not my strong suits. I promise to try very hard to be honest and brave in talking with you in private. I know I would need to always have to be brave facing the public world.

(Oh God. I would have to start by telling her I wasn't on a Fulbright scholarship.) Already my plus list was slipping into minuses.

The minus list was a lot longer than the pluses, as I knew it would be. The negatives included prosaic things I might readily improve on such as:

1. Don't know anything about lesbians.
2. Can earn money cleaning and caring for old ladies but otherwise have no idea of what kind of job I could do.
3. Have no real skills (except filing and very slow typing).
4. Can't cook except spag bol and chilli con carne, which is basically the same dish except one is with pasta and the other has chili powder and rice.
5. Can't drive.

I crossed out the statement 'have never made love with a woman' from the minus column as I just knew it would be no problem with Jenny. To be naked with Jenny would be as easy as prayer: simple, sacred, rapturous, blessed, oh blessed, benediction. I wanted to kiss Jenny, to kiss her slowly, to take Jenny's clothes off quickly and somehow to get out of my own clothes. I had never been naked with another woman, but I wanted to be naked with Jenny, to hold her and be held. I wanted the two of us to take all the time in the world.

The negatives included some intractable facts:

6. My family will not be good, it will all be tough there. I would prefer not to say anything at least for a while but understand I will have to. It will mean a lot of heartache for at least a long long time and maybe always.
7. Jenny's mother doesn't like Irish people or Catholics (possible triple whammy there as I presume she's not too keen on lesbians either).
8. I don't have any common sense. I don't know what it is that people generally think is normal, so I can get a lot of things wrong.
9. I find it really hard to have opinions, most things I am not very sure of.
10. I'm not discerning – I mostly like everyone, even the ones I know are a bit of a pain in the arse. I know I tend to waste a lot of time in hanging out and chatting.
11. People think I'm intelligent but I just got lucky in my exams. There is so much that I don't know, even about things that I'm supposed to know. I mainly wing everything but I'm probably going to get caught soon – like on this master's I'm doing – but I'll just put up my hands and say 'fair cop'.
12. I look organised and as if I have a plan: I have no plan, just alibis.
13. I can keep a place looking tidy but I'm not much of a one for actually cleaning.
14. I have a very strong imagination and live there a lot of the time – in dreams and books. I can find transitioning to reality a tough thing.
15. My friends say I'm too independent and won't lean on them or give them a chance to help me. I don't let them know about the shit until it's over. My new friends in Boston, Eily and Mels, give out to me for being 'proud'.

I hoped Eily and Mels would come to understand it was easier for me to keep zipped up and battened under hatches when trouble hit. I had no intention of ever changing that way of going on, it worked superbly well for me but I would have to change that way of dealing with the world if it upset Jenny.

I made lots of attempts to write out number 16, it remained vague but it was the most painful one to write.

16. I try and do the right things but I fail a lot. I wish I was a better person. I think if people really knew me then they wouldn't like me as much and the really worrying thing is I'm not often sure why I fail a lot but I do.

The minus numbered 17 was an imponderable but it belonged in the negatives category. I wrote in a detached, stoic manner:

17. I don't know what my friends will say if I get together with Jenny, they might need a bit of time but I can talk to them and I know they'll be fine eventually. And I suppose if they're not fine, then they're not my friends anymore.

There was one minus I was most reluctant to think about:

18. I have a strong anti-English prejudice/an Irish nationalism which comes in a knee-jerk and I know it is not my best side but will have to work hard to get rid of.

The truth remained I would find it very difficult to live in England. Actually, I would find it impossible. I had to give that fact its own space in the minus column:

19. Would find it difficult/impossible to live in England. If I lived in England and got any of the anti-Irish stuff, I would be afraid I would want to join the IRA.

The Brits enraged me: they assumed supremacy and they had no notion of recognising the damage they had done and were doing. Even the hunger strikers couldn't make them see. In fact, with each heart-breaking death, the Brits seemed to consider themselves affirmed in their reasonableness. If the Brits heard any moaning, they assumed whatever they had done or not done, whatever they were doing or not doing, or whatever they were going to do or not do, was infinitely better than anything that Irish morons might come up with.

Jenny wasn't a Brit, being a Brit was a state of mind. Jenny didn't do that Brit thing and she loathed Thatcher in more precise detail than I did. Jenny's Englishness – her accent, her awkward comportment, the precision of her manners, the no-frills, flat and factual appraisals, the astute wit of her humour, her emotional remove, her serious engagement, her assumption of security and odd trembling – all of this Englishness was strangely lovely and oddly restful. However, that being said, there were bound to be plenty of Brits in England and I knew I couldn't live there without being continually strung out on Class A fantasies of vengeful murderous atrocities.

I knew I could never give this list to Jenny, certainly not a list with numbers 18 and 19 on it. Would Jenny live somewhere neutral like Scotland? The few Scots I had met were like us in the same warm airy chat and the casual attitude to ferocious swearing. The Scots also seemed to share a glutinous appetite for the glee of wild stories and the odd bit of mayhem and it looked like they had even more capacity than Irish people to do the bitterly morose. We were merely mildly melancholy in comparison.

As I came to the end of my list, I had to face the fact it was all getting a bit ridiculous. Here I was marrying Jenny, I was marrying the woman without even having kissed her, and I didn't fancy my chances there.

I cuddled in further to the fur coats and found that my imagination produced no clear detail on what it might be like to be with Jenny physically, as her lover. However, my imagination provided a crystal-clear picture of what the domestic and mundane life with Jenny would feel like. I could feel that arc surge through me, and there was a way in which my life with Jenny was actually and simply happening. We read lots of books, talked about them, and wrote some of our own. I slipped into being in my imagined life with Jenny, this life that was already happening down some rabbit hole where six impossible things can be believed before breakfast.

In that realm I slept with Jenny and woke with her to begin another new day and Jenny would allow me to say to her how lucky I felt, how grateful I was to her. On those bad days that would visit, I would still be so very grateful.

# 5
# Whiskey In The Jar

I had very nearly forgotten I wasn't *actually* invited to the final day of the Fulbright Experience. Early the next morning I was back at the hotel, complaining there was no 'downtime' in the full inventory of talks planned by the Fulbright Commission. The day was devoted to a series of presentations on America's positive contribution to the world so that the Fulbright scholars could properly deliver the message to their home countries on their return.

The presentations didn't generate the effect desired by the organisers. The women running the event could sense the mid-morning listlessness of the students. One of them announced a coffee break and seemed to imply this was another thing Americans had given the world. The Turkish girl, Emre, and some North Africans were pretty put out with that quip.

'Ah lads, I think it was meant as a kind of an aside, a bit of a joke,' I said.

'I'm finding the neo-colonialism depressing,' responded Emre.

I nodded glumly. 'Let's not go there, though, we've the rest of the day to get through.'

I told Emre to get her friends over to Ireland. 'What passes for coffee in Ireland is truly shocking. It's hard to come by real coffee, not many have heard of the percolator. We mostly drink instant, which I don't think actually consists of any ingredient found in nature. I will give the Americans that much: the coffee is good.'

'Oh my dear friend, you make me weep. If you think American coffee is good, you are so much mistaken. Come with me to Turkey and I will show you.'

'That's a deal then.'

Emre and I sat next to each other for the next sessions and started to write notes to each other. Emre wrote scathing and quite brilliant critiques of the presentations (she was studying linguistics in Berkeley) and I tried to make her laugh. By lunchtime the general air of the students was peevish. I had finally allowed myself to feel how the relentless assertion of America's greatness was causing my bile to rise. I told Emre I thought the two of us were making a mistake in paying far too much attention to the presentations and I was going to get an overdue essay started during the session after lunch. Emre told me she was planning to tell the organisers she had menstrual cramps and needed to lie down.

She announced: 'I have never deployed that narrative before now, but I had decided I would allow myself two occasions in my life where I will indulge that discourse of feminine frailty and the proceedings of today demands, sadly, I will use half of my lifetime-allotted quota.'

'I hope you don't mind me asking this, Emre,' I said, 'but where was it that you learned your English?'

'Stockholm,' said Emre, as if it was very obvious. I nodded what I hoped was a nonchalant 'of course'.

I sat next to Jenny after lunch. Jenny, like most of the rest of the students, was in a bad mood. I tried to cheer her up by singing 'Land of the Free and Home of the Brave' over and over in an increasingly warbling falsetto, but I only succeeded in making us both feel worse. I had wanted to stay focused on how much I liked American people. They were astonishingly, uniformly intent on amplifying happiness.

They were keen to notice any positive qualities or actions and sing a chorus of high praise. All that positivity was the perfect antidote to being Irish. I told Jenny I wished every Irishwoman could get a chance to work in the States for a bit, all that precise attention to positive regard would be such a balm, such a tonic. Jenny said she simply found Americans to be too loud.

'Even in Harvard?' I asked.

'That's where I've been,' replied Jenny. 'And they make such a lot of references to God, even on their banknotes, which is alarming. I made the mistake of saying to a woman in my halls that I am atheist and she seems to have misunderstood that as an invitation for my conversion.'

'Tell her that you actually like how Jennifer rhymes with Lucifer,' I suggested.

'You don't seem to understand, my dear, how seriously she takes the business of God.'

The next presentation was on how America had saved Europe in the Second World War and secured the peace with the Marshall Plan and thereby inspired the Fulbright program. I noticed how Hans and Fritz maintained a dead-pan stare. They were bolt-upright, their spines stiff, jaws set.

'The Yanks don't seem to have heard the admonition, "Don't mention the war",' I said.

Jenny sank her head onto the back of the chair in front of her. She turned her face to me and whispered, 'I just keep thinking this will be another hour of my life wasted, another hour where I could be working on my dissertation.'

I whispered back, 'I don't know, Jenny, think of it as a tithe to pay the overlords. They are actually paying a small fortune in granting unbelievably generous access to their best colleges.'

Jenny was querulous: 'I can see they've successfully brainwashed you.'

I spoke slowly, I tried to joke but found myself speaking in low tones and with a searingly correct enunciation. 'My DNA has endured centuries of colonial brutality, so maybe that's why

I am used to bearing it.' I was surprised by the bitter edge in my voice. I didn't quite know where my spite came from.

Jenny blushed and immediately and loudly said, 'Sorry. I'm sorry. I am sorry.'

The students in front of us turned around and looked at us and the rest of their row shifted uncomfortably.

I could feel a strange anger rise in me. I couldn't look at Jenny and I stared instead at the fingers of my hands rigidly outstretched on the back of the chair in front of me. I had all kinds of rants shouting in my head, such as: at least the colonial fuckers here got rid of the ties back to England early, before they went on to fulfil their white Anglo-Saxon Protestant destiny of wiping out all the natives, starting with the ones who had fed them turkey over the first colonial winters. Thanksgiving, my arse.

Jesus. I had to drop the manic lecture.

'No, I'm sorry,' I said in a voice so low I didn't know if Jenny had heard me but I wasn't able to repeat the apology.

'Why do you say sorry?' whispered Jenny. 'I was the unthinking cow.'

'I just am. I shouldn't have bitten your head off. You're not actually Cromwell.'

'Cromwell?' said Jenny.

I saw Jenny continue to blush and realised Cromwell was probably one of the good guys in English history, bringing democracy and all that. I decided to spare Jenny the lesson on 'to hell or to Connacht'.

'Hey, look at us,' I whispered, 'aren't we after fulfilling the Fulbright vision: cultivating understanding across contentious cultures?'

'You put it far more poetically than they do.'

'Really? I thought I was just sounding fluent in Fulbright. Do you know until this morning I had no clue that there was an actual Senator Fulbright.'

'What do you mean?'

'I thought that Fulbright was spelled with two 'l's. I thought it meant that they had decided that you were all – well, fully bright, full of being bright, of brightness, smart, d'you know? Like a cheesy American slogan.'

Jenny couldn't stifle her laughter. 'Full-bright? As opposed to half-bright? Did you think there were half-bright awards?'

I shrugged, I was softly relieved Jenny was laughing. Jenny didn't realise her laughter made me stoned with happiness.

A few moments later Jenny turned to me and said, 'What do you mean, *you*?'

'Hmmmm?'

'You said "they had decided *you* were fully bright".' Jenny started to laugh again but stopped.

'Jen ... well. I suppose I would have to ask you, did you really think I was a Fulbright scholar?'

Jenny stared at me. It seemed she didn't know what to say. I tried to smile. Jenny had started to laugh but stopped when she saw my awkward attempts to shrug and smile.

'You are not a Fulbright student?'

'Eh ... not exactly.'

'Not exactly? Not. Exactly!' Jenny was failing to keep her voice in a low whisper. 'What else have you told me that is untrue? Have you been making fun of me?'

Jenny looked away and started squinting at the speaker who was wrapping up the event. She turned every few minutes to stare at me. Jenny seemed to be finding it difficult to speak.

Finally she asked, 'Why on earth are you attending this event?'

I lowered my head and started to examine my hands.

And then the presentation was over and the students went to get their suitcases, which were being stored in the lobby. Hans and Fritz had written their address and phone number on a piece of paper for me and they arranged to meet me on Wednesday night after their fencing practice. I hugged them both a couple of times. Jenny was one of the last students to claim her case. I stood beside her in silence and finally managed to ask:

'Jenny, are you at all up for going for a drink and I'll try and explain myself? It can be a cup of coffee or tea if you like?'

Jenny hesitated, and then I heard Eileen Joyce and Imelda Gallagher – my friends, Eily and Mels. I heard them before I saw them: they were singing a hearty 'Happy Birthday'. Hotel guests waiting at the reception desk dutifully joined in and with nearly the same gusto as Eily and Mels. 'Aren't Americans great all the same,' I thought before a shade of apprehension grew into tension as Jenny slipped around the back of me, moving from my left-hand side to my right. Jenny seemed intent on gliding steadily away, but Eily and Mels swooped in and cut off her exit. They fell on me with hugs. Eily was tall, broad-shouldered and rangy with short, floppy brown hair and Mels was a quintessential West of Ireland beauty, black long hair, pale skin and blue eyes.

'Come on, McCarthy,' declared Eily, 'we're taking you to The Shandy. Everyone's already there.'

Mels was figuring out how to transport Jenny, she told her: 'There's only room for three in the front of our van, but Ro and I can sit on each other's lap. We can easily fit your case in the back. It'll be grand. I'm Mels by the way.' She extended her hand to shake Jenny's.

Jenny stood motionless, it looked like she was about to shake Mels's hand but had become paralysed. Eily and Mels had come straight from work, they were still in their painters' overalls. Mels kept chatting to Jenny, who remained dumb and seemed a bit alarmed. Where had we met?

'This is Jen. I hadn't told her that it was my birthday yesterday. She might want to go home.'

'Come on. Come on with us, Jen. Have you been to the Tristram Shandy pub? It's over on Jamaica Plain. There's a session there,

there's one every Sunday and this will be a big one on account of it being Easter. Sure we'll make sure that you get home or you can stay over in my place,' said Eily warmly.

'Jen's English,' I said in an attempt to explain Jenny's obvious discomfort. I turned to Jenny and explained, 'A session is a music session, like traditional Irish music, live.'

'English! God, I haven't met an English person in years!' exclaimed Eily. 'Sure come on over anyway. There's a load of Easter eggs over there – like, proper Irish Easter eggs, chocolate that tastes like chocolate, Cadbury's like in England too. And there's going to be the birthday cake of course, for herself here,' she said, clasping me in a headlock, 'and twenty-two fucking candles and all on it.'

Mels gave her a sidelong look. 'D'you mean, like, the *surprise* birthday cake, Eily?'

'Oh fuck it,' said Eily with a dismissive wave of her hands: 'Well sure, Sully is supposed to be looking after it. So it might never happen at all.'

Mels rolled her eyes and gently shrugged. 'Genius, Joyce.'

'Lads,' I said. 'How come ye're working on a Sunday, and on Easter Sunday at that?'

'It's the Levines, Ro,' said Eily. 'We're back with them again, they love us coming on a Sunday. You know we can't do the Saturdays there and in fairness we left extra early on Good Friday: being able to drink a skinful on Good Friday and all of the pubs closed back home, it felt good, you know!'

'We had such a laugh over there today, Ro,' said Mels. 'We had brought over Easter eggs for the children. Anyway, they had a hunt for Hershey's Kisses all around the house, amazing it was, dressed up as rabbits and chicks and all they were, and they all had little baskets. But your one here,' she said, jabbing Eily in the ribs, 'she and Jim Levine got into acting out Christ's Passion, all the Stations of the Cross they did, or anyway the ones Eily could remember. Jim was Jesus, him being a Jewish gentleman of course, and your one played everybody else, and not a drop of drink taken, mind you, and all you could hear from her was, "Crucify Him! Crucify Him!" He told his children it was important to know how Christians think. Luckily the kids thought it was gas. But sure they're used to him.'

'It was a laugh,' Eily nodded with satisfaction. 'He might be one of "Boston's leading psychiatrists," but he's pure mad,' she said approvingly. 'Irish mad, I mean, not angry, just pure cracked. D'you know I actually seriously did like being Saint Veronica with the dishcloth.'

And Jenny was gone. She had slipped away. I could see her making her way through the revolving doors of the hotel, dragging her huge suitcase, making a swift exit out into the Boston night. I could hear my own heart beating through my ear drums.

'We could have given your pal a lift to wherever it is she has to go,' said Eily. 'Will I go after her?'

'Leave her, she's gone,' said Mels, 'I think we frightened the shite out of her.'

I tried to feel OK. I tried to smile for Eily and Mels, even as there was a searing in my lungs that felt raw but ancient.

I said, 'I think she thought that we're total madwomen, like insane mad.'

'They don't have the craic, do they? The English?' said Eily ruefully.

'I think we're too much for them,' I said.

'Come on youse,' said Mels, 'there's a rake of pints waiting for us.'

On the drive to the pub it was difficult to tune in to what Mels and Eily were saying. I was sitting in between them both in the front of the van and could hear their voices but couldn't make out the words.

'You're not with us at all, McCarthy,' said Mels softly. 'Are you alright?'

'Grand,' I said, though of course I wasn't grand, but I was just going to have to shelve the thought that Jenny was gone and

I didn't have her address or telephone number and Boston was a big place. The only way I could put aside that thought was to pledge I would find her, somehow I would find Jenny.

# 6
# She Moved Through The Fair

The Tristram Shandy had a special place in my heart. A bunch of fellas from Cork had got together and pooled their money and skills to create the kind of pub they would like to drink in. Most of them had been in Boston for two or three years and were tired of the Irish American bars, which often doubled as restaurants and which had non-stop TV coverage of basketball, baseball and American football. These so-called Irish bars could be reliably found clotting Boston's major arteries, but the Cork lads wanted a pub – not a bar, a pub. Somewhere you could have a decent conversation and some craic and no food except maybe a toasted rasher sandwich. Their vision was to have a place where you could listen to live music some nights and have the odd singsong. A proper 'local' where you could drop in and could see who else was there and chat or do the crossword from *The Irish Times* (which they would photocopy for the customers).

The lads took ownership in the week I arrived into Boston. I had bumped into one of them, Ciarán Sully, at the International News Stand in Harvard Square on my second day in the city. I had been sightseeing, or rather taking my bearings in the strangeness of Boston, and Sully had been picking up a Monday edition of

*The Cork Examiner,* which had the results of every weekend competitive sports fixture in the province of Munster. My parents were friends with Sully's parents, Maureen and John O'Sullivan. All seven children in the O'Sullivan family were known as Sully to their friends. I had succeeded in not having much to do with Ciarán Sully since I had seen him pull down his pants and jump around the living room at his cousin's birthday party when he was about six and I was four.

It surprised neither of us that we bumped into each other. It's the fate of every Irish person to bump into other Irish people in whatever foreign region we're roaming on the spinning globe. It doesn't matter how far away an Irish person strays from their native patch, the physical (or perhaps chemical) laws of the universe decree that that Irish person will inadvertently meet the nearest Irish person in the shortest amount of time possible.

I was doomed to meet Sully as his mother had phoned a few weeks before I left and had given me her boy's (last known) address and asked me to contact him. Poor Mrs Sully was anxious about Ciarán and had a hope I might take at least a modicum of responsibility for him, although of course this is not what she admitted in the phone call:

'Rosie, love, I'm going to make sure that Ciarán will take good care of you, let me have your address – I'll leave it by the phone so that whoever answers the next time he calls will give it to him and he's after being told he's to take very good care of you, love. And when he gets in touch with you, love, make sure and call me, you reverse the charges and don't worry about the time difference, just phone and give me all the news. Have a wonderful time over there, love, you're a great girl, your Mam and Dad will miss you but sure the Americans are great, and they love us, they love the Irish, God help them. You'll get on brilliantly I know.'

And now here he was in the flesh, Mrs Sully's Ciarán, her fourth boy and second youngest.

'McCarthy, girl! It's great to see you!'

I was surprised at the warmth of Sully's greeting. He even hugged me. Sully was chubby like all the other Sullys and they all had brown eyes and black hair like their father – 'Spanish Armada, from Kinsale,' according to Mrs Sully.

Sully had quickly roped me into helping him with his task of the day: he had eight large television sets he needed to get rid of, and he wanted to buy a fish tank for the Tristram Shandy. The TV sets came from the previous incarnation of The Shandy, when it had been a Puerto Rican dive bar festooned with TVs tuned to competing Spanish-language stations. The plan was to install a fish tank in the recess above the bar where the biggest TV had held pride of place. Sully had a half-assed plan that incoming students to Harvard might want the TVs and would pay for them. He had explained to me that in America you had to pay to get rid of electrical goods. However, we learned the students weren't expected back to any of Boston's two dozen universities for at least another week. We had found a skip ('they call it a dumpster here,' said Sully) around the back of what looked like a university science lab and had transferred the TVs accordingly, with as much wide-eyed innocence as we could muster.

'Just pretend you're thick if we're stopped, an Irish innocent abroad, like.'

This alibi which Sully recommended was one that he deployed for most occasions when he infringed on explicit law and general custom.

We had got stoned while choosing the fish tank and its intriguing accoutrements. I had never been much of a girl for dope or grass but Sully said 'when in Rome, girl' and apparently it was the done thing in Boston. Sully had informed me that they called them 'reefers'.

I had been impressed to see Sully had pre-rolled spliffs in a cigar case.

'There's a whole range of different patterns in the spliff papers here, girl,' said Sully. 'I love the ones printed with stars and stripes, especially in red, green and yellow, the Rasta colours.'

Being stoned had meant buying a fish tank became more complicated than it might otherwise have been. We nearly fell out over my strong take against buying mermaids.

'Mermaids are too spiritual for a bar, Sully!' I insisted.

We were both very happy with the wrecked pirate ship, the waving plants and the pink sand we chose. We never thought to buy fish.

Sully drove a large van called a Ford Transit, which was like the Hiace vans back home, except (of course, it being America) the Transit was higher, wider and longer. In the back of the van there was a mess of clothes, a sleeping bag, grimy pillows and empty and not quite empty takeout food cartons, which careened around the floor as Sully drove energetically around the city.

'Do you live in this van, Sully?' I asked.

'Well, only the odd night if I have to or want to. Usually there's a sofa to kip on. Though lads' girlfriends can get a bit bad-tempered about that after a few weeks.' He laughed.

'No wonder your mam has concerns about you.'

'Listen, girl, I'm doing grand, and you'll tell her that, and you'll say the same to your mam too if you're on to home. No point giving grist to their worry mill.' Sully smiled.

In those first weeks and early months in Boston I had spent most of my free time with Sully. There was a lot to do to get The Shandy up and running and he showed up at my house most mid-mornings or lunchtimes and I got into the van and ran various errands with him. The days inevitably segued into evenings and nights spent drinking and doing drugs of various kinds. Somehow or another I generally made it home and into my own bed before dawn for six or seven hours' sleep before Sully was at the door again. I knew no matter how drunk or otherwise out of my brains I got with Sully that there would be no romance and, more importantly, no coercion to take my clothes off. Sully was curiously passive when it came to women. He never made a move on a girl but was always happy to respond if any girl fastened on him, and the encounter was invariably a one-night stand.

Somehow everyone knew this about Sully and maybe this was the reason he was so often surrounded by a group of women. He seemed to have automatic, unquestioned membership of whatever girl gang was around. It appeared women accepted Sully was a good laugh, generally not a nuisance and handy in his way. A lot of the lads found his success to be both mysterious and at least a bit irritating, so Sully was duly punished by being teased. The lads liked to declare that from their point of view the best thing about hanging out with Sully was that he was the one who always got off with the ugliest girl and so they could get plastered and know they would be safe from that fate. Sully would often proclaim, even without any particular provocation and with not a little pride, 'A shag is a shag, lads, and I'm just not relationship material.'

Sully had managed to insinuate himself as a kind of 'middleman' for newly arrived Irish electricians, plumbers and carpenters. He called himself a 'building contractor' but not only did he know next to nothing about construction, he didn't seem to think he had to know anything. However, Sully did have a genius in landing jobs, he advertised widely and prided himself on what he called 'niche marketing'. In *Gay Community News* his business was called 'Stonewall Construction'; in the *Society of Friends' Newsletter* the business was called 'Simple Lines Design'; in *The Wildlife Trust Magazine* the business was called 'Whole World Environmental Construction', and on it went. I managed to avoid getting embroiled in Sully's dodgier business shenanigans once I got myself sorted with my cleaning agency work, but the wild nights continued as Sully would invariably appear either at the hotel or the library as my shifts ended or at my house if I had made it home without his interception. Once I had started to work for Clara Goldfarb and begun my studies in UMASS I had managed to ease out of hanging out with Sully. Initially he had tolerated my refusal to head off with him as a cranky phase I would inevitably emerge from. But since January Sully had slowly learned that I was no longer going to be a sidekick in his mad adventures. I had even turned him down for a skiing trip to Vermont, which would be augmented by acid. I mystified him by refusing. He'd offered me a return trip to New York as a birthday present, but I told him I'd prefer a night in The Shandy and he declared himself to be very happy with that plan.

'I'm delighted, girl! We've missed you there, ya know?'

And so here I was back in The Shandy. I had enjoyed a few nights on the tiles there since January but I was not the regular fixture I had once been.

There was a line of people waiting at the door. The Shandy now had the reputation of being one of the coolest places to be in Boston, not that there was much in the way of competition. It was a mystery to me how a city with dozens of universities and a population of tens of thousands of students could be such a bloody boring place to be at night. The American students' appetite for partying was subsumed in their desire to get good grades. Maybe it was having to pay such an enormous amount of money to go to college that made them very focused altogether. Of course, they weren't legally allowed to drink until they were twenty-one and that regulation, like all regulations in Massachusetts, was very well enforced. They might as well have rolled up the streets of Boston at 10.00 p.m. as the whole city was in bed, getting the necessary sleep for their 6.00 a.m. rise. The word was that New York and Chicago were much more craic than Boston. Still, Boston was where I found myself, and tonight I joined Eily and Mels walking past the line of punters who hoped to be admitted to The Shandy. The three of us walked straight up to the door where John-Joe stood guard. He was shivering in his bartender's T-shirt emblazoned with the pub motto *But I digress*.

'Lads,' John-Joe nodded by way of greeting as he opened the door for us. 'These are regulars,' he said to the people in the queue.

I could hear him advising the twenty or so people waiting that they would be better off trying for admission on another night, it was already too crowded inside and he had to give admission to the regulars.

'Will I make a punch, John-Joe?' I asked.

'I don't know, Ro, what do you think? Sometimes I think it only encourages them to keep coming along.'

'But sure that's the idea, John-Joe,' I said as patiently as I could.

'Alright so.'

It had initially been an idea of mine to give the people waiting in line who had no chance of getting into the pub a takeaway cup of hot toddy: whiskey and boiling water sweetened with sugar and slices of lemon studded with cloves. 'A good customer-relations exercise,' as Sully termed it. I told one of the lads behind the bar that a jug of hot whiskey was needed outside.

'What are you having birthday girl?' shouted Sully as he saw me enter. 'A pint of plain?'

'Your only man!' I replied.

It was good to be back in The Shandy. I had to admit it really felt like home, or rather how home is supposed to make you feel: safe, comfortable, happy among people who are looking out for you.

As we were waiting for the pint to settle Sully passed me a brown paper bag and said, 'Happy birthday!' The bag contained a deep purple candle in a tall glass jar and the plastic transfer image on the jar was of Santa Marta Dominadora-Filomena Lubana.

'My favourite!' I said as I hugged Sully.

'I was in that shop to get a few more of those candles for the statues there,' said Sully nodding to a number of shelves under the fish tank.

The fish tank, which still had no fish, bubbled on a shelf high over the bar. Underneath the tank there were a couple of shelves stacked with a motley crew of holy statues that had been left behind by the departing Puerto Ricans. There was a three foot tall statue of the Blessed Virgin Mary and four brightly coloured crucifixes with Jesuses on them who looked distinctly Latin. Someone had added a St Brigid's Cross made from rushes. None of the lads felt it was right to remove the holy relics, because what would they do with them? Because you couldn't put them in the bin. That kind of sacrilege would bring ferociously bad luck. The lads kept the Ricans' shoal of brightly coloured jars of holy candles replenished from a nearby shop run by San Dominicans.

'Would you say you are a believer, Sully?' I asked, as I caressed my holy candle.

'Oh yeah. I would, of course! Even though I don't darken the door of a church unless for a funeral or a baptism or a wedding. I didn't even go at Christmas to look at the crib. But yeah, 'tis important, like. I'll get back to it I suppose when I've kids. You'll have to do all that Mass stuff then anyway, to show them, and the genuflection and Confession for their Holy Communion. It won't do them any harm like. You probably think that's stupid!' he said, getting suddenly embarrassed.

'Not at all, boy, not at all I don't! I mean, I think I'm a believer too. I mean, the Catholic Church got me when I was young, I'm hardwired. I can't think outside how they trained me to think. And I like churches. I like when there isn't a Mass on. You can go in there and think. And light a candle. I think lighting candles works.'

''Tis no harm anyway!' he agreed.

I had hardly begun my pint when Sully was loudly ordered by one of the lads, called Mark, to go out to his van to get the birthday cake. As Sully was heading out the door, Mark came over to myself and Eily and Mels.

'That fella!' he exclaimed. 'I was out pricing jobs with Sully all day and I kept reminding him but he still nearly forgot to get a cake! We lashed over in the van to the Portuguese bakery in Somerville and got there just as they were closing up and putting everything away. The bakers said they had no big cakes left but Sully pulled a big white cake out of the window and kept dropping twenty dollar notes, but they still didn't want to leave him have it. He then dropped two fifty dollar notes on top of the pile and they agreed to let him take it away. You've got the most expensive birthday cake in Boston, Ro!' laughed Mark. 'I remembered to ask them for the candles. They didn't speak much English but we got the candles anyway.'

I was sent off to the loo while they were getting the cake ready and the candles lit. I came back out when I heard roars of laughter. Sully, the langer, had got the Portuguese bakers to sell him a display model, it was cardboard and old icing. Everyone there that night knew this was a story that was going to follow Sully for the rest of his days.

'No cake! We've no soakage now for the pints!' mourned Eily.

There was a load of musicians in the Tristram Shandy and the Irish traditional music session was well underway, the tunes were blasting their double-barrelled load of sadness and exhilaration. I realised I had missed hanging out in The Shandy. It was a relief to stand there swaying to the old airs amongst the banter and the bullshit. The blessing of getting drunk came on me quickly. I had never warmed to the lift and scrape of Irish traditional music back in Cork. Yet here in Boston I needed to hear that music played live around me, it had become as necessary to me as prayer. The biggest shock I'd had since landing in Boston was that I wanted to be back home, back on that island I had used all of my ingenuity to escape from.

I had seen some famous politicians up close and a bit too personal in some of the pubs in Dublin during my 'nearly a year' in the Civil Service. They were men who regarded drinking gallons of beer and pawing any women in their vicinity as a necessary part of their job description. They were gross. The politicians and their pals the priests insisted there would be no contraception allowed in Holy Catholic Ireland, leaving us young women shadowed by a terror about getting pregnant outside marriage and married women with the terror of more pregnancies. All my school and college friends had the same horror. It weirdly didn't matter if we weren't actually having sexual intercourse, we were still haunted by the fear we would 'fall' pregnant and bring shame on the whole family.

When myself and my friends had boyfriends and sex lives, our fears became more focused and acute. It was very difficult to get condoms, nearly impossible to get the pill, and both illegal and a sin to try to procure an abortion. However, there were always private English clinics for that secret, hasty, very expensive abortion and a whole system of mother and baby homes and adoption to hide the illegitimate births. At least you could rely on the nuns to help you hide your pregnancy and the fact you had given birth to a child. I could see no sane reason for staying in such a hole of a country that hated girls and women, and by last August I would have swum to Boston if it was the only way of getting there. Yet, as soon as I was on the shores of Massachusetts, I discovered that sanity and reason seemed to have limited powers. My viscera, and the soul I'd never realised I possessed, all longed to be back in Ireland.

It was still relatively early in the night but I was plastered and felt great. The pub went a holy quiet when Niamh Slattery finally agreed to sing. She asked me what I would like to hear and I said: 'She Moved Through the Fair'.

The minute Niamh started with her vibrato contralto, I was terrified I was going to cry, and not just an ordinary old tear or two, but a great big heaving sob. Desperate and all as I had been to leave Ireland, I had never realised I had a home, and what the meaning of home was, until I fled it. Even if Ireland was a soggy pit of venal corruption and half-assed ineptitude, well, it turned out that damp pit was home, my home. I seemed to miss everyone

I had ever known there and more besides. I couldn't even really pinpoint what I missed. I missed everything. Fuck it, I even missed the incessant rain. But I also couldn't go back, not yet. I had to go back with something, with money or some kind of an idea of how I was going to manage to live in Ireland.

The only way I was going to be able to stay in Boston was to have a plan, and my plan was the same plan as most of those around me in The Shandy: I would study and work and save as best I could. I would give it three years, five tops, if it meant I could save enough to buy a small house in Cork, and I should be able to do that within the five years if I kept the head down. Three years, or maybe five years, and I would be home.

# CAMBRIDGE & SOMERVILLE

1984

# 7

# Brass In Pocket

It had been nearly three weeks since I had last seen Jenny. I had met up with Hans and Fritz twice now, but they had had no sighting of her. It had taken me a few days to realise that the hot, raw pain in my chest when I inhaled deeply was not in fact a pulled muscle. That weird pain was caused by the feeling of missing Jenny. The realisation just seemed to make the feeling of lonely-longing much worse.

I tried to put aside those weird, achy-elated feelings. I was usually superb at this tactic of compartmentalisation, but in this case it didn't seem to be working that well. I would get sideswiped with a smack of longing. I contemplated going to the pub but knew pouring alcohol onto the pain would make it sizzle and smart all the worse and I would end up drifting into feral adventures and realising a day or two later that I was on the lucky side to be more or less intact. I had a clear, superstitious sense I might have used up a significant number of my nine lives. Whatever other fuck-up I would make of my life, I would face the mess of it all more-or-less sober.

I worked my cleaning shifts at the hotel in the early morning, leaving me time to get to my UMASS classes and do some study.

On the nights when I wasn't working over in Clara's or meeting up with the Austrian lads, I stayed in the library at BC once I had done my Monday and Tuesday evening shifts there – cleaning the toilets and hoovering my allotted floors. Reading mostly helped in absorbing the distracting pain and I also slept a lot – sleeping over books in the library was very comforting. One particularly painful evening turned into a rather restful night as I slept in a library armchair, open hardbacks making a kind of blanket for my lap.

The O'Neill Library in BC was a type of paradise, it had beautiful shaded light, acres of generous space, deliberate nooks, comfortable chairs, a galaxy of books available on miles of shelves and it was open twenty-four hours a day, most days of the year. But even here, in amongst the stacks of books, I could be ambushed by the piercing awareness that I should be with Jenny. And it was really bad luck that that week of all weeks I had to read Carson McCullers's *The Heart is a Lonely Hunter* for the class in American Gothic. It was full of searing shots about yearning and how very confusing and even lonely it is to be awash with sexual desire. All in all, I put down a tough week after my Fulbright Experience weekend.

At the start of the third week, my painful feelings were swept away by a growing sensation that became a certainty: Jenny would come looking for me. After all, I was easy to find. I had told Jenny I lived in a house on Foster Street, right next to the convent, and she had been very taken with the news I lived next door to a convent. That delusional certainty that Jenny would come and find me lasted nearly two days but burped itself sober during a night of fitful sleep. I began to learn one of the fundamental lessons necessary to become a true lover, that the defences of pride and wishful thinking must be abandoned. Once I had accepted the uneasy sensation of impending humiliation, I was able to develop an inspired plan of campaign. As was my wont, I made a list – it flowed easily.

1. Set myself up over in Harvard's Widener Library, near the Nineteenth-Century American Literature stacks and wait for Jenny to appear. If that doesn't work:
2. Go to the secretaries of Harvard's English Dept. for help (in my experience secretaries knew everything, everyone and every ploy for solving problems, and were generally very kind to people like me).
3. Stalk the graduate students' canteens at meal times.
4. Wander Harvard's student halls of residence and just simply ask if anyone knows of Jenny Archer.

This last move would take me into the zone of mortification, but it might just have to be done. It was Friday, and I would go over to Harvard on the following Monday and instigate my plan of action. However, I also had a slim hope I might bump into Jenny on this Friday night as there was to be an excursion of Irishwomen to a lesbian club and who knows, maybe Jenny would be there? Jackie, one of the women from the Tristram Shandy, had an older sister who was now a lesbian and was visiting from London with her girlfriend.

'She says she wants to introduce me to her girlfriend,' said Jackie. 'I'm the first in the family who is going to meet her, maybe the only one,' she said, a little shocked, also a bit confused, but honoured by the occasion.

There was lots of discussion about what needed to be done to entertain them. Apparently, there was a weekly lesbian club over in Cambridge (of course), in Central Square. A lot of the women in the pub and from the Boston camogie team promised to go and, of course, to keep the whole thing quiet (not to tell their fellas, even) to protect the news about Jackie's sister from getting back home to Ireland, which everyone knew could too easily happen. Clara Goldfarb was spending the weekend in her daughter's place, so I was free and had signed up to be part of the excursion. Jackie was gratified to see about twenty women gathered in The Plough and the Stars on Mass. Ave. all set to meet her sister and the girlfriend and to go dancing among the lesbians.

'Thanks a million for coming,' she said to each and every one of us as we filed out of the bar and walked down a number of blocks to get to the club.

'Not a bother, girl,' I said. 'Did I never tell you that I went to a lesbian night in Dublin?'

'Go 'way!' said Jackie.

'I did indeed. It was fierce rough, mind you.'

Jackie didn't ask what had brought me to that Dublin club, and I agreed with Jackie that the Boston lesbians were probably a lot more civilised than the Dublin ones.

The two dozen Irish women paid the entrance fee and then stood uncertainly just inside the doors of the club. It was a large barn of a place with no windows, and some giant glitter balls hung from the ceiling, bouncing off revolving coloured lights around the walls. The music was loud – Eurythmics. There seemed to be a lot of women already in the place and I spotted Jenny just a few feet away, standing a little apart from the tight-knit group of us Irishwomen lodged inside the door. It was as simple as a miracle. I was stunned to see that, in fact, I hadn't imagined Jenny, she was really a real person.

*Jenny!*

I tried to call to her, but all I could do was mouth her name.

She was with a group of girls who all looked like college students: the only word for them was 'preppy'. Jenny was laughing and all her friends were laughing and I took an intake of breath and made myself rush to say hello – if I delayed or dithered, I would be ruined with the nerves. I had to cross twelve or fifteen feet to reach Jenny, but it seemed I was in one of those Irish folklore tales where people perish on the mountainside because they arrogantly cross the fairies' hungry grass in the tiny field they know is forbidden, but they enter it anyway because it's a shortcut or night is falling, but the tiny field of hungry grass keeps extending longer and longer and longer and no one ever makes it across, they wither and fade in the lengthening time that never ends. I pulled myself out of the vortex in the nick of time and somehow reached Jenny and her friends. I smiled a silent hello and grinned as Jenny startled in shock at seeing me.

'Hello! What are you doing here?' Jenny asked.

'I came to find you,' was the reply, which might not have been the full reality of the situation but was the actual truth.

Jenny remained standing with her circle of friends but she turned her head and shoulders away from the group and towards me. She slowly smiled at my grin.

'I did wonder if I would ever see you again.'

'I knew I would find you. I wouldn't let you escape.'

'I wasn't running away.'

'How have you been?'

'Working. Harvard *does* have a good library. And you?'

'Well, I've cut down a lot on the amount of my usual dossing. I found the library in UMASS. I might even get my essays done, maybe even some of them on time.'

'You are really a student?'

'Yeah. Part-time, a master's. I'm going to be done in two years.'

I started making a long and much-rehearsed apology to Jenny. It was heartfelt, remorseful, contrite, but as I was talking, Jenny was smiling at me, not listening, tuning into Chrissie Hynde's mesmerising 'Brass In Pocket'.

Jenny leaned closer. I felt the electric shock of her fingertips on my left hip bone. I mirrored Jenny's soft sway to the music and gingerly placed my fingertips on her right hip. We started to breathe into being closer over the five stretched syllables of '... i-ma-gin-a-tion'. Our heads were about to touch when I became aware of Jackie on one side of me and Eily flanking my other side, and they were looking anxiously at Jenny's friends.

Jenny's mouth was close to my ear and I could hear her murmuring the song lyrics to me.

However, I could see what had made Jackie and Eily so nervous. Jenny's friends were gathered in a staring, scowling group, clustered around one particular woman who looked most distinctly aggrieved. All eyes of the group were locked on me and my hand on Jenny's hip, which I withdrew to my own side. I could see how nervous Jackie and Eily were as they shaped up to try and stare down Jenny's friends. Jenny took her fingertips from my hip but continued to sway to the music. Then she smiled lazily at me and I realised that Jenny had a few beers on her.

'Is that young one your girlfriend?' I asked.

Jenny smiled more broadly and gave a non-committal shrug. 'I wouldn't say that.'

'Would she say it, though?'

Jenny didn't look behind her.

'Maybe this is a rough place after all,' said Jackie anxiously in my ear.

'Ah, I don't think so,' I said as I stepped away from Jenny and nodded at her group of friends and nodded at Jenny, who turned slowly back into her group.

'Sure, let's find the bar,' said Eily in a louder than necessary voice, 'and we can come back and talk to these good women later on.'

'Jen, I'm going to get a drink and I'll be back to you later,' I said.

Jenny seemed rapt in her own private half-dance, even as the woman nastily staring at me stepped forward and slipped an arm around Jenny's waist.

'Jesus, Mary and Joseph,' said Jackie as they walked over to the bar, 'I'm not the better of that, McCarthy. For God's sake, don't be getting us into trouble with the locals and we only just in the door.'

Eily was kinder to me. 'I'll get you a pint,' she said.

I didn't want a pint. I didn't want to drink. I had been managing to dodge being in a round and had stayed sipping the same pint in

The Plough and Stars and I was far too stoned already after the encounter with Jenny. It was hard to concentrate on the conversation and banter. I tried my best not to be zoned out. I promised myself I would later replay the sensation of my fingertips on Jenny's hip bone and the sensational shock Jenny's touch had caused in me. I kept a sly eye out for glimpses of Jenny. I willed and prayed she would come over and talk to me (even with her girlfriend, if your one was in fact her girlfriend and not just a hopeful case).

The Irishwomen were doing their best to knock some fun out of the night and were having a laugh getting myself and Jackie's sister's girlfriend (whose actual name was Sandra) to repeat the same phrases as it was decided my Cork accent and Sandra's Caribbean London accent were really the exact same. Myself and Sandra cracked along, making our best effort to sound alike. Sandra was a laugh and was generally declared to be 'one of our own'. Jackie's sister, Martina, was very quiet though.

'She's been so nervous,' Sandra told me when we were in the long queue for the toilets. 'But you've all been brilliant. I can't believe we've been in an Irish pub. Martina won't go into a pub in London where there's going to be loads of Irish. It's been so fantastic here. Who knows? One day I might actually go to Ireland with her!'

I told Sandra she'd have a great time in Ireland.

'Really?' she said.

I was immediately unsure but said, 'Well, if I'm back there, I'll take you around and make sure you get treated well.'

Both Sandra and I could feel each other wincing.

I was going to say sorry, but I didn't want to make everything worse.

Sandra said, 'You know, I can't exactly see us going to Barbados together either. But maybe Jamaica or somewhere, so Martina can get a feel for what the Caribbean is like, for what my gran is like. You know the sad thing is I think our grandmas would really like each other.'

With the imminent moment of a third round of beers to be bought there was a conflab, and it was decided that as we had put in about an hour in the lesbian club it was now probably time enough to be going. Jackie's sister and Sandra both said The Plough and the Stars would be much more craic. I had run out of time to talk again with Jenny, but I got Eily to accompany me as I made a last-ditch effort at a courteous approach to Jenny among her not-friendly friends. I nodded a number of hellos at her pals, who remained stony-faced as I made my way towards Jenny. Eventually I caught her eye and she stepped towards me.

'Hi Jen, I don't want to disturb you now. But if you're up for it, I would like to see you again. Just a cup of tea sometime, maybe? I'm often over in Harvard Square.'

'She's not my girlfriend. I don't have a girlfriend here,' said Jenny in a rush. 'You're going! Why are you going so soon? Why don't you stay?'

'I can't really. I have to go with the lads. We're looking after a sister and her girlfriend who are visiting from London, so I have to go.'

'I don't see why you can't stay. There seems to be a rather large group of you. Surely there are enough to look after the visitors?'

'It doesn't really work like that. I don't want to be the one who starts to break up the night.'

'But you've found me.'

I laughed. I liked Jenny drunk.

'Can I find you again tomorrow night?'

Jenny gave a sigh. 'You really have to go?'

'Tomorrow night?'

'Hmmm, OK.'

'Pizzeria Uno? The one in Harvard Square? Do you know where that is?'

Jenny nodded her assent.

'At seven?'

Jenny nodded again.

'You kept bowing to all of her gang, you do realise that don't you?' said Eily as we walked out of the club.

'Ah I was just nodding at them, just being polite, like, showing them no harm intended.'

'You were feckin' well bowing.'

'Look, at least we had no trouble.'

'It seems you've got yourself some trouble for tomorrow night,' said Eily, squeezing my shoulder.

I hadn't quite realised Eily had heard what I had said to Jenny. I gave a shrug.

'I just hope you know what you're doing, McCarthy.'

I knew better than to reply.

# 8
# I'm Coming Out

I spent the next day shopping for hours for the perfect white T-shirt. I had bought clothes before, but only when I needed some particular item like shoes or pyjamas. I now knew I'd never actually shopped before. I had never had an image in mind of what kind of look I would like to project, but now I had a crystal-clear vision of the perfect white T-shirt, what it would look like and how it would feel to wear it.

I was triumphant when I found it: thick white cotton, a slight V to the neck, short sleeves that were gratifyingly tight on my slender biceps, it reached to the required half-inch below the top of the waistband of my well-worn Levi's 501 denims. I wore my red Converse sneakers, no socks, and I thought carefully about my underwear. I wore a small suede jacket from the Seventies which had been abandoned at the back of the large cupboard under the stairs in the house I was living in. I had gone to the Italian barber to have my hair cut and it was as close and as tight as a scissor cut would allow because he refused to use his shaving clippers on women. This was all totally new territory for me. Of course, I had put effort into dressing up on previous occasions, but only with the goal of blending in with whatever was the mainstream norm. I had never wanted to win attention. But tonight I was keen to look good. It was strange to know I wanted Jenny to think I looked good.

The sun had shone unexpectedly warmly during the week. I had become used to months of packed banks of dirty iced snow rimming the sidewalks. It was very odd now to see how quickly and theatrically the ice and grey snow meltingly disappeared, they offered themselves up to slush and gurgled down the deep drop of the storm drains. Spring had immediately arrived. Things which had looked dead, like the frost-burnt grass, were starting to turn infant green. Pewter clouds were thickening as I cycled from the tall house on Foster Street through Brighton Center to Allston and onto the banks of the Charles River, and pretty soon I was locking my bike in Harvard Square.

I was unusually early. I generally managed to arrive just in time, sometimes just a few minutes before, sometimes a few minutes after, but never late enough to have to apologise to worried Americans who began to inconsiderately fret a mere ten minutes after the agreed meet-up time. I skipped down the steps to the bar/restaurant, which was part of a chain expressly designed to appeal to the student market, serving a more pretentious-style pizza than the takeout chains and with the added attraction of many beers on tap. The room was quite small, with an oval bar taking up the centre of the room and booths around the four walls. I sat up at the bar counter, even with the knowledge I would most likely be told I couldn't be served a beer as I was alone. Massachusetts gloried in arcane laws about drinking alcohol, which had been on the statute books since the Puritans landed. The marvel was not so much these laws existed but that Americans took all their many laws and regulations seriously enough to obey them. I was in luck, though. I recognised the barman and he recognised me.

'How's it goin', Sailor!' he said.

'Grand, Soldier! And yourself?'

I couldn't remember where, how, why or when, but some raucous night in some pub or at some party we had established each other as Soldier and Sailor. He was a wiry, short guy, an inner-city Dub with a close-shaved head, a ready grin, a swallow tattoo on the fleshy mound of his thumb. He was older than me, maybe even in his thirties.

'You're far away from the ghetto,' he joked. 'What brings you to this part of town?'

'I'm here to meet someone.'

'A date?'

'I'm not sure.'

'Ah for fucksake. The Irish lads would have your heart broke. An American fella would never have you wondering like that. You'd fuckin' well know that you were after being asked out. We'd want to watch it or ye'll all be with the American lads in time. Fair fucks to you, though, for sticking with our own. You're better off in the long run.'

'No. It's not an Irish fella.'

'An American?'

'No,' said I, hesitantly.

Soldier cocked his head to one side and raised his eyebrows. He waited. He could sense a story was about to be delivered to him.

I swallowed and tried to cough up the simple sentence lodged in my gullet.

Soldier gave me the prompts. 'Not an Irish fella ...'

I shook my head and he waited before giving the next prompt. 'Not an American fella ...'

I shook my head and managed to say: 'An. English. Girl.'

Soldier leaned over the bar counter and locked me in an intense gaze. 'Deadly!' he said gravely.

He swung into action. 'Now what are you having to drink?'

'Can I have a beer?'

'Course – but seeing as how you are alone – if anyone asks, it was just that you were sitting with those two fellas over there and you moved here after you got the drink.'

'Yeah.'

'What's your poison?'

'A bottle of Rolling Rock, thanks.'

Soldier moved like a tango dancer to swiftly dip a beer mat, cold bottle and thick chilled glass before me. He waved away my money. He wanted all of the details and in the right order: the English girl's name, how I had met her, why I was not sure it was a date.

I answered in a shy rush. I had never said Jenny's name aloud to anyone before. I recited it with grinning pride.

Soldier smiled: 'Ah, you like her.'

I just nodded.

'But what do you mean you don't know if it's a date, Sailor? That's what's after worrying me here.'

'Well, I asked her to meet me but I'm not sure if it's a date.'

'Do you want it to be a date?'

'Yes.'

'Right then: make it be a date so.'

'How do I do that?'

A gaggle of Harvard boys arrived and Soldier got busy serving beer. The place started filling up and I requisitioned a booth. I placated the waitress by getting her to bring two glasses of tap water and assuring her my date (why not?) would arrive shortly.

I kept an eye on the door so I would be able to see Jenny enter and have time to compose myself. The thought crossed my mind that maybe last night she hadn't registered that she had said she'd meet up with me. I was swept by a confusing tide: relief, anxiety and sadness. Then, there she was. She had come in and I hadn't seen her, and there she was, standing at the booth, sliding into the bench opposite me.

As we were saying hello, the waitress promptly arrived with two chilled bottles of Rolling Rock. 'Courtesy of the bar,' she announced cheerily.

'I know the fella behind the bar,' I explained.

'I can't drink tonight,' said Jenny. 'I lost the entire morning's work due to a hangover and I still feel rather fragile. No drink for me, I'm afraid. I've to make up for lost time tomorrow.'

I pushed the bottles to the side and presented the menus. I was acutely aware of Jenny's knees not touching but so very close to my own, and I was deeply happy. I greedily stared as Jenny read through the menu. I loved Jenny's hands, they were kind of square-shaped, they looked beautifully capable. It was difficult to concentrate on what Jenny was saying. I listened instead to the depth of her voice, to the crispness of her accent, to the pivot of her phrasing. Soldier had dimmed the lights so much it was difficult to see the soft brown of Jenny's eyes, which was probably just as well. And then Jenny was telling me it was exactly sixty days before her flight home to England.

'You're counting the days?'

'I'm going to submit my final dissertation draft in forty-two days, which will give me two weeks for sightseeing and packing.'

'You're looking forward to getting home, so.' I couldn't decide if it was a question, an observation or a cry for help.

As the waitress was taking our order, Jenny stood up, leaving her bag and jacket on her side of the booth, and swung in to sit beside me. She looked ahead and gazed into the middle distance as if she and I were driving in a car. Her arm softened onto mine. She began to talk in a very low voice as if she was talking to herself but was happy to have me eavesdrop. This was something Jenny did throughout the Fulbright Experience. She did this thing of sitting beside me, slightly melting on to me, while she looked ahead and spoke of the things it seemed she didn't usually admit to herself.

'I just hope Susan has moved out of the house.'

That was another thing Jenny did – she would make a statement from the middle of something as if I already knew the beginning. (Who in the hell was Susan?) I waited for Jenny to continue, but Jenny just stared ahead as if she was on a car journey and mesmerised by fleeting scenery, the flicker of passing traffic, the shimmering blend of road markings, the metronome lull of windscreen wipers.

'Susan?' I ventured, puncturing Jenny's reverie. 'Is she your ex? The house? Did ye live in the same house?'

'It's my house. Rather, it's my aunt's, so it's a peppercorn rent. And Susan does have a job, one from which she can never be fired, not really. Unless they decide she's a danger to the children she teaches.'

There was more silence between us.

Eventually, Jenny said, 'I shouldn't have to ask her. But I expect it will come to that.'

'You haven't asked her to move out?'

'I think it should be obvious. She can't fuck her new girlfriend in our house. Though I suppose she's not exactly new now – the new girlfriend – I really am trying not to have to say "the other woman". Still. The point remains.'

'Just tell her to get the fuck out. That she's to be long gone and no trace remain by the time you're back.'

'Or else?' smiled Jenny.

'Or else there will be a pack of strong Irishwomen, led by me, Jennifer, and we'll be at the door rudely insisting that Susan gets the fuck out of your house.'

'I think she might rather like that scenario. I mean the gang of wild Irishwomen part.'

'I would make sure that she didn't like it.'

Jenny smiled. 'Are you my knight errant?'

'I would like to be.'

I was shocked by my own honesty.

The pizzas arrived. I abstractedly pushed a bottle of Rolling Rock to Jenny, who forgot her pledge not to drink, and the two of us started to eat the slices and sip from the bottles.

'You should just tell her to get out. Write a letter and tell her to be gone by the time you're back.'

'I really don't think I could do that.'

I shrugged. There was obviously some complicated point of English etiquette involved that was obscure to me.

I plunged in with the question I had wanted, needed to ask.

'Jen?'

'Hmm?'

'How did you know you were a lesbian?'

'What do you mean?'

'I don't know. Just that: how did you know?'

'I think being a woman who has sex with a woman rather clarifies the question.'

'But I mean beforehand,' I persisted, 'Did you always fancy girls?'

'What do you mean?'

'Like, for example, just supposing I thought I might be lesbian but I didn't have crushes on girls in school. Would that mean I'm not a lesbian?'

'I didn't fancy the girls in school,' replied Jenny.

'Really?'

'Yes.'

'Oh. Good.'

'But,' Jenny continued, 'if every girl who had a schoolgirl crush on another girl turned out to be lesbian, that would mean most adult women would be lesbian.'

'Why aren't they, then?' I asked.

'Maybe they are,' said Jenny.

I was confused. 'But if we didn't have crushes on other girls, does that mean we're not really lesbian?'

Jenny seemed to strangle a sigh. 'Look, you're lesbian if you're a woman who sleeps with women. Once you come out, that is. You could be closeted.'

'Coming out is telling people that you're lesbian and closeted is hiding?'

'Hiding or denying.'

'Why do you say come out, shouldn't it be come in?'

'What do you mean?'

'I don't understand why it's coming out, isn't it more like coming into yourself, coming into a lesbian life?'

'We say coming out, everyone says coming out, you could say coming in but I am not sure many would understand you.'

I felt I might be starting to annoy Jenny, but I needed to get things clear in my head. I persevered. It mattered more to be clear in myself than to steer clear of irritating Jenny.

'Is there a list?'

'A what?'

'I don't know, like, a list. A list of symptoms or characteristics, things you are or behaviours or attitudes that add up to being a lesbian?'

Jenny shook her head. 'I'm not really sure what you mean. Symptoms makes it sound like a disease, which it most certainly is not, unless being sane is considered pathological for women, which could be argued. A lesbian is a woman who has sex with other women, she prefers women.'

Jenny stared at me, then seemed to take some pity on me.

'Nature will out,' she declared kindly.

'I suppose, when I think about it,' I said, 'I didn't actually ever fancy boys. I mean, I like them, they are generally good craic and I have eyes in my head, like, some of them are so beautiful, but I always thought the other girls were faking an interest or exaggerating it, and I kind of thought eventually I would fancy the boys myself or the others would admit they were kind of messing about the degree of feeling they had. Did you ever have a boyfriend Jen?'

'Yes.'

'Well, I had one myself in college. But I had to. It was beginning to look very strange, like I was seventeen by that stage and I was coming in for a certain amount of hassle. You kind of had to have one because otherwise you would be in line for all kinds of attention.

Jenny began to rummage in her bag.

'Cigarette?' I asked.

'Yes, please.'

I produced my cigarette case, which held just eight fags. It was a bit of a pain having so few in the case but it helped with trying to cut down.

Jenny took one and I produced my brass Zippo lighter. Jenny smiled as she accepted the light.

'When's your favourite time for a cigarette?' I asked.

'Post orgasm,' said Jenny. 'Yours?'

'Eeh. I was going to say after dinner. I think I'll have to stick with that: after dinner. After a big meal, like, at whatever time that might be. But as you've brought up the subject of orgasm, I have to ask you, Jenny. What made you to decide to go for women?'

'Oh you have to ask me, do you?' She laughed. 'It's just obvious women are more intelligent than men, the conversation is much better and when it comes to sex men are just primitive shooting machines really.'

I took a cigarette for myself, lit it in silence and took a deep pull while I contemplated this information. Jen was quite a one. I was queasily unsure.

'I really liked Emmet, that was his name, my boyfriend,' I admitted.

'I should hope you liked him.'

'I mean, he was great to go out with – very portable, you know? I mean, you could bring him anywhere and he would talk to anyone.'

Jenny said, 'My last boyfriend read Economics.'

'Yeah?'

'He thinks the way to combat international capitalism is to develop local co-operatives. Self-sufficiency.'

'Very good. *Sinn féin*, ourselves alone. My fella wanted to be a stockbroker.'

'God!'

I wasn't entirely sure why being a stockbroker seemed to be such a bad thing in Jenny's lexicon, or maybe Jenny misunderstood the reference to *sinn féin*. This really wasn't turning out to be a date.

'What was his name?' I asked. 'Your boyfriend?'

'I had more than one.'

'The last boyfriend, the one who read Economics?'

'Cyril.'

'Cyril? Are people really called Cyril?'

Jenny didn't respond.

'Are you still in touch? I asked.

'I suppose so.'

I had a strange apprehension.

'Could you see yourself going back with him?'

'He does ask.'

'Does he want to marry you?'

'God! Cyril doesn't want to marry! Neither of us believes in marriage, it's a repressive institution, privatisation, exploitation. He just wants us to get back together.'

'And what do you say?'

Jenny stubbed out the end of her cigarette and drank her beer. I waited but knew I was not going to get a reply.

Eventually I said, 'I don't really know why I can't be with Emmet. He's beautiful. His face, his body, is very beautiful. To me he's not a primitive shooting machine, Jenny. I loved looking at him, touching him and kissing him, and he loved me, I felt it off him so clearly, it was simple for him, but it just wasn't simple for me. He kept saying we should just marry and I knew I would make his life hell and we would have beautiful children and I would be so cross with them all. I would be a lightning bitch. I kept splitting up with him, especially in the last two years. I think I was always half out the door and I didn't know why. He could have had his pick of anyone because all the girls were mad about him, but he kept coming back to me, and I was awful to him really. He used to just hang around and then we would end up chatting and we would kiss, he is really beautiful, and then we would be together again.'

'Do you love him?' asked Jenny crisply.

I was surprised at the tartness in the question.

'Of course I do. Of course I love him. If you knew him, Jenny, you would love him too.'

'I am not so sure,' replied Jenny.

I didn't care that I was blithely rankling Jenny.

'Ah but you would, Jen. You wouldn't be able to help it. Everyone loves Emmet. It's impossible not to.'

'What about this Fionnuala creature? Were you hot and cold with her?'

'Oh God, no. I fell for her in a completely different way. I mean total, totally. It was completely different. It was simple. Clear and direct.'

'There is your answer.'

'Yes,' I said, although I couldn't remember what the question was.

Jenny gave an exaggerated sigh. 'God, I am exhausted. I really rather overdid it last night.'

'Yeah, sure I'll get the bill.'

'I am going to go to the loo.'

'Grand.'

Soldier was over like a shot. 'Well done, Sailor, you're playing a blinder. The body language is beautiful.'

'Oh Christ no, if you knew how badly I'm doing ... I'm making a complete balls of it.'

'It doesn't look like that from where I am.'

'Ah no, Soldier, I think she's not over her old girlfriend yet. I'm not even sure if she isn't half-thinking of going back to her ex-boyfriend. And then I made a total hames of things by talking about my ex, who's a fella, who I definitely can't go with, although I have no real good reason. I'm not at all sure I'm even a lesbian. I'm not sure I make the grade, I don't know how you qualify.'

'Ah, hang on a second there, Sailor, you're getting yourself in knots and there's no need for it.'

I kept a weather eye out for Jenny's return from the bathroom while I gave Soldier my attention.

'One thing, Sailor, would you be a lesbian for that girl?'

'Definitely.'

The burst of absolute certainty surprised me. I smiled. Soldier nodded and I nodded back. The clarity flooded me with courage.

'I'm just going to find a way to let her know I like her and see what happens.'

'You can fucking do no more,' he said as he picked up the empty bottles and moved away to let Jenny back into the booth opposite me.

Jenny was remote, she did indeed look tired.

'Come on, darling, let's get you home.'

Jenny gave a wan smile. 'I am sorry, I am not much company this evening.'

'You're lovely company, girl. It's me who was dragging us down with stupid fussing about my ex-boyfriend. Crazy talk. I haven't seen him since the end of last summer anyway, before I came over here. I think I'm just going to have to accept that I'm doomed to like the girls.'

Jenny smiled sadly at the beer mat in front of her. 'Lucky girls.'

I watched as Jenny remained focused on folding the damp beer mat on precise axes. I loved Jenny's hair, the spongy mass of curls and the glinting blonde and copper colours. I loved Jenny's almond skin, her brown eyes, her lips. It was brazen to stare like that, I was drinking the sight of her, ingesting the shape of her. Warm puffs flooded my stomach and the pupils of my eyes bloomed. I was listing, tilting into a stoned state, and I would put the brakes on this later, but for now I gave myself over to wafting out of the booth after Jenny and following her up the stairs. I remembered to look for Soldier as I was going out the door. He gave me a grinning double thumbs-up.

The warmth and damp heaviness of the air hit us as we came out of the restaurant.

'Gosh, what a temperature,' said Jenny, 'this is not helping my hangover.'

'Close,' I said. 'In Ireland we call this weather close.'

'Same for us. And apt, it really is on top of us.'

'We can pick up my bike and I can walk you home,' I said.

'That seems rather redundant, if you have your bike you should cycle it home.'

'Well I can just leave it there so. It's grand where it is, it's locked, safe and secure.'

'Why would you do that? You would just have to walk back and get it once you've reached my halls.'

'I want to make sure you get home safe.'

Jenny laughed. 'I am perfectly safe.'

'Well, we could just chat a bit longer on the walk.'

'You know what you said about me writing a letter. To Susan?'

'Yes.'

'I think you're right. I think it's inevitable, really. And I am going to try and start it tonight. Actually, I am going to write it tonight. Get it all down. I am really not fit for much else. Think then I might concentrate better on what I have to do. More of a clean break.'

'Tonight?'

Jenny nodded.

'You won't want me yapping around you so.'

Jenny smiled. 'You don't yap.'

She slowly reached out and nearly touched the nape of my neck. I held still while Jenny withdrew the hand that didn't touch me. Jenny was already drifting into herself, into composing the letter that might not get written, might never be sent. She turned away from me and gave a silent half wave as she crossed the road.

I stood watching Jenny's slow walk around the high, red-brick wall of Harvard University. I watched how the Saturday-night people, mainly students in groups and couples, fizzled past Jenny without noticing her, without realising her loveliness. Jenny drifted in and out of view through the wash of streetlights and the shadows of the trees overhanging the wall. I watched until she was lost to my sight.

'Goodnight, sweet Jenny, and every blessing,' I prayed.

I stood in Harvard Square feeling the static prickle of the night and my thoughts. It took me a while to realise I was hearing thunder. The mugginess had buckled and was crackling. I unlocked my bike and began to ride under roiling clouds that I couldn't see but could feel above me.

The fat drops of warm rain fell unsteadily, unsurely at first, and as I crossed the bridge over the Charles River at Allston there was the sound of a thousand empty oil drums falling onto the asphalt as the thunder rolled and brought a deluge of warm teeming rain. I was instantly soaked, the gel in my hair ran into my eyes, the suede jacket was going to be ruined. Already I could feel my feet were wet through the Converse sneakers and I was never so integrated, so whole and clean and sure. I might not be a real lesbian, whatever that might be or look like, but I could be lesbian, adjective and adverb. I wanted to be with the lesbians. I wanted to romance and live there and learn from them and grow strange and old among that tribe. Jenny would never be mine, she was out of my league, but I wanted to be around Jenny and women like her. I could be, would be lesbian, if it meant I could be nearer to Jenny.

Maybe one day I would be with Jenny, maybe years from now, if I did a bit of growing up and wasn't such a fucking eejit, I would go to England and find the university Jenny was working in and just turn up and say, 'Hello, I've found you again.' Maybe I would bring a ring, a kind of a ring. Maybe I might be someone who could be someone and it would all, actually, all work out.

# 9
# The Weakness In Me

The following morning I arrived bright and early to Eily's and Mels's apartment. I had to tell them. They were my best friends in Boston. They had to know. But what exactly did I have to tell them? I wasn't quite sure, but talking with them would make it clear.

I rang the doorbell and had to press it a couple of times before a tousle-headed Eily arrived. She was wearing shorts and an XXL T-shirt from the Tristram Shandy with the quote: *Give me credit for a little more wisdom than appears upon my outside.* She was obviously just waking up.

'Oh, I'm sorry,' I said. 'I know it's fierce feckin' early.'

'Ah no bother, Ro, no bother at all. Come on in. Bring that small forest of the Sunday paper up off the step and in with you. Come in and sit down. I'll get the pot of coffee going and you can let me know what ails you.'

I sat at the kitchen table and said: 'Nothing at all is the matter, Eily. Honestly, I can come back. It's good news. At least, I hope you'll think it's good news. You have to know about it anyway. Now maybe you won't think it's good news and you'll have to see. You know, see about me.'

'Róisín, *a stóirín*, be kind to me now. You've got to talk slowly. I have a shade of a hangover about to bite my arse.' Eily pulled a gallon of orange juice out of the fridge and set about finding glasses.

'I'm not sure how to say it, Eily, except to say that back in Dublin I fell in love with a girl called Fionnuala. Nothing happened. But the feelings, the feelings happened.'

I had made a good start. It seemed I should begin with Fionnuala before getting into the confusing bit about Jenny because I was really not sure what was happening there.

Eily started to grin. 'Hang on a sec there, bud. Mels needs to hear this. She'll kill me if I don't call her.' Eily yelled, 'MELS! IT'S RO, LOVE, SHE HAS BIG NEWS FOR US!' Eily started to walk out of the kitchen. 'Stay there, Ro!' she said, 'and don't move an inch, we'll be right back.'

'Love?' I thought, Eily called Mels 'love'! My sense of confusion was whirling more. Eily came back with Mels right behind her, wearing boxers and pulling a large sweatshirt over her otherwise naked body.

I couldn't speak for a while. I stared at my pals. They were a couple. Eily and Mels were an actual couple. I could see it now. They just ... well ... they fitted together.

I started to slowly shake my head. 'Lads,' I began, and faltered. I tried again: 'Lads ...' I couldn't say anything else.

Mels understood: 'You mean you didn't guess about us? You didn't know?'

'No,' I said. 'Yes. I didn't know. I didn't know at all. God. That's wonderful.'

Eily sat on a chair next to me and started to rub her temples. 'Jesus, Ro! For a highly intelligent girl you can be a total thick.'

Mels was standing behind Eily and she put her hands on Eily's shoulders. 'Ah, leave her alone. Give her a chance. I keep telling you, Eily, that no one has cottoned on to us!'

'I think some of the camogie girls know right well!' retorted Eily.

'But you thought that Ro did, too!'

'I didn't,' I said. 'I didn't know.'

'It just doesn't dawn on people that lesbians actually exist, and that we're not monsters or look like we're in a porno movie,' said Mels, trying to reassure me.

'Are ye lesbians so?' I asked.

Mels, standing behind the seated Eily, smiled shyly, nodded and hugged Eily closer to her.

Eily looked up at her smiling and said: 'Fionnuala. She left a girl back in Dublin by the name of Fionnuala.'

'Well, I didn't really. I mean, we weren't an item. Exactly.' I didn't know how to continue. 'God! Are ye actually lesbians?'

Eily heaved a shrug and spread her palms to the ceiling. She turned around to Mels: 'Yes, yes, she's highly intelligent, but she's also a total thick.'

I realised my poor powers of comprehension had been a topic of conversation between the two of them before this morning.

'Well, as you know, Ro, we met in London,' said Mels.

'And it wasn't really far enough away from Mels's family,' continued Eily.

'So we came here,' finished Mels. 'In total, we're together three years.' Mels rubbed Eily's head. 'I spotted this one at a fundraiser for a fella who had an accident on a site. And I said to myself, she'll do nicely.'

'She completely seduced me!' declared Eily proudly.

'Did you know you were a lesbian, Eily?' I asked. 'How did you know?'

'Ah well, I'd shifted girls when I was a young one,' said Eily, 'But I didn't really think about it.'

'And you, Mels?' I asked.

'Always. I always was. Always knew and always knew to be quiet about it. But back to you!' said Mels. 'What made you come round to us at this early hour on a Sunday morning? What happened you last night?'

'Eeh. I'm not sure really,' I said. 'I mean, I just said to myself, well, lesbians are the people I want to be among.'

'Just last night?!' exclaimed Eily.

I nodded.

'Jesus, Ro! I could have told you!' said Eily.

Mels laughed, while I complained: 'Well why didn't you say something?! Why didn't you tell me about yourselves?!'

'Ah come on, Ro!' said Mels.

'What?' said Eily. 'Like, "Hello! Pleased to meet you. By the way, may I introduce you to my lovely girlfriend?!"'

Mels and I laughed.

'Alright!' I said.

'Anyway, we really thought we had given you enough hints,' said Mels.

Eily continued to shrug and raise her palms to heaven.

'And,' continued Mels, 'we thought if you picked up on the hints, you might be one of the friends of Dorothy yourself. What happened you last night to have the penny drop?'

'Did you shift the English one?' Eily asked.

'Eeh. No.'

'But you wanted to?' Eily persisted.

'Eeh. Yeah,' I admitted.

Mels tried to shush Eily, who punched the air and declared: 'Way to go, McCarthy!'

'You know, Ro,' Mels said, 'we thought you had great DP, but we weren't sure if you knew that for yourself.'

'DP?'

'Dyke Potential,' answered Eily. 'Ro, *a stór*, you are a total dyke. I know you didn't ask for my opinion. But there you have it. You're one of us!'

I had never been happier.

'God, I thought I was coming here to tell ye something and now my head is blown off my neck! In the best way! Group hug!'

Eily and Mels indulged me and the three of us embraced. I thought right at that moment we must be the happiest people in the happiest kitchen in Boston.

There seemed to be nothing for it but to go out to a celebratory brunch. We went to The Corrib and spent hours laughing over jugs of mimosas and rounds of French toast and pancakes. I had loads of questions, and Eily and Mels duly obliged with as much information and stories as they could supply. There were, however, times when Eily put her foot down.

'Ro! It really is out, not coming in. There's no point questioning it when that's what is said!'

It was decided I would accompany Eily that afternoon to a meeting of BQW.

'Boston Quality Women!' declared Mels. 'For the love of God! Could you credit that?!'

'Ah, darling!' pleaded Eily. 'The name was decided back in the fifties. And they're not that bad, really. You need to give them another chance.'

Mels turned to me. 'I will admit it is great for our business. Eily gets a load of good contacts from those meetings. But I can't be around her as she schmoozes. All of these old wans. Going weak for her!'

Eily raised her open palms, and shrugged. 'They all love a young butch!' she explained and I was happy to realise I knew what the term meant, in fact I could picture the scene.

'You take care, Ro, that you're not swallowed alive there!' teased Mels.

'Well, maybe Jenny will be there!' I declared.

I caught a half glance between my pals.

'Well, maybe,' they agreed wanly.

'You don't really approve?' I asked, as I realised the pair had already discussed Jenny.

'Well. It's not that. It's just, we worry for you Ro,' said Mels. 'That she might not fully appreciate you.'

I nodded. I knew Mels was being kind and wanted to let me gently know that Jenny was way out of my league.

When we left The Corrib and went back to the apartment, Mels found a nice shirt and chinos in her wardrobe.

'You can have these,' she said to me. 'I don't know why I got them. I never wore them.' She gave the clothes a fresh press with the iron and Eily put some gel through my hair. They agreed I looked 'smashing'.

Eily and Mels supplied me with a stash of their business cards and drilled me in how to act as their agent.

'There'll be drink at this,' explained Eily. 'They like their glasses of wine. So Mels will drop us over and we'll get the T home.'

I was very nervous walking in the doors of The Charles Hotel. I was nearly used to fancy places through my cleaning jobs, but I wasn't quite used to being a punter in swanky locations. And the weekend had been such a whirl. Here I was, all dressed up, going to meet lesbians. Maybe Jenny would be inside.

There were about sixty women in the hotel bar but Jenny wasn't one of them.

The glasses of wine were pretty huge and I was pleasantly squiffy in no time and it was fun. The lesbian ladies really liked me. I liked them liking me. They loved my accent. It was 'so cute'. One of them asked me if I was a poet. I said no, I preferred to write fiction. God! Why did I say that? It was too true a thing to be saying. I was nervous again and glad Eily put another large glass of wine in my hand.

'Come here, you're a big hit! Aren't you!'

'They all love a young butch!' I laughed.

Eily put her arm around me and gave me a playful pretend punch. 'Come on over here, Ro, remember we have a painting company to run. These women you'll be meeting are lawyers, and lawyers have clients, and clients listen to their lawyers' recommendations. Lawyers have given us our best contacts.'

Eily made the introductions:

'She's a literature student really, and too good-looking to send in to a lot of our jobs, we've too many bored housewives with houses they think need painting. I've got to protect my workers!' she joked.

I was bashful. I wasn't used to this. It was fun. But it was a bit strange, too. And Eily was totally at ease, she had the entire room eating out of her hand. I could see why Mels stayed at home.

'What's your name?' a tall, thin woman asked. She seemed old. Maybe mid- or late thirties. She had short, tightly permed hair. She wore a Lacoste jumper in a pink-and-green diamond pattern and navy trousers. And pearls.

'I'm called Ro, short for Rosemary.' I held out my hand to shake but the woman was holding two glasses of wine.

'Can't shake right now,' she said. 'Ro! That's a lot better than Rosemary. That's a name for grandmothers!'

I nodded. 'And your name is?'

The woman stared me down.

I repeated: 'And your name is …?'

'You want to know my name? Why are you asking?' The woman smirked. 'Why do you want to know my name?'

'I'm just interested …'

The woman interjected, '… you're interested! That's fast! I didn't know the women from the Old Country were so fast nowadays!'

I didn't know what to say.

'Terri. I'm called Terri and I'm Irish too. One hundred per cent. No mixing with the Italians in my family!'

'Have you ever been over?' I asked. It was the next thing you asked the Irish Americans, to be polite. 'Have you ever been over to Ireland?'

'Yeah,' replied Terri. 'It was a dump.'

I laughed. 'That's great! You're the first Irish American I met who has actually been honest! The rest of them all talk about the spiritual rush they felt coming up from the land as it welcomed them "home"!'

'I don't think it's cool to make fun of people,' Terri replied curtly. 'Do you think it's fun to make fun of people?' She seemed hurt.

I was embarrassed. 'God, no. Sorry. I genuinely meant no offence.'

'You can buy me another drink to apologise. That is, if you are genuinely interested in me as you said you were. Unless that was your idea of a joke.'

'God, no! Not at all!' I felt awful.

'House red,' said Terri.

I was going to point out to Terri that she already had a glass in each hand, but I decided to get her the requested glass of red and then scram. I went and put the order in and Eily came by and introduced me to a new clutch of women.

'Now she's only occasionally with us,' Eily explained, with her arm around my shoulders, 'because look at how handsome she is! We've too many bored housewives on our books! Our Ro would be in right danger if she was to be put to painting out in the 'burbs!'

I was suddenly tired and quite drunk. The women were all smiling at me. It was nice. I seemed to be a hit. I smiled back and found myself chatting. One of them asked if she could buy me a drink.

'Oh God!' I said. 'I nearly forgot! I have to bring a glass to someone, I forgot I was getting it.'

The women in the group smiled good-naturedly. I turned and got the glass of wine from the counter, hurriedly left a ten dollar bill for the bartender and went back to Terri. She was where I had left her, sitting alone. She had put on her coat and looked set to leave.

'You said you were interested.'

I was horrified to see Terri was tearful.

'But you're just one of those women who likes to make fun of other women.'

'I'm not, no! Really!' I said.

Terri waved away the glass. She seemed to be having a hard time holding herself together. I was very sorry for her. I put the glass down on the table. It seemed Terri had already had plenty to drink.

'Come on,' I said, 'let's go outside and get you some air, maybe a taxi to get you home.'

Terri tried to smile, but she got upset again and tried to wave me away.

'Jesus!' said Terri. 'I knew this would be too hard. But I pushed myself.'

'Come on,' I said.

Terri reached for my hand to help her out of the chair. She held onto my hand with both of her hands and we walked that way through the bar. I would look after Terri, there was something up with her. She was in a bad way. Eily came over.

'I'm going to make sure that Terri gets home,' I explained. 'I'm just going to get my coat and look after her. Is that OK? Are you alright here? I should be back in a little bit.'

'Grand so,' said Eily, softly adding, 'take it easy, bud.'

Once outside the hotel, Terri seemed to recover her spirits. Though the fresh air was making me feel quite drunk, those glasses were big (did I have two? It was never three!?) and the mimosas at brunch seemed to be having a belated effect.

'We don't need a cab,' said Terri. 'I live nearby, in Somerville, we can walk.'

'Eeh, grand so,' I said, 'though isn't Somerville a bit far?'

'It's not,' declared Terri as she clasped my arm, 'unless you've changed your mind?'

'I've promised to see you home safe and sound. I'm a woman of my word!'

We started to walk quickly, Terri had a very speedy pace. We clipped through Harvard Square. It probably actually wouldn't be long until we reached Somerville.

'You are single?' Terri turned to me with panic in her face and voice.

'Oh yes!' I said.

Terri smiled. I had a sinking feeling.

'I'm mad about a woman, though,' I blurted. 'I met her only recently.'

'What are you talking about?' Terri was upset again.

'Well, she's out of my league,' I admitted as we marched down Kirkland Street. I had rarely walked so fast.

'Are you sleeping with her?'

'God no!' I laughed.

'Why are you bringing her up?'

I didn't know what to say.

There was an uncomfortable silence as we crossed Beacon Street and then Somerville Avenue. Terri held onto my arm with both hands. I could see passers-by turn to look. They thought we were a couple. I liked that. Terri and I didn't look straight, and people gave us a second glance. One guy jogging past whipped his head back and gave us a bit of a sneer. I squeezed Terri's hands as she held my arm and hoped she hadn't seen the derision. We overtook two other women who were strolling together and as we stepped around them, for the first time in my life, I was given an affirmative nod of recognition by other lesbians. I was elated. This was brilliant! So much had happened in twenty-four hours. This day was HUGE!

'What are you laughing at?' said Terri, sounding worried.

'Oh! I'm just smiling,' I said.

'No! You were laughing!' snapped Terri.

'Oh! Well, it's just I'm very, very happy,' I said. 'I don't think I've ever been happier.'

Terri stopped suddenly and pulled me in close, she swivelled me against the wall of the building we were passing and I was being kissed, urgently. I was surprised.

'What's the matter?' asked Terri. 'Were you just playing with me?'

'No!' I said. 'I'm just surprised.'

Terri looked distressed. 'If you knew what my life has been like, you wouldn't treat me like this.'

I didn't know what to say. Terri was pressed into me and I loved the feeling of Terri's body trembling on mine. I was solid. I so rarely felt solid. I put my arms around her and she moved more slowly this time, she stroked my face and ran her fingers along the hairline of my forehead.

'I wouldn't take this behaviour from you,' Terri murmured, 'except you're beautiful.'

She ran her index finger along my lower lip and slowly this time, slowly, Terri leaned in closer to my face. Terri's breath gently touched my mouth and I parted my lips to receive the kiss. Terri didn't kiss me, she pulled back and smiled. Then she leaned in again and I closed my eyes and soon I could feel the softest kisses on my eyelids. Terri was murmuring in my ear and moving her body in slow grinding movements over my hips. I felt the faintest touch of fingers on the crotch seam of my chinos. 'God, this is good,' I thought. Terri's little finger was in my mouth and I gently bit and caressed it with my tongue.

'You're horny, little Irish, aren't you?' said Terri. 'Let's get you home.'

Terri clasped my hand and we started to run. I was laughing all the while. This was just mad, I thought. Terri lived nearby, on Avon Street. She pulled me up steps to a ground-floor apartment in a blue-painted triple decker and she pushed me back against the front door.

'It's locked, Irish! You've got to find the keys!' she said as she faced me and lifted her arms.

I had a feeling the keys were in one of Terri's fists but I played along, slowly putting my hands into her coat pockets: a wallet, a pack of tissues, lip balm, no keys. I shyly felt around the outside of her trouser pockets, back and front. No sign of keys. Terri swung round to face her door, her legs still straddled and her arms outstretched, she leaned on her fists.

'Why don't you put your hand inside my pants' pockets?' asked Terri in a low voice. 'Stay standing behind me,' she ordered, 'and put your hands, both of them, into my front pockets.'

I did as I was told. I got a surprise. I touched flesh and Terri's hip bones. Terri leaned her forehead onto the front door.

'Lower!' she said, and I obliged.

I slid my hands lower into Terri's pockets. There were no keys, no pockets, no underwear. Just sweet folds of heat and wetness. I knew by instinct what to do and I slid my fingers into where they belonged and within short minutes Terri had surfed my eager hand for her first orgasm of the evening.

At Terri's behest, I called in sick to Helen Keogh at the Plaza hotel at 5.00 a.m. the next day and I went back to bed with Terri.

Two hours later, Terri was putting nylon-stockinged feet into black patent pumps. She was a lawyer. She had to work.

# P-TOWN

# SUMMER 1984

# 10
# Born To Run

'It's been a week and a half, Ro! A week and a half! Where have you been, my buddy?!'

Eily and I were laughing as Eily held me in a soft headlock, she was mock punching my ear.

'Is that all? Sure that's no time at all, girl!' I laughed.

We were propped up at the bar counter of The Shandy with two pints of seltzer water, ice and lime cordial in front of us. It was mid-afternoon, mid-week, and outside the New England spring was in full, neon-green glory, blazing strong squares of light onto the bar counter through the small panes of the pub window.

'I feckin' waited for you for ages at the BQW, long after it was over! You said you would be back!'

Eily relaxed her grip and I sat up sheepishily, even as I was grinning.

Eily got a bit more serious. 'Mels and I were worried. Like, we called to your house a few times. Helen Keogh said you called in sick. Then we had to wait days before you were due to do your shift at Clara's.'

'I am sorry, Eily!' I was truly contrite. 'I thought you knew I'd be OK, that you'd seen me go off with Terri, like, and you'd get it.'

'Terri! Terri! Is that her feckin' name? I thought you said Cherry to me going out the door. No wonder none of the BQW women could help me out in tracking you down! Ro, *a stór*, you're family to Mels and me.' I was aghast to see tears in Eily's eyes. 'Just don't do that again, alright? Phone!'

I nodded.

'Now!' Eily gave me a real punch on my upper arm. 'I want the WHOLE feckin' story. You'll have to say it all again to Mels. But I want to hear EVERYTHING. When I say EVERYTHING, you know you don't have to tell me ALL of the details of the sex – though I'm happy to hear that too!'

'The sex … is … great. Just. Great,' I murmured.

Eily hugged me and whispered, 'G'wan! Ya good thing!'

'So, I'm in a committed relationship, I'm an actual lesbian! I'm with Terri and we're maho – that is – mon-ogamous. I've met her friends so you must meet her. We've been making plans.'

Eily smiled. 'I'm delighted for you, Ro. There is nothing better than finding the right woman, your someone. Life makes sense then.'

'Well, it's a bit hard for Terri. She never expected to be with someone who is so young. She likes the word gom. I introduced her to that word, and that's her pet name for me now.'

'You're getting her into the Cork slang!' laughed Eily.

'Well, she'll need to know what the natives are talking about when we visit.' I laughed.

'So you're right serious then, Ro?' said Eily gravely. 'Isn't gom a bit harsh on you, though?'

'Well, you know she hasn't had things easy. When she was in high school she had an awful time of it. Her first girlfriend started going out with Terri's own brother, the one just older than her. Can you imagine?'

'Christ!' said Eily.

'And that girl and her brother just made her life a misery. Her whole family, her whole school just mocked her and mocked her.'

Eily shuddered in response.

I continued, 'Like, none of it was easy. College and then law school and all the debt and shitty girlfriends.' I leaned in and spoke in an undertone: 'Eily, she even had to go to therapy. She's seeing a therapist!'

Eily nodded gravely.

'And then, just when she has her debts paid off and she's making something of her life, she falls in love with a twenty-two year old!'

'Well ...' began Eily.

I interjected in terse whisper, '*And* an illegal alien.'

'Right,' nodded Eily.

'So it's tough on her.'

'Hey!' And there was Terri! Beside us!

My groin expanded. Terri was hot.

'Hi, love!' I called. I was surprised and delighted. Terri was here. And she wasn't in her straight work clothes, she was wearing her cool golfing gear.

'This is Eily!' I said.

Eily had slid off the bar stool to stand up and she offered Terri her hand to shake. Terri looked Eily up and down before slowly shaking the proffered hand. As if they were making a deal.

'What's this?' Terri said pointing to the pints of seltzer water. 'I thought you guys were Irish! Where's the fucking beer?'

'Ah, we've gone native!' retorted Eily. 'No drunk driving, I've the van outside and a job to go back to. I just took some time out to meet my lost pal here,' she said gesturing with her thumb towards me. 'Missing in action, she was!'

'She's seen some action!' said Terri, leaning over and pulling me towards her. Before I knew what was happening, I was being kissed hard and urgently by Terri, who wouldn't or couldn't let the kiss stop. It was a bit embarrassing, but when I pulled away somewhat I saw Eily had turned towards studying her glass of seltzer.

'Are you guys just about done here?' demanded Terri as she pushed me away. Eily and I looked at each other in a pause.

'Eeh …'

'Ah, yeah, we are,' said Eily, 'though we've yet to hear all about you, Terri! But we should really wait for Mels to be here. Let's all go out for a drink this Sunday, after Ro's shift with Clara!'

I was nodding and grinning. 'Yes!'

But Terri shook her head. 'No can do this Sunday! Memorial Day Weekend! This lawyer has a holiday! We're going to my place in P-town!'

'P-town?' I asked.

'It was supposed to be a surprise, but it's ruined now!' Terri was upset.

'P-town? Provincetown? Oh! That's class!' said Eily quickly. 'Playground of the gays! Amazing to have such a thing! Me and Mels haven't been yet, but we're planning to go this summer.'

'We'll get to hang out there!' Terri said jubilantly. 'We're going to be there every weekend!'

'Great!' said Eily.

'I'm not going to be there every weekend,' I said quietly. 'I've got Clara to mind.'

I wasn't sure when Eily left, or even if myself and Terri left before Eily, as the row with Terri was so epic I couldn't remember much of anything after it. I thought we were going to crash a couple of times as Terri drove us back to Somerville.

I remembered wailing at one stage, 'But I want to do two summer courses at UMASS!'

Mostly I remembered being adamant I didn't want to go to Provincetown because I didn't want to leave Clara. Terri told me I was 'commitment-phobic' and I had 'relationship issues'. Terri adored me. Just adored me. I was beautiful, even if I was immature and maybe damaged. Most people couldn't love in the way Terri loved. Terri could see my beauty and potential even if I couldn't see it for myself. We would never get to see each other if I worked all weekends with Clara. Terri had to work all week. She just had weekends and a two-week vacation period in August. Terri was prepared to make the drive from hell every Friday evening to sit in the traffic jam all the way down the Cape from Boston. God knows how many fucking hours she would have to spend in the fucking heat in her fucking car, but she was prepared to do it for our relationship. She was prepared to get up at 4.30 a.m. on Mondays so she could spend three weekend nights with her girlfriend, and what was I doing for the relationship? Putting earning some cash before my girlfriend? I said Clara was like a grandmother but Terri said that was sentimental horseshit, more of my fucking bullshit and I knew it. If I was going to insist on staying in Boston for the summer, I could change my shifts to weeknights. I tried to explain to Terri what Jacinta was like and Terri kept saying, 'What!? What the fuck!'

I had to admit it all sounded rather pathetic.

Terri said, 'Get another fucking job, Ro, if you really want to stay in Boston. There are plenty of grandmas' asses that need wiping in this city, but get a job where you can have the weekend off and that pays enough so you can pay your half of the summer rental in P-town because that's where we're going every weekend.'

When the row was over and Terri explained how much summer rentals cost in P-town, I didn't see how I could afford to pay rent in Boston and P-town, even half a rent in P-town. Terri said I could move in with her, ditch living in that dump on Foster Street. Terri would give me a good deal on the rent for Somerville and P-town.

Terri said, 'I get why you can't tell those Irish guys you live with that you're a lesbian. They would get sexually violent.'

'No!' I exclaimed. 'It's just the word would be back home before I finished my sentence and I need to be the person to let people back home know. They can't hear it down the pub! Terri, those lads are sound! They wouldn't do a thing to me. They just wouldn't be able to help saying something. Or one of their girlfriends would pass on the news.'

'I know, honey, but you can move in with me,' Terri said. 'You need never have to see those guys again.'

I didn't know what to say, and so I said the wrong thing. 'But the lads are grand, I like living with them. They're hardly ever there anyway, and I'm near Eily and Mels.'

Terri started crying. 'You're not even passive aggressive,' she whispered, 'this is just abusive aggressive.'

'God, Terri, I'm sorry, I don't mean to be like that at all! Look, it's just I'm surprised, that's all. Everything is still so new. I'm in a new world. I'm still learning the language.'

Terri went quiet. 'This is so hard for me. I get you're immature, I really do! I make allowances! I know this is all new to you, honey. And I really do know how much I mean to you. I'm your lover!' Terri started to run her fingers down my spine, giving gentle rubs around my ass.

'You know I love you!' I said rather desperately. 'But—'

'But I know you're scared,' she said very gently. 'I know you're scared, Gom, and I know that means you're in fight or flight. You're shutting me out because you're scared. You're cutting off the one sure and good thing you have in this world because you're afraid of being hurt.' Very gently, Terri continued, 'This is just you, Gom! You put up barriers and make obstacles when your lover comes close to you because you're afraid of being hurt.'

Terri slowly leaned towards me and I kissed her. Slowly, she ran her hands up inside my shirt and expertly eased the clasp on my bra. Terri shuffled away my move to open her waistband, and she brought her hands to cup my breasts. She helped me shrug out of my sweatshirt. She gently held my chin and slowly pushed me away, she held me at arm's length. I waited while she gave me a soft, appraising look. To my horror, she burst into tears.

'I asked you to live with me! Don't you know what that means?' Terri continued to cry, I was not able to console her. I took her to the bedroom to lie down. Terri cried herself silent, she lay curled up in a foetal position. I lay behind Terri and I wrapped around her. We both fell asleep.

When I woke I saw the digital clock as it flicked to 21:04. Terri was still sleeping. I was wretched. My thoughts were churning and I could make no sense. I said a prayer: 'Please, God, forgive me. I don't mean to be such a horrible person. I know you forgive me for being a lesbian because you made me this way. I'm sorry I'm such a fuck-up in other ways, and you didn't make me to be like that. I will try and be the very best lesbian you made me to be.' I felt immediately better. I had never thought of myself in this way before, but what Terri had said made total sense. I loved Terri and here I was, even though I didn't mean to, I was pushing her away. I didn't really know what 'passive aggressive' meant precisely, it seemed to cover a lot of different kinds of my behaviour. Whenever I asked Terri what she meant by the term, she said my question was classic passive aggressive behaviour. What I did know was that I kept fucking up around Terri, but I didn't know why I made so many mistakes. Terri understood my failings, but of course she was hurt by me. The only thing for me to do was to work hard and show Terri I was worthy of her.

It was short notice but I organised to get the Memorial Day weekend off from working with Clara by swapping shifts with Helena Mulcahy. I worked that Tuesday, Wednesday and Thursday night with Clara before I left for the weekend with Terri in Provincetown.

I told Clara, 'I'm going to the Cape for the weekend with some American friends.'

'That's good, honey! It's good you make American friends and not be with all the Irish all the time. Where you going? Who are these Americans? Are they college friends?'

'Eh. I'm going to Cape Cod.'

'But that's a big place, honey. You know where on the Cape?'
'I think it's out towards the end of the Cape.'
'Truro? Provincetown? You going there?'
'I'm not sure.'
'If you're near Provincetown, you should go see a show. Me and Lenny loved going to the shows where the guys are girls and they sing all the show tunes. I don't know how they do it, even swimsuits!'
'Well, I'll go to that show if my friends are going to it.'
'You wanna go to the matinee show. We went in the day time. I think that town is a little too peculiar, you know, in the night time.'
I didn't know what to say.
'Who ya going with?'
'Terri.'
'Terry? Who's he?'
'Just a friend.'

Clara smiled, she smiled a very twinkly smile. She levered upright her La-Z-Boy chair, slid off it and hobbled slowly over towards where I was sitting. She gently stroked my face with her gnarled small hand.

'Your cheek is hot,' she said softly.

I nodded, feeling rather desperate.

'Don't worry, honey.' She chuckled gently. 'You tell me all about Terry when you're ready.'

I couldn't say anything. It was all such a whirlwind. I hadn't had much sleep over the previous nine days. I had no time to think. I helped Clara back to her chair and eventually I said,

'I will tell you everything, Clara, I promise. I just don't really know myself what's happening right now.'

Clara seemed a little surprised: 'Oh! Honey! You're so serious! Don't worry so much! You're young! You have a good time! Maybe you'll tell me more when you know you can depend on him.'

Terri phoned every night once Clara was in bed and I had gone into my own room. She introduced me to phone sex and I surprised myself by my fluency.

On Friday morning, I was bereft at saying goodbye to Clara.

'Honey! Honey! Why you so sad? You're going to have a good weekend with Terry! Holiday on the Cape! I see you next weekend and you tell me all about it!'

I pulled myself together and managed a cheery enough goodbye, but the truth was that I felt wretched. And I was scared. Scared that Clara would no longer feel warm and easy with me. I realised I had become quite dependent on Clara liking me. I needed some time to prepare myself for her dislike.

Getting into the car with Terri that evening, I still had a queasy hangover feeling that I was going to have to face Clara with news she might well be appalled by. Yet I soon forgot those feelings of dread once I was on the road to Cape Cod in Terri's fast car. I couldn't stop saying: 'My First American Road Trip!'

I put on a tape of Bruce Springsteen's album, *Born To Run*. Terri was reluctant at first, but I cajoled her into singing along, and eventually she sang with gusto.

Provincetown was as beautiful as everyone said. I was acutely aware I was a bit of an eejit, I couldn't stop saying, 'WOW! WOW!!' But Provincetown was perfect. The sunlight seemed to bless everything, it made the water shimmer, and it made the spring flowers more vivid, and it added a soft lustre to the freshly painted houses in the quiet lanes.

Terri had put a one-page CV together for me.

She explained: 'You know, you might be able to get work here. You can earn much more money here than in Boston and pay your half of the P-town rental. It's up to you if you want to pay dead money for a room you don't use in that dump on Foster Street. You can move in with me full-time in September if you're mature enough to make the move.'

Terri took me around to various shops and guesthouses to hand in my CV. I didn't think I would be able to get any work. Terri told me it was probably too late. But I was surprised I was immediately offered work selling on some of the stalls in Whaler's

Wharf and, if I wanted them, I could also have cleaning shifts at some of the inns. My new employer on Whaler's Wharf wanted me to start right on the spot and so I set to work while Terri hit the beach at Herring Cove.

That night, rather flushed with Californian rosé, Terri and I decided the best thing for me to do was to stay on in Provincetown. I would be able to earn a lot of money, so I could work less in September and focus on my studies. The lads on Foster Street would be able to find someone to take my room. On Sunday, when Terri called by the stall I was working on, it transpired we'd had another misunderstanding. I had assumed I was going back to Boston with Terri, leaving before dawn the next day.

'Grow up, Ro! You'll lose your jobs here and you were lucky to get them! They pay a lot more than your shitty jobs in the city!'

'I never talked to Clara,' I tried to explain.

'Phone, for Chrissakes,' said Terri, 'and do it today. Give that bitch Jacinta time to get a replacement. She'll be very happy to have you out of the picture. Go and make her day! And this is just so *you*, Ro! You don't face up to your responsibilities and you leave messes wherever you go!'

I regretted having shown Terri the list, the list I had made for Jenny before I copped on to myself. Jenny! God! I was deluded to think I would ever have had a chance there. It was amazing to me that Terri loved me.

The alarm clock went off at 4.00 a.m. the next day. Terri swore as she got out of bed and swore as she tiredly made her way to the bathroom.

'Chrissakes, Ro! Are you just going to fuckin' lie there?'

I got up, not entirely sure what I was supposed to do.

'Make some strong coffee! I got a horrible journey to do.'

I made the coffee extra-strong as Terri was having her shower and poured it out for her in her favourite mug. She started to sip it as she dressed.

When she was going out the door I attempted to give her a goodbye hug. She shrugged me off.

'Chrissakes, Ro! I don't have time for fucking right now!'

'It was only a goodbye hug,' I meekly replied.

'Oh fuck you too,' she wearily responded as she closed the door behind her.

I could hear her revving the engine as she reversed out the drive. I felt bad I hadn't gone out with her to wave her off, and rushed out to try and catch her and wish her all the best for the long journey. I ran out just in time to see the tail-lights turn right at the top of our little road. I waved anyway, even though I knew she wouldn't be able to see me, even if she looked back.

I didn't want to phone Jacinta without talking to Clara. I started my trial as a cleaner for an inn at 7.00 a.m. and was done by noon, but had to go to Whaler's Wharf to open up the pewter figurine stall where I was due to work until 9.00 p.m. During the afternoon I got a bundle of quarters and went to the call box near my stall. I nearly sobbed when I heard Clara's lovely voice and, to my horror, I found myself lying to Clara.

'Honey, honey, what is the matter?' Clara exclaimed as she recognised my voice and heard my anguish.

I wasn't able to answer.

Clara continued, 'Jacinta has been saying a little that something is wrong with you. I could see you've been what they say stressed these weeks. You looked to me like the lovesick and then you tell me about Terry and I think it's maybe your boy is some trouble for you? But Jacinta last night tells me you might be maybe some kind of sick? Honey, I have money – we can have a doctor.'

I didn't know what to say to Clara, and I didn't know what that weapon Jacinta was up to, but the truth was that I really did feel sick as I began to lie to Clara.

'Yeah, I'm sick.'

'Honey!'

'Well, no, I'm fine really. Just a bit sick, I mean, I think I should go home to Ireland to get myself checked out.'

'Oh?!'

'Yeah, I'm going to stay there for the summer. Yeah.'

There was a silence then, which I rapidly filled.

'Clara, I'm really, really sorry not to have told you anything. Not to have been able to tell you in person.'

I could feel sobs snag my breath. I held it together. Here was a chance to stay in Provincetown for the summer. Sort myself out a bit and tell Clara when I was ready for the fallout.

'Look, I've gone down to New York, Clara, because I can get a cheap flight from here to England and then the boat back to Ireland. Yeah.'

'Honey! Your school work! Your summer courses!'

'Lookit, I'm going to be back in Boston in September for sure. Yeah. Like, even if I have to come in over the border from Canada, I'm going to make my way back to Boston, Clara. I'm going to see you again.'

And that's when I really began to cry.

'Honey! What's the matter with you? What are your symptoms? There are much better doctors in Boston – they are best in the world. Come back here and I will get you the best doctor! You gotta stay in school, honey! That's your future!'

I was too shocked at myself to say anything. I could hear Clara's distressed breathing on the phone and I couldn't say anything to relieve her anxiety. I was numb, zoning out.

Clara broke the silence, in a low voice she said, 'Honey, you're not to worry. But when you get back home, you phone me. Call collect and we can talk and you can tell me everything – everything about Terry and how you are.'

I still couldn't speak.

'You make me a promise, Ro. Make me a promise that you will phone me – call collect – but you phone me when you're back in Ireland – in a few days – phone me and we will talk.'

'OK.' I had only a few days to figure this out.

'Say, I promise!'

'I promise.'

'You're such a beautiful person, my Ro. I am not going to let anything bad happen you. You know that?'

'OK.'

There was a silence then. The automated phone voice said I needed to put another 75 cents into the slot for another three minutes. I could hear Clara's jagged breathing through the line and the shrieking phone beeps and I remained numb and stuck to the spot as the call got cut off.

I returned to the pewter figurine stall in a semi-comatose state. Michael, who sold all kinds of crystals and semi-precious stones from the stall opposite me, came over and asked me what was wrong.

I couldn't say anything, just 'I'm a horrible person'.

Michael said nothing, but he hugged me. He was tall and skinny and awkward, he smelled of turpentine and cigarette smoke. I noticed a streak of blue paint across his ear as we hugged. He was about my age, maybe a bit older, and he seemed to be very gay.

'Thanks,' I said as I released myself from his bony embrace.

'It's not easy,' he said.

I nodded.

'When we're through here and have locked up, come with me and have a beer with my friends. You'll like them. We're all misfits.'

Misfits.

I got back to trying to busy myself with the stall. Repeating the word 'misfits' lulled me into a kind of calm, but then I had a flashback of the eager way I had lied to Clara and I thought I might throw up. I pulled out my jotter and wrote a letter to Clara.

## KATHERINE O'DONNELL

*10 Center Street*
*Provincetown*
*MA 02657*
*May 28th, 1984*

*Dear Clara,*
*I've just put down the phone to you and I'm ashamed of myself. I lied to you. I have ended up in Provincetown because I am in a relationship with a woman called Terri (she's actually 100% Irish). We are very much in love and if I worked weekends in Boston we would never get to see each other and I wouldn't have given our relationship a chance.*

I winced when I read it back. I didn't want to imagine Clara reading that. I scrapped the letter and started again.

*Dear Clara,*
*I've just put down the phone to you and I'm ashamed of myself. I lied to you. I am not at all sick. I am very very sorry for telling such an awful lie. I have ended up in Provincetown. I'm really not sure how I ended up here but I know I'm a lesbian and I'm finding it hard to tell people – even you who likes me and who I love so much. I am so sorry I lied to you and I am so sorry not to tell you all of this in person. I'm very sorry Clara. I would love to be spending weekends with you but I think I should stay here and sort myself out and I'm so obviously fucked up (please excuse the bad language but I haven't been able to think of how else to describe myself). I'm not asking you to forgive me because what I did was terrible. Never ever worry again about me.*
               *Ro*

I thought about asking Michael to read the letter to see if it was OK, but he was intently smoking and reading a glossy art magazine, scarcely glancing at the potential customer who was stroking the large lumps of rose quartz on his counter. I decided I didn't want to deliberate any further. I got Michael to cover for me while I ran to the post office, bought an envelope and stamp and sent my confession to Clara.

Running back to Whaler's Wharf, I made a pledge: I was going to use the shifts on the pewter figurine stall to write individual letters to my family and friends back in Cork. I would tell them I was lesbian. I would come out, I would be absolutely out. I would never tell that lie again. I made a list of all the letters I had to write, fourteen in total. I was heavy with dread. I started with the one that was going to be easiest but that would force me to follow through on writing all the other excruciating letters. I jotted down the note I would send my younger brothers, Mossy and Ger:

> *I've big news: I'm in love with a beautiful woman, Terri (actually three of her grandparents are Irish – all from Kerry, but besides that she's sound – you'll love her). My life makes sense now. I'm very happy so don't be worrying about me. I'm going to write to all the rest of the family throughout the summer so you won't have to keep this a secret for too long but don't let on until they bring it up with you. I miss you all the time and think about how much you would love it here – how much I would love to have you here with me. All my love, Ro xxxxxxxxxxxxoo*

I stared at the note and crumpled it up. It was impossible. I was going to have to phone them. It didn't take many minutes before I thought about how that was also going to be also impossible. No privacy. I would be standing at a public phone and it would cost a fortune. I would need shoals and shoals of quarters to feed the phone. And what if they were shocked? Or disgusted? Or thought I had lost my mind? Or thought I was just messing? A phone call would be a disaster. I should probably just go home and tell the folks and let the shit hit the fan and deal with the fallout while I was home and then get the hell back to the States.

It had been well over an hour since I'd made a sale. I was going to have to concentrate on making eye contact with people who were quietly perusing the stall, engage them in small talk and make them feel happy about buying a figurine. If I wanted to earn commissions, I was going to have to deliver sales. I stood up from the seat where I had sat scribbling notes and making lists and resolutions, but immediately I felt sick. I crouched down on the floor and found myself hugging my knees and rocking back and forth. This was all going to be very tough.

# 11
# Love Is A Battlefield

I had very little time off between my multiple jobs but I loved being in Provincetown. I loved waking up there and going to sleep there and the glorious days and nights in between my waking and sleeping. Everyone who worked in P-town was lesbian or gay, or as good as. It thrilled me to be immediately part of the community of misfit workers who were from all over the States, they were still arriving, many of them returning for their tenth or more season. 'Swallows,' I thought, 'we're swallows.'

My first night in P-town after Terri had left, Michael had taken me to meet his friends after we had cashed out and pulled tarps over our stalls at Whaler's Wharf. Michael was an artist, a painter, working at part-time jobs to keep himself in oil paint and canvasses.

'I've set up a studio space out on the porch of my house share. Lots of agents and gallery owners come here, especially in September, so I want to have a collection to show if I can get anyone interested to come and have a look.'

I liked Michael, he was serious, nearly grave, he seemed very focused and he was sweet to me. On our walk to the house he shared with his friends, he gently questioned me about why I had been upset during the day and I ended up telling him about lying to Clara.

'I rushed off a letter to her then, confessing everything. That's why I had to go to the post office. Thanks for looking after things.'

'You did the right thing, writing to her. You will kill yourself if you lie to try and hide. It will feel like safety for a while, but you will find that you will be in a prison and breathing poison. Don't do that to yourself, Ro. It will kill you.'

Michael's house was at the far east end of town. The night air was warm and carried the faint scent of garden flowers as we walked along narrow Commercial Street. The black waters of the harbour occasionally came into view on our right, behind the clapboard houses and small stores that lined the street. We eventually came to a small, low, wooden gate with a painted rickety sign of a skull wearing a pink pirate hat and eye-patch with pirate crossbones.

He lifted the latch and we walked along a private dock. I could hear music, someone was playing a guitar.

Michael said, 'Walk to the end of the dock, Ro – it sounds like Joni is there. I need to go get some beers.'

Michael shimmied up a wooden staircase, it looked like his house was on stilts, built above a narrow dock. I walked slowly to the end, towards a guitarist who was lost in music-making, a beautiful human with long flowing hair and high cheekbones. It was dark, there were little candles in jam jars and the water lightly slapped time under the dock. There was a boy standing out on the balcony above, he wore a long flowing white shirt and he seemed to be filming with some kind of a video camera. The guitarist had their eyes closed, they couldn't see me, I wasn't sure if they were male or a female. I stepped in and sat down close and they started to sing Joni Mitchell's 'A Case of You'. I couldn't help myself, I joined in.

I had a magical evening with Michael and his friends. Michael's friend from high school was Joel, an intense boy with heavy, dark-rimmed glasses who had a very nasally voice and was studying theatre at Princeton University. There were two

Michaels, my painter friend was known as Mini, even though he was by far the tallest of the six boys, his skinny frame making him appear very long indeed. The other Michael was a writer (although working as a waiter in Ciro & Sal's restaurant for the summer) and the boys liked to call him 'Maxi', but he did his best to resist the moniker and insisted that he must be called Michael or MichaelC to distinguish himself from Mini. MichaelC was the shortest of the lads, thick-set, black-haired with a deep baritone voice. He wore a white, tight-fitting T-shirt, baggy black shorts and black Converse trainers. I was wearing a sloppy white T-shirt and black cut-off jeans shorts, with black Converse trainers.

'Oh my God!' declared Joel, 'here is living proof that Maxi dresses like a lesbian!'

The boys laughed and Maxi/MichaelC said: 'These guys are forever teasing me about my styling choices.'

'What styling?!' some of them replied in chorus.

There were also two Johns. One of the Johns, the guitarist, was called Joni and his boyfriend, Russ, had the most delightful Southern accent, which he exploited fully for maximum laconic camp effect:

'Ro? Oh my dear, I do hope that your surname isn't Boat!'

I laughingly replied: 'Ro is short for Rosemary.'

Russ seized on my name and emphasised it as two words: 'But Rose Marie is such a beautiful name, why ever would you allow anyone to foreshorten it?'

From then on the boys all called me Rose Marie.

The second John was, startlingly, from County Cork. He was John Kerrigan, from Kinsale. We were both shocked to meet each other. I had never met anyone gay from Cork, the city or county. I had never even imagined there would be a Cork lad who was gay.

The first thing I asked him was, 'Are there any lesbians in Cork, do you know?'

'No idea,' he brusquely replied with obvious discomfort.

Russ announced: 'You must forgive our friend's curtness, dear Rose Marie. He can sometimes revert to being Shamcock John. We all here are doing our best to train him in, but he can be Straight-Acting John if we don't keep right on top of him.'

And with that Russ swung an arm around John's neck and draped himself across him, swinging one of his legs around John's hip. All the boys, including John, laughed.

'Sorry, Rose Marie,' said John. 'Nobody knows back home. So, like, it's a bit sensitive, d'you know?'

'Yeah. Me too,' I replied.

John looked immediately and obviously relived.

'Though I'll be telling them, like, as soon as I can,' I said.

John tensed. 'Well, I'm not going to be saying anything. Like. Ever.'

I nodded. This was not going to be an easy friendship, which was a pity. It was so lovely to hear even a soft Cork accent and he looked a bit like my brother Mossy.

It was a magical night on that dock, meeting those boys for the first time. I mean it was magical in a quite literal sense, as in something transformed within me. I was met and accepted for who I was and that steadied me and allowed me to bloom.

Joel and MichaelC and I got into a big conflab about Arthur Miller's short story 'The Misfits'. I was highly gratified to be among boys who were equally addicted to fiction. And Joni and I sang in harmony while Mini sketched us. And Russ delighted me by saying shocking things and yet being very kind. He asked me about my life and seemed interested in anything I told him. Russ had an antique dickie bow left un-tied hanging from his neck, he wore an immaculately white, cotton, oversized grandfather shirt and round, rimless wire glasses. His hair flopped from side to side in a long blonde fringe over his beautiful fine cheekbones. He was from Baton Rouge, Louisiana, and spoke with a languor and humour that was mesmerising.

Over the course of three hours, Russ gently brokered conversation between me and John Kerrigan. I learned that John had graduated from UCC the year before me, but it wasn't surprising that our paths had never crossed as he had been an Engineering student and I had never even been into the School of Civil and Electrical Engineering building.

Graduates in electrical engineering could find immediate lucrative employment in the world of 'computing', as everyone called I.T. back then. John had got a sponsored visa, gone to Boston the week after he'd finished his final exams, and got a job with a small firm founded by MIT graduates. He was being paid a massive salary to fix problems they were having with 'code'. When there was a problem he worked night, noon and morning so that when there wasn't a problem he could take days or even weeks off at a stretch. He was renting a room, or rather a couch space, with the rest of the boys and he would come and go from P-town to Boston over the summer.

That magical night transformed me. I became immediately, and with relief, more confident, settled and deeply happy among my queer tribe. I belonged with the lesbians and gays and the other queers, this was the family I chose, this was where I would grow and become wise. That night I fell in love with those six boys, my kin. I knew we would be friends for life.

The boys gave me a bike that was creaky and old and a bit too big for me, but it meant I could nip out from Whaler's Wharf for an hour or so in the afternoon. Michael would look out for any customers who might browse my stall, and in any case there was never all that much business in the afternoons because all the lesbian and gay holidaymakers were at the beach. I would cycle out to Herring Cove, to the women's part of the beach, and sunbathe and earwig on the lesbians' conversations and have quick dips in the sea.

On Friday, at the end of my first week in P-town, I received a letter. The writing on the envelope was spidery, an old lady's hand. My heart was yammering as I slowly opened the letter. There was the briefest note on headed notepaper, the address was that familiar one in Brookline.

*Dear Ro,*

*I am happy you are healthy. That is a big relief. I am an old lady and I knew many homosexual ladies and men in my lifetime, they were my best workers. Good people. Everything is good. You should not worry about telling me anything. You are a good girl. That cannot change. Phone me. At once when you get this letter.*
*Your friend, Clara Goldfarb*

I ran so fast to the pay phone by the post office that once there I realised I had forgotten my wallet. I raced back home, so happy, so elated, I wasn't even breathless. I skipped with joy on the spot while phoning and talking with Clara. It was a short call, she had already been making plans. She had arranged to have her grandsons, Arthur and Max, drive her down to P-town. She would book into an inn and stay a night and would get the ferry back to Boston. Art and Max would collect her from the port and drive her home. She would take me and friends out to dinner in the Lobster Pot. We settled on a Wednesday visit in a few weeks' time.

I was giddy with excitement. Back on my stall in Whaler's Wharf, I shared the news with Michael/Mini and he joined in my elation.

'Hurrah! Hurrah! Hurrah for Clara!'

I celebrated the great day by writing to Jenny, a very long, newsy letter recounting my first adventures. I hoped it would reach her care of Harvard English Dept.

*Dear Jenny*

Then I squeezed in *est,* so it read *Dearest Jenny,* but that was a bit much so I scrapped that and began again.

*Jenny, just on the vague off-chance that you're wondering where I might have got to, I wanted to let you know that I arrived in Provincetown, at the tip of Cape Cod, on Memorial Day weekend. I decided that I'm going to stay and you must come and visit. Come during the week, as my girlfriend, Terri, will need all my attention at the weekend.*

A bit awkward but fine. Jenny would be more likely to visit once she knew I had a girlfriend and she was no longer in danger of me making moony eyes at her. I wrote about how beautiful P-town was and how I liked to explore the place in the early dawn and after 9.00 p.m. when the Whaler's Wharf closed but all the art galleries were still open and the lesbian and gay holidaymakers were queuing up to get into the late drag shows and comedy shows.

*I have made some friends too – some gay boys, there's a gang of them – we're the 'Misfits'.*

I decided to end the letter there.

*Sorry for the quick signing off, Jenny. I'm not even sure this letter will reach you. R.M.*

I folded the letter, and put it into an envelope. I pulled it back out and wrote a final phrase.

*All my love.*

I was elated, four days later, to receive pages and pages of a letter back from Jenny. *Dearest R.M.*, wrote Jenny. Large parts of the letter were detailed accounts of what she had read and what she had thought about her reading in the previous week and I was fascinated with every pedantic scrap. I wished she was right with me so I could ask her questions. The last page became surprisingly personal:

*I am so very glad that you wrote, R.M. I had begun to think that you had forgotten me. I appreciate that you are in a new relationship and I know that people can disappear for weeks and sometimes months when love is first new. But I have so little time left here and you are the person I most enjoyed meeting during my time in Boston. I find that you are someone I confide in and I can find it most awkward to take people into my confidence. It was always such a bugbear of Susan's. I really did not, indeed DO not feel, that I kept secrets from her – I always felt that I told her everything but that I lead a rather uneventful life. However, I see now, in how I speak with you, what Susan meant. It is so easy to speak with you. I used to think that I was rather affectless, but you bring forth my awareness and it transpires that I have feelings, many of them! After all! I find I quite like this new me, maybe it is a mixture of being in America and having you as a friend, that I am now quite garrulous with emotion. I talk to you constantly in my head.*
    *If I am to catch the last post I must stop now.*
                      *Fondly, with great fondness,*
                               *Jenny*
                                 X

It took me a while to catch my breath. I started writing back immediately, there was already so much to tell Jenny. I told her about all the boys and how Joel and MichaelC and I had formed a reading group together, we were going to spend the summer reading writers who had lived in Provincetown, starting with Eugene O'Neill and then Susan Keating Gaspell (who Joel said he 'adores') and next we'll read Norman Mailer, although MichaelC worries I will hate Mailer. I told her how Russ is so wealthy that he doesn't really have to work. His father threw him out of the family home at seventeen and pays him handsomely to stay away. Russ, however, does run a small bar with capacity for just twenty people or so, eight sitting at the counter and a dozen or so standing behind. It is always packed, with many waiting outside, attracted by the howls of laughter from the punters inside and Russ's reputation for making the best cocktails in town. Russ's boyfriend Joni is very quiet, has long, nearly waist-length hair and is so beautiful he combines the best of femininity and masculinity. Joni likes to play the guitar and sing. Joni works in sales at a gallery in the east end of town. I wrote about what I was reading and what my jobs were like and stories that the boys and my customers had told me. I told Jenny about my routine with the boys, then I signed off:

*I talk to you in my head too Jenny. Constantly. I love talking with you all the time –*

*All my love, RM x*

I received another long letter from Jenny in reply and so it began. Soon we were not even waiting for a response and most days we put a letter in the post to the other. My new friends thought it hilarious that their Rose Marie had the hots for Jenny. I objected to the phrase 'the hots', but had to give way as it was better than the cruder alternatives proposed. And so what if I liked Jenny (yes, a lot!)? Nothing was going to happen, there would be no romance. I was in a monogamous relationship with Terri, whom I loved dearly. The boys thought it hilarious when they realised I had to mouth the word 'mahogany' in order to pronounce 'monogamy' – there had been a lot of new terminology to learn over the past month or so and I was still not fluent.

'Don't let Terri hear you comparing monogamy to a kind of furniture!' laughed the boys.

Terri had refused to meet them. 'Gom! I haven't driven all of the fucking way from Boston to waste precious weekend time drinking with gay men! You do know, Gom, they're even more sexist than straight men, who at least pretend to like women to get into their pants?'

I made the big mistake of arranging that John Kerrigan and Russ might, accidently-on-purpose, bump into myself and Terri when we were having a late-night drink at the Pied Piper bar. Terri had said she wouldn't mind meeting John Kerrigan.

'My God!' Terri said, 'what's happening in the Old Country? I wish my Listowel grandfather was still alive – it would kill him all over again to meet fags from Ireland!'

Russ and John Kerrigan had played their part beautifully, they were there before I arrived in from closing up at the Whaler's Wharf and I greeted them before I made my way over to Terri.

'Hi, darling!' I said, kissing Terri's cheek. 'Look who I met on my way in! My friends, John from Cork and Russ.'

Terri nodded. 'Yeah, I saw you.'

I took that as my cue and waved the boys over, but even as they were making their way across the bar I realised the meeting was a big mistake. Terri was quite drunk.

'Cock. Cock. Cock,' she muttered as they arrived, 'that's all they ever think about.'

'Cock,' Terri said as she drunkenly shook Russ's hand. 'Cock,' Terri slurred as she waved after John Kerrigan, who was already leaving the bar. Russ offered some pleasantries and managed to depart graciously. I gave up trying to explain to Terri why I was offended on my friends' behalf. I didn't want an epic row. The boys came to understand their Rose Marie was only available to play with them during the week. Whenever any of them came across Terri and me over the weekends, they learned pretty quickly to leave after saying 'Hi'.

I generally thought it was funny the way the gay boy gang teased me about my 'English sweetheart Jenny', but their attitude to Terri was a bit depressing and confusing. The boys didn't say much when I spoke about Terri, besides a few eloquently raised eyebrows and loquacious shrugs and sighs. It did seem that older gay men and older lesbians weren't especially fond of each other. Some of the posher older gay men had straight women in their entourages, whom they mockingly referred to as their 'fag hags'. The younger guys called these women 'beards'. I couldn't see what fun these high-femme heterosexual women might have had with those old gayers as they were so often the butt of bitchy and lewd jokes once the men started drinking. It seemed the older gays liked to assert their masculinity by having these pretty women patently adore them yet treat them almost as badly as any boorish straight guy might.

Russ had developed a reputation for refusing to serve men who made sexist jokes in his bar: 'When you are more comfortable with your feminine side, gentlemen, you may return to this bar.'

He would put the offenders' drinks into takeaway glasses, refund them the money they had paid and patiently wait for them to leave. I was there one time when a man who looked about sixty was making a joke about flipping a girl over and pretending she was her brother. Russ whirled him out of the little bar with such deft alacrity that the man was on the street before he knew it. His drunken companions started to complain, until Russ announced he would refund the punters and close down immediately if there were even two people who thought he had been unfair.

'Now, raise your hands, gentlemen, if you feel I was too harsh in cutting off that line of amusement.'

He waited. No one raised their hands.

'Brothers, we are deluded if we think hating on women will earn us the respect of the straight boys. They will hate us anyway. We are deluded if we think that hating our precious femininity will protect us from the hatred of straight men who work so hard to distance themselves from their own feminine aspects. Let us embrace our inner Queen. Repeat *Amen*, gentlemen, to my prayer:

"I embrace my inner Queen."'

Only a few of us said *Amen* and Russ's inner Southern Baptist Preacher came to the fore as he repeated louder and with a pulpit fervour.

'Gentlemen, I say to you: I embrace my inner Queen.'

More of us said *Amen*.

Russ kept working the crowd and within a few recitations we were all shouting: *AMEN!* to Russ's chanting:

'I embrace my inner Queen.'

'AMEN!'

'I LOVE my inner Queen!'

'AMEN!'

'My precious femininity is the very best part of me!'

'AMEN!'

'A woman gave me life!'

'AMEN!'

'Lesbians are Goddesses!'

'AMEN!'

'Free cocktails for everyone in this bar!'

'AMEN! AMEN! YEAH! HELL, YEAH! AMEN!'

Russ and I tried to make sure we had a dance together every day – whether it was on one of the A-House dance floors or at the Pied Piper or the Crown and Anchor, at The Boatslip or as he opened or closed his bar. Russ would try and persuade the DJs to play that classic Donna Summer track, 'I Feel Love'.

Some of the DJs would object: apparently Donna Summer had made some anti-gay remarks at her comeback concert the previous year, but Russ always protested her innocence.

'I do not believe that Ms Summer is in the slightest bit prejudiced towards homosexuals. I believe that she has been maligned most vilely!'

If we got our way and got our track played, we would close our eyes and swirl around and around and around. Whenever I opened my eyes, in whatever dizzy corner of the room I found myself, Russ would be right by me, circling around me, smiling, eyes closed, mouthing the words. It was our song.

One night after we had indulged ourselves in a couple of twirling dances, replaying the song in Russ's empty bar, he told me of the night he had left home.

'We were all dancing to this divine noise, around and around the house, out around the porch and back indoors. I had just graduated high school, the summer was ahead, I was seventeen. Me and Mama, and my sister Charlotte, and Mimi and Louise who helped Mama, we were all dancing and we were singing loudly with Ms Summer.

'As soon as ever the track ended, I lifted the needle and started it again. And Papa came home from a ride on one of his horses and found us all, whirling dervishes. I had put on some outrageous eye shadow and the lightest dusting of rouge on my cheeks and Mama's deep red Chanel lipstick. I looked mighty fine. And Papa just exploded. "I'll clip your wings, my boy!" he shouted. Papa never shouted. He had his riding crop in his hand and I thought for a moment he was going to strike me. He had never struck me (or to my knowledge had never struck anyone), but then I had never heard him raise his voice before and anything was possible now. Papa went to the record player and ripped the vinyl from the wheel. There was such a tearing noise. He had ruined the record. Ruined our dance.'

Russ continued: 'I shouted back. I said, "HOW DARE YOU!" I don't know what else I shouted. He yelled again at me. Mama and Charlotte were crying, Mimi and Louise were trembling. He told me that, if I couldn't be a man, I should leave his house and learn to live like one and not come back until I was ready to assume my responsibilities. I left there and then. I went first to my Grandma's house, Mama's mother. The next day my father arrived and we made our arrangements. He would pay me my entire four years of college tuition in full, in a lump sum, and he agreed a monthly stipend I could live on and he would pay my health insurance. We would conduct all future correspondence not through his local lawyer but through his lawyer in Washington D.C. It was up to me to manage my own affairs from now on. I would be welcome home once I had "proved myself to be a grown man and not a boy who brought trouble on himself and dishonour and trouble on his family".'

'Jeepers!' was all I could manage in reply. Russ told the story in a strangely disconnected way and not with his usual camp delivery.

'The previous summer I had got into all kinds of trouble with deliciously bad boys who I had met in my high school. But some of their older brothers learned of our playtime and appointed themselves the Righteous Lord's Anointed, and they sought to stamp out our evil ways. I had gotten beaten up pretty badly at one stage. Some of those good ol' boys had the audacity to come driving by and hollering at our house. My father had to lean exceptionally hard on the local Sherriff's office to ensure that the message was clear that no further assaults on me or on my father's house would be tolerated. I think Papa was dreading that there was going to be another steamy summer of gay boy madness.'

'What did you do then? Where'd you go?'

'I was true to my foolish gay teenage nature. Why, I blew a lot of money on taking myself off to Venice as if I was a Medici prince!'

I laughed, 'Were you Henry James or Thomas Mann?'

'Rose Marie! All I know for sure about either of those fellows is that they never had anything to do with Motown!'

I laughed again.

'Rose Marie, please! You must not confuse me with our literary friends, Joel and Maxi. I am not in the slightest bit literary. I am purely a dedicated devotee of disco.'

'How long did you spend in Venice?'

'Not long, once I heard about the island of Mykonos! I went there for the summer and then spent the second half of what you call the autumn, and then winter and springtime, visiting all of the cute boys I had met from all over Europe. It was my Grand Tour! Alas, I never made it to Ireland, all the cute Irish boys I met lived in London.'

'What was your favourite place?'

'Right at the very end I visited Paris. All the other places I went to I would visit the art galleries and I could never figure out what was so great about this European fine art! In Venice, there was nothing but giant canvasses of sky with the buildings and gondoliers and people at the markets all squashed into the bottom of the pictures as tiny exact miniatures. In Amsterdam, all the paintings were black except for the odd face lit by a lantern or all the ladies were dressed in terrible dresses and reading letters. In Madrid, there were lots of paintings with interesting dwarves and paintings by artists who were tripping on hallucinogens across the centuries, so that was nice. But in Paris, all the paintings were painted by people who obviously were suffering from cataracts. I was *weary*! And then I went to La Museé des Beaux-Arts and I met a painting that helped me understand the world a bit more.'

Russ paused dramatically.

I took up my cue: 'What was that painting?'

'It is *Landscape with the Fall of Icarus* by Bruegel the Elder and everyone is very busy in it. The ploughman who takes up most of the scene is working hard at ploughing on a headland. In the sea down below him the fancy ship must have witnessed the amazing sight of Icarus, a boy who flew too close to the sun, falling to his watery death. The wax on his homemade wings has melted, but nobody notices his white legs crashing into the green water.'

'Oh.'

'Yes! My, how I laughed and laughed! And then I saw it was sad, too.'

'Yes.'

'I bought two large postcard copies of it in the gift store and I sent one to Mama. I wrote: *Mama, I realise now that every true thing has more than one meaning.*

'That's very philosophical, Russ!' I said laughingly.

'I agree, I have been most precocious,' he said with camp satisfaction. 'I think I peaked right there in my philosophical education! Maxi and Joel were very excited to see my framed postcard of that painting. They showed me a poem about that picture by that English gentleman faggot, W. H. Auden, and it's the only poem that I have ever entirely enjoyed.'

'So, hang on then … you write to your mother?'

'Of course I write to Mama!' he exclaimed. 'Though …' he paused. 'I don't address the letters to our house. She is devoted to my father and he to her and I don't want to cause any more upset between them.'

He paused again.

'So I send her cards and letters care of her favourite florist in Baton Rouge. Whenever she goes there, he lets her have whatever mail I've sent and he makes her a corsage and sends me the invoice.'

'That's incredible service from a florist!'

'He's one of our gay brethren, Rose Marie. He thinks he is *highly* discreet, but his gayness positively *flames*!' said Russ with a flourish. In a softer voice he added: 'He is indeed most awfully kind to me and Mama.'

He smiled and asked: 'One more twirl of Ms Summer?'

'Absolutely!'

## 12
## What's Love Got To Do With It?

Clara made a great splash when she visited. The day of her arrival I had taken the afternoon and evening off work and I had also got someone to cover my following morning cleaning shifts. I was expecting that her grandsons, who had driven her down from Boston, would stay and hang out, but she waved them off once they had dropped her to my flat.

'Good luck, honeys! Thanks for the ride! See ya tomorrow evening at the port!'

I thought Clara might want a nap or to sit in the shady garden. In fact, I was hoping that she would want that because the mailman had just dropped off a hefty letter from Jenny and I wanted to settle in to read it quickly then re-read it slowly. However, even before her grandsons had finished reversing their car up the small lane in front of the house, Clara linked my arm and said, 'Show me the sights!'

So we went straight to Russ's bar, which wasn't all that far away from my flat. She wouldn't let me use the wheelchair I had borrowed from Adams Pharmacy, so we hobbled along and got there and one of the men at the bar counter immediately relinquished his seat and helped Clara climb up onto the stool. And that was the way it was for the entire time Clara was in

P-town; troupes of gay men positively doting on her. I suppose she reminded them of their grandmothers or their mothers, and you just don't really see little old ladies in P-town. They were all queuing up to talk to her. To find out who she was and why she was there.

Russ made a big fuss of her, doing a whole doubling and trebling on his accented Southern charm. 'Why, Mrs Goldfarb! I am honoured and most delighted that you have visited my bar. You are my most cherished guest, Ma'am. I shall right now invent a cocktail in your honour! And if you like it, Mrs Goldfarb, maybe you would consider allowing me to name it after you?'

Clara simpered. I had no idea that Clara would ever be able to simper, but she positively simpered under Russ's drawling, flirtatious flattery. She tried the golden-colour cocktail three times before she considered herself fully satisfied. Russ then shut up his bar, insisting all of us had to put our drinks into plastic carry glasses and he took us all in for free through his bar into the tea dance at The Boatslip.

John Kerrigan, MichaelC and Joel were already there and they flocked around Clara, buying her multiple cocktails – she insisted each one had to be a different colour from the last. Nobody ever actually dances at the tea dance but when Tina Turner's new song 'What's Love Got To Do With It?' started being blasted, Clara began to shift her bottom from side to side.

'I like this song!' she cried.

John Kerrigan dutifully accompanied Clara in her bottom shaking, holding her hand and guiding her in a few twirls. I was really redundant. I felt like a foot soldier in waiting to an Empress. She was mobbed by gay men. As the day went on, she got more raucous and flirtatious with them.

'I'm here to show you what you're missing, gay man!'

Of course, they all absolutely loved her and she loved bossing them around. She even got John Kerrigan to go get his motorbike to come and collect her and bring her to dinner in The Lobster Pot.

'I got really bad arthritis, you know?! I can't walk that far!'

She had to ride side-saddle. I was terrified she would fall (and on my watch too). She agreed to let Russ hold her hand as John Kerrigan went at a crawl up Commercial Street. She kept getting John to rev the engine of the bike. She loved the roar. She waved to the populace of P-town like they were her subjects. John Kerrigan, myself and Russ went to dinner with her and she milled into some Bloody Marys and ate a lobster the same size as herself. We got her back to her inn and I helped her to bed.

I ran home, eager to begin reading Jenny's letter, which began as was now usual: *My Dearest R.M.* Her opening sentences threw me: *Would you mind awfully if I came to visit you? I promise it would be a lightning visit, just a day trip. I might come on the 8.30 a.m. ferry and leave on the 5.30 p.m. one? Say Thursday a fortnight from now?* I didn't even read the rest of the letter before I had written, addressed and put a stamp on a postcard which said: *YES!! Come visit Thursday week, I'll meet you at the ferry dock! XXX R.M.*

I dropped that card into the post box in front of the post office very early the next morning, then I rushed to Clara. I was terrified that she would be violently ill with alcohol poisoning but there she was, sitting up in bed, surrounded by the pillows I had banked around her the night before and as fresh as a daisy, already impatient to start the day. I had got her a room with a large shower and while she was sitting on a stool and showering she made me phone the boys' house and ask them to come to breakfast. So MichaelC and Joel and Joni and John Kerrigan came down and joined us both for breakfast on the porch of her inn. She insisted we all had to have champagne in our orange juice. John Kerrigan took her on the bike again to the ferry while Joni was elected to hold her hand and MichaelC carried her bag.

'Are you going to write a story and put me in it?' she asked MichaelC.

'Do I have your permission for that?' he asked (I thought a bit too eagerly).

'Just make me taller and with bigger boobies,' she replied.

I went onto the ferry with her to settle her in and I was thanking her for coming to see me. She got all serious and patted my hands and said the most curious thing:

'You should marry that John Kerrigan. That way you can both live in Ireland.'

'Clara! That's mad – pure mad, like – like, nuts!'

'But honey – how else you gonna go home? And you wanna go home, right?'

I didn't know what to say to her then and the hooter was going and I had to run off the boat otherwise I would be at sea with her and on my way to Boston.

I began to get nervous when Eily and Mels were due to come for a week's holiday. I began to worry that they too would hate the boys like Terri did. They were coming the following Monday after Clara's visit. I told them that they could come on Friday and get a lift down with Terri, but they insisted on coming at the start of the week.

'We'll have a chance to see you first for ourselves and, sure, you'll be wanting to spend the weekend just with Terri,' explained Mels on one of our weekly phone calls. Eily and Mels had the number of the pay phone in front of the post office and they never failed to ring at the same time, after I finished work on a Wednesday night. They even stuck with trying to get through when there was someone else ahead of me already deep into a call. The three of us would talk for an hour or more, unless there was someone else who came along and wanted to use the phone. I had filled them in on all the boys and they said they were dying to meet them and hang out, but I was nervous all the same.

Joel came with me in the taxi to meet them off the plane from Boston at the airfield. We watched as the tiny plane made a bumpy land and Eily and Mels, with four other people, hunched their way out. Eily made a great show of kissing the ground like she was Pope John Paul II.

Mels rushed over: 'Ah! You must be Joel!'

'Yes! How did you know?'

'Ro is so good at describing people, I just thought it must be you.'

'I told them how handsome you are,' I chipped in.

Joel beamed. Eily followed behind us, having grabbed her and Mels's rucksacks from the plane's hold.

'Let me see, are you Joel?' Eily asked.

'Yes, I am!' said Joel, looking very pleased.

'Yeah, Ro said you had those kind of heavy glasses.'

Joel laughed and I loved him more.

The taxi dropped us all off at the Dusty Miller Inn on Bradford Street, where Eily and Mels were booked in for the week. I appreciated that they had come to P-town in June, when the weather could still be unpredictable, and that they were spending so much money when they should have been managing all their painting crews of Irish students over in Boston on J-1 visas. I knew they wanted to make sure I was really OK, which made me feel both awkward and gratified. I had tried to reassure them on the calls that I was grand, but they could hear that I missed them.

When we arrived at the inn, Joel insisted I should stay with Eily and Mels and that he would take care of our shared cleaning shift by himself. When I went later to the Whaler's Wharf to sell the pewter figurines, Joni was already there and shooed the three of us away. For the next few days Joel, John Kerrigan, Russ and Joni covered what shifts of mine they could manage so I got to have bursts of holiday time with Eily and Mels.

And we had a ball. We hired bikes and cycled through the dunes and scrub oak woods of the national seashore park. We tramped around the miles of beaches from Long Point all the way back into town. We cycled to Herring Cove with a picnic and we swam in the sea.

'They call it the ocean,' mused Mels. 'We really don't give it the respect it deserves by just calling it the sea. It's the same ocean, that North Atlantic, that is rolling the big waves into my hometown, Bundoran, right now. Amazing to think of it.'

At night we had dinner in a restaurant and we went to see a show in the Crown and Anchor or to whatever movie was playing that night in the hot cinema upstairs at the Whaler's Wharf. We saw the latest Hollywood movie, *Indiana Jones and the Temple of Doom*, with a raucous lesbian and gay audience.

'It's amazing how different Harrison Ford looks when you've got the gay boys carrying on!' said Eily. 'I'm sure now if I watched that back in Boston 'twould be a totally different film that I saw.'

We spent every night with the boys, sitting on the dock after everyone was finished work. Laughing, chatting, singing, sipping beer, having snacks. One hilarious night Joel gave us all Tarot readings and most of the boys got card number 13, a skeleton riding a white horse with a sickle. Joel insisted that it was a card about letting go of 'attachments' but the card itself said: 'DEATH'. Russ made us all laugh by imagining a series of ways that the boys could all die together.

'Joel,' Russ said, 'do you think a freak wave will take us all during our synchronised swimming practice?'

Russ was one of the organisers for what he and some friends were beginning to call the 'Esther Williams Water Ballet and Bathing Suit Competition', which seemed like it would actually happen at Herring Cove on the Fourth of July.

'No!' said MichaelC, 'we will all die of Popper-induced heart attacks in the A-House, Macho Bar, dressed only in a leather thong, a feather boa and dancing to bad disco.'

'Now that's a scene worth dying for!' said Michael/Mini. The boys liked to tease Mini for his predilection for the older leather queens in the Macho Bar, which is where he had hooked up with his sugar-daddy, Tony.

'Hmmm, so long as it's not GRID,' said John Kerrigan.

'What's GRID?' asked Mels.

'Gay-related immune deficiency,' replied John Kerrigan. 'Older gay men in San Francisco, L.A. and New York have a strange incurable cancer.'

'Oh John!' exclaimed Joel. 'You and GRID! It's NOT GRID! It's called AIDS! And what is it with you? You really want to go with that right-wing Neo-con God's Judgement on the Gays! It's negative propaganda.'

MichaelC seemed to agree with Joel, 'Yeah, anything to scare the gays and make us more monstrous. Haitians have the same kind of cancer, it seems to be about using drugs.'

'If it is GRID that mows us down, at least we will be very old queens with our own special disease earned from decades of going to the bathhouses and taking poppers,' said Russ, languidly.

'What's poppers?' said Eily.

'Leather cleaner!' I answered.

MichaelC released a little glass vial from the small pocket in his jeans' waistband.

'Available at most newsagents' stands for just five dollars,' he said. 'Come dancing with me later and we'll check it out. Once you sniff it deeply through your nostril, you'll get a lovely, short, euphoric high that gently relaxes the anal muscles.'

'Now be the hokey!' said Eily, camping up her Irish accent. 'I'll be having a go off that surely! As soon as we hear that Pat Benatar number – we'll be off!'

'Love Is A Battlefield' was the misfits' song that summer.

Another night, Russ took Eily with him to cruise the Dick Dock. I could see John Kerrigan's disapproval, but I knew that Joni also liked to sashay off with different men. One late afternoon it had taken Joni and me well over an hour to go a relatively short distance in town as Joni returned appreciative gazes and entered into chat and made what seemed to be appointments to hook up at another time.

'I'm with my friend right now,' I had heard him say and I tried to turn away from hearing the murmured arrangements for later.

In spite of John Kerrigan's tut-tutting, it was clear that Russ and Joni were deeply in love with each other. They were always leaving little gifts for the other on their bed or on the double hammock at the dock that seemed to be exclusively theirs.

MichaelC and Joel told me that they assumed that John Kerrigan had a closeted lover back in Boston.

'Or else he truly is a shamcock!' MichaelC declared. 'He hardly turns his head to look at any guys here.'

I watched how, over the course of a few days, the girls slowly relaxed into being more affectionate with each other. By the third day, they were holding hands. They allowed themselves to gaze at each other more and just smile at each other. I was beginning to be grateful that I was going to have to work all of my own shifts over the weekend. The girls should be enjoying some time just with each other and not have me as the eternal gooseberry.

On the Thursday evening, Mini presented the girls with some pencil sketches he had made of them which he had washed with faint blue watercolour. Eily was not far off tears.

'You've made us look so lovely,' said Mels.

'But you are!' exclaimed Mini, and the rest of the boys concurred, with Russ and Joni exclaiming, 'But you are, Blanche! You are!'

The boys took turns to gaze at the sketches and hug the girls.

Nobody said anything, but we knew that this was my last night with the group. Terri was going to be in town on Friday evening and would stay until early Monday morning. Eily and Mels would fly out on Sunday afternoon. The two of them planned to take Terri and me out to dinner on Saturday night, but I didn't think I would see much of them otherwise and I certainly wouldn't be with the boys over the weekend.

Our Saturday night dinner at The Mews went off well, or at least I thought so. Terri was in flying form. We all had too much wine to drink. I was relieved. The evening hadn't started out well between Terri and me. I had come home from the glass studio with just time for a quick shower and change, but I found Terri sobbing on our bed when I came in the door.

'I just can't take this, Gom,' she kept saying, between heaving sobs.

'What, what, my love – what's the matter?'

'I just can't take this – this …'

I waited until she got the words out. I knew what they would be. My heart had already sunk.

'You're going to leave me.'

'Of course I'm not going to leave you!'

'You say that. But you're so young and immature. And you're so good-looking. I see the way other women here look at you. You know it!'

'But love, I don't! I don't see anyone looking at me! I love that you think I'm a beauty, but love, I'm yours. You're not to worry. I don't want to be with anyone else.'

The drama went as it usually went, with Terri crying her heart out and me feeling ever more sad and inept. There seemed to be nothing I could do or say that might reassure her. I hated that I unwittingly gave her so much doubt.

'You've so many secrets from me.'

'I swear I don't have secrets from you.'

'I never know what you're thinking. And when I ask you, you just talk about some books or something somebody said to you. And I just know that's not the whole story.'

'But it is! That and white noise – there's not a whole lot going on with me otherwise.'

'I know you've doubts about us.'

'I swear I don't, Terri! I swear I don't.'

By the time I had held, hugged, kissed and stroked Terri into a soft orgasm we were already very late for our dinner date with Eily and Mels. There was no time for a shower. I couldn't find the clothes I had laid out. Terri had put them into the washing machine, which had gone through a cycle and they were soaked.

'I thought they were laundry, Gom!'

I jumped into a half-clean T-shirt and some baggy Bermuda shorts of Terri's that were too big for me but I cinched with a wide belt. We were nearly forty minutes late. Eily and Mels looked smashing, they were dressed up, and they were very forgiving, of course. Their good form was probably helped by the fact that they had already finished a bottle of sparkling wine. I was surprised they had already drunk so much. Terri said she wasn't going to be long catching up.

'Ro here has joined the Prohibition! She hardly drinks at all now!' said Terri.

'Yeah!' agreed Eily

And Mels said: 'Well, sure isn't she drunk on love! And here's to the two of ye!' she declared as she raised her glass.

Everything was going well until Clara's name got mentioned. Terri really didn't like me talking about Clara.

'Oh Jeez, Gom! Don't go all sentimental now!'

'What do you mean?'

'She's your fucking employer, for Chrissakes, not some amazing person. And you don't even know if she'll have you back to wipe her ass in September!'

'What do you mean?' I repeated, feeling disorientated.

'She might like boogeying down in the Boatslip with cute gay guys, but will she really have you back to sleep over now she knows you're a big old lesbo?' Terri shook her head at me in disbelief.

Mels and Eily looked uncomfortable. Eily started to peel the label from one of the wine bottles on the table.

Eventually Mels said, 'Well, Ro, Terri's got a point. Lots of people go strange. I've had it myself. Back in London. I lost that childminding job I had.'

I nodded, I remembered the story.

'Like they were fine with me and Eily and all,' continued Mels, 'but, you know, they were worried about the children and the way they looked up to me, you know, the influence. You know, if Clara's family get wind of it, they mightn't like it,' she said gently.

Eily squeezed Mels's shoulder and looked very upset.

'Clara won't be ruled by her family,' I replied. 'She's eighty-one years old and her bones are shot but she rules her family, not the other way around.'

Terri said: 'You live in a fucking dream world, Gom!'

'Lookit!' interjected Eily, 'You're a fucking very brave hoor, McCarthy! Most of us never say a fucking word – and you're not like that.'

'I just think we're amazing,' I said, feeling quite stupid and speaking in a low voice. 'Like, we've come through so much to get here and to stand up for love. To find our way through all of the stupid shit we've been told about men and women and what our bodies are for and what a good life is and still we managed to find each other and be brave and live what's true.' Terri was rolling her eyes.

'Alright, alright!' I said softly, reaching across the table to take her hand from her glass and hold it in mine. 'I'll shut up.'

'Wait till they hear there's a dyke in the family back in the old home-place!' she laughed. 'That will cure all your pretty speeches.'

I smiled ruefully and shrugged, 'Yeah. I suppose so.'

The tension evaporated and Terri and Eily spent the night teasing me about my various stupidities. It was fun. It was so good to see Terri happy. I hoped she would begin to really trust me. I hoped she would see that I was utterly devoted to her alone.

# 13
# Every Breath You Take

The boys kept quizzing me about Jenny and what seemed to amuse them most was that Jenny was English. They couldn't believe their Rose Marie was crushed out on an English woman. So when the boys heard that Jenny was coming to P-town for a day trip, their excitement ran out of control to become a running joke, and, because these were gay boys, the joke had high production values. They decided the day of Jenny's visit was to be themed 'The Potato and The Crown' to honour our respective countries. They made T-shirts designed by Mini who made a tiara for himself with little French fries as a motif.

And that strange day finally arrived: the day when Jenny would arrive by ferry from Boston to Provincetown. John Kerrigan came to collect me at my apartment – he seemed to understand I would need company to ensure I would get to the pier on time. When we arrived, Joel and the two Michaels were already there, wearing their T-shirts picturing a potato wearing a crown ('painted Dutch Old Master style,' as Mini said proudly). I was a bit surprised they had shown up. I realised they were there both as a sort of queer guard of honour on my behalf and because they had got swept up in the detail of the pageant design.

Standing on the pier, I was acutely aware of the surface of my skin, of how the hair on my arms and legs tickled with the breeze. My yammering heart was beginning to cause me discomfort as I watched the hulking Boston ferry slowly pull up to P-town's only large pier. I tried to stop bouncing from one foot to the other but merely managed to slow down my bouncing. John Kerrigan was holding my hand. He was very sweet: he wasn't laughing at me.

As the ferry came nearer, I saw Jenny standing on the top deck and I started to grin and feel stoned. The boys realised I had spotted Jenny, but I couldn't respond to their requests to point out Jenny who was busy talking with someone on the top deck. I watched Jenny trail through the top cabin into the bowels of the boat and out of sight, and I held my breath until I saw her again emerging onto the gangplank. Jenny was still deep in conversation with another woman who looked like a dyke: she had short hair with a massive curly fringe and was wearing a big chunky jumper.

The boys and I heard Jenny ask her friend, 'Do you mind if we go directly to a place called the Whalers' Wharf?'

'Jen!' I shouted, louder and higher than I intended.

'Oh hullo!' smiled Jenny shyly. 'You're here! How nice!'

Jenny and I strode quickly towards each other and in sync we both stepped back from what must have been an inevitable embrace. We stood smiling at each other without saying anything. I couldn't say anything because I was grinning so much.

'These are my friends,' I said, gesturing aimlessly towards Joel, the Michaels and John Kerrigan. 'These are some of the boys I wrote to you about.'

Jenny hardly looked at the guys. She gave a vague nod of recognition and continued smiling at me.

'Oh yes,' she said.

'I'm Michelle,' said Jenny's companion. She had a guttural, weird accent.

'This is Michelle,' said Jenny. 'She's the reason I came.'

God, I thought, so Jenny has a girlfriend.

I tried my best to say 'hello' to Michelle but very quickly learned it wasn't entirely necessary for me to struggle to engage in conversation as Michelle confidently took charge of the situation.

Michelle shook my hand and announced: 'I am from Mont Réal. I am a Harvard doctoral student and nearly finished my studies there. I am writing the definitive biography of Madame de Staël. I am bi-sexualle.'

We started to walk down the pier and Michelle turned to lock me in her gaze: 'I realise lesbians find it difficult to accept the arc of my libido but I love people for their minds and not their genitalia. Genitalia are merely a means towards expression. So.'

Apropos of nothing, Michelle recounted her plans to complete postdoctoral work in Yale. By the time that we had reached the end of the pier all the boys had vanished, except for John Kerrigan.

He squeezed my arm and whispered in my ear: 'Are you alright, Rose Marie? Will I hang on with you?'

I shook my head. My heart was about to burst with the immensity of Jenny being so close to me, but there was nothing John Kerrigan could do to help me.

'You're grand, thanks,' I murmured, though as I watched his strong and true frame glide off, I almost called him back.

Michelle, the girlfriend, was still talking. This was not going to be an easy afternoon.

I tried my best to be tour guide. I started by having Jenny and Michelle pause to look at the traffic cop who singlehandedly directed human and motor traffic at the busy crossroads at the top of the pier. He pirouetted in clockwise fashion on the balls of his feet, making 270 degree rotations, and he conveyed his elegant ministrations to the traffic by means of precise, white-gloved hand gestures and eloquent toots on his whistle.

'Welcome to P-town,' I said to Jenny. And then, trying to include Michelle in the conversation: 'Nobody minds waiting here.'

I brought the visitors down the throng of Commercial Street and squeezed them into Adams Pharmacy where we got seats at the Formica and chrome soda fountain. MichaelC was inside, listening to his Walkman.

I slurped chocolate malt and listened to Jenny and Michelle as they realised they had both seen the same performance of the same play in Boston months before. I gave myself a strong lecture: of course Jenny would have brought a girlfriend. Sure, for fuck's sake I had a girlfriend myself. I was Jenny's friend and whoever Jenny loved, well then, I would do my best to love them too. It was just as well Jenny had brought her girlfriend, now everything could be mature between us. I had just got too caught up with all of the boys' banter and hadn't thought any of this through properly. I hadn't prepared myself to be a grown up. I was such a feckin' eejit. Jenny would be appalled if she could hear the kinds of things that were going on inside my head. I would cop on to myself and make sure these women had a good time before they got back on the evening ferry.

I was surprised by a kiss on my temple. It was MichaelC, making his way past. He stuck out his hand and introduced himself to Jenny and said some pleasant things I couldn't quite tune in to. I hoped Jenny wouldn't make any comment about his potato and crown T-shirt. Jenny seemed to be introducing Michelle. Michael kissed Jenny on both sides of her cheeks and went out without acknowledging Michelle's existence. I knew then that I would love MichaelC forever.

As we left, Jenny turned to me as if discovering me by chance and asked to be brought to the Whaler's Wharf.

'I would like to see where you work and meet the characters I've learned about through your letters. They are so eccentric and so funny – you have such a gift for comic caricature, R.M.!'

Dread rose up my swallowing gullet. What the fuck had I actually written to Jenny? I didn't think I had written amusing letters, I had actually worried they were a bit too heartfelt and sincere. I tried to distract myself from the prickling swarm of fear that buzzed around me.

I first took Jenny and Michelle to Chris Pearson's glass studio, where I had a job wrapping copper foil on the edges of the glass pieces Chris had cut for his elaborate Tiffany-style lamps. Russ was in the studio with Chris, shooting the breeze and having fun. Russ wore a crowned potato T-shirt, on which he had stencilled a red-spotted bowtie.

'You must be Russ!' exclaimed Jenny, as if she was being reunited with a long-lost friend.

'Why, if it isn't Jenny Archer!' exclaimed Russ. He took her hands and kissed them and strangely that was not at all odd.

'Jenny! We've been waiting for you!' said Chris as he perched himself on a high stool.

Jenny excitedly replied that Russ and Chris looked exactly as I had described them and that the little studio was as wonderful as my letters had depicted. I was stunned to see how relaxed, how happy Jenny suddenly seemed.

Russ invited Jenny and Michelle to stroll up to The Boatslip with him and me for the tea dance.

'Are we going to your bar?' asked Jenny excitedly.

'In your honour, dear Jenny, I am keeping the bar closed today so that we can circulate and converse. I find it is good to keep irregular opening hours for the bar. It keeps the customers' appetite keen.'

Michelle said she was going to wander around Commercial Street and she would meet Jenny at 5.15 p.m. at the front door of the Boatslip, to see if she was going to get the ferry back to Boston. Jenny said of course she was going to get the ferry back. Michelle laughed and said she thought Jenny might change her mind. Michelle and Chris shared a near imperceptible but utterly distinct flicker of a wink. I saw that flicker-wink and realised with a shock of elation that Michelle was not Jenny's girlfriend. A flock of birds beat through my chest. This pedantic, pain-in-the-arse French-Canadian had appointed herself Cupid. I realised Jenny would never have made the journey without Michelle taking charge. I struggled to close my mouth. I struggled to lift my arm to link with Russ who had already linked Jenny. I found myself walking out onto Commercial Street with Russ leading the way for me and Jenny.

Michelle was waving a grinning *Au Revoir*.

Jenny piped up, 'I would like to see the rest of Whaler's Wharf and meet the other people R.M. works with.'

Russ bid a graceful retreat, reminding us we were welcome to join him for a rainbow of vodka jellies in The Boatslip, and then I was alone with Jenny. Alone, among the throng of Commercial Street: the gay holiday-makers and straight day-trippers who came to see the gays. Jenny and I weren't able to elegantly negotiate the space between us and we kept bumping into each other as we turned into the Whaler's Wharf and wandered from stall to stall, meeting my colleagues and marvelling at the souvenirs. Jenny linked my arm.

Now, Jenny needed to use a loo and asked if she could use the one in my flat. Was it far? I gave some sort of a nod. I wasn't able to speak. Jenny was linking me. Jenny had casually threaded her right arm through my left arm and was leaning in and talking to me, her voice was so lovely. She was smiling and laughing and chatting. There was a bubble of light around Jenny and me as we made our way off Commercial Street. There was nothing else really present in the bright world but the two of us walking together. We ambled up the quiet lane towards the flat, and drifted into a peaceful quietness, we didn't speak and it was perfect.

Jenny followed as I went down the steps and opened the door to the flat which comprised one large room.

It took a moment to adjust our vision to the dimness. On three sides of the room, tiny windows near the ceiling let in a sharp light from the garden path around the house. The room was chilly, with no furniture except a futon double mattress that lay directly on the concrete floor and an oversize Victorian dark wood cupboard. Next to the bed there was a torch and some tea-light candles in glass jars.

'Where are your books?' asked Jenny

'Everything I own, books, tapes, clothes, pens and jotters, my electric kettle, and all my tea-making equipment are all in that cupboard,' I said. 'And the loo and hand basin is just through here,' I said as I opened a white door in the wall near the wardrobe.

'I'll fill the kettle and make us a cup of real Cork-Kenyan tea, Barry's,' I said, 'while you use the loo.'

I heard Jenny say, 'May I?' as she opened the wardrobe.

'Are these all your books?' Jenny asked. 'And all of these clothes?'

'Well, just a few things are mine really,' I said. 'Most of the stuff is Terri's. All of the lesbian detective books and the books on business are hers. I never realised there were so many books on how to succeed in business. It just shows my ignorance. And Terri owns all of the clothes that have the alligators and polo players on them.' I laughed.

Jenny didn't laugh.

I elaborated, 'You know, all the Lacoste and Ralph Lauren stuff is hers and the Benneton stuff too and the golfing gear.'

'Oh yes,' replied Jenny, 'she comes here on weekends.'

'Yes. This is our first home together,' I said.

There was silence while I waited for the tea to draw in the pot. I used a strainer while pouring and I handed Jenny the best China cup with two UHT milk capsules on the saucer and motioned for her to sit on the futon mattress. Jenny sat down on the floor. Wordlessly, I took two pillows from the bed and got Jenny to sit on one while I sat on another.

'Your first home?' asked Jenny.

I didn't know how to reply.

'You're very serious about her.' Jenny appeared confused. 'I'm very sorry. I have just forgotten her name. What's your girlfriend's name?'

'Terri.'

'I am very sorry,' Jenny said in a formal voice. 'I do know her name, of course, I just forgot for a moment.'

Jenny was silent.

'Well, I'm going to move into her apartment when I go back to Boston in September,' I said.

Jenny remained silent and I knew I had a choice. I could lean forward and touch the very outer curls of Jenny's beautiful hair and that would betray Terri. I knew if I leaned towards Jenny, that Jenny would lean into me. I did not know how our bodies would fit together, but I knew we would fit, and we would feel strong and blown apart with each other. In our kisses we would lose the knowledge of where our bodies ended and began. The heat and the hunger and the drenching would dissolve our outsides, we would be turned inside-out.

That would betray Terri and my chance for stability and safety and a real relationship with a woman who was prepared to stand next to me, to sleep and wake with me, to make plans for the future with me and who would let at least some of the world sometimes see that I was loved. And Jenny ... Jenny was leaving.

I was suddenly strangely angry at Jenny. In her letters she had even said it was good for me to have an older lover. Her girlfriend Susan (who had still not moved out from the house back in Cambridge, UK) was the same age as Jenny, but one of the nice things about Susan was that she wasn't a student, she had a real job teaching in a primary school and it was nice to be with someone who was a grown-up. Jenny had confessed to me that her Harvard girlfriends were boring, but she also seemed to be happy with the attention she received and the romances she was having and she seemed alternately happy, sad and furious about going back to Susan. Whatever was variously going on with Jenny, her passion was focused on other people, and she had seemed to have had interest in nothing but a friendship with me. Why in God's holy name did she wait until the last hour before the ferry was leaving to begin to signal she might actually think of me as more than a friend? Or did she?

I stared at Jenny and as suddenly as my annoyance and confusion had risen, it crashed and fizzled away. I was now flooded with love. From within my churning thoughts and bodily craving there bloomed a calm, expansive gentleness that shone through and hovered over me and through which I was able to gaze at the wonder of this woman next to me. This was a form of love I had never been in before and through this aspect I saw Jenny, all of her, and felt every facet of Jenny radiate through me. All of Jenny's visible and invisible edges and curves, knots and freedoms, presence and gaps touched and moved through me. I called on all of the goodness of every realm, of all galaxies to encircle and protect precious Jenny. I knew then that love means clearing and keeping a space for the other.

'Come on, darling,' I said softly. 'We've got to get you on that boat.'

# BOSTON & FIFE

# 1984-1985

# 14
# Two Tribes

I went back to Boston in September and moving back in with the lads in Foster Street was very disorienting. It took me days to shift from thinking that a femme woman doing her make-up on the T on her way to work wasn't a drag queen. It took me days to get used to young straight people, that is all the students around Boston. They were everywhere, holding hands, embracing, kissing, and they just looked so strange. Within that first week I told the lads that I was a lezzer and that I was going to move in with Terri in Somerville. They tried not to be shocked and to be sound and they all offered to help move me over, even though I had very few things to move. I felt a little sad waving them goodbye on the Monday evening I left. They had chipped in and bought me and Terri a bottle of Jameson Whiskey and a few cases of beer.

'Lads, ye're very decent. Ye're all pure decent,' I said at an awkward moment as we were all standing on the porch and trying to say goodbye. We shook hands and hugged slightly and then I got into Eily's van and went to Somerville.

I took on a full slate of courses in UMASS so that I could graduate the following summer, and I went back to minding Clara. There was no question but that Clara wanted me to be her carer and her daughter seemed to have no issue with a lesbian looking after her mother. Anyway, Clara was the boss and she paid me double the going rate.

I spent three weekend nights and many weekend days looking after Clara. The time I spent at Clara's meant that I wasn't available to Terri when she was off work and this was the constant source of epic rows between us. I knew it was very poor form on my part, but it made financial sense, the job worked really well with my studies, and anyway, I loved Clara and I wouldn't give her up.

One night, pretty soon after I had come back from P-town, Terri rang me at Clara's very late in the night. She was drunk and shouting at me. I could hear Clara had woken up and was fumbling in her bedroom to try and pick up the phone there. I hung up and went in to Clara to tell her not to worry, it was just Terri on the phone for me. I apologised for waking her and as I was assuring her that everything was OK, Terri was already ringing back. I rushed back into my bedroom and when I picked up the phone Terri was already screaming obscenely. I hung up and took the phone off the hook so there would be no more calls coming through that night. I went back to Clara, soothed her and made her comfortable.

I lay awake on my bed most of the night. It felt mostly so good to live with Terri but it could also be so tense. I lay on the bed feeling the weight of the tension like a concrete block on my chest.

I phoned Terri very early the next morning. She didn't pick up and I left a message on the answering machine: 'You phone here like that again, Terri, and I am not coming back to your apartment. I will move out.'

I hung up.

It was the one and only time I threatened Terri with moving out. She never pulled that late-night phone stunt again.

While Terri worked long hours and I worked weekends, we really just had weekday nights to spend with each other. It was much easier to find time to spend with John Kerrigan as he had such a flexible working situation. He liked to drive his motorbike out to meet me by UMASS Library and we would go from there for a walk around the beaches in South Boston. Castle Island beach was our favourite. Early into my time back in Boston, John Kerrigan let me into a secret: he introduced me to Neeraj, his boyfriend.

'Rose Marie, this has to be a secret. I mean it. It would just kill Neeraj's parents. They're the same kind of people as my family. It really would kill them.'

Neeraj was as tall and well-built as John, from the back they looked very similar in their preppy chinos and button-down shirts. But Neeraj's beaming smile, brown skin and silky black hair was quite the contrast to John Kerrigan's pale, slightly worried expression and his tousled clumps of brown curls. Neeraj's parents had emigrated from New Delhi to California's Silicon Valley when they were newly married, and his father worked in the Xerox lab. Neeraj was completing a Doctorate in Physics when he met John.

I got Neeraj to tell me how he had met John Kerrigan, and it was the typical start to a gay boy romance: all competition and testosterone. They had seen each other in a club, they were circling around each other when another guy made eye contact with John and began to make rapid advances, touching him, stroking his back. Neeraj cut in and started kissing the boy who had been coming on to John. Such is the way of men.

Neeraj told me, 'Me and the other guy started to head out of the club and I motioned to John to come too. He seemed to go off to get his coat. At least that's what I hoped he was doing. Me and the other guy waited for him outside. I was just about to go back inside and look for John when he arrived. The three of us began to make out, kind of wildly, outside the club. It was so dangerous, gay-bashers everywhere. But it was so hot. I knew I didn't want to share John. Those freckles! Those long eyelashes! And he was so shy, which was a big turn-on because I could see he wanted me. I got rid of the other guy. We went to John's apartment and I never left. We acted just like lesbians. You know, on our second date we brought the moving van! I just moved in and we never let go of each other'

I loved how open and free Neeraj was and talking to him, I got to know John Kerrigan better. John was so relaxed when Neeraj was next to him. In their yuppie two-bed apartment on Cambridge Parkway, I loved to watch how they would grab and hug each other in amazement and gratitude that they had found each other, utterly forgetting for a few moments that I was there as a witness. I loved to bask in the heat of their excitement in finding each other and the joy they had in their astonishing, never-to-be-imagined, perfect good luck. I understood their joy: after a lifetime of caution in every move they made in front of other boys and men, they could now move freely with another man, even if it was just in their own apartment, or in gay clubs, or in the homes of friends, or in resorts like Provincetown, or Fire Island, or South Beach, or the afternoon of a Gay Pride March. They now had a home, nearly a world, where they could walk, talk, sit, listen, stand without searing self-conscious monitoring of every posture and move of their bodies, every cadence of their voice. They had each found a man who loved every gesture of their body. In the way of all young lovers, they rejoiced that they now had a stability that would last forever.

John's insistence that Neeraj's parents would be killed by the news that their son was gay did not seem entirely well-founded. Shortly after meeting Neeraj, he filled me in on his family and showed me lovely framed photographs of his parents and his sister, Sunita, when I was at their apartment waiting for John to come home from work. He plainly adored his sister.

'Sunita's so smart, and you can see how beautiful she is. She looks just like my mom was at that age. She's getting her master's in science education in Berkeley right now and once that's done she'll get married and teach high school science. Sunita's much smarter than me but she didn't want to go on and do a doctorate, she's excited to be married and start a family.'

'Who's the lucky boyfriend?'

'You see ...,' Neeraj seemed unusually stuck for words. 'My parents are arranging the marriage for her. We will all go to India for the ceremonies. Maybe next year or the year after.'

I was a bit taken aback.

'My sister is very happy with this arrangement. She's a quiet girl and she's dated some boys but doesn't like that dating culture. She knows my parents will find her someone completely compatible who will love her. On the Indian side of my culture we love the person we marry, not marry the person we love – what comes first is the marriage and then the love.'

'I suppose that seems fine by me, Neeraj. I mean, what do I know? But, like, can you get divorced?'

'Yes, of course you can get divorced!'

'Well, in Ireland you can't get divorced.'

'Really?'

'Oh yes. No divorce.'

We were both silent for a while, each contemplating the weirdness of each other's customs. I think Neeraj's lot had things much better sorted than mine.

'I was going to let my parents arrange a marriage for me before I met John.'

'No!'

'Yes!' Neeraj laughed. 'I knew I was gay, but I never fell in love before I met John. I just assumed I would marry some nice girl, make everyone happy and have fun with boys on the side.'

'God!'

Neeraj laughed at my shock. 'Well, you know, I just thought it was a sexual fetish thing. Whenever I visit India, there's plenty of men giving me *that* look. When you follow them, it's clear what can happen. I never did anything there because my Hindi isn't that good and I didn't want trouble. I just kinda thought being gay was like, you got married and you continued to have sex with men. I went to some bars and clubs when I was in Caltech. It didn't occur to me that I would or could fall *in love* with a guy – I thought it was all just *lust*. It wasn't until I came to Boston that I met any gay *couples*. And now I plan to do the honourable thing. Once my sister is safely married, I will introduce John to my parents. I don't want to wreck any of the plans being made for Sunita. My parents will be upset, but they will say this is what happens when you raise a child in America. And in time they will love John when they see how much I love him.'

Then Neeraj asked me: 'Have you ever met John's mother?'
'No, never.'
'Is it difficult being a widow in Ireland?'
'What do you mean?'
'Do people shun her?'
'Because she's a widow?'
'Yeah.'
'Ah no. Not at all.'
'John says that she has had a hard life.'
'Well, John's father died young and she was left with John and his two sisters and they were all quite small, I mean, John is the eldest and he was only seven. So I imagine it was tough enough financially, maybe, or tough due to loneliness. But I gather John supports her a lot now, I mean with money, and he talks to her a lot on the phone and visits of course.'

'Yes, he is a very good son,' said Neeraj with obvious pride. After a while, he asked softly, 'John will never tell her about me, will he?'

'Maybe in time,' I said as gently as I could.

At the end of September, Russ and Joni moved to Boston. First they stayed with John and Neeraj, and then they took a short lease on a small one-bed apartment at the top of a Victorian red-brick in the

South End. Russ laid out his more long-term plans to John Kerrigan and me as we celebrated their arrival to Boston with a cocktail at the new gay bar, the Club Café, where Russ and Joni were both working. They had a plan to save money and go to Europe to travel there the following spring. They were going to stay away as long as their money lasted, and after that Russ was going to arrange to meet his father.

'I'm going to lay out our plans and ask for his blessing.'

Their plan was to open a small gay bar in New Orleans. Russ had a few locations in mind. Joni and he would also purchase a building with a wraparound porch and run it as 'Icarus: the Premier Gay Inn in New Orleans'. Once the businesses were established, Russ would go to college part-time and study Business and Finance.

'I'm going to equip myself to be able to look after the family investments and care for my parents when they are old and provide for my sister's family should she have any children.'

John Kerrigan was as surprised as I was to hear this plan.

'I can't believe you will study Business,' was all I could muster.

'I think it's a great plan,' said John, 'but do you really think your father will be OK?'

'I think Papa will be ready to have me back.'

'As his *gay* son?' said John incredulously.

'As long as I don't trail trouble to the door, I think he'll be very happy to no longer be estranged. After all, I've always been his gay son.'

John and I nodded dumbly. I don't think either of us believed a grand reunion was possible. We had never seen a prodigal queer child being welcomed back into the family fold.

'But before all of those *serious* plans commence – my Joni must see Paris and all its delights! And he must see all the other beautiful places I saw in Europe.' Russ continued with a rising crescendo, 'And that way we can both ruminate on the beautiful things we've seen in our youth as we tighten our belts, get our noses to the grindstone, and into all those other *manly* poses of businessmen as we set to work on being shining examples of success in the State of Louisiana's hospitality sector!' He stood and flung his arm high like a flamenco dancer in a flourish finish while John Kerrigan and I applauded.

John was given to worrying about my relationship with Terri, but then John was given to worrying in general so I didn't pay too much attention to him when he would say, 'It really shouldn't be this hard, Rose Marie. You really should not be this tense.'

I had made a mistake in confiding in him that Terri had phoned Clara's late at night. He got the whole story out of me, including that I had promised her I would leave if she did that again.

'I think you should leave anyway,' he blurted.

We were walking around Castle Island on an unseasonably warm October day. I said nothing. I had said too much already.

'Look Rose Marie, it's not that I have anything against Terri, but it's just not good that you can't admit to her that you meet with your friends in the evening before heading home because it will make her angry. Or you can't tell her that you and I meet up because even that will make her angry.'

'I never said that!' I protested.

'I know you didn't,' John said softly. 'But I can tell. It's obvious.'

I felt too embarrassed then to say anything. John put his arm around my shoulders and hugged me close.

We walked on in silence. I felt bereft. I didn't want to leave Terri. I couldn't bear that upheaval and I knew how upset she would be and I really and truly did love her.

'I would love if you had someone like I have Neeraj. I would love that for you. Like, are you able to look at Terri and say: "yes, she's the one"?'

'That only ever happened me the once. I saw a girl standing by a massive big pot plant in the Copley Plaza Hotel.'

John smiled at me: 'Let me guess. Her name was Jenny.'

I said nothing but gave a rueful smile.

'You can definitely have that kind of feeling again, Rose Marie. And that's all I would wish for you.'

I gave a non-committal shrug and said nothing but thought to myself that kind of thing probably only happened you once. We reached his motorbike in silence and he gave me a lift back to the library.

I persuaded John to let Eily and Mels meet Neeraj. With Russ's and Joni's move to town, we were quite the gang now. Some of us met most days in the early evening at each other's apartments but I never had them come to Terri's apartment. I always made sure to be back at 8.30 p.m. and tried to have a dinner underway for her when she came home from work around 9 p.m. However, that autumn, the conversations among our gang became increasingly apprehensive. Russ called us all to come around to their apartment one Friday afternoon in October before I went to work with Clara. Mini wanted us all to be gathered because he was phoning from New York. Russ put the call on speaker through the answering machine. We were all there: me, Eily, Mels, John Kerrigan, Neeraj, Joni, Russ.

'Hi!' Mini said.

And we all yelled back: 'Hi!! Hello!'

Russ was wafting around, supplying us with gin and tonics, although he didn't seem in his usual happy form.

'Guys, I talked to Russ and Joni during the week and they thought it would be a good idea for you all to hear what I've to say.' Mini sounded very serious and also upset. 'Guys, it's real. GRID is real, although it's really called AIDS, because it's not just gay men. But it's lots of gay men here in New York and not just older gay men. Young guys too, our age. They are very sick and about five or six thousand are already dead now between L.A. San Fran and New York. You're not going to hear it on the TV or in the newspapers. They don't give a fuck about us or the Haitians.' He paused and said: 'Guys – Tony – Tony's very sick.'

Mini's voice broke. He was struggling to keep it together.

I eventually asked: 'When you say Tony's sick, like, what does that mean? How is he sick?'

'Hmmm, pneumonia and KS lesions, like skin tumours all over his face and back and chest and arms. He has lost so much weight. You guys would be shocked.'

There was a silence.

After a while, Mini continued: 'There's a group here, Gay Men's Health Crisis. It *is* a crisis, guys. Look, we didn't take it seriously all summer. I know we thought those guys from New York who came up in August were just hysterical queens. But we've got to be careful. I've mailed Joni and Russ a package with more information – it's those flyers we saw in August – you can still have sex, but you've got to be careful. There's probably a group in Boston too – check it out guys. Please, be careful.'

Joni passed around the flyers from the Safer Sex Committee of New York: *Healthy Sex is Great Sex*. John Kerrigan and Neeraj arranged to go down and see Mini, and he told them they could stay with MichaelC. The rest of us were rather silent.

I had to leave shortly after the call with Mini ended. I was very sorry to hear about Tony. I had only met him in the A-house dance floors and a few times when I called to his house to help Mini with processing photos. Tony seemed very nice. He was old, in his forties, with a lightly shaved chest and a dark moustache, he kept his hair tightly cut, his temples were silvering. He was generous with his time and encouragement to us young ones. His house was packed with guests all summer who looked exactly like him: middle-aged trim guys, white, black and brown, with moustaches and beards. Men who liked to wear leather going out and checked shirts and Levi's when walking their cute dogs.

What amazes me now is that even after that call, I didn't quite realise that Tony was dying. Of course I knew that some men had died from GRID/AIDS, but it didn't dawn on me to think my own friends were in any way in danger, even with Mini's crystal-clear warning. My head was full of Terri, my studies, carving out time with Eily, Mels and the boys. I had no foreboding sense of imminent disaster. I was young.

# 15
## Karma Chameleon

After Jenny left Boston and went back to England, we wrote constantly to each other. Jenny wrote to me care of Clara's address. When the letters arrived Clara would tuck them into the drawer where the tablecloths were kept.

We loved writing to each other. Occasionally I would paste Jenny's A5 letters onto an A4 page and write replies to her comments and questions around the margins. She loved getting those letters in particular.

Jenny had got a job in St Andrews, a very prestigious university, but back then it was hours and hours from anything like a place where you might meet a lesbian. Jenny was bored and lonely and unable to finish writing her book on Emily Dickinson, which made her so anxious that she found it difficult to find the concentration even to read. She started to spend most of her time going to the cinema and watching videos, getting the university to buy her box sets of classic films.

*All I do, my dear R.M., is muddle through my teaching and write to you.*

Jenny was far more forthright in her letters than she was in person.

> *Breaking up with Susan was physically painful. My muscles between my ribs ached so much I thought I must have pleurisy which I had continually as a child until I went to boarding school. I insisted that my GP organise an ultrasound. I was a little embarrassed to realise that the pain was merely heartbreak. Our friends really have no sympathy for me as ostensibly we had broken up before I went to Harvard which is over a year ago now. Moreover, they rightly discern that I never really thought that Susan and I are altogether a good match, so I really can't fault their impatience. I am quite relieved that I never confessed to anyone other than you that what initially attracted me was her name: Susan, and thinking of Emily D.'s big love, Susan Huntington Gilbert. I haven't been quite able to tell those friends of ours how much the home-making part with Susan was the thing that I loved most and miss now as if it is some living thing that died. That house we rented from my aunt was my first ever domestic home and it was an astonishingly wonderful thing to have. The house where I was a child with my parents – that was not remotely a home. That was a cold house – freezing – materially and metaphorically. School was more of a home, I got a taste for homes there. I heard other girls' tales of homes. Susan and I made a home that was warm, it was a shelter, a shelter from storms rather than a nexus of bad atmospheres.*

Over the months it became clear that Jenny's pride saw her withdraw from her friendship circle. She didn't ask anyone to come and visit her in Scotland, and after a disastrous trip down to London for a thirtieth birthday party, she didn't again make the effort to travel to see her lesbian crew.

> *I was so very tired by the time I arrived, I was anxious about preparing some university lectures I had to give but I couldn't focus on them over the long train journey. I could only afford the time to spend a night in London before hauling myself back up the country again. And, R.M., I got so very drunk. My alarm clock woke me early to get the train and I found I had got sick into most of the plant pots in the living room. I was sleeping on the couch. I vaguely remembered getting up to vomit through the early hours. I found myself hoping that it was someone else who had vomited. But alas it was only me who had been quite so disgusting. I left rather hurriedly. I've phoned and written an apology since. I am not sure that it has been altogether accepted. It pains me to write this – but you must understand why I cannot take your advice to stay in touch with that circle. It was different when we were all living in the same small city and all in college. All our contexts have changed now and those friendships have changed and I can do nothing to keep them.*

Jenny's letter, after dutifully spending Christmas and New Year at home, was the most joyful letter she wrote during that first year she spent in St Andrews:

> *My mother says that we no longer need pretend that we are close. It was her parting gift to me as I waited to get a taxi to take me to the train station. It was a lot better gift than the slippers and pyjamas she gave me – both in sizes too small and in styles more fit for a little girl than an adult woman. I asked her to clarify what*

*she meant: did she mean I did not have to visit on the holidays? And she said, 'That's exactly what I mean. Please phone around birthdays and holidays but don't feel that you have to come here. I think it's quite alright not to come. Having you in the house makes your father more fractious. He's really not too much to handle when it's just the pair of us.' I tried not to grin. What a relief. I feel as if I have been released from a rather grim bondage. My life is lighter now, it is my own to live.*

Jenny was lonely in St Andrews and felt quite marooned there, but Cyril, that persistent former boyfriend of hers, began to routinely visit by taxi – a helicopter taxi. Cyril told Jenny that on the last Friday of every month he would fly from London to Edinburgh and from there he would visit St Andrews on the 'copter and continue to invite Jenny to climb aboard and spend the weekend with him. Jenny wrote and told me she was quite enjoying snubbing Cyril's offer, even if it was wonderfully romantic.

The next letter I received from Jenny was the shortest one she ever wrote me.

*Dearest R.M., Is there any way you could come visit me? We will both be finished with college work in June. I could help towards the travel costs. It would help so much to be able to look forward to seeing you. I miss you terribly. Terribly. Jx*

John Kerrigan insisted on paying for the flights, he organised the set of lies to be told to Terri and told me to learn them off: he was paying for the trip because it was a graduation present for my great result in my master's so far; there was to be an interview in London for a lucrative scholarship; if I got it, I would have a lot of money and a visa to live for four years in the States. It was a story Terri was keen to see fulfilled. I felt guilty that I felt absolutely no guilt about lying to Terri as to the real reason why I was going off to the UK, and Russ spent an afternoon laughing at the contortions of Catholics. I had a week between summer courses in UMASS. I was also on some painting shifts with Eily and Mels's company but they enthusiastically encouraged me to go.

And so it seemed to be sorted with remarkable ease. I would visit Jenny. If it went badly wrong, I could go to my old school pal, Gemma, who lived in Birmingham. In any case, I would visit Gemma overnight after visiting Jenny for a few days and come back in via Canada. John and Neeraj would drive up in John's Chevrolet and collect me at Niagara Falls. All my pals, Eily, Mels, Russ, Joni, John and Neeraj, knew the plan. Even Clara knew all the details. I wasn't sure exactly what Clara thought about it all as I was so awkward confessing to her why I needed the time off. She made no comment then, but on the last evening I had with her before my trip she gave me an envelope with £200.

'Do something nice with Jenny, honey,' she said, patting the envelope as she put it into my hands.

So everyone knew I was off to visit Jenny – everyone but Terri.

# 16
# All The Way From America

My journey to Jenny was epic: Boston to Heathrow to Edinburgh, bus from the airport to the train station, two changes of trains, and there was Jenny, waiting on the platform. I was amazed at the miracle of seeing her again after nearly twelve months apart. I knew I was in Scotland, it was teatime and it was summer, but other than grasping those facts, I was nearly delirious with tiredness and the pleasure and wonder of Jenny.

I rushed up the platform and stopped a few feet from Jenny and stood grinning and grinning while she shaded her eyes.

Without saying 'Hello' Jenny asked: 'Did you get my Bloomsday letter? June sixteenth?

'Eh, no. June tenth was the last one. But you know they can take a week to arrive.'

Jenny moved towards me and swung me around so the sun shone on my face, and now it was my turn to squint. I still couldn't stop grinning, even though I knew I looked like a total eejit. I didn't care. Here was Jenny, next to me.

'I wrote to let you know I've been sleeping with Cyril. For nearly a month now.' Jenny spoke formally, solemnly. 'He's going to arrive tomorrow. You'll meet him then.'

I hugged her. 'You're here, Jenny! And I'm here!' was all I could say.

Jenny appeared to be about to cry. 'I have missed you so, R.M.'

We walked out of the train station and I just could not stop talking. I knew I should be paying more attention to the lowness of Jenny's mood, but I was sloshed with happiness. I didn't care about anything other than the miracle that Jenny was alive and well and wanted to see me, and besides, I was still with Terri. I did have one vague and inarticulate promise to myself (and maybe it was a half-hope): if Jenny seemed to want to kiss me, well then, it would happen, and anything and everything else Jenny might want to happen after that kiss would certainly happen too. However, I was preoccupied with a crystal-clear and firm vow there was something I would tell Jenny on my visit. I had even tried to practise coughing it out, but mostly I prayed I wouldn't chicken out of saying it. The only clear motive I had for my epic journey was to tell Jenny this one thing.

After we had our tea I fell asleep while Jenny was showing me some books. In my travels I had lost a night's sleep. I rested my head on Jenny's shoulder and I was asleep. Jenny shrugged me awake as best she could and led me up a narrow staircase and showed me into the single room at the back of the house, which overlooked a small fishing port. I managed to squirm my way out of most of my clothes. I left on my T-shirt and boxers and was soon asleep on top of the eiderdown, yet I kept jerking awake with a terrible dream. I was walking into Jenny's room, getting into her bed and Jenny didn't want me there. It was awful, every fifteen, twenty minutes I jolted awake.

It was about 10.00 p.m., still quite bright outside and I had been crashing awake with the awful dream for about three hours and I knew I would lose my mind if I couldn't settle in to sleep. I needed to tell Jenny I was afraid I was going to sleepwalk into her room. I stumbled out of my room and stood on the tiny landing. Jenny was in her bedroom, the door was open. She was in bed, reading. She was wearing an old-fashioned brushed cotton nightdress with long sleeves. Her curtains were drawn and she had her beside lamp on. I leaned against the door frame of her room and stood on the threshold. I pressed my left foot against my inner right thigh. I had done this pose in the only yoga class I had ever attended, they called it 'the tree'. So I stood like a yoga tree, just staring at Jenny, who stayed absorbed in her book. I closed my eyes and may have nodded off. When I next opened my eyes Jenny was looking at me inquisitively.

'Anything the matter?'

'Not a thing, except I keep jolting awake.'

'Oh dear. Jet lag.'

'Well, I suppose.'

'Anything to be done to help?' Jenny asked.

I could tell Jenny wanted to get back to reading her book.

'Not a thing. Except I have to tell you something so I can get a good night's sleep.'

'Hmmm?' Jenny was sliding back into reading, surreptitiously letting her eyes follow the tantalising print under her fingers.

'I love you.'

That was the thing I had firmly promised myself I would say to Jenny. The thing I had tried to practise saying, but I didn't realise I was actually going to say it right then and out loud.

Jenny was staring at me uncomprehendingly, as if she hadn't quite heard what I had said.

'I love you,' I repeated, beginning to grin, realising what a total tool, a complete langer, an utter gom I was, standing on one leg, leaning against Jenny's door frame, banjaxed with exhaustion.

But, in fairness, it just had to be said. I had a strong hunch that unless I told Jenny I loved her, I would start to get contorted in how I thought about Jenny and how I wrote to her, and Jenny wouldn't know what was wrong and it wouldn't be fair. So she was going off to be with a man – well, some lesbian had to let her know she would be missed from the tribe, that there was a flame for her, somewhere.

Jenny started to smile slowly, she began to blush a bit. I was surprised to see she was pleased.

'Same,' she said and she looked me right in the eyes and I could see it was true. Jenny did, in miraculous fact, love me, even if she didn't want to say it out loud.

I was very, very, very happy.

Jenny waved me off. 'Now sleep well,' she said.

I woke the next morning with Jenny at my bedside telling me my old school pal, Gemma, was on the phone. I went downstairs to take the call, feeling a herd of small children had run over me. Every part of me was sore, I was enervated with exhaustion. Gemma was checking to see when I was going to arrive in Birmingham.

'Eeh, I'll be arriving today, Gem.' I was a bit surprised at my decision, but I decided on the spot I wasn't really up to meeting old Cyril. Best to head off.

'Ahhh,' said Gemma, 'well, I'm delighted to be having extra time with you, Ro, but a bit sorry and all for you. Sure we'll talk later. Give me a ring when you land into Birmingham Central. I'm just half an hour away. I'll come in and get you.'

I had to rush then. I told Jenny I was going to head early to see Gemma. Jenny just nodded. Within twenty minutes I had dressed and got a cup of tea and some toast into me and was walking out of the house with Jenny, who insisted on carrying my small knapsack to the train station. I was too tired to take it from her. Jenny linked my arm, which for a few moments made me one of the happiest young lesbians on the planet.

I said, 'I'm a bit sorry that I won't get a chance to meet Cyril and check him out to make sure he's even half good enough for you.'

'I think you and he would actually get on. Oddly.'

'Oddly, I'm sure!' I replied.

Jenny fussed over me as I sat on the train, checking I had the packed lunch she had made for me and that I had sterling currency. She even checked I had my passport and flight ticket to Canada. She fiddled with my shirt collar, unfolding it and folding it again.

'I love you,' she said.

'Same,' I replied.

Jenny smiled and held my shirt collar between her thumb and fingers. She hesitated in her smiling, she slowly leaned closer, she kissed my brow and did not look at me again as she let go of my shirt collar and pulled back and left the compartment. She had left the train and was walking resolutely down the platform when the driver gave the last call for all people not travelling to disembark as the train was about to leave the station.

# BOSTON & NEW YORK

## 1985-1992

# 17
# True Colors

After I came back from my visit to Jenny I remained weirdly 'stoned', expansive with having been around her, and that feeling lasted most of my first week back in Boston. I was grateful that Terri was generally uncurious, she asked me very few questions and once she had vented on my failure to win that 'fancy scholarship', which was the lie we had all told as the reason for my trip, she seemed to forget that I had ever gone. But ten days after I was back I woke up with a horrible tight feeling across my chest. I sat up, the digital clock glowed 4:02 a.m. I could hardly breathe. I didn't know what was happening. It took some moments to figure it out: Jenny was gone.

That was all. Jenny was gone.

I made my way to the bathroom and lay on the floor. I stopped fighting the tears and they came with sobs. I waited it out. I stayed there until I heard the alarm ring for Terri's early rise and I got up off the floor and made my way back to bed.

I began a practice then of counting the ways in which being with Terri brought so many benefits to my life. It was good to have someone to hold, someone who would be there, an anchor in all the confusion. She taught me how to cook, how to use herbs and taste as you go. Before we turned out the lights for the night, we would read through cookery books together and plot meals. We slowly worked our way through Italian cooking before learning Vietnamese and then Thai. When we went out to fine restaurants we savoured the food to figure out the flavouring and method, we would chat with the chefs if we could and try to recreate the dishes at home.

Terri was very patient in introducing me to baseball that summer of 1985. It took me about two seasons before I accepted that while it wasn't hurling, baseball had some merits. I eventually joined her in being a Red Sox fan and having a season ticket to Fenway, singing 'Sweet Caroline' at the 7th inning stretch, eating hotdogs and drinking weak, warm beer under the Citgo sign. Those were happy days.

We played on the same softball team, called the Navratilovas, every Wednesday evening during the summer and early autumn. Our colours were red, white and blue (the Czech flag colours! we insisted), but most of our teammates envied the kit of the Bread & Roses team from Cambridge who wore lavender. Those B&R women were our arch rivals. They came to the games on bicycles or in battered old station wagons with bumper stickers that read: *My other car is a broomstick* or *One nuclear bomb can ruin your day* or *Love your Mother* with a picture of planet Earth. By day, the B&R women were non-descript university administrators, librarians, lab technicians and academics, but come Wednesday evening they were loud, swearing, aggressive and downright mean softball opposition. They claimed they were so well-bonded as a team that they were on the same menstrual cycle.

'That's just psych ops,' insisted Terri.

But of course that information worried me and the other Navratilovas.

I once casually asked my teammates if there was a softball league for straight women before being met with incredulous laughter. We were apparently playing in the one and only Boston women's league, which I had assumed was exclusively a queer women's league, but in fairness to me, every team seemed to be entirely composed of dykes, trans- and bi-girls and *two* of the teams even called themselves 'The Other Team'. Joni elected themselves our cheerleader girl and water-boy and completed those tasks with great devotion, patiently spelling out 'Give us an N! – through A! – V!-R!-A!-T!-I!-L!-O!-V!-A! and S!' If they got tired they sometimes merely spelled out M-A-R-T-I-N-A. Sometimes Russ came along too, and the pair were quite a lovely sight in their little cheerleader dresses and oversize pom-poms. Russ also liked to wear a mauve T-shirt with the slogan, *Nobody Knows I'm a Lesbian*. Terri was never a big fan of Russ and Joni but she appreciated that their antics disturbed the opposition, plus the rest of our team really loved having them around. 'Good for morale, I guess,' Terri would mutter.

Terri and I loved that our team took the softball business very seriously and that we collectively sought to win every play. The two of us went over the best and worst plays of the game for days afterwards. We shopped for hours to update our kit. I only sometimes missed playing camogie. In time I learned to relish the sounds of softball: the clunk, pop and team gasp when a perfect strike was hit; the dim shouts heard from outfield; the sliding crunch of getting to base just in time. I loved that moment in the evening when the bases were loaded and I went in to bat. I loved kicking up the dust in sliding into a base and I loved stealing runs. But most of all I loved standing in the outfield, waiting to catch a hit, watching the dramas gather and roll in the in-field before the summer sun set in its quick Boston orange dusk and the night began as pink and mauve.

Joel came to Boston in the autumn of 1985, he had been accepted into Harvard Law. We were all surprised he was going to law school and not heading to New York or L.A. to make theatre. He confessed, 'My folks find it hard that their only child is a fag. Getting accepted to Harvard Law softens the pain.'

'But my dear, you are not merely accepted to the law school. You're now going to have to become a lawyer,' Russ softly pointed out.

'I'll figure something out. I'm glad to be with you guys in Boston. I can volunteer with Harvard's theater program. I really didn't think my folks would take it that hard. You know my uncle is gay, my mom's favourite brother, my dad's favourite relative! But it seems that no Burrowitz grandchildren is a big blow. Who knew? Going to Harvard Law makes them happy, and they'll pay, so that's three more years to figure things out. My mom even said maybe I would meet a nice Jewish lesbian there who wanted kids!'

We all laughed, except for Joni who said, 'Wow. I think that would be neat. I think it would be so nice to be a dad, or a mom.'

Russ put his arm around Joni's shoulder and hugged him close.

As the autumn turned into winter our gang became increasingly worried about AIDS. We heard more and more stories of the men we knew from P-town who were beginning to get sick. The gay newspapers, such as *Bay Windows* in Boston, carried more articles about the impact of the disease. Gay bathhouses in San Francisco had voluntarily closed down and there was a campaign to close down the bathhouses in New York.

Russ disagreed. 'But these are the only places where all of those closeted married men will learn about the disease – where safer sex can be encouraged and practised. The inevitable result of closing the bathhouses is we go back to the parks and bushes and piers, not so safe at all, my dears!'

My gay boyfriends were all healthy. There was some worry that perhaps the infections caused by HIV took years to manifest, but whenever I freaked out and rang them to ask how they were and if they were practicing safer sex, they generally seemed amused. Except for John Kerrigan. 'I'm worried enough, Rose Marie, don't be freaking me out further.'

I regularly met up with my friends on those weekday evenings when I wasn't playing softball or at a Red Sox game with Terri. Our entire gang met most Friday late afternoons before I went to Clara's, and Russ and Joel both liked to tease John and Neeraj for their constant gym workouts. Russ would invariably greet them by saying: 'My, aren't you two the most *divine* Muscle Marys.' And Joel would cajole them into letting him wrap his hands around their biceps, or shins or thighs, becoming increasingly more outrageous until John was shouting and Neeraj laughing.

In truth, John and Neeraj did indeed look utterly smashing. John even began getting his clumps of curls properly cut. They both (unsuccessfully) pretended to be nonchalant about their toned physiques. I decided that Russ and Joni were beautiful, they had bravely blossomed into their full natures, while John and Neeraj had sculpted themselves handsome. And Joel – well, Joel had a nerdy-boy clever sweetness that seemed to mean he was never without some other earnest boy orbiting him with interest.

Working the weekends with Clara was the highlight of my week that winter of 1985. Although Clara was not without her edges: she bullied me to apply for a place on the PhD programme in English literature at Boston College. I wept through closed eyes as Clara put the completed application form into the envelope.

Clara had insisted on me doing multiple drafts. 'Why do you keep doing the messing up?!' she had bawled at me.

I knew I didn't have any chance of being awarded a scholarship. When I saw the thin letter with the crest of Boston College as it lay among the pile of junk mail and flyers on the mat outside Terri's apartment, my heart sank: such a simple rejection to so much hard work and Clara's confection of hopes. I couldn't open the letter I held in my shaking hands and so I stuffed it into the pocket of my overcoat and instantly forgot about it. That might sound unbelievable, but it's true. As I stuffed the letter down into one of the deep pockets of my duck down jacket I was already forgetting I had seen that university crest on an envelope. Even taking off my coat in Clara's, I forgot what was burrowed in amongst tissues and subway tokens.

Over the weekend Clara suddenly turned on me and asked me if I had heard from BC. We were sitting in the La-Z-Boy recliner chairs, digesting our fillet steaks and enjoying the afterglow of Burgundy. I had an uncertain memory of a thin envelope and, as the memory of the letter began to take shape, I started to inhale and begin to form the words of some class of an evasion.

Clara cut me off, 'The head of the English Department tells me the letters are all sent out. I was expecting it to arrive today.'

'You've been phoning them!' I squeaked.

'Yes, and they don't like it,' said Clara with a shrug that was her quintessential mixture of nonchalant yet brazen smugness. 'And the secretaries say a lot of nonsense, they say I'm not you, they say I should not be canvassing them. So I phone the head guy instead and he's a lot nicer, but with him I know to be a little soft-in-the-head little old lady yadda-ya and he tells me the acceptance and rejections letters went out on Wednesday. So the letter arrives? Yes?'

It was one of those moments when Clara left me speechless.

I levered myself off the La-Z-Boy chair and padded over to my coat in the hall and dug in, got the slip of the letter. I got Clara's reading glasses from the sideboard and handed her the letter. She read out the first line and then she started crying, and then she kissed me and hugged me and cried again. I was invited to accept their offer of a scholarship. I could let them know by phone call or letter.

We phoned the number there and then and doubtless left one of the longest and most incoherent messages ever put on that answering machine. We got cut off. We squabbled and I insisted on writing down what we were to say. The phone kept shaking in my hand. I read out my acceptance and then handed the phone over to a demanding Clara.

'Rosemary McCarthy says yes, she will be your PhD scholarship,' said Clara. 'She says yes. Rosemary McCarthy says yes and she will send a letter, too. She says yes.'

So by the following September, in 1986, I was all set to become a doctoral student in Boston College, and Mels had been accepted into UMASS to study nursing.

'I'll be the only thicko amongst the lot of ye now!' said Eily proudly.

Mels would still work on managing the painting and decorating business, which I had seen first-hand was making a lot of money, but she would no longer do painting shifts. They were planning to move back to Ireland. There were always jobs for nurses at home, but they didn't know how a painting and decorating business would transfer.

'Irish people do their own painting and wallpaper hanging,' explained Eily to the boys. 'We'll need to diversify!'

While the New Year of 1986 had started out so auspiciously with our college acceptance letters, that spring and summer were cruel seasons. The first to develop symptoms was Joni. He began to have gut problems and lose weight. It took three months back then for a definitive HIV test result, and he didn't bother to take the test as it seemed clear he had the virus. When Joni had left his home in Minnesota in 1981 he was just seventeen. He had got a greyhound bus to New York, hoping to find community, work, a place to live. He found that New York landlords wanted references from previous landlords, first and last months' rent, plus a big security deposit. He got work washing pots in a kitchen and found community and rough sleeping on New York piers where he supplemented his income by turning tricks. We reckoned that he'd had the virus for a while.

We were all freaked out by Joni getting sick. John Kerrigan and I had a massive row.

He said, 'I suppose it was inevitable,' in a tone that was one of his self-hating, straight-acting modes that was beginning to grate on me.

'What do you mean?' I asked crisply.

'You know,' he said defensively.

'What?'

'He was a rent boy.'

'So what? He would have had sex anyway, he only charged because he needed money.'

'Well.'

'Well what?!'

'It's inevitable then!'

'The only thing that's inevitable is that nothing is being done about it! Jesus Christ, John! This fucking president and his disgusting government and most of America are only all too delighted! A couple of thousand are dead and thousands more infected and it's no problem at all to them is it? Haitians and the homeless, hookers, heroin addicts and the homos. They really believe that God is on their side and sent a plague to kill ye. To kill US! Awwww, it's a shame though about the "innocent" haemophiliacs!'

'Stop it, Rose Marie,' John said softly.

I was so angry I could have punched him. I saw he was distressed but couldn't stop one last shout.

'Sex! John Kerrigan, sex! It's an adventure! Just seeking and finding experiences outside the descriptions and prescriptions of the horrible ways we were raised! Just *inevitably* guilty of searching for and finding pleasure! Just guilty of wanting someone's heat, skin, attention, touch, even for a little while, some connection. Some *fucking* connection! The luckiest adventurers, like our Joni, were just guilty of finding *love*.'

'Stop it, Rose Marie. I said *inevitable*, not that Joni was guilty of anything. Some things just logically happen. There's a pattern to things.'

John Kerrigan was weeping. That made me stop. I looked at him and felt wretched. And then I fell on him in a hug, saying, 'I'm sorry, I'm sorry, I'm sorry.'

I could feel our fear combine to beat through our chests.

Mels and I quickly became active in AIDS activist and service organisations, most of which had lesbians in key positions. Joni, in particular, loved that so many lesbians were involved in AIDS campaigning – 'So much dyke power fighting AIDS! We will definitely have a cure with so many lesbians on our side!'

MichaelC and Mini were constantly on the phone, letting us know the latest news from N.Y.C., and we told them anything we heard in AIDS activist circles in Boson. Mels and I travelled down to New York to go to AIDS Coalition To Unleash Power (ACT UP) meetings during 1987, and we got involved in setting up the Boston chapter. I was careful never to be involved in activist work at Terri's apartment during the times that she was home as it upset her to see how agitated I could get, but also it was yet again another way of me being removed from her. On the other hand, Jenny nagged me in her letters to take my writing, my study and my AIDS work 'seriously'. So under her direction I bought a steel office cabinet and in the tiny 'spare' room of Terri's apartment, which I had taken over as my office, I began filing and archiving whatever I came across in the world of AIDS activism.

When Russ learned what I was doing he was curious: 'Why are you so careful to keep all this stuff, Rose Marie?'

'When this war is over, we will want to write the history, and we may lose the war, but I'm not going to have those fuckers write the history.'

'I don't know if fags and dykes will ever get to write the history, dear Rose Marie,' said Russ languidly, 'but we will certainly make the art.'

While Joni got sick first, it was Joel Burrowitz who died first, in 1988, aged twenty-five. Initially, his parents planned to bring him home to Manhattan, but he asked that they let him stay with us in Boston. His mom rented a lovely three-bed apartment in

Cambridge and it was an open house. All of us came and fed them both, cleaned the apartment and helped Marsha Burrowitz nurse her boy. Joel was blind for the last few months of his life and he got most of his visitors to read for him: newspapers, novels, poetry, scientific research papers on HIV and AIDS, books on the Kabbalah, Louise Hay's books and *Variety* magazine.

MichaelC phoned every evening from New York and Joel got him to repeatedly and slowly recite Lorca's poem, 'Ditty of First Desire', until he fell asleep or had had enough.

Joel's Dad, Alan, came on the shuttle flight from New York every Friday evening, leaving early on Monday morning. Every Friday, before I went to Clara's, I watched him come in from the taxi he had taken from the airport and rush to kiss Joel, then Marsha, then Joel again, and before he took off his work suit he would go out to the porch on the deck of that Cambridge apartment, lean his forehead against one of the wooden posts and sob. He cried deeply for about five minutes, wiped his face and then went into his family.

In the final weeks he also stayed full-time in Boston, as did Joel's gay uncle Marv, who kept repeating: 'It should have been me, I wish it was me, it should have been me,' until Mels or Russ would gently lead him away to stop his refrain.

In those final months, after he went blind, Joel spent his days manfully fighting the fear of dementia. Each day he would battle the fear of losing his mind. His struggle was frightening to watch. He often won through humour, or convoluted reasoning about madness, or channelling a courage to accept whatever else fate would bring, but sometimes his fear and the horror of his blindness made him turn like a roasting carcass on a spit. The helplessness of watching him on those bad days is with me still.

I have hardly ever seen women cry, but when it was clear that Joel had died, Marsha's wailing shocked me. I realised with a jolt that she had been hoping that she could keep her boy alive. For months she had kept the house running, and Joel nursed, and the platoon of friends fed. And for all Joel's dying it had still been a loving house filled with young people's friendship, joy, play and laughter. I saw Marsha had hoped, and maybe believed, that in all the living we were collectively doing we might love Joel into staying with us as he so much wanted to.

Joni Brunstrom was nearly twenty-five when he died, a few months after Joel. His parents came to visit him in Boston from Minnesota and persuaded him to move home, even though Russ, who had been his lover for six years, and John Kerrigan and me and other friends were caring for him. We were paying for the apartment and medication, complementary therapies and food. Besides Russ, there was a rota of carers who loved Joni and we were plugged into AIDS charities and services that helped us with everything.

I visited Joni during his first few weeks back in Duluth. I was shocked to see that his parents had insisted he cut off his very long, very straight blonde hair and, worse, they had given this dying, androgynous, effeminate boy a military buzz cut. He wanted me to take him back to Boston. He said he had had a crazy, deluded hope that by going back to his childhood home he would get better, that his illness would have all been a bad dream once he woke up in his boyhood bedroom.

Joni's parents had told him he would get cured at home, they knew a pastor who could cure AIDS.

'I kinda believed them, Rose Marie. My mom always had a way of making me feel better.'

It turned out the pastor's church was a long drive from Joni's family home and he was put into his parents' station wagon to be driven to the cavernous church where the pastor had the teeming congregation pray not for a cure for AIDS but to 'drive out' homosexuality, which they seemed to think was a synonym for AIDS and for all diseases and ills of the godless. After the third trip, once Joni had been brought onto the pastor's stage and displayed as an exemplum of God's hatred of homosexuality, his parents had decided not to make any more journeys to that pastor's church.

It is one of the most shameful episodes of my life that I let his parents talk me out of renting a car to bring Joni back to his home to die among his friends, his chosen family, to be with Russ. I was the last of Joni's queer family to see him alive. They called the local police when Russ and I came to the house just two weeks after my initial visit. It was a good job Russ was driving us back to the airport as he had prior experience of how to drive when cars with no licence plates are trying to run you off the road. After that attempted visit, Joni's biological family wouldn't let his queer family visit or even talk to him on the phone and we had to assume our letters and care packages were not being passed to him.

Given the violent hostility of the local police, it was too much to ask AIDS activists in Minnesota to try and make contact, so I phoned the family pastor. Well, look, I was desperate.

The pastor said 'Hello' when he answered the phone and 'Yes' when I asked if he was Pastor Jensen and 'Yes' when I asked if he was pastor to the family of John Brunstrom who was ill with AIDS. He said nothing while I introduced myself and pleaded he pass on my love, and Russ's love, to Joni, to John. Before the pastor put the phone down, he quietly said that he would pray to Jesus and ask him to show me how to turn away from the perversion of my homosexuality. He told me if I prayed to Jesus, he would come into my heart and heal my sickness.

AIDS activists based in the Twin Cities were able to confirm Joni was dead about a month after his passing.

I hated Joni's cruel parents and smug siblings, but the loathing that gave me such solace seemed to pain Russ. He would say, 'I don't want to lose you too, Rose Marie.'

Russ would have me rehearse how frightened Joni's parents must have been, how their entire culture told them their son was possessed by evil and if demonic possession wasn't their fault, then they must blame Joni's lover and friends. Russ would prompt me to repeat how I knew Joni's parents thought that curing him of homosexuality was a crucial part of how to love and care for him, to prepare him for the only world they knew. Of course, I knew that Joni's parents lived in a world that never let them know that they had an especially blessed and beautiful spirit come to them in the guise of their youngest girly boy. There was nothing in the worlds inhabited by Joni's siblings, his three older brothers and the sister he adored, that ever let them know the obvious queerness of their youngest brother was something to be protected and cherished. Everything, everything, told the Brunstroms their youngest son, their youngest brother, was cursed. But still, even I had to admit Bill and Rose Brunstom loved their boy, and in spite of all of the cruelty caused by their utter lack of understanding and acceptance of who he was, it was always clear John/Joni loved Bill and Rose. Joni always talked about his parents with such love. And although he knew his brothers and sister were ashamed of him, Joni also knew his siblings loved him as he loved them, and all that love was the nub of the tragedy. There was all that love generated from and through them, and still that family could not find a way to withstand hating the gay.

Russ asked me to visit the Brunstroms again, but to wait for a decade or so. In my twenties, a decade seemed a lifetime away.

'You're the one who is going to survive all of this,' he said.

'But so are you!' I wailed.

'I plan to thrive, Rose Marie, but just in case I get hit by a Boston Trolly car, make me a promise to visit Bill and Rose and Joni's brothers and sister and all of the nieces and nephews he will never see. Keep going back until you find them softer, and talk to them. Talk to them then about Joni and how much love he brought with him.'

I would ritually and blithely promise, not expecting that I would ever be without Russ.

I was so young back then, when those boys were dying. I was green growth, pliable and malleable, and very lucky that Russ Edouard

Belafonte took charge of turning me towards the direction of peace, of understanding, of acceptance. He almost succeeded in helping me face grief, he certainly helped me as a young dyke in learning a plethora of skills to face being denigrated and even hated. Russ gave me many tips on how to survive the onslaught of those years and I am grateful to him to be living, to be still standing, without more significant contortions than I have. Back then I was embarrassed that I was heading into my mid- then my late twenties and I just faked being an adult. My strategy was to keep up appearances until eventually I would achieve what I imagined was the steadiness, the stability and security that was the possession of all grown-ups. I didn't realise then being adult is merely a communal charade.

MichaelC phoned at 3.00 a.m. on 24 April 1989, he was crying: 'He's gone, Rose Marie, he's gone.'

MichaelC and his boyfriend Mark and other friends were with Mini/Michael Green when he died in Williamsburg, Brooklyn, aged twenty-seven. Mini was an art director in an advertising agency in New York. I have two of his paintings, two canvases that were not for sale in his first and last solo show in a SOHO gallery. They are abstract oil paintings but they encapsulate a Provincetown summer – Michael caught that transient light of sunsets on the outer Cape, a particular flooding honeyed light that does not linger like an Irish sunset. The outer arc of Cape Cod makes a tentative curl far into the North Atlantic and there, in that part of the globe, at the end of cloudless summer days, the sun can momentarily electrify the waving green grasses on the dunes, warm the shimmer on the salt water and bring nostalgia briefly to westerly rooms. So very few people in the world are able to capture the light of such a moment, but Michael caught it in paint to preserve and transmit to us all.

Michael was one of those who died as he lived: with grace and quiet attention. At least he was spared the fate of a multitude of others who died ashamed and scared.

# 18
# There Must Be An Angel
# (Playing With My Heart)

It was a haven, a sanctuary, an oasis, a beautiful dream to study Literature at the Jesuits' Boston College, amidst all of the craziness and sadness of the life and deaths I was living. BC's Gothic buildings and quads were very much like University College Cork – if UCC had a number of those growth-hormone injections they give to American cattle

    I began to read the novels of Kate O'Brien and John Broderick, a lesbian and a gay man who wrote exquisite fiction, written at a slant to the thrust and torque of twentieth-century Ireland. I settled into their work and came to understand so much about all the sad and heavy baggage I was carrying almost unbeknownst to myself. My so-called cultural heritage: so much hope and cruelty, rage, secrecy, lament, wildness, strength, suffering, poetry and acrid poverty; so much melancholy and laughter; so much tangled belonging and yearning. It was just seven miles from where I lived in Terri's home in Somerville to BC, but the leafy quietness of Chestnut Hill was a world away from Terri's ongoing disappointment with me and the illness and passionate strategising that pulsed through the rest of my life.

Within a few months of going to classes at BC I learned I was referred to as 'the girl with the leather jacket,' which in one respect shows you how genteel the place was: there was only one female student tripping around the Arts faculty wearing a leather jacket. Yet the phrase 'the girl with the leather jacket' actually underscores the politeness of the people at BC, as no one referred to me as 'the girl with the shaved head, the eyebrow piercing and the Doc Martin boots,' which was how I rocked around the environs of Chestnut Hill in those days.

Activism pulled me out of my books more often than was good for my progress with my studies. I thought of my work with ACT UP and AIDS activism more generally as my job, my obligation, the big 'ought-to-do' in my life, and my time studying was my self-indulgence, my leisure, the ultimately inconsequential time out of the real affairs of the world. I was embarrassed I didn't seem able to meet any deadlines. However, I did write all the time, so I always had things to give the professors at BC when they pulled me into their offices and inquired why I had not submitted the required assessment and essays. I was never entirely clear why those professors seemed to like my work. The whole system felt like everyone was collectively abandoning their duty to make the real world a more bearable place to be. It was surely fundamentally wrong to be wallowing in the pleasures of reading and the delights of writing. My friends were struggling to live, they were dying, and me and my kind were hated.

I also knew I didn't belong at BC, that there had been some kind of mistake. Ever since my first day there in the autumn of 1986, I was always on the alert for the inevitable tap on the shoulder. It would be a kindly old Jesuit. He wouldn't have to say anything – he would just have to nod and I would know I had to leave. I hoped he wouldn't say anything, that he wouldn't spell it out. I would let him know immediately I was all set to leave, that I fully understood I didn't belong.

Most of my AIDS activism took place in Boston, but the epicentre of the devastation and the resistance was in New York.

A few times a year, once I could organise it with Terri, I took the bus, or Russ or John drove me down to N.Y.C., to stay with MichaelC and his boyfriend Mark, who were both deeply involved with ACT-UP and AIDS services. On my forays to New York I met loads of Irish gay guys, a few were around my age but mostly they were older.

Many of them had been closeted back home and had left Ireland in the aftermath of vicious murders of gay men in Dublin in 1982. In one case, convicted gay-bashers were given suspended sentences and a victory parade by their neighbours. In another, Garda detectives roused themselves from inaction and seized the opportunity to track down every gay man in the country. Gay sex was illegal back then and hunting for a murderer, who might have been a serial killer of gay men, became conflated with compiling a registry of queers. The Guards turned up at schools where men were teachers and at the other places the gays worked: the banks, the shops, the factories, the hotels, pubs and restaurants, hospitals, farms, colleges, family businesses. They even turned up at the men's homes, at tea-time, when they were with their parents and siblings or with their flatmates, and, of course, some of them were at home with their wives and children. For the men who were deeply closeted the Garda investigation terrorised them. Once they had been paid a visit, once they had gone to the local Garda station or were invited up to Dublin to Pearse Street Station 'to assist with enquiries', their boss, co-workers, or family were freaked out that these men were not merely suspects in a murder hunt but deceptive gays to boot. There weren't many options open to them, especially if they had been pressured into naming the men they had sex with. So they emigrated to London, to New York, to be unknown in large cities. Having been betrayed and having betrayed in turn, these Irish gay men were wary about making friends. They kept their anonymity more strictly. But they were shortly to find their silent arrival coincided with the stealthy advent of AIDS. I met a number of Irish men in New York who had emigrated between 1982 and 1983, and by that time many were HIV positive.

In June 1990 John Kerrigan, Terri and I travelled down to join the Irish Lesbian and Gay Organisation (ILGO) contingent in New York for its first outing at the Gay Pride parade. Terri actually seemed to like John. He was 'mature,' she said. We tucked in behind the ILGO banner and, from the moment we set off down Fifth Avenue with the bland banner announcing ourselves as the Irish Gay and Lesbian Organisation, we attracted an amazing reaction. There were exuberant shouts, cheers, whistles and ringing applause, well above the already loud decibels of the enthusiastic onlookers. ILGO was causing quite a stir. Apparently it was entirely surprising to New York that such an organisation existed. There were people jumping over the barriers to join.

'Are you Irish? Are you really Irish? My boyfriend's Irish! Seán! Seán! Come over here! These guys are really Irish!'

Lesbians who had left Ireland in every decade since the 1940s were helped to clamber over the barriers, many of them weeping, they came with their girlfriends and friends and started to walk down the Avenue with us.

'All my grandparents are Irish! I can't believe this!'

'My mom is from Cavan, she says I'm to say nothing to our family back home. Wait until I tell her this. Wait until she sees these photographs!'

It was a long parade route and a number of the early 1980s exodus who joined in met men they had last seen in Bartley Dunnes, or The Bailey, or Le Chateau, on the docks of various Irish cities and towns, or around Phoenix Park or The Gym sauna.

Friends who were caring for a guy who was in a wheelchair, undoubtedly with AIDS, followed ILGO for blocks and got the crowd to insist they move the barriers to allow him enter the avenue and join. As we continued down the long parade route, the cops began to assist in moving the barriers on the sidewalks as there was a continuous crush of those who wanted to come through. ILGO became hundreds and hundreds strong, there must have been a thousand, most in tears, by the time we reached the end. It was the biggest gathering of Irish queers, ever. Terri had sobbed most of the way down the avenue. I held her hand. I wasn't crying, I was grinning. This was a movement, a revolution, now this turn had happened the world had changed, and it was beautiful.

ILGO applied to walk in the New York St Patrick's Day Parade in 1991, because that would also be wonderful. Terri couldn't believe how stupid the idea was but I wasn't the only naive eejit who was surprised when ILGO was denied entry to join in the parade with their organisational banner. However, one of the Manhattan branches of the Ancient Order of Hibernians (AOH) invited ILGO to march with them behind its banner. I wanted to swell the ranks of ILGO, so I got a bus from Boston to join them. Terri wouldn't go and she begged me not to go.

'Someone is going to be killed,' she kept saying.

I had got used to ignoring Terri by then. I went anyway and didn't even feel guilty, in fact I had to hide my exasperation when Terri said: 'Gom! Gom! I don't want you to die!'

I knew it was going to be fine. New York's first African American mayor, David Dinkins, was also going to march with the AOH group, which included ILGO. It was important to be there. It was going to be a great day.

That parade was hell. Walking the long route down Fifth Avenue on that day was hell. The New York St Patrick's Day Parade is deadly serious and it remains the world's single largest ethnic celebration. It goes on for hours, around 150,000 people march and over a million onlookers are said to line the parade route. It is televised live in all its martial tedium and has been annually rattling through Manhattan since the mid-eighteenth century, and in 1991, I can tell you that New York St Patrick's Day parade generated hell.

For hours the crowd screamed at ILGO and threw horseshit and pizza slices and beer cans at us, and they lobbed bananas at the mayor.

'AIDS! AIDS! AIDS!' they yelled in triumph. 'Shame! Shame! Shame!' was their furious curse of disgust. 'Mayor Dinkins, one-term mayor!' they chanted, not as a threat but as a promise they were to see fulfilled.

I couldn't tell if they were all drunk on beer or on hate. Perhaps it was a potent cocktail of both. They looked like my brothers. They looked like my sister, my cousins, my neighbours, my school friends. They were Irish, American-Irish, but Irish nonetheless. They were young and old, male and female, and they jeered, swore, raged, mocked and screamed at the Irish queers.

'Go home!' they screamed, as if Irish queers' home was not shared with them.

'Go home!' they yelled, as if anyone would ever have left home if it was not already a place where hope was a scarce commodity.

I made myself smile and wave in that wrist-swirling, vaguely dismissive manner of the British royal family. It was the closest I could get to answering back. The worst moments were standing stopped at the intersections of the streets that sliced through the canyon walls of skyscrapers, where the funnelled winds stripped what skin we had exposed. It was in those moments, while we were standing still, that I couldn't help but notice the blanched faces of fellow queers among the screaming heads of the onlookers. One dyke walked for blocks shadowing ILGO's progress from the sidewalk, I caught glimpses of her every now and then. How did I know she was lesbian? Well, lesbians always recognise their own kind. That magic power is called gaydar. Twice I saw the pain in young sissy boys as they stood watching ILGO, surrounded by their family members. My gaze fell on a tomboy girl and we nodded to each other. Her mother gave her a reactive thump and I tried to pretend I was nodding to someone else.

Afterwards, when it was all over, I took the bus back to Boston. I kept nodding, replaying that look of recognition with the young tomboy, nodding again in pretence towards her mother that it was someone else I recognised who stood further back in the crowd. All the other bus passengers seemed to be asleep, but my pale nodding head haunted me, reflected in the beaded rain on the coach's window while the interstate traffic flashed by.

# 19
# You Spin Me Round
# (Like A Record)

I became a stalwart of the Boston chapter of ACT-UP, exhausting myself in a dervish of activities but mainly working with the Treatment and Data affinity group. The work was constant, and even when I was over with Clara, I was answering the phone to fellow activists and working late into the night there after Clara was in bed.

Working diligently on ACT-UP's treatment and data campaigns was not without its rewards. I had a facility for understanding badly written medical literature and summarising it to make it comprehensible for a wide audience. I worked on teams focused on education programmes and learned how to conduct surveys and interviews to gather data that would be respected as reliable. But none of it, none of it, felt enough. It never felt like I was doing enough. Legions died while my comrades and I tried to shatter the wilful ignorance that buttressed the powerful.

However, ACT-UP also did spectacular, life-affirming, exhilarating, creative, direct actions that sustained me. I travelled fairly frequently to New York and D.C. for die-ins, political funerals, media jamming. I loved our joyful, sexy, wild parties, where those who could still dance danced through the rattling of pill boxes and in the company of so many fighting to live. We laughed because for some of us there would be no tomorrow. But there was this glorious now, a space and time for us that we had created together, and we relished every beat. I was there. I saw it all.

The letter-writing between Jenny and me continued unabated all through my activism and my failing studies. Jenny decided that she didn't like lecturing. She had started to do film reviews, initially for Scottish newspapers and then as an acerbic commentator on a late-night BBC TV arts show broadcast from Edinburgh. Suddenly, in the summer of 1990, she left university life and Scotland, she moved to London and moved in with Cyril, but only while she was trying to find a flat of her own. Her relationship with Cyril, as she described it in her letters, seemed to be more 'off' than 'on'.

Cyril seemed to have forgotten his student enthusiasm for co-ops and the end of capitalism. He had an esoterically precise and lavishly lucrative job in the City of London and he lived in a big house in a beautiful square in North London which had a library room for Jenny. They had a key to the private park, shared with their neighbours, who lived in the other large houses that encircled the leafy park with its grass tennis courts behind ornate iron railings.

When I wrote back, I said that I'd thought Cyril was a class of a socialist economist and was into co-operatives. Jenny replied:

> *Oh Cyril had a leftish socialist phase in college but I think that was to get rows going and maybe to worry his father (if his father ever took notice). Cyril says that people try out being different people in college and that's how he rationalises my lesbianism – he's wrong of course but he remains entirely incredulous that he might ever be wrong.*

I was very grateful that Terri had never met Jenny, and that I had always managed to barely mention Jenny to her, so Terri never knew Jenny might in any way be someone who pulsed along my veins. I often had to remind myself that by every rule, legal and moral, I was technically faithful to Terri, but I began to face up to the fact that in what I felt for Jenny I was betraying Terri.

Even though I partied hard with the radical faeries and the fags and dykes of ACT-UP, I never took another woman except Terri into an embrace that ended in a kiss. I remained faithful even after I learned Terri had had sex with an ex, or 'just drunk sex' as Terri called it. The truth was I didn't feel jealous – and of course my lack of jealousy upset Terri a lot. The care and attention that should have gone to Terri went to the friends I ran around after, particularly Sully and John Kerrigan. I understood I was responsible for the horror in which Terri found herself: to be utterly in love with someone who was so undeserving. I knew I was guilty. I was hiding a secret from Terri: I was entirely in love with someone else and I was hiding that fact, but I knew that Terri could sense it. I just hoped that Terri would give me the time to figure myself out so I would not continue to be an ongoing disappointment.

Perhaps the most perfect times I had with Terri was watching TV. We loved to curl up on the sofa and talk at the TV together. We both agreed that television was an interactive medium – of course you're going to loudly talk out your critique, assent and dissent with the TV set. The only time we were silent was 'the holy hour', as I called it: Monday (later, Tuesday) nights at 10.00 p.m. when *Cagney and Lacey* aired on CBS. When would they ever get together, we wondered? Or at least, when would Cagney realise she was lesbian and Lacey realise she was bi? When in goddess' name would they kiss?

Terri had a tough time with her family. Simply put, it was obvious that they didn't like her being around. When I was there I was able to mediate things a bit, oil to the mechanics of the situation. I was also able to assure Terri after family events and gatherings that she was not imagining things, that the slights and digs were real. Some of the exclusions by her family were petty, such as nobody taking her photo at whatever event we were at. Once, I saw them all laughingly fall into place while Terri was at the loo, 'quick, while she's not here,' to take a multi-generational photo of the entire gathered clan, dispersing when she came back out into the yard. Other exclusions were harder to bear, such as being the only sibling not invited to a cousin's wedding or a niece's Holy Communion. She did her level best not to react to the unkind mockery, but if she made any protest I saw the consensus immediately close on the line that 'Terri has ruined everything again'. Some could clearly see that she was being made a scapegoat, but they did nothing. I suppose they hoped that leaving Terri be the target, meant in that family's pecking for ranking, they wouldn't end up at the bottom of the heap. I understood she was afraid of even more derision if she introduced me as partner. I tried – only once – to tell her that closeting probably wasn't helping. I felt so sorry for her.

And I did love being with Terri, although she would ritually have meltdowns when I was due to go away to an AIDS conference in New York or D.C. She would start weeks in advance, having loud conversations with her friends on the phone who agreed it was highly suspect or inconsiderate that I was going away, and she would work herself into a crescendo of lament that I was intending to leave her 'for real'. It was exhausting, but after two years or so I eventually learned not to engage, to zip up and weather her operatic rhetorical storms. There was just one time, very early on, when I acquiesced and organised for another colleague to go in my stead to a meeting in N.Y.C. I thought Terri would be delighted, but she merely said:

'Why does it always have to be so hard, Ro? Do you get a kick out of seeing me hurt? If it was so easy for you to get someone else to go [*it wasn't by the way...*], why didn't you do it earlier?'

I heard her on the phone to her friend Cheryl later on that evening:

'All of a sudden, she's able to stay in Boston after all. That crucial meeting isn't so *crucial*.'

Damned if I did and damned if I didn't – so from then on I stuck to my guns in terms of fulfilling my travel commitments, and over the years I just learned to disassociate when she started on her spiels. They seemed to have nothing to do with me really, or else they were about making me feel wretched, but I didn't want to think too much about that possibility, so I simply didn't ponder whether Terri got a kind of satisfaction in berating me and seeing me spun out. And so we ambled on for years.

When I was about five or six years into being Terri's girlfriend, some young dyke asked me what was the secret to having a long relationship and I think I shocked her by replying 'Having a busy life and a poor memory'. But perhaps most crucially, being with Terri kept me feeling safe and on the straight and narrow, or as close to straight and narrow as a young dyke AIDS activist might be. Terri and our friends kept me in Boston, which I knew was an altogether more sober place than the wilds of New York City. I had an apprehension that if I went to live in Manhattan's East Village among the junkies and homeless, the Ukrainians, the artists, AIDS activists and the coolest dykes in the world, it would soon prove too difficult for me to find a way to stay on the ground.

Eily, Mels, Clara and the boys were all still in Boston, so that was going to be where I was rooted. They were family. Over the years, I really began to consider John Kerrigan as my brother. Whenever we were out and about on our walks around the beaches of Southie people asked if we were brother and sister and we liked to say 'Yes'. It wasn't obvious that John Kerrigan lived with shame and fear. However, shame and pride, fear and bravery were the four cardinal directions around which John Kerrigan's life spun.

John Kerrigan's bosses were content to have him work away from the office. They seemed to consider him a type of genius who must be given special privileges. John never told his bosses he had a HIV-positive diagnosis, which had, in fact, motivated his insistence he work away from the office.

Neeraj was John's first lover. That is if we were to discount the time he had sex when he visited London over the October Bank Holiday weekend in his final year at UCC. John went to Hampstead Heath then, as it was the only place he had ever heard of as a meeting place for gay men. He told me that he was so ignorant he had never heard the phrases 'cruising ground' or 'trick' and there he was with no language, no etiquette, yet he was cruising, looking for, or to be, a pick-up, a hook-up, a trick. On the heath he met a man who asked him if he wanted to go to a gay bar. John said he didn't know if he was gay and he didn't want to go to a gay pub. The man told him not to go with guys with an American accent. He brought John to a sauna and John learned there that he was definitely gay, although it was going to be well over another year before he actually kissed a man. (That always made me sad, imagine having sex for the first time but without any kisses?) So after that London adventure it was going to be a year before John Kerrigan had his first kiss with a man, and that man was Neeraj.

Neeraj was the first to develop symptoms, the first to get sick. John was still very healthy, but severely malfunctioning due to guilt and shame. He decided that he was the one who had infected Neeraj. He decided that the man he had sex with in the London sauna was from L.A. I learned again that there is no point trying to reason with the irrational.

John's self-disgust raged when he was drunk or high. Neeraj did eventually get John to stop drinking and drugging. There were times when I wondered why Neeraj didn't just break up with him, but they got through those months of madness. John stayed sober and just lived with his story that he had given a death sentence to the man he loved.

I was surprised when Neeraj moved into an apartment by himself, very close to where he had lived with John. Also, John appeared to be paying the rent so they were not split up. In fact, they seemed more immersed in love than ever. When I called around with a phallic little cactus I had got as a kind of housewarming present for Neeraj I found that John was there too. Neeraj seemed a little tired, he lay stretched out on the couch, his head in John's lap while John softly stroked his hair. The boys asked me about Clara and the latest gossip from the Boston ACT-UP chapter.

'Please! No actual activism news!' protested Neeraj as I began to tell them about an event Mels was organising. 'I just want to hear the sex scandals and love stories!'

Neeraj was in his new home less than two weeks when he took the overdose that killed him. He left a note for his parents saying he was sorry, he had fallen in love with a woman who had ultimately rejected him, he wasn't able to focus on his studies, he had fallen too far behind to ever catch up. He thanked them for being the best parents in the world.

John met Neeraj's parents and sister at the airport and guided them through the arrangements for the cremation. They were very touched that John had managed to find someone to chant Hindu prayers for the dead. John begged Russ and Eily and Mels not to come to the cremation and said we would organise another memorial service for Neeraj. I was surprised John invited Neeraj's parents and sister back to his apartment after the ceremony, but that was nothing compared to my shock at Neeraj's mother offering congratulations on my engagement to John when he was driving us all back to his flat in his big black Chevrolet SUV. ('So butch!' Neeraj would tease whenever they climbed into that vehicle.) I caught a flash of John's fearful gaze in the rear view mirror. 'OK,' I silently nodded at him, 'I'll do this.'

It was awful to see the apartment utterly stripped of the plethora of framed photographs of John and Neeraj. The Tom of Finland poster in the bathroom was gone, the video collection was nowhere to be seen, the piles of magazines on either side of the sofa were stripped of all of the fashion, fitness and gay titles. Even the original poster for the movie *Funny Girl* had been removed from the kitchen. I couldn't speak. Neeraj's lovely parents thought I was very shy. They said Irish and Indian cultures had the same high value placed on family. I couldn't say a word. His sister Sunita also said nothing but trembled slightly throughout the visit. She looked even more beautiful than the photographs Neeraj had shown me. When we silently embraced as they were leaving, I thought she was about to say something, but she held back whatever she was about to utter with a shake of her head.

John stayed remarkably healthy. That is, he stayed physically healthy even with binge drinking, chain smoking, tsunamis of self-loathing and carrying a grief that was utterly palpable but totally unarticulated. He kept asking me to marry him.

'You can get legal that way, you'll be able to inherit the flat, my money, you can look after Russ then.'

'Stop it, John. You can live with AIDS. People are actually living with AIDS. It's not an automatic death sentence. There will be treatments,' I said, and I believed that. 'There will be a cure,' I said, though I was never sure, yet that was what we had to demand, to hope for, that had to be the horizon we sailed towards.

John would snort, get pissed off and huffy and a week later would ask me to marry him again. I wouldn't do it. I knew he would kill himself soon after.

I wanted John Kerrigan alive more than I ever wanted anything, and the news on his health was all good: he had no discernible symptoms and his T-cell count was always high. There were PWAs (people with AIDS) who were living longer than expected, who seemed to be beating the virus. Research was underway.

Eventually he succumbed to my nagging and agreed to go back home to Cork for a holiday. During the weeks John was home, his mother told me he kept having dizzy spells. She sent him to the doctor. He told her the doctor said he was anaemic and he could do with a blood transfusion. He said he would organise it when he went back to Boston, but as it was his last two days in Ireland he didn't want to waste the days he had left. He wanted to go to Fota Island where he had camped as a boy scout. He organised to meet one of his sisters there, at the new wildlife park, but he headed off early. He was walking near the train-tracks. He had his camera, it seemed to be thrown clear. They processed the film. He had taken lots of pictures of the estuary, the mud flats, Harpur's Island. Maybe he was trying to photograph the migrant seabirds? A lot of the photographs were out of focus, nothing but bright light. He must have had a dizzy spell as the Cobh train passed. It was instant. That day, 12 June 1990, was the first anniversary of Neeraj's death.

At the funeral his mother kept saying softly and proudly: 'He never gave me a day's worry all his life. Never a moment's worry. Since he had his first job at the petrol station he gave me money from his wages. He was always sending money home. He was always the perfect son.'

John Kerrigan lived and died as the perfect son.

John Kerrigan's death broke my heart.

# 20
# Smalltown Boy

All of John Kerrigan's affairs were in order. Terri took me to the reading of his will. It was in a large, bland office in one of those corporate buildings near Downtown Crossing. I would never have found my way there. I felt like I was sleep-walking. Terri was so sweet and gentle and kind with me in those immediate weeks of the aftermath. She had really liked John. He was always quite formal with her whenever he came to visit or to pick me up to go somewhere. He would ask her respectful questions and remember what she had told him the last time they had a conversation. He sent her birthday cards and Christmas cards and Good Luck cards if our softball team got into playoffs. She really liked him.

I had no tears. I was numb.

The attorney told us that John had willed his photograph album and all of his personal effects to me, and that John had made special mention that he wanted me to wear Neeraj's tuxedo jacket. Everything else went to his mother.

When I was going through his things, I found an envelope addressed to me and Russ. It was sticking out from the top pocket of Neeraj's tuxedo jacket. There was nothing but an ATM card and a note with the pin code, which said:

*All our love, Neeraj and John.* There was $148,763 in the account. Russ's father had cut off his allowance when the health insurance bills revealed that he was on AZT. Russ communicated with his father through an attorney's office in Washington D.C., 'which is as far north as my father has ever travelled,' said Russ. That attorney's office sent Russ a letter to say his father noted he had AIDS, he was sorry that there was no cure, and he hoped Russ would not suffer too much nor for too much longer. He said he was cutting off funds as he did not want any 'vultures' to continue to draw on the money after Russ's 'demise'. He added that it would not be 'honourable' for Russ to visit home to inflict the signs of his disease on his mother and sister's memories.

I was shocked to read the letter, but Russ merely said: 'He was a good father when I needed a father.'

Russ lived on John Kerrigan's money for another two years.

In the end, it seemed Russ lasted a long time, he nearly made it to thirty years of age. He became wise, or perhaps it was the long illness that allowed everyone to notice how wise he always was. Even when he was patently dying, everyone who spent time with Russ left him feeling happier in themselves and with the world. The most detailed memory I have of Russ is at a party in a beautiful Victorian brownstone house in Boston's South End. It's September, but the night is warm, and Russ is standing on a small balcony. His central IV line in his chest makes a little bulge under his immaculate white shirt, he is wearing a dark purple silk dickie-bow, his beautiful face is marred with KS lesions, his hair and skin and frame are thin and old both from the toxic drug AZT and the virus that it is trying to poison. He looks as if he's 102 years old, but he's smiling. As ever, he's smiling. Our song started to play, the song where we would seek out and find each other to dance with if we were not already swirling, eyes closed, around each other.

'This is a song for all ages. Dance for me, Rose Marie.'

It was the Bronski Beat version of our favourite Donna Summer song. We had given each other the same Christmas present in 1984: the album *Age Of Consent*. So I danced for Russ and pretended that he was strong enough to dance with me in the ways we had loved to dance in so many queer spaces in New York, Boston and P-town. I closed my eyes and swirled around, mouthing the words of 'I Feel Love/Johnnie Remember Me'.

When I peeped through my lashes I could see him, with his eyes closed, swirling his hand and arm, singing along.

Clara and Russ died within weeks of each other. Russ went first. His tiny apartment in the South End had no air conditioning. He claimed Yankee summers held no challenge for a boy from Louisiana and saunas were his spiritual home. The window of his bedroom opened onto a fire escape, and I sat out there for most of what was to be his last day. The sun had set behind the dense cloud of that oppressively hot day and the night was swaddled with damp heat. Russ had been dying for days, breath gurgled through his racked frame, he had stopped speaking, his eyes were mostly closed. There were three fans moving hot air over his body. The fans couldn't seem to cool the air, but they took some of the damp moisture out of the room. I sponged him down with iced water and softly patted him dry with a baby towel. I had lollipop sponges I dipped in cold mint tea and gently ran inside his mouth and tongue. I had to keep the tin of Vaseline in his tiny, noisy fridge and with my little finger I dabbed that Vaseline on the parts of his lips that had not already burst. I didn't allow anyone else to touch him. I knew he was intent on dying. A few weeks earlier I had noticed that the framed postcard of the painting of Icarus that had always been on his beside locker was now gone. When I asked him, he had said, 'I sent it as a farewell card to Mama.'

Sitting on the fire escape, I could hear the sounds of the Boston Pops Orchestra playing an open-air concert to an appreciative audience on the Charles River Esplanade. I was listening to the epic swell and battlefield bang of the '1812 Overture' when I realised something had happened inside the room. I clambered back inside and saw that the crowd of people who had been coming and going and hanging around for the previous months, weeks, and especially the last number of days, had now all gone. Only Mels was left in the room and the dull laboured air had changed: it was now light, soft and full of trembling. Russ was sitting up in bed, full of life and smiling. He seemed to be smiling in greeting. He was looking into the distance, as if watching people who were coming from over the brow of a faraway hill. I had the distinct impression of the room expanding, being flooded with joy.

'Wonderful,' said Russ.

He lay back down, closed his eyes.

I didn't look at Mels, I wasn't able to. The gurgling of breath continued and I don't know when it stopped because I left Russ with Mels to get on with dying in his small bedroom, which was thick with spirits who brought such radiance and flooding peace. I knew as long as I stayed beside him he would linger to keep me company, and I knew he had to leave and go to … wherever. I crawled out the window and sat on the highest step of the fire escape. Over the rooftops of the South End and Back Bay I could see the upper reaches of fireworks. I had forgotten it was the Fourth of July, Independence Day. I sat outside on the steps of the fire escape and watched as the fireworks exploded and fizzled and the orchestra, far off on the riverbank, played in accompaniment to the thumps and thuds of the exploding colour. Eventually, Mels was there too, she sat below me, holding on to one of my legs, sobbing. I was too exhausted to move, to move down next to her, to comfort her.

Towards the end of August we took Russ's ashes to P-town. MichaelC had organised everything. In the morning we went to the Unitarian church for Eily and Mels's re-commitment ceremony (the third of many they would go on to have). After lunch we went back to the church for a hilarious and sad and packed remembrance ceremony for Russ and Joni, which was organised by the Club Café staff where they had worked. A troupe of gay synchronised swimmers, in monumentally flowery swimming caps and silver lamé bathing costumes, scattered some of Russ's ashes in a surprisingly solemn ritual at Herring Cove. Afterwards, we all went back to the Boatslip for cocktails and a tea dance.

MichaelC had organised with the current renters of the boys' rickety house on the dock to let Eliy, Mels, me, Terri and him and his boyfriend, Mark, have a private hour there from 11.00 p.m. until midnight. He brought the old sign the boys had hung on the gate: a skull wearing a pink pirate hat and eye-patch with pirate crossbones. I tried to sing a 'A Case of You' but largely failed, so the six of us hummed our way to the end. MichaelC, Mark, Terri and Eily cried a lot, but Mels and I were out of tears. I hadn't cried in years, not since Joel's passing.

We let some of Russ's ashes onto the wind and into the ocean. MichaelC, in his deep voice, recited the poem Russ described as being 'by that English Gentleman Faggot, W. H. Auden' and which he said was the only poem that ever made any sense.

The poem describes the painting by Bruegel the Elder that Russ loved, where everyone in the picture is just getting on and doing their thing. They may have heard a boy shout or may have heard a splash but for everyone in the picture it just wasn't important or urgent enough for them to pay any attention. Everything and everybody is turned away from witnessing the disaster.

And that's really how it was back then. The world did not deign to notice all the dying boys.

Eily and Mels drove me to BC just before the start of the semester. I needed their help to get there because I had to go and meet my dissertation committee in person to tell them that I would be dropping out of the PhD programme. I owed them that much, to show up in person to say I was quitting. They told me that, while I was terribly slow, what I had written on my thesis so far was 'stellar'. I will always remember that word. They asked what was wrong. I was surprised by the question and confused by my answer, because I said nothing was wrong, but maybe, really, that was true. I meant there was nothing wrong that could be righted. So there was nothing more to do but to get out of there, to get out of that lovely academic office, the shelves lined with double stacks of books, the art, the lamps, the plants, the coffee tray, the soft chairs. I just had to get out of there, out of the English Department in Carney Hall and across the campus, out the main gates, to the White Mountain Ice Cream Parlour where Eily and Mels were parked and waiting for me.

Eily drove while Mels held my hand. They brought me over to Clara's, where I was due to spend the night.

Clara had had a 'mild' pneumonia since the end of June. She had given us some bad scares during the summer and we had to change the rota so that someone could stay awake and be with her as she struggled so much with breathing at night, but she had recently made a significant recovery and seemed to be her old feisty self again.

'Honey, what's the matter?' You look like the shit!' she said when I arrived.

I tried to banter back: 'I'm worn out with the worry that you are going to pop your clogs, and what will I do for work then? I'll never get a gig as easy as this.'

Clara shrugged. 'Oh honey, I must have done something very bad. God has cursed me. I think I'm gonna live till I'm a hundred. Maybe even 102!'

Later in the evening, as I was about the turn out the light, she said: 'Wait honey! I wanna talk with you.' She patted her bed and got me to sit down next to her.

'Honey, tell me, what's the matter? How is Terri – is anything the matter?'

And I heard myself saying that everything was the same as ever: great. So it was just half a lie, that everything was the same as ever was true, but it wasn't great. I was just shit at being a girlfriend. I had promised to change, but I didn't know what to change into.

Clara then said: 'And your studies, Ro? Is everything OK there? Is it too hard?'

'No, it's not too hard.' Technically, that was true. I just hadn't the heart to tell her I'd quit.

'And how's my beautiful boy Russ?' said Clara, 'Is he getting worse?'

Clara had been so gravely ill in June and July there had been no way I could have told her anything then. She had recently started asking again about how Russ was doing. This time I told her the total truth, no half-lies and no withholding. 'Fine,' I said, 'he's fine.'

That was true. He was fine. He had lived a full and good life and he was done and he was gone and he was fine.

I was surprised to see tears stud Clara's eyes. She hugged me then, one of her lovely warm hugs, and I was hollow, empty, or maybe I was full, packed tight, maybe everything was frozen stuck.

'Don't stay awake on that armchair,' Clara said. 'Take your shoes off and sit up on this bed.'

And that's how I slept that night. Within minutes I was crashed out, propped up on a mountain of pillows next to Clara.

When I woke the next morning. Clara was already awake. I hadn't turned off the lights, the lamps and overhead lights still blazed in the heavily curtained room.

'I've slept the sleep of the dead,' I said.

Just two days later, Clara passed. I wasn't there. Helena Mulcahy went to make Clara a cup of tea and when she came back Clara lay smiling on her bed, propped up on multitudinous pillows. Dead.

The funeral was small, quick and lovely, just like Clara. I had been to countless funerals, but this was the first funeral where the dead person was old and had talked about being ready and wanting to die. I felt weirdly happy as the rabbi led us in the Kaddish. As I threw a handful of earth on her casket I even smiled, as I swear I could hear her voice calling, 'So long, sucker!'

Clara's family had invited all the carers to join them at a nearby restaurant. I had already made my excuses to Sophia and the grandsons because a plan had begun to form in my head. I had a long walk from the cemetery to the Green D Line stop at Chestnut Hill. Once the T reached Downtown Crossing I changed there for the Red Line. I got out at Porter Square and walked to Terri's apartment, the place where I had lived for almost eight years and had never managed to call 'home'.

I walked through the rooms as if I had never lived there, as if I was seeing the walls and the furniture for the very first time. I picked up my passport. I packed up the things that had belonged to John Kerrigan and Russ and had been entrusted to me: photograph albums, home videos, mix tapes, letters and cards they had each sent and received from Neeraj and Joni. I packed up Clara's record player that her daughter had given me and a small carved wooden box with the last of Russ's ashes. Everything fit into one medium-sized suitcase. I put on Neeraj's tuxedo jacket. The clothes and books I owned, I just left behind.

I realised, with waves of shock, that leaving Terri had been on my mind for years, ever since I first began to notice Terri sometimes pretended to be upset just to make me feel bereft. And she seemed to enjoy how horrified I was when she said I wasn't committed to loving her and putting her first. Often I just couldn't avoid the clear evidence Terri was working herself up into a lather because she was bored or hungover, or because I was just too damn content or calm or sad, and Terri didn't want that.

I walked through Terri's apartment and my legs shook with the dreadful awareness that I had been too frightened and too guilty and too confused, I had kept myself too busy to allow for the realisation to hit: I needed to break with Terri.

I phoned Aer Lingus and bought an expensive one-way flight back to Shannon, due to leave in a few hours. I withdrew the total amount of money in my bank account ($436). I wrote a cheque clearing out what was left of John Kerrigan's legacy and on my way to Logan airport I put that cheque in the mail addressed to the AIDS Action Committee at Fenway Health Center. At Logan I rang from a payphone and left a garbled message on Eily and Mels's answering machine, and that was how I left Boston.

On the plane home I wrote Terri a letter full of remorse and apology, telling her I wouldn't be returning to Boston. It was an utterly unforgiveable thing to leave so suddenly, to give such an horrific shock to someone whom I had repeatedly declared I loved. Terri always said I would leave her, and she had been ultimately proved totally correct. It was true, Terri was right, I was a total shit who didn't know what it took to be in a committed relationship, who didn't know the meaning of love.

# BALLYVOLANE

## 1992

# 21
# Hanging On The Telephone

I was back in Cork less than a week and by a minor miracle my mam and dad were both out of the house that Saturday lunchtime when Terri phoned. I woke up to the ringing phone, I listened to the answering machine click and beep and I heard my dad's voice:

'Ehhhhh. Hello! Listen. There's no one here, like. So. If you want. Leave a message and hopefully someone will take it down and tell me. Otherwise. I don't know. [Pause] Maybe try again and see if I'm in. Good luck!'

I laughed to hear my brother Mossy's voice also recorded on the answering machine message: 'Da! Da! Press the button there now! You're finished. It has to beep!'

My father's voice was recorded again: 'This is a total langer Dan of a birthday present, sure no one ever phones me.'

BEEEEP.

I went into shock when I heard Terri's voice.

'I believe this is the McCarthy household? My name is Terri! I was your daughter Ro's lover for the past eight years! But I came back to our home four days ago to find a NOTE left on the refrigerator! A NOTE! After eight years! I was YOUR DAUGHTER'S LOVER! And she just left me with a NOTE!'

I ran down the stairs, barely able to breathe in fright, as Terri's voice filled the hallway and the answering-machine tape.

'YOUR DAUGHTER EATS PUSSY! RO McCARTHY EATS PUSSY! RO McCARTHY LIKES EATING MY PUSSY! SHE LOVES EATING MY PUSSY! IT MAKES HER SOOOO WET!'

I snapped the tape out of the answering-machine, but my relief was short-lived as Terri's voice kept coming through the machine's speaker and my sister Mags slowly walked into the hallway from the kitchen and heard Terri yell:

'RO McCARTHY LIKES TO WATCH GAY MEN FUCKING. SHE LOVES TO WATCH GAY PORN. I hate that porn, but still I bought her videos for Christmas. I even bought her a Tom of Finland Calendar. She loves to watch BIG DICKS FUCKING. SHE STRAPS ON AND SHE FUCKS ME!'

I found the volume dial and turned it down.

Mags was at my shoulder, ashen-faced. 'Is that the fuckin' bitch that you've been crying about?' she said. 'The Terri wan?'

Mags picked up the receiver and got an earful of Terri in full lewd mode. She held the phone away from her for a few moments and then shouted into the phone, 'You! You're one filthy, dirty, disgusting whore!'

I could hear Terri rev to full throttle (and lewd) mode. I was going to be sick.

Mags slammed down the phone. She pulled the answering machine plug out of its socket. 'You can unplug the feckin' machine, Ro!' she said, but the phone was already ringing again. Mags stared at it for a few moments and then turned to me. 'Do you have this mad bitch's family's number back in Boston?'

'Eh, no.'

'But do you know their address?'

'Roughly.'

Mags lifted up and promptly put down the receiver, hanging up the call. She lifted the receiver again and quickly punched in four numbers.

I could hear someone say: 'Hello, International Directory Enquiries?'

Mags said, 'Hi, hello. Listen, I need to phone my aunt back in Boston.' She put her hand over the mouthpiece, 'Where does her family live?'

'Worcester,' I replied.

'She's actually in Wooster, my aunt,' said Mags to the operator. 'Yeah, Massachusetts.'

I said, 'They live in West Boylston. Her parents' names are Pat and Eva McNutt.'

Mags's eyes spoke volumes.

'West Boylston is the street name, and my aunt's name is Eva, and my uncle's name is Pat and the family name is McNutt,' said Mags. 'Yeah, I know,' she said, 'tis a bit unfortunate alright. No, you're grand, that's not actually our own family name. Yeah, you're right – they should have taken the chance for a change at Ellis Island. Yeah. Yeah. I know. Sure some people are dopes.'

The operator said there were two Patrick McNutts in West Boylston, Massachusetts, and Mags said one of the numbers was probably her cousin Pat, and she would take both numbers as she wanted to let her aunt know someone was dying back in Cork. The operator, who was evidently in the job for the bird's-eye view it gave him on international personal relations enquired who was dying. He ventured it might be a grandparent.

Mags replied, 'No, 'tis my younger sister Rosemary, she's dying.'

The operator was patently shocked and very, very sorry and gave the telephone numbers, which my sister wrote down on the notepad next to the phone.

'Yeah, 'tis awful,' said Mags, a bit too brusquely I thought, given the sadness of the situation. 'Yeah, you can hear all the clicks on the line,' she said to the operator. 'The phone is ringing off the hook, yeah. People are so good. Yeah. Thanks a million. Bye.'

As soon as she put the phone back in its cradle it started to ring again.

'Mc-Fucking-Nutt!' was all she said, staring like a beagle at the phone.

She picked up the receiver and Terri went straight into a foul-mouthed description of something I considered sacred.

I sat down at the end of the stairs in the hallway of my family home and put my hands over my ears. I was dying. Mags was right. I *was* dying.

Mags let Terri go on, putting her hand over the receiver so Terri wouldn't hear Mags's enraged breathing. Mags held the phone away from her and then she put it under one of the pillows on the old kitchen chair which was called 'the telephone seat'. Mags picked up the handset once in a while, but it seemed Terri was still screaming. Eventually, Mags picked up the notepad and recited the telephone numbers. She kept loudly repeating them. I lifted my hands from my ears. Mags had Terri's attention.

'You are one vindictive, savage whore. I just thank Jesus and his Holy Mother that everyone in this house is out the door and gone to town! Now listen, girl, I have a tape of your load of shit that's on our answering-machine here and I swear to Christ that I'll be making copies of it and sending it to your boss and to West Boylston in fucking Wooster and to your fuckin' mam and dad and they're the ones who will hear it, not my mam, not Ro's mam. Two can play your game, Terri girl, but I guarantee ya – there will be only one winner!'

Mags obviously had Terri's complete attention.

'Now you know, Terri girl, that myself and my fiancé Brendan are going on honeymoon to Boston. If you give my sister any more grief, if you phone this house again or you go next to, nigh, or near our mam and dad, I'll be into your work office, and I'll be out to fucking Wooster and there won't be a langer in the joint that won't know about you, girl. And that's a solemn fucking promise, girl. D'ya hear me?'

Terri seemed to be silent.

'I think you heard me, Terri Mac Nut-Job.'

Mags put down the phone. She sighed and sat on the telephone chair and was quiet.

'Are they all like that?' she asked eventually.

'No.'

'You do know you actually are good-looking, Ro,' Mags said. 'Like, I mean, you're better looking than me, except I know how to make an effort.'

I nodded.

'You could easily get a fella. A nice fella. Like Emmet was only gorgeous.'

I nodded again.

'What happened to you, Ro? Besides the study, you were always so normal! You were happy, Ro, and look at you. You're just not happy now!'

I had told Mags all about Terri, but I hadn't told her about the boys, about ACT-UP, what it was really like being queer. That there was a real happiness, an ecstatic joy to finding your own tribe, and it was magical to be part of a movement that was about making space for all the differences to flower. That it was lonely to be away from all that possibility. I hoped I'd find that tribe in Cork and if I didn't, I would have to leave again. I just didn't know what to say, and Mags didn't ask me anything. Maybe Mags didn't know how to ask, what to ask.

'I AM happy, Mags,' I said.

'You're not, girl, you're just not!'

'Look, you're not to worry about me.'

'I can't help but worry about you!' I was shocked that Mags wailed. The McCarthys are not a demonstrative family, but I did my best to hug my sister.

Mags shuffled me off after a few moments and said: 'Promise me one thing, Ro!'

'Of course!' I declared.

'That you'll grow your hair. Just for my wedding. You can cut it all off again then, if you want. The photos will all look crap if the bridesmaid is a baldy.'

'Grand,' I said. I knew I owed her.

That wasn't quite the last of Terri. Months later, about two weeks after Mags and Brendan came back from their honeymoon (New York, Boston and Cape Cod), Pat the Post brought a package one Thursday night into Cork's gay bar, Loafers. Pat worked in the General Post Office and relished introducing himself as a 'mailman'. The other gay men (behind his back) called him Straight-Acting Pat (*Straight-Acting* was a key phrase in the personal ads Pat placed in the back pages of the *In Dublin* magazine under the name Mailman Matt). Thursday night was 'women's night' in Loafers and the little back room was reserved for dykes. I was perched in my usual spot, on the threshold between the back room and the main bar. Pat called me outside into the beer garden. It was raining and cold and Pat was anxious.

'D'you remember how, months ago, you asked me to keep an eye out if I saw a letter or package coming from Boston to your mam and dad?'

I was going to say no, but then I remembered: 'Ah Pat, I was only joking. Well, I was a bit paranoid, like. I was a bit rattled about an ex that I did the dog on, to be honest.'

'Ah fuck it, Ro. I'm after pulling a package from Boston addressed to your house, to your mam. It really is totally illegal to do that. I would get the sack, only they know I would never do something like that. That I've never done something like that before. Fuckit, I won't again either! Look, you're going to have to take it from me now and slip it into your folks' post. I can't take it back. I never would have done it but I took you very seriously, girl. You seemed fierce scared, like.'

When I saw the handwriting on the package I gasped.

'Oh Christ!' I whispered. 'Pat! Thank you!'

'What's in it, girl?' he asked.

He waited while I opened the package. It was full of photographs and a letter addressed to my mother. The photographs were largely photos of me: laughing, nearly naked on Herring Cove beach; lifting up Russ's mini kilt at Boston Gay Pride to reveal the tattoos of the two W's perfectly placed on either cheek of his ass; smiling up at Terri from a bank of pillows on a bed; photos she took of me coming out of the shower, generally a bit mortified but so happy to be desired. There were photos of me being arrested at one direct action protest or another.

Mam and Dad would have expired on the spot if they had seen those photographs. For a start, the naked snaps would have humiliated all of us. But my parents would have been terrified to have seen all the photos of my arrests: my yelling and roaring, the placards I carried, the defiance and rage on my face, being handcuffed and hauled up off the ground by four cops, being lifted into the Paddy wagons. (There was one photo of me drenched in blood. Would they be alright if I explained it was just pigs' blood?) There were a few photos of me and friends, clearly marching down Fifth Avenue, clearly in front of St Patrick's Cathedral, with our T-shirts off, no bras to be seen either, with tiny pieces of masking tape over our nipples and we're laughing and pointing to the long line of cops in riot gear.

There would be no way to convince Mam and Dad that there was a delicate choreography to being arrested for civil disobedience in the States: this was the free speech thing they kept talking about; it was a dance, a performance of sorts; that there was a whole team of people behind the protestors, including lawyers; all that happened was a couple of hours in jail and a quick appearance before a judge, who would sentence us to do community service with some charity or group associated with the cause they were championing. My dad had been promoted all the way through to being an inspector in the Guards. He wouldn't believe that all that civil disobedience stuff is routine work for American cops. It was a million miles from the practice of surreptitious surveillance, hard and soft leanings on people and the mutuality of swapped favours that had structured his policing career.

I finally mustered: 'I owe you big, big, big time, Pat!'

Pat was reading the letter to Mam. He held it from him at arm's length.

'God, girl. What did you to do your one? I'm sorry, like. I just started reading it and I couldn't stop, like. Jesus!'

'I don't want to read it, Pat.'

'You're right, girl.'

Pat took out his Zippo lighter: 'I'm happy to send it into ash here and now if you like?'

I nodded, and soon the letter was curling into flame. Pat put it into an ashtray on one of the tables and we sat on a bench in the dark beer garden, the rain falling softly, and together we watched the densely typed pages turn black. Soon there was a soggy mess of ash lying in the ash tray and floating around the table. We were silent. Pat lit a cigarette.

Eventually he said, 'D'you know, I can ask one of the supervisors to pull any more letters. He's a married fella and a closet case and I won't have to tell him anything. Just say there's "nuisance post", you know? It happens occasionally, that we're asked to pull stuff. For the Guards, like. I can just ask anyway.'

I could say nothing.

Pat shuffled up the photos, which were spilled out on the table. The light rain was beading on the glossy images of my former life.

'There's some nice photos of you there, Ro,' Pat said.

I shook my head. 'I don't want them. I never want to see them again.'

'Grand, girl.' he said.

We sat outside in the fizzling rain while Pat patiently burned the photos, which curled and charred and drifted in black whispers around the small garden and its high stone walls.

# CORK & LONDON

## 1993-1997

# 22
# A Case Of You

It took a while for me to stop feeling jumpy about Terri. It was the first anniversary of Russ's death and I was in my mam's back garden, gathering handfuls of mint to make a julep to toast his memory, when I realised it was nearly a year since I had left Boston and Terri hadn't arrived in Cork, nor sent any more letters, nor made any more phone calls, and she was unlikely to do so now. I smiled. I couldn't think of John Kerrigan without feeling there was a stake of pain shooting through me, yet a glimmer of thought about Russ always seemed to bring me gifts of one kind or another.

Mostly, people leave the countryside or small-town homes to go to big cities so they can become anonymous, become new. I left Boston and New York to return to Cork and sink back into the inconsequential life of Ro McCarthy, where there was nothing expected of me, which was just as well as I had nothing to give. My new/old life was more comfortable and more liberating than anonymity and the promise of reinvention. I rarely mentioned 'the States', and if I did it was in some oblique way. Hardly anyone thought to, or knew how to, ask about what my life was like 'over there' and the few who tried to enquire were met by deft evasions. People soon forgot I had ever been away.

I settled into being 'a bit odd, but harmless, nice really, Ro McCarthy *(d'you know she's a lesbian?)*, mad for reading books, talks a bit like one too!' Nobody I knew was trying to complete a PhD or had even thought about such a thing, and I liked it that way. I settled in to fading into the background, being a bit overlooked and sometimes even forgotten, and I began, myself, to forget. I forgot mostly everything. But I never forgot Jenny.

Even after I moved back to Cork, Jenny and I still wrote weekly letters to each other. We wrote about everything except what we felt for each other. Jenny once wrote: *I don't know if I like or dislike the ways in which my English reticence is matched by your Irish evasion.* I smiled. For such avid letter writers, we were poor communicators.

In the first few years I was back in Cork, I periodically got a Slattery's coach service, leaving at 4.00 a.m. from Patrick's Quay, behind The Metropole Hotel, which would board the ferry in Rosslare and cross into Pembroke in South Wales and trundle its way into England and on to London. The constant cigarette smoke from the other passengers made me feel nauseous, but that twenty-four-hour round trip journey to see Jenny was totally worth it, even just to see her for a late afternoon and evening before it was time to get the return coach back. We considered it best to meet for only a few hours. Although we only referred to it obliquely in our letters, we always had to factor in what Jenny called a *hangover effect*. The hangover effect was a kind of raw longing that often took a few weeks to dull, marked in the letters only by euphemistic references to *reticence and evasion*.

I thought I should help by writing out what we were to each other. I wrote:

> *There ought to be a more accurate, handy noun, a more correct label than 'friend' for what we are to each other. We're part of a certain group of people who*

*could do with a word which encapsulates that long-term angled relationship where two are bound together by an awareness that they might have been lovers, and if they don't remain vigilant and maintain a kind of gap, that there could be awful slips; slips that would crash and wreck each other and the precious people around them. We share a creaky, chancy vulnerability with each other, an attraction that we can't dissipate or change and that keeps pulling us towards one another. We have a beat between us that is not simple, not rhythmic, but it's strong and compelling, and it keeps moving through us in spite of various attempts on both our parts to scourge its pulse and momentum.*

There was a delay in reply from Jenny. When she did write, she didn't respond to my suggestion we needed a different word other than 'friend', and I didn't broach the subject again. We continued to send letters again.

A few months after my attempt to address and name the feelings between us, William, one of the handsome young barmen in Loafers, sent word that there was an urgent message from my friend Jenny. She had phoned the pub, hoping that I would be on one of my shifts working there, but had to make do with leaving a terse and precise message with William: *R.M., please come and see me, as quickly as you can.*

'She got me to transcribe it exactly and read it back to her. She was very fussy about the commas,' said William.

'She is very careful about commas,' I said.

So of course I went, that very night at 4.00 a.m. on the Slattery's coach. There was a mad pro-life activist at the bus stop who was trying to pass photographs of fake abortions to women getting on board. The rain was lashing as we puddled our way onto the coach and it got worse as we made the long journey to the port in Rosslare. It was so stormy that we expected the ferry would be cancelled and myself and my fellow passengers stretched out on the slatted wooden benches in the embarkation area. However, about an hour later we were roused: there would be a crossing. They really should have delayed that ferry further. There was a stench of vomit and moans of fear as we pitched our way slowly across a heaving Irish Sea.

I usually met Jenny in the café of the National Portrait Gallery. I had never been near the neighbourhood of the house she shared with Cyril. By 8.00 p.m. I was finally walking towards Jenny's address, along a quiet, tree-lined street. And soon I was at the house she lived in. I stood at the wrought iron gate and looked at the impressively large Edwardian, two-storey-over-basement home. Across the short stretch of lawn ran a black-and-white tile path to a flight of steps and a large, black, gloss front door. There appeared to be just one lit room, on the first floor, which revealed book-lined walls and a writing desk with a lamp. I could see no other sign of life. I stood holding the metal spikes of the gate, trying to gather my courage. This was awkward. I was acutely aware that there could have been some kind of misunderstanding. Yet again I pulled out the message that William had carefully transcribed: *R.M., please come and see me, as quickly as you can.* I had Jenny's phone number, although I had never phoned her. I would go and find a phone box somewhere in this classy suburb and phone her from there, but then I heard that lovely voice say:

'R.M.!'

She was silhouetted by a street light. Her lovely curls were shorn, her hair looked like the fleece of a newborn lamb. We stepped together, our foreheads lightly touched and we stood there, holding hands. We had never been closer.

'I hoped you would come.'

'Of course I would!'

'R.M., I'm pregnant.'

I was silent.

'Unexpectedly, of course. There never seemed any need for birth control as sex is a rather rare event.'

I couldn't speak and her tears were quiet. I touched one of her tears with my finger and brought it to my own cheek.

'I have always wanted children. I don't quite know why. Mothering is not a strong tradition in my family.'

'You will be such a good mother, that is one very lucky foetus.'

'I always imagined we would, some day, in our own slow way, be eventually together.'

'Same.'

Jenny smiled and said: 'What shall we do?'

'Well, can you really give up all this?' I said, gesturing to the house and the street.

'I really don't know,' she said, with an honesty that pierced me.

'I don't see how you can,' I said slowly. 'But you do know, don't you, that—'

'HEY!'

Jenny and I pulled apart from each other and it was Cyril who was jogging towards us, wearing expensive running gear, sweating. I don't know how I knew it was him, but somehow I did. His shapely head was shaved to a bristle.

'Hullo?' he said to me with a studied politeness.

'This is Rosemary McCarthy,' said Jenny quite formally, and she found and held my hand again.

'Ah!' said Cyril.

After a pause he said, 'My competition,' with an assured smile that revealed he assumed victory.

'There's no accounting for taste,' I said evenly, very glad that Jenny held my hand fast.

I was acutely aware of how awful I looked: no sleep, no shower, reeking of second-hand cigarette smoke, with patchily cut short hair and sodden clothes. I looked out of place on the beautiful street in my denim jeans, black jumper, old leather jacket, with my trusty knapsack. I felt a kind of shame as I stood in front of Cyril in my leaking Doc Martin boots. I hoped he couldn't tell I was wearing plastic bags over my socks. I could feel the mark of Jenny's tear drying on my cheek.

'How are you, my love?' Cyril asked Jenny brusquely. 'Feeling any better?'

'Yes, fine.'

'She's had some tummy trouble these past few days,' Cyril announced to me proprietarily.

The three of us stood in an awkward silence.

'Coming in, then!?' said Cyril to Jenny in more of an announcement than a question.

'In a mo,' she said.

'You too, Rosemary, you are welcome to stay,' said Cyril.

I admired how Cyril pitched the invitation. While the words seemed to be issuing a welcome, his tone managed to convey that he would like me to promptly slink off to whatever hole I had emerged from. I was tempted to call his bluff but instead said:

'I'm grand, thanks, Cyril, that's very kind of you, but I'm staying with friends over in Hackney and they're expecting me.'

'You're "grand" are you?' said Cyril, pointedly smiling. 'Hackney? I see! Very well, nice to meet you then. Do you plan to stay with us another time? We would enjoy your visit.' And I understood that he wanted me to toddle off to whatever dyke squat would have me in Hackney and never trouble his sight again.

'Need a shower,' Cyril murmured to Jenny. He nodded at me and opened his heavy wrought-iron gate and bounded swiftly up the path and high steps into his house.

Jenny was silently weeping again. We stepped together and held each other close.

After a while I said, 'Jenn, love, choose me if you can bear being poor. I'll disappoint you in many ways, because that's inevitable, but in all the big ways I'll stay true.'

'We'll be poor?' said Jenny with surprising excitement.

'Well – neither of us earns much, so we'll be poor for at least a while, and possibly always, although I can try hard to earn better money.'

'OK!' she said.

'Being poor is not as much fun as they let on it is,' I said, laughing, feeling ridiculously happy and very, very scared.

She kissed me, holding my face and closing her eyes. Eventually, I closed my eyes too and it was everything, more than I had ever imagined.

'Amazing, amazing, amazing,' she whispered in between kisses.

We staggered in towards the bushes growing through the wrought-iron railings. I felt my heart and breath tumbling over inside me, I was flooded with love, beaming bright expansion.

Jenny pulled at my small rucksack and jacket – I shrugged them off as she wanted. She pulled at my jeans waistband and found my shirt under my jumper. She pushed her hands up under my shirt and T-shirt and found my breasts.

'No bra, good!' she whispered.

Her fingertips delicately shook on the tips of my nipples. I thought I might faint. And we were kissing again.

One of her hands left my breast and grabbed one of my hands which she brought under her skirt, I could feel heat, wetness. I was stoned but something was wrong, I knew it.

'Woah! Hang on!' I said, slightly pulling away, reluctantly withdrawing my hand a little. 'Not here. Not like this! We need time, a room, our own place. I want slow love. We deserve that.'

We steadied ourselves. We stopped kissing but held each other tight. I was surprised to be an inch or two shorter than Jenny. I had always assumed I was taller.

Jenny shuddered. 'I want you,' she said simply.

'You've actually got to say goodbye to Cyril first. This might get very messy otherwise.'

'I am always surprised at your clear good sense,' Jenny said. She started weeping again.

'I've been so ill with morning sickness and I have not slept much this past week.'

I kissed the tears on her cheek.

'I will tell him tonight. I can move my things to the house in Somerset. Will you come and find me there?'

'Of course.'

We had one final long kiss. It was physically painful to stop holding her and step back. We stared at each other.

'I love you,' we said in unison. It was a seal, a bond.

I picked up my jacket and knapsack without looking again at Jenny. If I looked at her, I would never leave. I turned and walked away and in spite of longing to, I never looked back.

I walked the miles back to Trafalgar Square through the night for the Slattery's bus with the incongruous sign *Cork & Tralee*. Nobody was expecting me in Hackney. I had to get back home in time for my next shift in Loafers. I was elated and terrified and remained that way for days.

A few evenings later, I was opening up Loafers at 6.00 p.m. and I could hear the phone ringing as I fiddled with the locks. I knew it was Jenny. The phone kept persistently ringing as I stood before it. I eventually answered.

'R.M.?'

'Hi, Jenny.'

'I am afraid I can't choose you.'

I really don't know what she said next, or if I said anything at all. A letter I received a few days later spelled it all out very clearly.

> *I don't think I would be good at being poor. I have no practice and, I think, very little aptitude. I just don't know how it could be done. When I imagine being a mother, I imagine a life of plenty.*

*I also did not imagine how upset Cyril would be. I thought he was rather more serious about a lover he has had for a while. Someone quite unsuitable, but still. He cried and cried which was quite alarming. He wants to be a Father. He really does. And it is technically, in some respects, his child. He went on about maintenance and visitation rights and spoke about lawyers. It was all rather grim.*

*The morning sickness has been lasting all day, for a fortnight now, and I haven't been sleeping at all well, which is not to make excuses. I know you would stay true in all the important ways, always. You are the freest person I know, and the bravest and the kindest. If I was to choose you, I would become a much better person, and be more free. But I don't want really to be a better person and I don't even want more freedom than I already have. I want myself and this child growing within me to be safe. More than anything I want safety. I will stay with what I know.*

*And most of all, I know that I can't promise not to disappoint you, and not just in the small ways but in the big ways too. You see the best in me and I think you bring the best in me to the fore, but I am much more venal and a coward than you can imagine. Ultimately, I cannot promise to stay true.*

I read the letter through quickly and then got to work setting up the pub for the night. We were busy. It was past midnight when I sat on the humpbacked Clarke's bridge on my way home from work. The River Lee whispered over the nearby weir as I re-read the letter. I made my way back to my bedsit flat and opened the window. I lay on my bed fully clothed, staring at the ceiling. I felt I was tumbling, round and round and round. I got up and sat by the window and watched the sky. I wished I hadn't forgotten how to cry. I thought the tumbling feeling would go or it would be easier, the tumbling feeling, if I was able to cry.

Letters were somewhat more intermittent after that, especially after the baby, Emily, was born. Two more children, Katherine and Gilbert, arrived in relatively quick succession.

# SOMERSET

# 2006

# 23
# Blue

There was one, and only one, occasion when I went to visit Jenny, Cyril and the children, and that was when I joined them in their cottage in Somerset for a weekend during the summer in the early years of the new millennium.

When I arrived on Friday evening, Cyril had a brutal hangover he couldn't seem to cure, yet he got plastered again. Both he and Jenny drank pints of champagne before turning to dusty bottles of French red. They declared themselves impressed that I wasn't drinking, but I knew they were merely being polite. I knew I was being a bad guest: it's no fun to be getting pleasantly sloshed yet have to relate to someone who is demurely sipping. But it made my stomach queasy to see the unthinking speed with which Jenny and Cyril downed the drink – they hardly swallowed, they just poured it down their gullets. I fought hard not to close up and zone out. I maintained a steady patter of questions directed at Cyril and Jenny about their house. The lamps in the room cast more shadow than light. I couldn't actually see their faces as they talked across each other for nearly two hours about the renovations and extensions they had made and intended and were still debating: they seemed to have a precise chorale of disagreements. I counted down the minutes until I could politely find my way from the sitting room through the rambling tight corridors and into bed.

The next day Jenny was up early and seemed as fresh as a daisy, while Cyril was again as sick as a dog. So Cyril lay on one of the big couches in the larger sitting room while Jenny and I took the children on what turned out to be a day-long picnic. We had a small meadow and a riverbank to ourselves. That day was idyllic. Jenny and I lay alongside each other, chatting under the shade of a giant willow tree. We moved in and out of the river with the children, we played rounders and fed them. After lunch Jenny and the children and I lay on the rugs and they demanded I make up a story on the spot. I mashed what I could remember of classic Irish myths and legends with the freedom of knowing none of my audience had ever heard about the characters and tales. I started with the Children of Lir, with Fionnuala and her brothers.

'Fionnuala!' giggled Katherine. 'That's a silly name!'

'Your Mummy laughed at that name too, when she first heard it,' I replied.

'A silly name for a silly woman,' said Jenny sleepily. The rosé she'd had with lunch seemed to be wiping her out. She curled behind and put her arm around me, pulling me towards her and tucking into my back. 'Only silly women let you go.' I could feel her warm breath on the nape of my neck.

The children nestled in around us and I continued telling stories. My audience fell asleep and soon so did I. All of us slept deeply and didn't begin to wake up until the shade slid and the hot sun began to inch along our exposed skin. Jenny and I rearranged our camp further into the canopy of the willow and began to cool off again in the shallow river. We didn't think to head towards home until we realised dusk was bringing mauve shadows and a slight chill.

Somehow our bodies had become aligned over the course of the day and neither Jenny nor I was surprised to find we cycled home hand-in-hand along the towpath. My bike had full panniers with all the gear and a seat with one child, Katherine, on the back. Jenny had her youngest, Gilbert, in a perilous seat where a front basket might have lodged, and her eldest, Emily, held the huge folded blankets while seated on the backer behind her. Yet somehow Jenny and I still managed to cycle and hold hands. When we needed to push the bikes up a steep bit, it hurt to have to pull apart, yet we were vigilant not to drift into holding hands after that.

Cyril was pale with anxiety by the time we came back. He said it was quite late.

I was relieved to get straight to my bedroom. I opened the window to the night sounds and lay fully clothed on the bed.

The children woke me very early the next morning and we all went downstairs where I found things in the array of cupboards to feed them a kind of breakfast while I gave them another requested instalment of the saga I had been telling them the day before. When Cyril appeared, I asked him to take me to the railway station. He drove me all the way to Bristol so I wouldn't have to wait at the local station. I was in that car for over an hour while Cyril steadily and relentlessly seemed to praise me but in fact left me feeling roundly and subtly mocked, with no grounds for protest. Cyril had a dizzying manner of asserting his supremacy by gracious self-deprecation. I had never come across this mode of total power assertion before. It was confusing at first, but I was left in no doubt Cyril would use his money, his contacts, his charisma and trusted strategies (including indefatigable stamina) to cheerfully crush me if I encroached again on his family, and he would be watchful. By the end of the car trip I had an insight into the recipe of temperamental qualities that enable certain kinds of men to establish and maintain their empires. And I knew I was no match.

I sent a perfunctory 'Thank you' card to Cyril and Jenny, but I didn't send any letter, and it didn't surprise me that Jenny took months to write, although I compulsively checked for post, sometimes a couple of times a day. A card eventually arrived, *It's been difficult R.M. All our broken hearts heal unevenly and slowly*, and there was a list of some random words about the towpath.

I never learned to stop feeling lonely for Jenny after that visit. Once or twice a year, I send Jenny a slab of fiction and a letter and a collection of cards I have written but not posted. Jenny sends me random cards occasionally, with oblique notes. Jenny rarely writes letters but when she does they give reticent news, detailed appreciation for the fiction I sent and long lists of precise questions on the state of my health and recent reading. Jenny sent me an iPhone when they were first invented and explained what Skype was and suggested we might have Skype conversations, but the iPhone is still in its box. I phoned Jenny from my folk's house to say there's no point having a smartphone when my building doesn't have WiFi. I thought Jenny seemed quite relieved. I'm sure sending over the smartphone was a quickly regretted whim. The letters and the cards that are still sometimes sent must be enough.

CORK


2015

# 24
## Don't Leave Me This Way

I keep a photograph album that records that P-town summer of 1984, it's one of my few treasures. Yet I never open the heavy, padded cover to lift the cardboard pages on the ring binder. I never look at the sun-drenched photos of the boys, the sea, the shacks and dunes, the sunsets and waving grasses. I don't need to look at the photos because those images are etched on the insides of my eyelids. When I think about the summer of 1984 I think of it as a prelude, the time before, the Garden of Eden innocence before the fall into knowledge. 1984 was long ago. Somehow I managed to get carried along with time as it flowed and I managed to garner some knowledge. Everywhere I could see how power worked to maintain those on top while keeping many on the margins and pushing some beyond the edge. In the second decade of the new millennium, in 2015, I was a woman in late middle age, a very different person from young Ro.

I am intimate with failure. I have failed at most things. I have no savings, I have never learned to drive, I don't play any musical instruments, I can't speak a second language, I haven't travelled much, I have no house plants nor pets, I have forgotten how to cook and I am an idiosyncratic dancer. I can't knit, sew, sing, draw or put up shelves. Eily and Mels had reason to call me the world's slowest house painter. I take my bike to the repair shop to get the tyres pumped. Department stores overwhelm me. I find mirrors intimidating. I don't have a social media profile or presence. I can never name more than three government ministers and there have been times when I have forgotten to vote. My nephews and nieces tell me my phone and computer are antiques. I can often take too long to reply to emails and text messages, and when I do text back, I'm told my messages are too long and too fussy with punctuation. I own a television but not the remote control that might make it work. I like listening to voices on the radio, but people familiar with me know I won't usually know anything about the match, or celebrities, or soap operas, current affairs, the tragic disasters in the news, global politics, or imminent weather fronts. Any jobs I've had, or house shares or flats I've rented, have never required me to sign a contract, so it's been largely inconsequential to anyone else if I come or go. With such a CV, it's hardly surprising I have failed to maintain what in the world is called a 'long-term relationship'.

Besides being good at failure, my most significant success is in being a good friend: I show up, I respond, I am interested, I care, I remember. I am also successfully self-sufficient, so if you have me as a friend there is the added bonus that I am not high maintenance. I am a great reader, I am very successful at that. I am an all-round great audience. I love live performances of every kind: music, plays, dance, sport. The accomplishment of the performers isn't why I'm there. I'm there because there are real people who are performing and I have yet to get tired of being grateful and surprised by people who let us join in their explorations of the beating hearts in this swirling world. I love to look at anything people call art, although I never think to judge it – it simply makes me happy that people will share the art they make in an effort to touch me, to move me. (It might also be noted, even in passing, I am a really good, if not an excellent, maker of lists.)

For the past twelve years I have been successful at keeping the same job: I work as a care attendant in a nursing home at night, twelve-hour shifts, one week on and one week off. I love my job, even if the wages aren't all that good, and even as I am constantly reminded by my mother and others that it's a 'waste' of all my years in third-level education. I love the work, I bring comfort and calm and good cheer to people in acute need of those three benefits. My work expands my heart and allows me the headspace to daydream about ideas that intrigue me. I may not be much good at writing fiction, but I am happy to be successful at having the time to read and write. For over seven years I have managed to keep the same bedsit flat, on the top floor of a house on Summer Hill North. Many may not rank a seven-year tenancy of a studio flat in Ireland's rundown second city as an achievement, but to me it feels like deep success.

I love the view I have from my flat. It sweeps down over the railway station whose tracks glisten black and mercury in a shower of sunlight after those bursts of rain which slip-jig in from the nearby Atlantic. I can see the sagging docks and the old port where the north and south channels of the river Lee meet again to flow on a wide meander nine miles down to the harbour mouth. I like to keep the window of the flat open so I can hear the sounds of the small, twisty city below; to smell the mixture of traffic and river; to daydream over the weedy walls and quiet buildings. I can hear the public address system of the railway station, which is precisely far enough away both to be heard yet incomprehensible. I am soothed by the Cork accents of the pigeons who strut around the roof by my window like men going to a hurling match, nodding their flashing pinky-purple-green heads at each other and chestily rumbling, *How's it goin', boi?!* I like to watch the weather come in on the clouds and the way the changing light changes everything. From my perch I can hear two nearby churches and a convent ring their bells, each marking the hour on a different minute, which is a quintessential

Cork experience – non-conformist independence amid staunchly loyal traditions. Sitting at my window, I feel a type of loneliness, a singular aloneness, that makes me feel secure and that the world I am in is full of possibilities. I know myself by my loneliness. This is me. This is me.

By 2014 I had an exceedingly happy life. I had plenty of time for reading, writing, going to films and chatting with friends. I had a weekly routine of shopping in The Quay Co-Op and English Market, visits to the library, rowing on Saturday mornings on the river, visiting my folks on Sundays, going to music and spoken-word gigs with the nieces and nephews. My year was punctuated by going to the Cork Women's Fun Weekend and the Listowel Writers' Festival in May, three weeks at the anarcho-feminist Women's Camp in July, which was entirely blissful, and I regularly managed to spend ten days or so most Septembers at a beach where Sappho lived on the island of Lesbos, a place I laughingly liked to call 'my ancestral home'. With my core tribe, that is about sixteen middle-aged lesbians, I celebrated the winter and summer solstices, Hallowe'en, multiple birthday parties and hikes, year-round sea swims and summer camping in east and west Cork.

And then, early in 2015, I became a junkie for canvassing on the marriage equality referendum and even I came to realise that I was having some kind of burnout. At Easter, my pal Chris declared that she was worried about my health and she persuaded me to take a holiday: to go to Connemara and visit Eily.

I arrived to Eily on Easter Saturday and even before I had brought my knapsack into the bedroom I was to sleep in, she took me into the back bedroom. It wasn't the room she usually slept in, but it was the nicest room in the house. There was a large, built-in wardrobe on the right wall, with white folding louvre doors, which took up the full width of the room. The double bed was dressed in Foxford blankets and Laura Ashley sheets and pillow cases, which matched the curtains and the shades of the bedside lamps on the pine lockers on either side of the bed. There was a deep pink carpet with strong brush marks from assiduous hoovering. There was a framed picture of a large pencil sketch with a light blue watercolour wash of a young Mels, smiling shyly, looking directly at the viewer as she leant back on Eily sitting behind her, holding her in a soft embrace. The young Eily was gazing adoringly at her Mels.

'You keep this room so perfectly, Eily,' I said weakly.

'Sure, herself would slaughter me if I let the standards drop,' Eily said cheerfully.

Eily slowly folded open the doors of the deep wardrobe – there was a space in the middle of all of the garments, which hung on the railing that ran the full width of the wardrobe, and in this cleared space sat a kitchen chair. On the back wall there was shelving, where there were neatly placed collections of shoes, soft toys, books, magazines, rolled-up posters, photo albums, vinyl records, CDs and tapes. Eily switched on a light and a fluorescent strip-bulb lit up the wardrobe space. She pointed to the chair.

'Sit down on that there and have a chat with Mels. She's been dying to talk some sense into you. But tell her everything yourself, tell her all of it. She loves the bones of you, Ro – you know she'll give you great advice.'

Eily started folding back the doors.

'I'll leave you in peace. Come out when you're done. But take your time. No rush. You know the pub stays open all hours here. Have a good chat. Here, look it, I'll turn the light out. I think off would be better.'

There was a flickering *thunk* as the fluorescent bulb cooled and a magnetic *click* as the last fold of the louvre door found its place. I sat on the chair, in the darkness, amongst Mels's clothes hanging to either side of me and with all of Mels's bric-a-brac arranged on the shelves behind, all the precious detritus of her life. I did what Eily usually advised me to do: I closed my eyes and made deep inhalations through my nostrils until – though embarrassing to admit it – until I would swear on my life I could actually smell Mels next to me. Mels was present enough for me to talk to her. It could be a group delusion of two – me and Eily – but for me that wardrobe was one of the world's most sacred, holy spaces with all of the magic of sacredness, all of the tenderness of sanctity.

That particular night, as I sat inhaling Mels, I got stuck in trying to figure out how long it had been since her death. It took me a while, but I eventually reckoned it was nearly seven years since Mels had died, two years before the civil partnership legislation was passed. Of course, the total lack of any legal structure didn't stop Eily from constantly making marriage proposals to Mels, who had an octopus's collection of rings by the time she died. As the years went on they felt more and more married to each other, deeper into being a partnership, and so they had a number of commitment ceremonies. Each ceremony marked what they felt to be a shift and a change, a deepening.

My favourite ceremony was their first, in the Unitarian Church in Provincetown on 14 July 1987. Eily's and Mels's commitment ceremonies always followed the same pattern: they celebrated their achievement in getting their lives in sync with each other, affirmed they were planning their future lives with each other and asked for help from their friends, their community, in building a shared life together. At their first ceremony Joel was already quite ill, but he was there and so were John and Neeraj, Mini and Terri, who all sobbed the entire way through. MichaelC, Russ and Joni and I could not stop grinning. We felt such delight.

Once they moved back to Ireland in 1995, to Mels's home of Bundoran, Eily and Mels stopped their commitment ceremonies. Instead, they began to talk about their wedding. Initially 'the wedding' was talked about as 'just a small do', but of course the wedding hormone attacked and their 'very simple, no major fuss at all' bash morphed into the classic Irish rural wedding: three hundred-plus guests, a weekend of activities that included a massive marquee in the garden, a full bar, a terrace of portaloos, a disco, a wedding band, a ceilí, a champagne reception with a string quartet, a full sit-down four-course meal, and a ritual comprising readings, songs, a boy soprano, an uilleann piper, two harpists, candles, hand-fastening, rings, a comprehensive series of vows and a closing kiss. They were going to combine the wedding with the blessing of their house by the parish priest of Bundoran. The plan was that once Fr Timmy had doused all of their rooms with Holy Water and led a recitation of the rosary, then they would start with the wedding.

In the fervour of their planning, they had never checked with Fr Timmy that he would segue from a house blessing into a lesbian wedding ceremony. I did raise the issue that Catholic clergy were expressly ordered not to get themselves involved in blessing lesbian or gay unions. In time, Mels made a party piece of Fr Timmy's near-death experience of choking when he realised that after blessing their house they thought he was going to oversee their wedding rituals, and that's how I became their 'high priest'.

I was deeply thrilled to perform the priestly duties for Mels's and Eily's wedding. I might even admit I came into my own. I channelled the wisdom and grace of Russ Belafonte in managing to mention, and thereby include, Mels's mother and father and some of her aunts and uncles who had refused to attend. For all my rational objections to the ludicrous posturing of weddings (etc.), I did feel honoured to be the high priest at Mels's and Eily's wedding. (I like to think these feelings are merely complex and not contradictory.)

Eily and Mels had been living in Bundoran for about nine years when Mels got the diagnosis of ovarian cancer. She was young and it wasn't a bad cancer, so the prognosis was good, according to Eily. Chances with ovarian cancers are slim, so the prognosis was bad, according to anyone who had a Google search engine.

The two of them had made a small fortune with their all-women painting crews in Boston: enough not merely to put Mels through her nursing degree but more than enough to build a house and establish a large hostel and award-winning restaurant with a popular pub in Bundoran. They had built a steroid-sized bungalow, a Texas ranch really, six miles out of town with spectacular views of the North Atlantic and with five en-suite large double bedrooms. They were both tremendously proud of the place, though Eily would make some sort of apology for the scale, 'Mels has a load of nieces and nephews, and Mam and Dad will be coming up and might live with us eventually, and hopefully Mels's parents, too.'

The hope that Mels's parents would retire to be cared for by Eily and Mels was magical thinking on Eily's part. Mels's parents were not best pleased with her return with Eily in tow. It wasn't the done thing, even in the mid-nineties: two out lesbians setting up shop and living together, without discretion or shame or by-your-leave. Eily is butch, and back then she looked a dead-ringer for the young Brad Pitt as he lit up the screen in *Thelma and Louise*. Mels was petite and a west of Ireland beauty – dark black hair and blue eyes and pale skin. Even people largely oblivious to sexual energy could sense these two were hot for each other, and what would be considered admirable for a straight couple was precisely what seemed to damn this pair: they were too materially successful and too obvious with their love for each other.

I always thought Mels's sisters and brothers might have done more to make peace, particularly as they were so happy to offload their children to Eily and Mels. Whenever I visited, there were squads of nieces and nephews around their house or being ferried by Mels and Eily in their minivan. There were lovely meals all together and everyone helped with the tidying up around the place, marking off their jobs on the roster. There were nineteen nieces and nephews and they all seemed to have a permanent berth in a cot or bunk-bed in that house. Every year Eily and Mels would bring clutches of them to Women's Camp and they always stayed the entire three weeks. I liked watching those children grow. It was a bit miraculous to see them shift and change and I loved seeing how Eily and Mels providing such shelter, both thoughtful and instinctual, protected the greenness in their growth.

There was a good showing of dykes at Mels's funeral, but something was wrong with Eily on the morning of the funeral: she couldn't sit up straight and I initially thought it was an expression of shock, but then Eily told me one of Mels's sisters had given her a tablet to help with the grief. The tablet must have been a horse tranquiliser. Eily was so badly stoned I ended up having to help her get dressed: a white shirt and black tie and black chinos, she had new black leather brogues ('Mels ordered these online for me,' she mumbled). I went out and bought her black socks.

'You're too 1980s with your white sports socks,' I told her.

Eily and Mels had been careful: there was a big life insurance payout due to cover all of the inheritance tax Eily was going to be lumped with as the sole beneficiary. There was very orderly paperwork left for the executors, me and Eily's brother, Seán. The solicitor seemed decent, but he warned Seán and me that some of Mels's sisters had already been in to see him.

As Seán, Eily and I were leaving he mumbled, 'The Gallaghers aren't too happy with their mother and father and their children not getting so much as a mention. But we're watertight. The will is an accurate record of Imelda's wishes.'

That's when Eily started her mantra, 'Sure, Mels knows that I'll be looking after her mam and dad. She knows I'll be looking after the kids. She expects that. I'll never let her down. I'll be looking after them all for her. She'll be their angel in the spirit world and I'll be looking out for them down here.'

I began to wonder whether I should suss out which sister had the strong Valium.

On the bus back to Cork after the will reading, the restaurant manager and some of the pub and hostel workers texted me to say Mels's family were taking sofas and TVs and beds from her house. Seán and I did what we could. The solicitor, in fairness to him, wrote strong letters, but those sisters and brothers of Mels were united in insisting their sister had given verbal bequests, and before long they said the furniture had been theirs all along.

It took just about a month for Eily to be bullied out of the businesses. There was obviously a plan that had been previously made and it was executed with immediate precision. Myself and a big crew of lesbians went up for Mels's month's mind mass. There was some priest, not the nice Fr Timmy but a relation of the Gallaghers, doing the honours. Eily was a wreck. All the dykes got a fright when they saw her. Her hair was turning grey, her skin was grey, she was stooped and was beyond skinny, she was a living image of the word gaunt. Afterwards, some random neighbours showed up for the gathering the lesbians had organised back in Mels's and Eily's house, but none of the Gallaghers came and most of the community stayed away. Apparently, there was a gathering back in Mels's parents' house, but Eily hadn't been told of it and none of the workers in the restaurant, pub or hostel had tipped me off. When Eily was putting me back on the bus to Cork a few days later she gave me one of her great hugs, and that was when I realised the full danger of the situation: I could feel Eily's heart shake in my own chest, Eily's blood was trembling.

I phoned Eily most days. Things were getting worse. And then the evening came when Eily asked me to come up. She had to move. Seven-and-a-half hours later I was being driven by our pal, Ruth, through the gates of Mels's and Eily's ranch house. It was the early hours of the morning, before dawn. Eily had carefully boxed up all of Mels's clothes and gear. Ruth and I helped her to finish packing the mini van. We threw as much stuff of Eily's as we could cram into Ruth's car. Eily said one of Mels's sisters was going to move in and turn it into a B&B and after that nobody said much. We knew none of us would be coming back to that house.

In spite of all of the public swearing of Mels's and Eily's love, in spite of their carefully considered and crafted vows, in spite of all of the celebration, in spite of all of the affirmation they seemed to get, ultimately Mels and Eily had no contract of marriage to protect them from the impassive cruelty of fate and the formal logic of greed.

And so here I was, sitting in a cupboard, inhaling the spirit of a dead woman, ritually communing with her ghost as I had done over the past number of years. I told Mels I had bumped into her niece, Sharon, who worked in Cork, and that she was pregnant, which meant Mels was going to be a grandaunt for the fifth time. I didn't tell Mels that Sharon had tried to avoid me but that I had seen Sharon first. I didn't tell Mels I had made her niece blush when I asked her why she hadn't contacted Eily, why none of them had contacted Eily, even though they were mostly all adults now.

'Sure, Eily shacked up with a Polish one just months after my aunt died,' Sharon retorted.

'Well, for a start, there was a time when Eily was also your aunt. And moreover, Mels herself told me Eily would have another partner in no time. I didn't believe her, but of course she was right, she knew Eily too well. And if there is such a thing as an afterlife, I'm certain Mels is cheering on Eily and Marta and their daughter, Anna. Eily is convinced Mels brought Marta and Anna to her. And that's just Eily's way, Sharon, and why would you begrudge her happiness? Why would you deny her that?'

'I wouldn't,' snapped Sharon, 'none of us would, but none of us wants to see her again either.'

She walked away from me and she didn't look back. I watched her steady march along the meandering pavement of Patrick's Street until she drifted out of sight.

As I sat in that cupboard, replaying the grief-struck hostility of that encounter, yet deciding not to share it with Mels, I became quickly and entirely confused. Was Mels, in fact, all-seeing and all-knowing with an all-encompassing view from the dead nowhere which might be everywhere? Or was Mels dependent on me bringing her the news? Was my discretion ill-founded and could

Mels hear my thoughts on meeting her niece, even though I kept physically silent? Could Mels read my mind in the way she had when she was alive?

Did Mels know how much I missed her, especially now in this awful referendum campaign? Did she know Eily went out every day with a bread knife in her van to hack down the awful posters protesting against equal marriage? Did Mels know Eily hopped up onto the roof of her van and cut clear the plastic ties by which those posters hung from the electricity poles? Did Mels know which neighbours put up those posters every night? Once Eily took down the posters early in the morning she came back home to collect Anna, the girl she called her daughter, to drive her to school. When Anna first saw those posters on that grassy road, she said she felt like someone had smacked her face. Eily was eventually visited by an embarrassed garda who had driven over forty kilometres from the nearest police station. He said he had been told to warn her it was an offence to take down the posters. Eily told him she hadn't taken down any of the posters. He beamed a smile and said he was glad to hear that.

'Be careful now,' the garda said as he left. He also squeezed her shoulder and mumbled, 'Hang tight.'

Did Mels know Eily's father was no longer going up to his local for a pint to watch the main evening news with his mates? Could Mels please help?

I sat in the cupboard feeling ridiculous, lost, confused and deeply annoyed with myself. I realised the regular pilgrimages I made from Cork to the wilds of outer Connemara to commune with the ghost of Mels/Imelda Gallagher were now at an end. That chapter was over. Everyone had to get through this stinking time without Mels. I knew I would never again sit in that cupboard. Mels was gone.

# 25
# Bang Bang
# (My Baby Shot Me Down)

I went from Connemara to Dublin. I still had a few days before I had to go back to work and I knew Chris could do with more of a break from my ranting, and besides, Dublin was in need of canvassers. I went to stay with my pal Angie and her girlfriend in Rathmines. Angie rolled her eyes when she saw my small knapsack contained a heavy stash of Marriage Equality flyers and badges.

'You still have that banjaxed knapsack, it's as old as I am, that thing.'

'I love it, Angie, it brings me good luck on my travels and it's never, ever been stolen from me.'

'I might have an answer to explain that miracle,' said Angie, laughing. 'But it's true then!' she continued. 'I'd heard you'd lost the plot, girl, and become a compulsive canvasser. Was it for this that Robert Emmet died!?' Angie said as she picked up the campaign literature.

Yet, Angie came out with me to the district of Stillorgan on a bright spring evening to join a well-organised canvass. Angie noted that the bigger the house and the longer the owner took to arrive to answer the doorbell, the more likely we were to get a definitive No.

'I have read all of the literature and I have made up my mind and the answer is No,' said one woman as Angie and I stood on the granite steps at her large front door.

'I always find that you never have a water-pistol handy when you need it,' said Angie as we plodded down the flight of steps to the cobble-locked driveway, where muscle-bound jeeps stood parked.

House after house in Stillorgan it was much the same answer – *No* or *My ballot is private*, or they gave polite silent nods or mumbled *I'll see* when asked what way they were voting. A campaign tallyman kept a running score. Angie and I reported the silent people and the mumblers as No.

Angie and I received a lot of lectures on the finer points of homophobia from the denizens of Stillorgan. Time and time again we heard that a phobia is an irrational reaction or hatred and the Stillorgan citizens declared themselves to be of sound mind and entirely rational: it was just good sense to treat different groups of people differently. I told Angie they had the exact same lines in Bishopstown, down in Cork. It must be something they've all heard at their golf clubs. Treat the lesser people to less respect.

'No,' said Angie, 'that's what the Catholic crowd are saying on the radio and TV.'

'Oh, right,' I said, 'I'm not actually able to turn on the radio and TV.'

'You're better off, girl,' said Angie.

Angie and I started canvassing with a lesbian couple in their early thirties, who were both very pretty, one had long red hair and the other had long dark hair. They had come to canvass directly from work. They wore heels and beautiful skirts and blouses and short jackets. They were sweet with each other and proud they were six years together. They had engagement rings. They had held off from having a civil partnership because they wanted to have a full and equal marriage.

'They are a totally different species from us,' I said to Angie as we stood at the gate of one particular house and let the younger women walk up the garden path. Angie and I stood waiting to commiserate or celebrate on their return.

I continued, 'I don't mean that they are a different species just because of their age either, we just don't have anything in common with them. They are in a totally different world from us.'

They were called Paula and Claire. Once Paula had come out, it had taken her parents four years before they would let their daughter spend more than two hours with the family. They were afraid of Paula's influence on her younger brother, but he came out as gay anyway. Claire's family was declared 'very supportive' but she wasn't out to her grandparents, two of whom were still alive, and this made her feel awful, especially as they liked Paula so much. Her mum said it would kill her Granny. Paula said it was fine to say nothing to Granny. On hearing this, I relaxed a bit with Paula and Claire – there's nothing like a common experience of homophobia to bond even the most unlikely allies. I showed them how to push a flyer into a letterbox without losing skin and bruising knuckles, and Angie charmed them with stories of Cork dyke-scapades in the 1990s when Paula and Claire were just small girls.

Yet again, I marvelled at Angie's way with strangers: within twenty minutes of meeting her, Claire and Paula loved Angie. She had them laughing so much they had to sit down on the kerb as she described the time she had waved off eight lusty lesbians from Loafers, who were travelling over to London full of high anticipation of the delights that lesbian scene would present.

'Well, there was great excitement altogether! They were all set, they had taken down addresses from the pals in London over long-distance phone calls that just drank their pooled stash of fifty-pence pieces. But when they came back, there wasn't a whole lot of chat from them about how they had got on.' Angie was laughing so much she found it hard to continue. I helped her out with the story.

'Eeh, we couldn't find our way to the first club venue,' I reluctantly began, 'and I was the one elected to go and ask for help with directions, and to be safe we pretended the address we were looking for was the venue for a twenty-first birthday party. We eventually managed to find the club door and ring the doorbell and someone peered out through a spy-hole. There was a bit of outraged muttering behind the door and then there was full-on angry shouting that there was no way we would be allowed in.'

'They were wearing leather!' interjected Angie.

'Well, some of us had leather jackets and some had leather trousers,' I clarified. I couldn't really continue with the story and anyway, Angie was dying to tell the yarn.

'The London women told our little band of Cork heroines it was obvious they were part of the evil, gay, male-infected tribe of dykes who were into sado-masochistic sex!' Angie started laughing again.

I took it up again: 'We didn't know anything about the arguments, the sex wars in London. We just wanted to get inside the door and meet women wider than our own circle. We did our absolute best to let them know we were ignorant Paddies who knew no gay men whatsoever and nothing (at all, at all) about S/M. We thought we were being charming with our *plámás*. But they were having none of it. One woman inside the door said we looked as if we were into butch and femme role play.'

I dried up, I couldn't continue.

Angie took over: 'In spite of many subsequent tribunals, it could never be established who it was exactly that mumbled "Ah for fucksake, like" but everyone heard it and this simple prayer provoked the slamming open of the door and the emergence of three women in flannel shirts. They screamed at the Cork women to stop being violent and that they would call the police if they continued to loiter at the door.'

'We scarpered,' I said, 'and set about getting to the lesbian S/M club then, which entailed a long haul across London. And they were lovely but very cagey as anti-S/M lesbians had stormed in and broken up the joint a few times, protesting against the violence of the S/M club.' Paula, Claire and Angie could not stop laughing but I continued anyway: 'The S/M dykes seemed genuinely sorry to say they now had a strict policy: it was full leather and fetish gear only. With the help of some customers already inside, the Loafers women cobbled together three such outfits, so three went (gleefully) inside.'

I left Angie with the punchline of the story: 'And the rest of them went to a ceilí in Kilburn!'

Even I had to laugh again at that.

Claire and Paula would have listened to Angie talk all night, but I pointed out we had fallen behind the rest of the canvassers and I hustled the others to catch up. Clare and Paula walked up one drive, and Angie and I went through a neighbouring gateway.

A handsome, well-toned man in his late thirties opened the door. Children's toys were strewn across the large hallway behind him. He greeted us cheerily. He had a lovely smile. Angie and I were painfully smiling our canvass smiles. He said that before we said anything he would have to let us know he and his 'good lady wife' would both be voting No. They had 'tonnes' of gay friends who agreed with them. He reminded us that the politician Leo Varadkar, who had recently come out as gay, had previously given a speech in the parliament saying that every child needed a mother and a father and he had to agree with Leo: it was cruel to deny children the love of a father and mother. Same-sex marriage was a social experiment too far to inflict on children. The handsome, smiling man was 'all for love, in whatever fashion'. It was just that he had to think of it from the point of view of the children because he was a dad himself. Angie and I nodded. I asked him if we could leave a flyer with him. He refused, smiling.

'No point, I'm afraid.'

Then he seemed to have second thoughts. He asked us to hang on and wait. He shouted: 'Rua! Saoirse! Malachy!'

Three smiling children appeared, as if on cue from central casting, aged between five and twelve. Then his pretty wife appeared, and the Labrador dog wearing a rainbow kerchief around the neck. His 'good lady wife' was introduced as 'Tina' and he explained to the children that Angie and I were a loving lesbian couple who deserved their respect. He asked the children to shake our hands, and we solemnly shook the children's hands. He told the children he had explained to the 'lovely ladies' why he and Mum were voting No in the upcoming same-sex marriage referendum, because he and Mum wanted every child to have a dad to mind them. The children looked fearfully at us, they obviously had never been introduced to father deniers (or stealers or killers) before. Somehow we got ourselves off the front door step. Handsome Dad watched us walk down the steps from his door and out his drive and he actually waved at us.

I eventually said, 'You know, Angie, that's my first time seeing you lost for words.'

'Your first time seeing me quiet? Be careful what you wish for, Ro,' Angie said weakly. 'He thought we're a couple.'

'The worst thing he said was "lovely ladies",' I said.

'God yeah – that was bad alright,' agreed Angie. 'Come on, girl,' she said, 'let's get out of this hell-hole.'

I had a difficult job getting Angie to canvass Ballyfermot the following evening. I was addicted, I had to get back out there. I managed to persuade her that Ballyfermot would be as kind as other communities where people knew the taste of hard times. And sure enough, we had a lovely, redemptive evening along the miles of terraced houses in Ballyfermot. Everyone said Yes, except for one old fella who was out walking his little dog. He told us in no uncertain terms he was voting No. Angie pointed to the tiny dog he held on a pink lead, whose coiffured fringe was held in place with an exquisite diamante clip.

'Eh, does your dog know the way you're voting? You'd better not tell her, because I think she'll be very cross with you,' said Angie.

The old man was shocked. 'That's no bitch,' he said. 'My dog is a DOG: male!'

It was the second time in two days that I saw Angie at a loss for words.

Everywhere we went that evening people said: 'Fair fucks to ye, standing up for yourselves. It's about time someone did.'

The mammies of Ballyfermot talked about their lesbian daughters, granddaughters, nieces, aunts, sisters, their gay sons, grandsons, nephews, uncles and brothers. They talked about their trans relatives and friends and neighbours. The women of Ballyfermot talked quietly, but openly, about the dead ones: AIDS, suicides.

Some older men of Ballyfermot told us how they had been taken from their mothers and their fathers and put into the monstrous industrial schools. They said, 'The Church and the politicians said our families and our mothers were unfit too.'

However, we did have a startling couple of moments when a fit-looking middle-aged man answered his door and promptly ordered us off: 'Get away! Don't waste your breath!' I was surprised as he had a *No to Water Meters* poster in the front window and the houses of the protestors against water privatisation were adamantly Yes.

'We've six votes here,' he said as he pointed us out towards the road, 'and we're all Yes. We've no time for ye here.'

'Ah! We're looking for Yeses!' we chorused.

'Deadly!' he said instantly.

He swung his front door wide open and shouted into the house: 'The marriage equality people are here looking for our votes. What do we say to them?'

His wife and grown-up family must have been clustered around the kitchen table. 'Yes!' shouted one and then they all joined in: 'Yes! Yes! Yes! Yes!'

'Will you definitely get down and vote?' I asked anxiously.

'We're all registered in this house. We all vote.'

'Do you have any idea what the Ballyfermot turnout might be?' I continued my anxious questioning.

'Well you know, love, the turnout is never high in Ballyer. Even for the general elections. And this is a referendum.'

'I know,' I replied, 'you need to come out in big numbers so we don't lose by such a big margin. Losing by a small margin will be OK.'

My new friend nodded sagely. 'Yeah. This is going to be very tight. I'm glad you recognise you've a fight on your hands. I wouldn't believe the polls.'

I told him I didn't believe the polls.

# 26
# Take Me To Church

When I got back to Cork, it was less than a month to go before referendum day and I continued to obsessively, neurotically canvass. However, six days before the referendum, Chris called a halt to my activities.

She had tolerated me swinging by her house on a daily basis and she had listened to my monologues on how the canvass had gone. I always had a list of heart-stopping encounters. Chris never gave much of a reaction to my recitations, except for the account I gave her of the girl in her school uniform (she might have been any age from thirteen to sixteen) who had cycled after me once I had left her house. I had spotted her about ten minutes earlier, looking out from her bedroom window. I waved up at her and the girl had waved back. Presumably it was her older brother who answered the door. He was also in a school uniform. He was a tall, bashful lad. He took the flyer I offered and when I asked him if he had a vote he said he didn't, he was only seventeen. I asked him if his parents were available and he said no. I asked him if he would give them the flyer and he handed it back and said no. I asked him if he knew what way his parents were voting as I was keeping a record of each Yes and No as I went from door to door.

The boy blushed furiously and shook his head.

I said, 'I take it they are No.'

He nodded in the affirmative.

One of his parents shouted: 'Kevin! Why are you so long at the door? Come inside!'

I apologised for keeping him and said: 'Goodbye,' and added: 'Good luck.'

His sister had some urgent need to come flying after me. She screeched her bike to a halt and only just in time, I thought she was going to knock me down.

'I wish I had a vote!' she shouted. 'I'd vote Yes!'

I smiled. 'Well, if we have to fight this fight again, we'll be counting on your vote the next time.'

'My brother is gay,' she said. 'He doesn't know I know, but I do. He answered the door to you. My parents made him answer the door. They got texts to say you were coming.'

'You've a lovely brother,' I said, 'he was very polite.'

'Do you think we'll lose?' the girl asked.

And without missing a beat I lied to her: 'Oh, we'll definitely win. All the polls say we'll win.'

'We have to win,' the girl said.

'Don't worry,' I continued to lie, 'it's in the bag.'

The girl nodded and turned her bike and started to pedal off.

'Be extra nice to your brother now!' I called after her.

She stopped and swivelled around to look at me.

'I'm being very, very careful of him,' she said.

I was shocked to recognise her fear.

'Tell him that you know and that you love the bones of him, and that there's loads and loads of support. That everything will really be OK. Tell him that it really will be OK. Tell him he just has to do the Leaving Cert and, once he has his Leaving done and he's able to leave home, he'll find there is plenty of support. And your parents will be fine with it all eventually. Honestly.'

The girl nodded gravely: 'I need you to be right,' she said.

'Why did you lie to her?' Chris asked. 'Why did you tell her you were certain the referendum would be won?'

'I lie to everyone about that: it's the best campaign strategy. You have to believe you can win to keep doing it.'

'But you think we'll lose.'

'Yes. I can't see Ireland being the one and only place in the world where a public vote on gay marriage actually wins. But raising consciousness, building a movement, that's always good. I can't have the young ones lose heart because I can see things more clearly. And it might be close. We might not lose by much, and there are now plenty of young leaders and I'll be on hand to support them. To keep going.'

Chris sighed, 'Hmmmm.'

Chris hadn't had much of a reaction to my tales over the long months of canvassing, but that eventually changed on the night when I came into her house full of the joys from canvassing the suburb of Douglas.

There had been a large group mustered for the canvass and I was asked to walk along with a husband and wife. It was their first time canvassing and they needed to be shown the ropes. The wife was petite, very pretty and chatty. She told me her husband, Liam, was a principal of a boys' secondary school and she was a primary school resource teacher who specialised in teaching autistic children. They had made a long drive from a large town in west Cork to canvass one of Cork City's most affluent suburbs.

'Why did you not join a canvass nearer home?' I asked.

'Our son has recently come out to us,' she said, 'and so I was determined to show him we support him. He doesn't want us to say it to anyone just yet. We're going to leave him tell people in his own time, but I was determined to do my bit to get him his rights.'

I looked at Liam, the husband. He leaned into me and spoke in a conspiratorial tone and his wife turned away and affected not to listen. 'I thought the people in Douglas might be, well, easier, for Fiona. You know, it's different in boys' schools. She went to a convent school. She hasn't ever really heard how cruel, how crude it can be.' He nodded at me and stepped back.

I gleefully announced to Chris that Douglas was just like Stillorgan.

'At more than a few doors we heard the phrase, *You can't be encouraging them*, often allied with the injunction, *They're more to be pitied than despised. They can't help it, d'you see?* My new best friend Fiona got quite shook!' I laughed.

I described to Chris how I had deliberately and carefully stoked Fiona's horror.

'Chris, it was JUST like teasing a fish with bait, waiting for that swallow and then gently, gently tugging, enjoying the very slow reeling in! I got her to talk about her gay son, Peter – It was SO easy! He is SO much the apple of his lovely mammy's eye. He's the eldest, her right-hand man, a wonderful older brother, don't you know! Doesn't he want to be a primary school teacher just like his mammy and he hopes to do his training at the very same place where Mammy had trained: Mary Immaculate College in Limerick. And isn't he just mad for the rowing! Oh and of course he's great at that too! And he doesn't want to be too far from his local club and the river that flows past their lovely house! And of course he has already qualified as a piano teacher, he has already done all his City and Guilds exams and he has begun to take on pupils, neighbours' children. Oh! He'll probably get an A in music in the Leaving!'

I rejoiced in a falsetto tone, mocking Fiona's enthusiasm and pride in her boy.

'Stop,' said Chris.

'I know,' I continued, 'old Fiona gave me all the information I needed!'

'Ro,' said Chris in a quiet voice, but I was already interrupting her.

'Chris! You should have seen dear little Fiona's face! There was one nice lady who said to us: "I do feel sorry for them …". She was snipping some flowering foliage from a bush in her front garden. She cut some for us to take away as she had plenty and it smelled so wonderful and it wouldn't last much longer. So Liam, the husband, begins to look a little less worried that lovely Fiona is going to collapse with a nervous breakdown. But I just knew Gardening Lady would come through. And she did! She did, Chris! She said: "… however, we've to be careful." She lowered her voice and said: "We actually think that there's a gay man teaching in my sons' school. I mean, everyone says he's gay." Then she says, "Though it doesn't seem as if he brings anything into the classroom, but you know, you would have to be worried. We keep an eye, we make sure and ask the boys questions and let them know they can come to us with anything. Though now he does seem to be an excellent teacher, very dedicated, over and above. And that's the thing, really, I mean the boys idolise him and if he came in talking about his partner …" Gardening Lady raised her eyebrows and tilted her head to one side and said: "I mean, if he came in and started talking about his HUSBAND!" Gardening Lady shrugged and snipped another bloom and concluded: "Children are very impressionable".'

I re-enacted all of the drama through Chris's kitchen and living room, following Chris out to her back garden, continuing with venomous excitement:

'Ah Chris! You. Should. Have. Seen. Her! It didn't take all that long for Fiona to go from crumpled to weeping and close to broken. Hubby Liam was completely silent and seemed to be aging before my eyes. He walked with his arm around Fiona's shoulders. He held her close into him.'

I pantomimed the upset of the couple – throwing my arm out as if I was husband Liam, as if Fiona was tucking into my extended embrace.

'So, Liam kept murmuring something in Fiona's ear. I think he was trying to get her to stop walking up to the doors of Douglas.'

I took Chris's shaking of her head as encouragement to continue.

'This is the best bit, Chris! I asked Fiona if the teacher training college in Limerick still required a letter of recommendation from the parish priest. She looked at me perplexed, said she didn't know. "Good job your son hasn't come out then," I said, in as even a tone as I could manage. I thought I was going to laugh right into her crushed face! I also managed to ask about the other boys in the rowing club. Did she realise they were going to feel lied to? Though I said all that would sort itself out in time, all of that unease in the changing rooms.'

I shrieked harshly as I related the adventures of Fiona and hubby Liam at the doors of the Douglas bourgeoisie.

'She had no fucking clue! She had absolutely no idea! She hadn't a notion what her son faces on a daily basis and what he's in for next. But she's getting the picture now!'

I was sitting at Chris's garden table. She stood up to put her hands on my shoulders.

'Stop,' she said, 'you've got to stop this. Stop.'

I took a breath. Chris kept her hands on my shoulders. Chris, who never, ever, ever cries, had tears running down her face.

I didn't understand. It took me a few silent moments. I heaved a big sigh and realised it was a sob. Chris hugged me.

'Stop, Ro. Just stop.'

Somehow I had ended up contorted. I had wanted pretty and sweet and unconscionably ignorant Fiona, so delighted and proud of her beautiful son, to suffer. I had wanted her to have a little taste of the pain that her kind, the straights, had inflicted. Still inflict.

I had never been more lost. I had a knack for finding people like Chris and Russ who were gentle and focused on bringing more light and oxygen and space into the world, and I had walked with them towards that horizon. Now, I didn't know where I was.

I worried that marriage was only going to benefit lesbians and gays who already had plenty of assets in terms of property and pensions and social capital. I had signed up for a vision of lesbian and gay liberation that did not seek a cosy nod of recognition by the 'haves' but wanted nothing less than a complete redistribution of social goods for all the marginalised and despised. Nobody spoke in that way anymore. I was lost. All that had guided me in my past was now gone in this awful present and I had no future hope to steer towards.

I went back to work for a few nights in the week before the vote. While I was getting the residents ready for sleep, I noticed how soothing it was to bring my attention back to them, those who needed me to be gentle and careful and strong and patient and safe. There are no differences between the bodies of old men and old women – like infants, everything is soft and loose and folded in wrinkles. Hair is sparse and thin or stiff and brittle. When older people are waiting to die their eyes are cloudy, their fingers count pleats into the blankets and they listen to other voices. As older people fade from this world, their bodies are often cramped in pain or in memory of pain or in anticipation of pain but they still like to be touched, to be softly touched. Yet even in my most absorbed moments of caring for the residents, I knew, all along my large intestine, that the referendum would be lost, and that I would be stuck in this sickening struggle for many more years. Because this marriage equality, this sell-out of the radical lesbian, gay, trans and queer liberation movement, was where the battle lines had been drawn against the homophobes.

I generally loved the quiet of the corridors when all of the residents were sleeping or trying to sleep. I liked the gleam of the polished lino, lit only by the desk light at the nurses' station, and the dim green glow of the exit-door signs. But once my general duties were done, I was too wired to write fiction as I sat on call. I couldn't even read much.

For the last six days of the campaign I didn't canvass, but I probably wasn't shocked enough at how crazed and contorted I had become. I kept myself busy by obsessively writing notes, lists and exhortations for the ongoing campaign, which was going to need to resurrect itself immediately when the No vote was announced.

# 27
# She Keeps Me Warm

Chris agreed to come with me to the counting of votes in Cork City Hall. The boxes would be opened nationwide at the official count centres at 9.00 a.m. I made sure to get myself in front of a box that held votes from Churchfield. I had just one question: had the working class turned out to vote? I was standing next to a party activist from the Fianna Fáil party and I knew he would be able to tell on sight if there was a big turnout.

'That's massive,' he said as soon as the box was opened, 'looks like 60 per cent turnout.'

I nipped over to other boxes from the solid working class areas of Cork and it was the same story: they had come out to vote.

The tallymen were marking the votes as they were being laid open and brought into Yes and No bundles before being properly checked by count officials. The inner city areas were resoundingly 'Yes'. It was about fifteen minutes into the count.

I started jumping around the hall, shouting, 'Yes! Yes! Yes! We've won! We've won!'

My pal, Toddy, was looking ashen. She was doing the tally at a box from middle-class and older Bishopstown, where it seemed a conclusive No.

In less than half an hour after the boxes were opened nationwide it was clear that the resounding Yes from the urban areas in Cork, Dublin, Limerick, Galway and Waterford allied with the massive youth vote was going to swing the day. There was solidarity among the most disrespected, there was support for the queers from Ireland's young and they had voted. I saw that. I saw that.

Chris and I left City Hall and wandered, mostly silently and somewhat dazed, across the glinting branches of the river to the Cork campaign HQ on the North Mall. Old friends leaned against the sun-warmed low granite wall of the north channel of the Lee and chatted with the dozens of people milling around. People were happy but very tired, there was a mellow atmosphere. We spoke softly to each other, many said they were looking forward to sleep, to rest at last.

The TV broadcast of the results from the country's count centres was being projected onto a very large screen set up in the open-plan area downstairs in the HQ. The place was packed with people sitting on the floor or standing around the sides or at the back of the room, watching the coverage of the count and the broadcast of the rainbow-clad crowds gathering in the grounds of Dublin Castle.

People were invited to record their thoughts and feelings on a large roll of paper on a table in a side room and I found myself standing by the table but unusually stuck, squirming an impotent biro around in my hand. By teatime, one more result had to be officially recorded: the count from the city and county of Cork. I couldn't stand still long enough to focus on the TV screen. Chris said she was going to head home the minute there was an official count given. I said I would walk with her as far as Patrick's Bridge and then head up to my flat.

I was alone in that side room with the big roll of paper and other people's writing when I heard the loud cheer from Dublin Castle on the TV and a more muted cheer, then some applause from the crowd in the room watching the coverage. I was writing at last. Of course I wrote a list:

Joel Burrowitz died first.

John/Joni Brunstrom was twenty-four when he died.

Russ Edouard Belafonte took charge of turning me towards the direction of peace, of loving understanding, of acceptance.

Mini/Michael Green was twenty-seven when he died.

Neeraj Acharya and my lovely John Kerrigan.

Imelda/Mels Gallagher.

I started writing the list of the suicides and those who had merely gone away, abroad, or into a bottle or into a small and quiet life.

Eventually Chris came and watched until I had finished writing and then we left the building.

'Only 38 per cent of them hate us now,' I said to Chris as we walked along the river.

''Tis an improvement, I'm sure,' she replied.

'Of course they won't admit to hating us,' I continued.

'No. They are very reasonable, after all.'

'It's going to take a while to get over this,' I said.

'Yes. Many wounds are fresh with the young ones. They took quite a battering on the doorsteps by all accounts. Discovered all kinds of things about their neighbours that they might not have known.'

'I'm glad you didn't go out on the canvass.'

'At least one of us had to try and preserve the sanity, keep the old wounds tightly bound. Somebody had to watch *Miss Marple*, you know!'

I smiled. 'I'm sorry I went so crazy.'

Chris squeezed my arm. 'So long as you're not crazy enough to fly to England and get down on the knee to Jenny – I can live with any other craziness.'

I put my arm around Chris's shoulders and gave her a squeeze. 'Well, I think I am actually overdue one of those particular meltdowns! But luckily I always have you to talk sense into me and anyway, you'll be glad to hear that this particular year I'm too exhausted to summon any energy in that direction.'

We walked on in companionable silence until we came to Patrick's bridge and our separate ways. We hugged and parted.

Crossing onto MacCurtain Street, I came across two young men in their early twenties, walking hand in hand towards me. They were only slightly self-conscious, but I could see this was a new experience for them. I stopped in my tracks, they drifted around me, smiling a silent 'hello' once they recognised me as an old dyke. I pressed on the metal fasteners of the leather band I wore around my wrist. It was a cock-ring, now an old-fashioned one, that had belonged to Russ. I summoned his ghost to me.

'Aren't they beautiful?' I asked him.

'Beautiful,' he replied.

# DULUTH, LOUISIANA, NEW YORK, BOSTON & P-TOWN

## 2015

# 28
# I Feel Love

In the immediate weeks that followed, I tried to write about how awful the Marriage Referendum was. I thought I would open up a blog page and post up my piece on what it was like to be canvassing with ghosts; to be one of the walking wounded yet required to act pretty and be nice; to never, ever whisper the word homophobia; to pretend straight relationships actually make sense and queers are simply an ever-so-slightly odd version of same. I would write about what it was like to work hard towards a goal that sells us all short, to pretend optimism for the good of the comrades, to take again the frontline flack for the sake of the younger ones, to canvass while not believing for a millisecond that the day would be won. I got a taste of what it was like to have a life without hope, to feel that it was impossible to reach safety.

I remained frighteningly unable to write anything for months. Throughout the canvass and afterwards, through June and July, I was walloped with writer's block, but eventually I started writing again in August 2015. I started writing *Slant* when I was on the plane from Shannon to New York, with a number of changes ahead of me before I would reach Duluth. Chris had encouraged me to go back to the States, and she had even got the rest of our friends on board to tell me to go back and face the past. She was right, they were all right, of course. I had to press the reset button and go back before I could go forwards.

Joni's parents, Bill and Rose, now in their late seventies, were going to collect me at the airport in Duluth. I had a photograph album for them, only lightly censored, with hundreds of photographs of their John, our Joni. I had a DVD with nearly two hours of footage of John/Joni I had transferred from video shot lovingly by Russ. It began with a small snippet of almost total darkness except for a little glimmer of light, which I knew was a candle in a glass jar. The sound is perfect, the sea exhales under the dock and Joni is playing the guitar. He is singing and a girl comes to join him and they harmonise on the lyrics of 'A Case of You'. In the rest of the video clips Joni is mostly in the middle distance and unaware the camera is trained on him as he strums his guitar or lightly sways his long and graceful limbs along the dunes of Provincetown or the banks of the Charles River. He would never let Russ videotape him up close, but Russ was able to tape Joni while he slept, his long hair flowing down his back or fanning the pillow, grainy daylight flickering in the window.

I spent just an hour with Joni's parents. I stiffly presented them with the photos and DVD and then we just sat in silence in their family room. A giant TV screen presided over the low sofas. The sound was on mute but Fox News poured a speedy, botox-filled, blonde spew over our silence. Every ten minutes or so Joni's father, Bill, let out some startling, shuddering sighs and seemed about to speak and then didn't. He was a large old man in a brightly coloured checked shirt, his denims were hitched right up his midriff, held up by old-fashioned braces. His wife, Rose, was a slight woman who sat perched on the edge of her seat, her gaze focused on her husband. I gathered she wanted him to say something and she wouldn't, or couldn't, speak unless he did. I finished the ginger ale soda they had offered me and said I'd better call a cab to take me to my hotel. As I was stepping out of their house and into the waiting taxi, I did what Russ had asked me to do, I said:

'You had a beautiful son, John. It was clear he loved you very much. And we loved him. His friends loved him.'

Bill turned away quickly and walked into his house.

Rose gave a tentative half-wave: 'I'm sure you did your best, honey, I'm sure you did your best.'

Except for that burst of writing activity on the plane to Duluth, I continued to have a scary leaden freeze, the white noise of writer's block, all through that grief-struck fortnight of my American trip. I spent days with a blank jotter on my lap. On the trains down from Duluth all the way to Baton Rouge to meet with Russ's sister, Charlotte, I could not write a word.

Charlotte lived in Russ's old family home, a gorgeous wooden two-storey house, painted white, with verandas and a wraparound porch. The house was just a few miles outside the city and the garden sloped down to a small river. There was a long avenue of trees that led to the house.

'That right there is the start of the Mississippi Delta,' Charlotte laughed, pointing to the river as she was showing me around the garden. Charlotte described herself as 'happily divorced, thrice. Each divorce happier than the one before.'

Before I brought my bag to my room, Charlotte mixed me a sweet-tasting, muddy-looking cocktail and my two days with her became a blur of laughter, weeping, storytelling and a glorious remembering of Russ.

'I was ten when Russ left and I *adored* him. I was always so lonely for my big brother. When I was twenty-two and was finishing college I was resolved to ask Papa where I could go find him. I just knew he had some way to reach Russ. But when I came home from college I found that Papa had been telling everyone in the district that Russ was training to be a commercial pilot! I just *knew* that was not true! Papa had been drafted to Vietnam, he was a Navy pilot. All the folks around were saying the same thing: "Isn't that the darndest thing! Like father, like Son!" But Papa was a *terrible* liar. Papa tried to tell people that Russ had died in a training accident on the Fourth of July, that his plane had crashed.'

I was silent for a while.

'Families said all kinds of things back then,' I said.

'I know. He was always trying to protect me and Mama. But I guessed Russ was gay and Mama told me that it was true.'

I noticed that Charlotte couldn't seem to use the word AIDS. I decided against naming 'it'. Eventually, I told her that once Russ had passed, I had posted a sealed letter that Russ had written to his father, care of the attorney in Washington D.C.

'I sent my own note, too, asking what we ought to do with Russ's ashes, but I never heard back. We had our own ceremony in Provincetown, on Cape Cod, in a place where we all first met each other. But I've kept some of his ashes to bring home. I have them with me here.'

'You are a darling,' said Charlotte. Then she sobbed and I was afraid she would never stop.

'Poor Mama! Poor Papa!' she kept repeating.

I was feeling very weary. Poor Mama and poor Papa could have brought their beautiful son home and made him comfortable, let him die at his beloved home, let him know for sure with a thousand actions in those final months and weeks that they loved him. I kept silent. It was exhausting to bite back all the recrimination and sadness and let Charlotte take her role as if she alone was heartbroken.

'We'll scatter Russ's ashes on the veranda,' said Charlotte. 'Tomorrow night, your last night here, we'll have a ceremony and we'll drink French champagne.'

The next day, I asked Charlotte if she had ever found the final letter that Russ had sent to her father.

'No, I have not. But I have all the letters and cards he sent Mama. He sent them care of the old florist in Baton Rouge. Let me get them for you.'

I spent the day reading through the tender, funny, wise and outrageous letters Russ had sent his mother every few weeks over the dozen years he was away. I read them chronologically. It was painful to see how his handwriting had deteriorated as his illness worsened.

*Dearest Mama.*
*I often think of that evening when Papa and I had that <u>stormy</u> row. Could I have done anything that would have changed things? Could Papa have done anything to change things? I often think I <u>might</u> have done something, one small thing, that would have changed everything or Papa might have done something, one small thing, that would have changed everything but I can't think what that one thing might have been – because then I wouldn't have been me and Papa wouldn't have been himself and I would never want Papa to be other than exactly who he was all my life: the best father I could have had.*
*My friend Neeraj told me there are parallel universes and our lives are playing out in multiple other dimensions in other parts of space/time. Maybe, Mama, in another part of the cosmos young Russ didn't wear eye shadow that night or didn't turn on that music or didn't yell back at his father. But Mama, worse things could have happened, given my nature and how young I was. I could have skipped out of that house one night to meet a friend and never lived another night longer.*
*Worse things could have happened, given my nature and how young I was and how fearful Papa was. It took me some years to realise that Papa has been very fearful.*
*I'm so very glad I lived in our universe and everything played out exactly as it did. I have had wonderful adventures and felt so much love. I thank*

*you and Papa for making me, for loving me as a young boy and setting me free about my life. I had the most – the most – <u>beautiful</u> life.*

*It doesn't seem like I will actually get home for a visit but I know my soul will dance on the veranda and I am looking forward to that free feeling. I believe we have souls Mama, I know you believe that too, so I hope it is a comfort to know my soul's home is right near you, and Papa, and Charlotte.*

*Russ*

I kissed his last signature. 'Good night, sweet Prince,' I whispered.

That evening, I gave Charlotte the box with Russ's ashes. She turned on the record player, put on Donna Summer, and we solemnly, slowly danced, eyes closed, around the veranda, and I felt the slender presence of Russ dance around us, whispering the lyrics.

I had an almighty hangover on the flight to New York, so I wasn't surprised I couldn't write anything then either. My old haunts in NYC were no longer dangerous territory, the pavements were filled with white people walking impossibly large dogs, considering the probable size of their apartments. I stayed with MichaelC and Mark, they had a lovely old walk-up, rent-controlled apartment in the East Village. For years MichaelC had worked as a staff writer on various TV shows broadcast from New York, but he had had one major literary commercial success and that novel was now going to be made into a Hollywood movie. He was excited to tell me about who had signed contracts for the cast.

'Meryl *fucking* Streep! I can now afford to spend the rest of my life writing books only literary queers will read!'

We were sitting on the tar roof of his apartment building, looking across to Tompkins Square Park point, when Mark came home from his work and joined us up there with some nice chilled Californian sparkling wine and three lovely glass flutes.

'We have a lot to celebrate Mark!' I said as I saw him arrive. The boys clinked to my being back in New York and I made a toast to Mark's undetectable HIV status. We had got that good news some time ago but this was my first chance to rejoice with them.

'Amazing! Amazing! Amazing!' I said as we clinked our glasses. 'Weren't you the smart boy not to start on AZT!'

I was the lucky one who stayed well for so long and then the cocktail of drugs came in when I needed them ...'

The three of us were silently thinking about the legions of unlucky ones and MichaelC tuned into our thoughts to say:

'I have no idea why I never got infected. That was just luck. I had much, *much* more sex than Joel, probably tricked with many of the same guys.'

He teared up, Mark hugged him.

'Jeez, I can't believe I can *still* get upset about that,' he said.

After a while I said: 'Guys ... d'you know, I haven't cried since Joel died.'

'Oh Rose Marie!' they chorused.

'That can't be good,' said Mark.

We went off the sticky roof and into their apartment, where we had a lovely meal with a proper Italian tomato sauce over our homemade ricotta ravioli, all made according to MichaelC's family recipe.

After our meal, MichaelC brought out a large artist portfolio with MG stamped in large, faded gold lettering. We looked through Mini's work for the rest of the evening. There were some truly gorgeous black-and-white photos. There were surreal photos of me and Russ posing for Mini with our dyed, leopard-spotted, close-cropped heads, looking like feral twins. There were other photos I didn't realise Mini had taken, where I was sitting with John Kerrigan as we dozed together on the double hammock under the rose trellises in Tony's garden, lit and darkened by the summer sun and the tender shadows of the full-blown flowers. I felt very odd looking at those photographs.

'Are you OK, Rose Marie?'
'I feel a bit weird.'
'You're crying, Rose Marie,' said the boys in unison.

I got the bus, finally, to Boston, still stuck in my writer's block. I doodled sometimes, intricate, obsessive inked circles that wound their way into dense puckerings all over the once-blank pages, but I still had no words.

I had never gone back to Boston, not since that day we buried Clara. Boston hadn't changed much except that the Irish-American working-class enclave of Southie, which was still white, was now full of what the former denizens would have called Yuppies.

Terri agreed to meet me. I think I caught her off guard. I got her work phone number from LinkedIn and the morning I was leaving Michael's I phoned her at work. There might have been other people around. In any case, she agreed to meet me at the Club Café that evening at 6.00 p.m. All the way up on the bus I asked myself why I was doing this. I had written to Terri only twice, they were long, long letters of apology and explanation. I heard nothing back from the first letter I sent. I wasn't sure it had ever been read. I wrote again a few months later. The second letter arrived back to me complete with dog turd that had thankfully dried up on its return journey. This was probably not going to go well, but I wanted to know that I had done my utmost to resolve things between us.

I got there early and really wasn't sure she would show up but in fact she was already there when I arrived and she looked the exact same, right down to wearing golf pants and a Lacoste T-shirt with the collar turned up, except her hair was fully grey and she had more wrinkles around her eyes and mouth.

She seemed to have a speech prepared. I was still pulling out the chair to sit down when she told me that she was a partner in a law firm that specialised in patents and copyright issues. I was taking off my jacket and settling my bags down when she told that she was married to a nurse who worked part-time in the local hospital and who had given birth to a boy aged nine and a girl aged seven; that they lived near her wife's parents; that I looked the same and that I had ruined her life. On that declaration she started to cry, pushed her chair back, stood up and strode off to the bathroom to compose herself. I don't think I even got to say 'Hello'.

I was going to follow, to try and comfort her, but my dominant inner coward thought it was probably going to work out better for me if I stayed in a more public place than the bathroom.

After a while, through the window I saw Terri leaving the restaurant. I was suddenly furious. I ran after her and caught her before she had made it to the end of the block.

'HANG ON!' I skipped ahead of her and blocked her path. 'You were just going to walk out on me like that?!'

'That's what you did to me!' Terri yelled. 'You just left! Leaving me with just a NOTE!'

'But Terri! You weren't happy with me! I was such a constant disappointment to you!'

She stopped walking, stood looking at me with her arms folded and gave the oddest smile, she said, 'Remember how I used to say you would leave me?'

'Yes. Of course I remember. You said it a lot.'

That odd smile flickered again. 'I never thought you would. Leave.'

I was hit by the same old wave of confusion that had hit and submerged me whenever I was trying to connect deeply with Terri.

She continued, 'And I read all your letters and faxes and your notes and diaries.'

I was instantly guilty about the notebooks and Jenny's letters, which I had kept at Clara's.

'Well, that's OK, I suppose. Welcome to my boring life.'

'You thought I was psychic. You thought I knew what you were thinking or about to do before you told me.'

I nodded dumbly. It had been one of the flashpoints. Terri would ask me to do something nice with her and I would excitedly agree and she would ask if I was free. I would respond by saying I would check my diary, but even if there was something pencilled in I would see if I could change it. I would come back and let her know I had a commitment of one kind or another but I would try and rearrange things, and she would be heartbroken and upset that I never let her in on what was happening in my life. I had secrets. I wanted to leave her.

'Terri, we're middle-aged women. We loved each other deeply once and I was trying my best to connect with you. We went through a lot together. I am very, very sorry for walking out and just leaving a note. I will always feel ashamed of that. It was a horrible, horrible thing to do. I am very, very sorry and I always will be sorry. Do you think there is any way you can forgive me?'

'FUCK YOU!'

I persisted. I had travelled a long way in literal and metaphorical ways. I had to ensure there were no further things left undone.

'Is there no way to wish each other well? We don't have to have a friendship, but it would be good, don't you think, to wish each other well?'

She stood looking at me with incandescent contempt.

'Terri, you have a happy life now. Can you ...'

She cut me off:

'A happy life? A happy life? Are you insane? You know what my life has been like! I have to work so hard! Do you think anything in my life is easy?! You don't have kids! You'll never have kids! You don't know how hard it is to raise kids! You are still such a fucking stupid fuck! You've made a fucking mess of your life, Gom! You're such a loser! My friends always said you were dragging me down! You're such a fucking loser! Who the fuck has a happy life?!'

I stepped away from her to let her pass, feeling a strange peace, grateful again for all I had in my life, for all its rich relationships and, yes, for my happy life. I walked back slowly to the restaurant to get my bags and see if there was a bill to pay. Terri shouted more things at me as I was walking back. I'm not sure what she said. It didn't matter. I haven't heard from her since and I don't think I'll contact her again. As I said, Boston hadn't changed much.

I couldn't find the courage to take the T out to Boston College. I sat in the underground station of Kenmore Square for nearly two hours watching all of the B, C, and D Green trains clang their way through the station, but I wasn't able to get on one of them.

However, I decided I was, after all, able to do a trip back to Provincetown.

The ferry was filled with queer holiday-makers, making the most of the last days of summer. I settled on the top deck and let the winds blow my thoughts towards the ever-present past. When I disembarked, I immediately rented a bike on Commercial Street and started cycling around. P-town was exactly as I remembered it. There were places, sounds and smells I had forgotten but it was all there, all still intact, waiting to coalesce in bombs of memories that ripped me apart. I cycled out to Herring Cove and sat on the beach and watched that immense optical illusion of the sun setting out on the ocean, knowing stars were already visible in the night skies on that same ocean as it flooded by Roches Point and into Cork harbour. We are on a turning globe and we bury our lives seeking stable forevers.

I sat with my jotter, which had an old postcard from Jenny tucked into the sleeve. It was a picture of the river towpath near her house in Somerset. She had broken some months of silence to send it to me after the weekend I spent there with her and the children and hungover Cyril. On the back she had written one of her oblique, almost cryptic notes. I've learned the hard way not to respond directly to those messages of hers, but I keep my sanity by writing my would-be replies onto those cards she posts to me, and I fix her letters onto larger pieces of paper like I did when we were young ones and I write all over the rare letters she still sometimes sends. It's my way of having the conversations we can't have. Sitting in Herring Cove as the earth turned from the sun and towards the lesser stars and moonlight, I re-read that old postcard and the note, unsent, I had written in return. I realised I would have to start there. My reaction to that awful referendum wasn't going to make sense unless people knew something of the longer story, something of my longer journey, how my heart was formed and broken, broken open. Jenny wrote:

*Towpath*
*Now I know why it is called a towpath.*
*Strong*
*Long*
*Longing*
*Prolonging*

There's an analytic philosopher who asks the question: are fictitious characters as real as humans who have actually lived lives? After much careful consideration he concludes: yes, characters in novels are as real as those who read the novels. He's wrong, of course. Fictitious characters live on in the imagination of readers and never die, they are immortal, not like mere human mortals, they are always alive as long as there are readers who believe in their existence. I want that for my friends, to make a story where they will forever be alive in strangers' hearts, minds, imagination and memory. I want Eily and Mels to be forever singing me 'Happy Birthday' in the lobby of the Copley Plaza Hotel; I want Mini/Michael Green, who smelled of turpentine and cigarette smoke and befriended a confused young woman, to forever be recognised for his kindness; I want Sully to be remembered as a (perhaps slightly flawed, but definite) hero; I want the absolute legend Clara to be always swaying her arthritic hips to Tina Turner on The Boatslip; I want Neeraj and John

Kerrigan reaching for and finding the other with eternal delight in their classy apartment; I want to preserve as long as this print exists the image of Joni and Russ in their cheerleaders' dresses as Terri steps up to bat for the Navratilovas and the twilight causes the bank of floodlights to bang and click and hum into light over the dusty field; I want Joel to be always lulled asleep as MichaelC's deep voice recites Lorca's poem.

I want me and Jenny to be forever on that summer evening towpath.

I started to write then:

We were pushing our bikes up the steep walkway from the towpath. You were ahead of me.
*I love you. I love you.*
I don't know which one of us said that first, but I know the other said it second. Or maybe neither of us actually said it out loud and it was just in the air, on the tip of our tongues, under our breath.

And then I said, 'I think I mean something different every time I say that, *I love you*. I think it's a different thing every time.'

You turned towards me in a half-pause, 'I mean the same thing every time.'

And I knew that was true.

I knew that was true and I ached, because I uniquely loved you every struck moment, and you loved me constantly.

I wrote then about one young woman seeing another who stood at angles to herself in a hotel lobby. I wrote until it was dark and in the following days, which became weeks, months and years, I kept working as best as I was able to finish this, *Slant*.

# Acknowledgements

If you're like me, acknowledgements are where you judge whether to spend time with the rest of the book. A special welcome to that reader.

*Slant* began in January 2016 when I arrived in Oxford on research leave from University College Dublin. I had planned to write about eighteenth-century Ireland but was invited to teach feminist philosophy instead. So, I thought about bodies, gender, and care for the world and other humans. By spring, students were falling in love and the lecture topics and the crashing rush of young romance became strong influences on this book.

I had planned to go to Oxford to escape Ireland's commemoration of 1916. I was sore with Ireland. I had worked for years with four super-humans, Claire McGettrick, Maeve O'Rourke, Mari Steed and Jim Smith, to advocate for justice for women held in Ireland's Magdalene Laundries. We had some success but by 2016 we were combatting the Department of Justice's intent on undermining the redress scheme. Mary H., a former Magdalene, told me: 'If the women and men who fought in 1916 could have seen ahead the state of the place they sacrificed themselves for, they would have rolled over in their beds that Easter Sunday morning and taken a lie-in.' Mary spoke truth. I was battle-weary and many friends who had been active in Ireland's Marriage Equality campaign in 2015 seemed also to be suffering burnout.

I began to think about revolutions and the toll they take on foot soldiers. Two (non-victorious) history books that helped to form *Slant*, were Sarah Schulman's monumental *Let the Record Show: A Political History of ACT UP New York, 1987-1993* (Farrar, Straus and Giroux, 2021) and the tender *Rock the Sham! The Irish Lesbian & Gay Organization's Battle to March in New York City's St. Patrick's Day Parade* (Street Level Press, 2005) by Anne Maguire. Thus, Ro McCarthy began to introduce herself. She was going to be that stalwart, unglamorous, dedicated activist, one of those many unsung heroes who are the backbone of every social movement.

My plan to escape nationalism by going to England in 2016 resulted in me missing some thoughtful events in Ireland on democratic futures while having to remain a silent guest amidst Brexit mania. I decided Ro must be an economic migrant. I would show the humanity of 'illegal' workers. And Ro and an Englishwoman would fall in love. It would not be straightforward.

*Slant* was a very wonky text that somehow burped loud enough through the slush pile to catch the attention of Aoife K. Walsh of New Island Books. I will be forever grateful to Aoife that she allowed *Slant* under her skin and found me the superhero, Rachel Pierce, to guide on rewrites.

Apologies to the garage band, No Dead Lesbians, with whom I play arrhythmic bass. I am very sorry one of the lesbians had to die. I could never entirely control the narrative; other wills sometimes came to dominate.

I could not have written *Slant* without the friendship of Rosaleen McDonagh who has inspired and sheltered me since we met decades ago.

I could not have written *Slant* without belonging to UCD School of Philosophy. Before joining in 2015 I did not have hope enough to imagine such a supportive and dynamic culture.

I would never have been an academic or have had the bravery to write fiction without being mentored by Colbert Kearney. His wit and kindness have been a constant resource.

I would not be as happy as I am without the friendship of the class of SAC '83 (let me mention just three: Deirdre Somers, Miriam O'Flynn and Aisling O'Callaghan); I would not be as happy as I am without my neighbours in Wellington Square and having a place that is deeply home. Thank you, Arthur Leahy, for that and for so much more. I would not be as happy as I am without the Triratna Buddhist Sangha (those who go to Paramananda's retreats will recognise his influence). I would not be as happy as I am without the good times I have with my parents, my brothers and the next generation of O'Donnells.

And finally, I dread to think what my life would be without the tribe of middle-aged lesbians of Cork. Thank you all. You will see that this book is written for you and for the children we have raised.